A Very Crowded House

Kelly Elizabeth Huston

Edited by Ash White | Cover and format by Watermount Publishing

ISBN: 979-8-9877885-2-3 (e-book) | ISBN: 979-8-9877885-3-0 (paperback)

Library of Congress Control Number: 2023917204

Visit www.kellyelizabethhuston.com for author information

To all the people for whom I'd unquestionably wield a shovel.
You know who you are.

Prologue

IT WAS THE SUMMER I learned to tie my shoes because my big sister Genevieve refused to do it for me anymore. I conquered riding a bicycle without using training wheels because training wheels were for babies. My two front teeth fell out, and I saw my sister kiss a girl for the first time, but not the last. It also meant the beginning of my love for fireworks and the unfortunate start of the Monsters finding their way to our summer safe-haven.

We were suffering the hottest day of our summer stay so far, and nighttime brought little relief. Despite the fully opened windows with drapes pushed wide, the night air, too thick to move, hung in the eaves of the upstairs bedrooms. It suffocated us in the dark with the added cruelty of the screeching tree frogs and their unique brand of rhythmic torture. I lay atop my sheets and considered sneaking to the end of the hall, where a sunroom offered windows on three sides and perhaps a chance of a mild crosswind.

Rules about leaving our rooms once we were sent to bed had been clearly outlined, but the night's heat smothered us, and my eyelet-trimmed Raggedy Ann nightgown clung to my belly; my blond curls stuck to the back of my neck. Dangerously dangling my feet off the side of my four-poster, I assessed the benefit to harm ratio of breaking those well-defined bedtime tenets. Having weighed my options and determined the possible consequences, I slid down the mattress until my bare tiptoes hit the wide planks of knotty-pine floors, prepared to suffer the penalty if it meant a breath of fresh air.

At the moment of impact, when flesh met wood, everything changed.

Frozen to my spot, the stifling heat of the night no longer my concern, I held an inhale in the hopes I had misinterpreted the sound, but I knew I hadn't. A door slammed, and a door slam marked how it always began. My new hope was for another door to slam, the front-entry, the backdoor, any portal that let him exit the house before things escalated. But someone had lifted the charm thanks to me and my yearning for a gentle breeze. The price would be paid. The Monsters had found their way to our once-peaceful summer sanctuary on Market Street. Life, as we had always wished it, was no longer.

To be clear, until that long ago summer, the Monsters had never come to the Hamptons. At least I never heard them until that swampy July night. Maybe we could chalk that up to a solidly built shingle-style "cottage" of five thousand square feet or that summertime in Amagansett meant running free dawn until dark and then sleeping hard after all the sun and sea air. But I believed guardians had enchanted the big, old fairy tale house with its mullioned windows, cedar shake, and bright white trim. Secret sentinels kept it protected on an expanse of the softest lawn bare feet ever scampered across, while tiny pixies glimmered around nearby greenery in a dreamy twilight dance show. The magic hour. Then again, I was only six. Whatever the reason, until that July, summers in Amagansett were the best weeks of the year, the best weeks of our lives.

That sweltering airless night, as the thumping on walls and the smashing of glass amid shouts and screams commenced, I burrowed under my bed with down-filled linen wrapped around my ears to block the horrifying noise.

A firm yank on my ankle startled me out from under the pillow, but I swallowed *my* scream.

"Jojo," my sister Genevieve beckoned in a loud whisper.

"Don't grab me, Gigi." I swatted back and shimmied out of my makeshift foxhole. All my curls stuck to my head, matted down, sweat-soaked from hiding under the fine linens.

"Come look. Plug your ears but come see." Genevieve walked to the double-wide casement window, and I watched my sister remove the screens to sit on the windowsill. Her version of blonde lay straight in the nighttime light. Four years older, she knew everything and had no fear. Fingers, firmly in my ears, muffled the Monsters thrashing below us. I tiptoed to where she sat. Fireworks brightened the distant sky with white, red, and blue. Colorful sprays of fire arced through the air, overlapping, popping, and whistling in the moonless night.

"Gigi." I watched the colors reflect on her glistening face. "Gigi," I repeated, then bit my bottom lip, waiting to make my confession.

"What, Jojo?"

"I broke the magic, Gigi. I'm sorry, but I broke it."

Genevieve smeared the sweat and tears across my cheeks and shook her head. "It was bound to happen, Jojo. No one to blame but the Monsters. Now, no more tears and stop biting your lip. Watch the fireworks."

1

Jocelyn Durand

I REMEMBER THE DAYS when the racket wouldn't stop. Neighborhood kids running through the house, plastic light-up toys, powered by vicious Energizer Bunnies, squawking constant noise, blared music or television, and the phone ringing twenty-seven times a day, at least. Sure, when earbuds arrived on the scene, and my son Gabe got a cell phone, things quieted some. Still, the tromping up and down the wooden stairs, beckoning shouts through closed doors, and a near-constant thump of a basketball, soccer ball, or a tennis ball on the driveway—too often a bedroom wall—inundated our charmed existence. And did I mention the drum kit I could still kill his Aunt Genevieve for buying him?

Those were the moments I dreamed of quiet, wishing for Calgon to take me away. Naturally, I also loathed the nights when I lay awake, desperate to hear the rumble of Gabe's rusted muffler pull into the garage, telling me he had survived another night of teen driving. So yes, some quiet you don't want to relive. But to tell the truth, I've longed for this day, the stage of my life with few disruptions, no persistent noisemakers or usurpers of my time and attention. The day when I'll pick up my writing career again and *surely* it will be as easy as that. *Think again, Jocelyn.*

Of course, the landscape had changed since those chaotic days of carpools, sports practices, and after-school clubs. The 1920s four-bedroom, three-bath Tudor outwardly looked the same, though we completely renovated the indoors. But I hadn't imagined I would be alone in this more serene chapter. My ex-husband Will had always starred in that movie-in-my-mind of what Act II would look like. To be fair, he still plays a role in my life since the *Second Act* began, but as a background player, maybe a somewhat regular walk-on, but certainly no longer the leading man.

Don't cue the violins. They aren't necessary. I married extremely well, but I divorced even better. Will and I remain close friends. And the change in the *figurative* landscape I mentioned became quite literal, compliments of the man Will left me for. A landscape architect, Raphe, built and continues to maintain an outdoor paradise behind my house that flourishes beyond compare. No doubt to assuage his guilt for stealing my husband of twenty-four years. And if it makes him feel better, who am I to get in the way of that?

As I sat on the flagstone patio in my Westchester oasis, I enjoyed a cup of coffee and my New York Times crossword. The coo of mourning doves with the low hiss of the in-ground sprinkler, watering the luscious green space, accompanied the quiet in my meticulously cared for backyard. See? I'm doing *just* fine. It was early morning, but in an hour, the June sun would shine high enough to make the lounging spot untenable until Happy Hour when wine on the then-shaded terrace served as the perfect end to a summer day. I breathed a sigh of relief when a ringing phone interrupted my wistful thoughts of five o'clock.

"Gigi, little early, isn't it?" I answered my big sister's call on the first ring.

"To start drinking? Yes. To call my kid sis? Also, yes. But I know you're *always* up at the crack of dawn, Jojo." Gigi possessed an uncanny knack for knowing when to call and what to say, and she purred it in a low, sexy Kathleen Turner rasp with a hint of Long

Island I had long since lost.

"Guilty, counselor. But why are *you* up this morning?" I sipped my coffee, relaxed on a cushioned chaise.

"Laney is beside herself. It's rare, but never a good look on her. Her bestie had the gall to marry, then jet off on a honeymoon to Greece with no discernable return date. Plus, the bride is notorious for never carrying a phone."

"No phone? I'd be lost without mine. My whole life is in this thing."

"Yeah, well, Laney is driving me nuts, so I gently encouraged her to go to the office and foster some other needy writer's career." Gigi's wife, Laney Li, was a five-foot-nothing spitfire of a literary agent.

"Gently, huh?" I gave her a verbal poke.

"Not really, no. Speaking of, are you writing these days?" She returned the favor.

I sighed, "Not really, no." We sat in a comfortable but long silence. "Gigi?"

"Hm?"

"You know you don't have to call me all the time, right? I mean, I'm fine. Alone? Yes, but fine. Between you, Gabe, and even Will, it's like constant surveillance." That's how it had always been. Like they've been in cahoots, on a check-in rotation. 'Cahoots.' Now, there's a great word more people should use.

"I have no use for that ex-husband of yours, but hey, when's my *brilliant* and *gorgeous* nephew getting home?" My sister side-stepped my observation, but the new topic wounded my heart.

"He's not. My *fair-to-middling* son got an internship for the summer. In North Carolina. Yaaaay." I joked, of course, but the late change in plans disappointed me.

"Can't help but notice your less than enthusiastic cheerleading routine, Jojo. That's not like you. And stop biting your bottom lip. I can practically hear it from here." She wasn't wrong.

Summarily chastised, I released my lip and adjusted my attitude. "It's fine. I thought Gabe and I might have some time. Head out to the summer house for one last family hurrah. Whatever. He said I should go anyway, but I assured him I wouldn't." I paused before asking the foolish question. *Don't suppose you've considered going out there? To the summer house?* I knew better than to ask. Gigi conveniently begged off, unable or unwilling to make the two-hour trip to East Hampton most times. If she did, the visit never included an overnight. The sleepy little hamlet of Amagansett was either too quiet with no traffic noise, too loud with its tree frogs, or had too much green grass Gigi swore exacerbated her allergies. It didn't.

"Nope. No plans for that," she dismissed the notion. "But you should definitely go."

"Are you and Gabe in cahoots?" *Ah-ha.* "I'm not going out there by myself, Gigi. Raphe will take care of the grounds. Some of his crew, anyway. It's fine if no one goes this season."

"Good lord, Jo. *Cahoots?* And really? Poor Raphe and his guilty conscience. How long are you going to milk the home-wrecker routine?"

"Shut up. Raphe loves me. And if he and Will ever split, I think I'll side with Raphe just for the landscaping perks."

"See, there's a joke in there somewhere, but it's too damn early for me to find it." Her laugh hinted the joke might be dirty, but as usual, I didn't get it.

"Okay, why'd you call, Gi? Is there a problem, or you just bored?" I set my lukewarm coffee on the stones at my freshly pedicured feet and stepped out to feel the cool fescue still damp with morning dew.

"Bored? As in-house counsel at a talent agency, life is never boring, Jojo. Surreal? Often, but never humdrum."

For years I clamored for any tidbit of celebrity gossip and, attorney-client privilege aside, Gigi shared it, but these days I had enough of my own small-scale scandal to reflect on, so the chinwag had lost its appeal.

"Then what?" I asked, distracted by the tickle of my foot, the soft blades of grass grazing it.

"Hold on, incoming call... *Huh*, it's Laney. She never calls. I should take this."

"Okay."

"Hey, go to the summer house." Genevieve pushed once more.

"For the last time, I'm *not* going."

"Fine. Then write something."

"Love you, Gigi." I brushed over her suggestion.

"Love you, Jojo."

I returned to my crossword only slightly agitated my sister had ruined my timed speed, but in three more clues I'd complete another puzzle.

Twenty years ago, I wrote a book. A fluke in my opinion, but if I've learned anything about the publishing business, it's that my opinion isn't worth much. Writing stories wasn't something I did as a child, but when Will and I met during freshman year of college, he encouraged my creative side, though I never thought I would do anything about it.

We married young, right out of school, and traveled the world, in love *with love*. Then, when it came time to start a family, we had a tough go getting pregnant. The inconsistency in our sex schedule was likely the culprit and, in hindsight, should have been one of many red flags. Many, *many* red flags. Anyway, it finally happened, but not without a price. Doctors confined me to strict bed rest from eight weeks on. I stood to shower and use the toilet—nothing else. And while Will doted on me like the devoted husband and proud papa-to-be, it was a maddening time. I found solace filling blank pages with words. Hopped up on pregnancy hormones with nothing but time, I wrote like wild, and in the end, a highly regarded, critically, and then commercially acclaimed novel emerged. No one was more surprised than me.

The book launched a brilliant start to a young writer's career, or so the industry thought. In reality, I wrote the proverbial one-hit-wonder. Maybe that's going too far. Failed attempts at another success would be necessary to prove true lightning in a bottle, and those attempts never happened. Not in earnest. Nope, I took one look at my son Gabriel's baby blues, and *that's all she wrote*. Literally. To this day, Jocelyn Atwater's debut novel (published under my married name), having won notable prizes and awards, is a perennial, highbrow book club favorite, and an often-studied work in university Modern American Literature classes. The tale of two young sisters growing up in an outwardly idyllic existence, when their picture-postcard life is anything but ideal, told a very adult story, rife with symbolism, magic, and monsters. Smart people said so, anyway. Again, no one was more surprised than me.

A crack of thunder startled me out of my trance. To the west, a storm I hadn't seen brewing roiled with dark, angry clouds and a sudden uptick in the wind. At the edge of the patio stood a two-hundred-year-old white oak, its trunk over three feet in diameter with impressive leafy limbs that spanned wide and high atop the house. The crown jewel of my garden of Eden. The whitish undersides of the bright green, round-lobed leaves bared themselves in the abrupt, gusty breeze. A sure sign of an imminent downpour. I should have guessed. Inches of rain had fallen every day this week, and my left arm had that bothersome barometric ache, but the morning sunshine duped me into thinking the unusual spate of days upon days of showers had run its course. No such luck.

When the first splat of fat drops darkened the blue-gray slate, I darted to grab my crossword and coffee mug before I found shelter indoors. Catching the screen door with my foot to avoid its slam, I witnessed the skies send down yet another deluge. For the fourth time in as many days, I chided myself for neglecting to turn off the automatic sprinklers that continued to soak the already well saturated grounds around the house. To make matters worse, the chaise cushion would also get waterlogged since I failed to grab it in my rush to stay dry. It had been the soggiest June I could remember.

"Aww, poop." I watched as the hydrangeas took a beating for another day. It may have been the morning's sunny tease, but the downpour looked harsher than any of the others that week. I closed the door and poured another cup of coffee. My phone signaled a text from Genevieve.

Gigi: Work emergency. Left coast variety. I'd tell you all about it, but I'd get disbarred. ;) Out-of-pocket for the next few days. Laney too. I'll call when I get there. Tmrw, latest. Hey, so about the summer house?

Me: STOP! Quit calling me for no reason. And seriously, I'M NOT GOING!

Gigi: Good. Don't.

I rolled my eyes and tossed my phone onto the quartz counter. It landed with a *smack*. Taking another sip of coffee, I trudged the basement stairs to swap laundry from the washer to the dryer. It wasn't a California celebrity legal crisis, but it was my life.

2

Asher Cray

IT HAPPENS TO *EVERYONE* eventually. Isn't that the lie we tell ourselves? The first time we can't— I mean, you reach your mid-forties, and things don't always work like they did in your younger days. Back in my twenties, I could go all day and night, it seemed. Nothing slowed me. Even in my thirties, my drive surged, relentless. And if I felt my performance waned, the shortest of breaks... a quick shower, maybe a snack, the occasional catnap, and I rebounded right back at it.

The reasons for my sudden— incompetence could be any number of things: lack of sleep, stress, hell, it could be the summer heat for all I knew. I hadn't imagined it would happen like this, not that I dwelled much on this particular scenario. Who would? But it seemed to me there would be a slow decline, a petering off, not an abrupt inability to—perform. And now I couldn't get out of my head, which only made matters worse. The memory of my last time ran on a loop. The last time? Jesus Christ, not *the* last time. Was it?

I looked at my watch and then ran my fingers through my graying hair. A vigorous scalp rub provided momentary relief to my throbbing— The elevator dinged, and I launched out of my chair, eager to see the only woman I knew could help with my little *um*... problem. Instead, a custodial worker appeared as the doors slid open. I stayed on my feet and gave a weak salute with a nod. He returned the non-verbal greeting and pushed his garbage bin and tool caddy by me. My chin hit my chest.

Plodding down the hall toward a wide window offering an impressive view of Lower Manhattan, I waited for my savior. Despite the early hour, traffic inched through the Financial District. Thirty-eight stories gave a dizzying perspective. My stomach lurched, and I stepped back from the glass. "Jesus, Ash. Get a hold of yourself, man." I strained for a deep breath but forfeited that exercise when another mellow *ding* announced the elevator's return. I jogged the carpeted hall to meet my ace in the hole.

"Asher Cray? Did we have an appointment?" Laney Li exited the elevator, ubiquitous phone in hand. Her frenetic thumbs almost blurred with their speed as she spoke. "Pretty sure I'd remember if we did. Sorta pride myself on keeping up with my clients, my favorites, anyway. Joking, of course. Wait. Aren't you supposed to be in L.A.?" She continued to text while I stood paralyzed in front of her. Phone to her side, Laney craned her neck to meet my pleading eyes. I stood more than a foot taller than the pint-sized woman, but I trusted no one more when it came to...

"I can't write," I blurted.

Laney's brows raised as she sidestepped me and hurried to her door down the hall. "Okay."

"No, not okay. I mean I. Can't. Write." I punctuated the confession. "There's nothing flowing here, Laney. Nada. Zip. Like for a while now." I took long strides to keep at her fast-moving heels.

"I see." She unlocked her door and flipped the switch to light the foyer of her office suite.

"*Uh*, your casual tone makes me think otherwise, Ms. Li."

"Asher, it's going on twenty years now, and we've been over this. It's Laney or Laney Li, *never* Miss Li, and this may surprise you, but— not the first time I've heard this from a writer client. Other popular authors who have written longer than you, more books than you. Trust me when I say, while your CV shows you to be an incredibly talented and prolific novelist who spends more time *on* the New York Times bestseller list than *off* it, you are not exactly unique, big guy. This, too, shall pass." She busied herself around the office, opened the blinds, booted up her computer, and flipped through junk mail.

I sank onto a smooth black leather sofa across from her sleek glass and chrome desk. Laney Li in furniture form. My palms pressed into my eyes. "When a man comes to you, practically on his knees with a—performance problem—a creative muscle dysfunction... I'm not sure telling me I'm *not special* is really the way—I mean, far be it from me to tell you how—"

"Hey Ash," Laney interrupted. "I'm your agent, not your fluffer." Laney stared, steely-eyed.

I threw back my head with a laugh, finally able to get that deep breath. Elbows to knees, I held my head again, massaging my temples.

"We good?" My agent rocked in her desk chair. Smiling didn't come easily to Laney, but she did her version of it now.

"We're good. Better anyway. Thanks."

"And what about L.A.? Thought they were going to woo you into script approvals."

"Aw, Laney, I couldn't give a crap. I'm a writer, not a movie maker. And if I can't write, then I don't know what the hell I am. You're welcome to make the deal on my behalf. I trust you. But the window's closing. End of business two days from now, I think. Sorry. Guess I dropped that ball too."

"I don't care about the flick biz, but really, Asher. How bad is it?"

I stood, feeling caged. "I don't know what's happening. I've never—"

"Never?" Laney gave me a side-eye look.

"There are two things I have never had a problem doing. And the second one is writing." I paced in front of her desk.

Laney let loose her loud honk of a laugh. "Says the man I know has been single for over a year and even then... Glad to see you're keeping up the persona, outwardly anyway. Maybe you just need to get—"

"All right, Laney Li," I jumped in. "I think it best we stick to one problem at a time, and I pick the writing. I can handle the other one on my own."

"I'm just saying, maybe your handling the other one *on your own* isn't—" My agent's hand gesture wasn't Disney-approved.

"Jesus, Laney Li. You're on fire today." I resumed my head massage.

"You know what I think you need, Ash?"

"Yes, Laney. You've made that clear."

"No, seriously."

"Please don't tell me to go to *shul*." If an award for world's most-lapse Jew existed, I'd be a frontrunner.

Laney rolled her eyes. "Give me a minute." She reached for the phone, never more than an arm's length away, and dialed. "Genevieve... what do you mean, I never call? I call sometimes. Did I interrupt something?... Jojo, *huh*? That can't be a coincidence. How about you and I hop a flight to L.A. to hammer out a lucrative deal for Asher Cray? Wanna bat around some movie producers?... Um, today... No, I'm not kidding. We'll be back in two days, three tops. Now here comes the big ask..." Laney pulled out a bottle of dark liquor and two short glasses. It wasn't eight a.m.

Nope. No one I trusted more.

3

Jocelyn

I TOOK A WRITING class once. Check that. I *registered* for an online writing workshop, and I eagerly sat through the introduction and first lesson but didn't get much further than that. Not only because my life brimmed full of a miracle baby boy and the household duties I took seriously like a Martha Stewart-acolyte, but I also found the litany of *never-ever* rules, and *this-is-the-only-way* instruction squelched any desire I had to write. And honestly, my desire ran in short supply. *Never, ever* start a book with someone waking up. *Never ever* write in passive voice. *Never ever* use an adverb. I mention this because the morning of the disaster—and I'll get to that—I woke out of a deep sleep with a jolt and such a feeling of foreboding I couldn't help but think, *Wow, this feels like a horribly clichéd way to start a story.* But much like the online writing workshop, I didn't get much further than that.

The initial noise was the wind. A wailing siren. Like nature's warning bell of fast-coming destruction. The shriek didn't ease its way. It started and remained at top volume until it stopped in an eerie silence. I'd have appreciated the alert if it had given me time to do anything except utter the start of the *never ever* spoken phrase, "What the—?"

A cacophony followed. The snap of branches and the oddly high-pitched squeak of nearly one-hundred-year-old roof rafters buckling under the weight of a two-hundred-year-old white oak tree mixed with the wind's howl. I don't recall the *sound* of the trunk's collision with the masonry of the first-floor sunporch, but I felt it like it crashed into my chest. The shatter of window glass screamed like banshees cackling through the air before daybreak. Catastrophic damage resulted, but luckily the worst of the impact missed my bedroom.

I flew out my bedroom doorway, narrowly avoiding a large chunk of falling plaster when I looked up to see leafy limbs and stormy pre-dawn skies. Rain fell on my face, and my toes squished in the carpet. I'm not sure how long I stood there, but my hair and nightgown soaked through—a fact I would recognize later when a young first responder who'd come to my rescue struggled to maintain eye contact. The thin, pale pink knit clung to my skin, accentuating every curve of my body, making it clear I wore nothing underneath it. In time, I would be thankful for many things affecting the early morning misfortune, my vigilant upkeep with a regular lap swim routine not the least among them.

Eventually, I stood in a fireman's spare turnout coat in front of a rain slickered police officer trying to answer his questions: *Anyone else in the house?* No. *Any pets?* No. *Can we call anyone for you?* Two firefighters lifted me off the ground as I tried to dash past them for the house, desperate to find my phone. No civilians could enter the building until an engineer cleared it as structurally-sound.

"That *building* is my *home*," I shouted over the rumble of the idling fire truck engine. "That's where I *live*."

"Well, ma'am, you're *half* right." The safety officer's apparent attempt to lighten the mood failed.

In the immediate wake of the calamity, I walked away with two things: my purse, unharmed, safely hung in the kitchen by the back door, and my own raincoat, both fetched by a rugged emergency crew member. The bag held my wallet with ID, credit cards, and some cash, plus my house and car keys. Like the kitchen, the garage survived unscathed, and so did the Volvo inside it.

My phone, suffering a different fate, lay abandoned on the second floor. Thanks to my ex-husband's insistence that cell phones were sleep disruptors, our family kept a charging station in the upstairs hall where we plugged in every night to charge and grabbed again come morning as we hurried down the stairs to start our days. Living alone, I maintained the habit. A fireman braved the newly open-air top story in search of my device, that held every phone number and email address I could ever need, and the only way anyone knew to get a hold of me. I breathed a sigh of relief when the burly young man held it as he emerged from the rubble and jogged my way. Relief quickly morphed into disappointment when I saw the cracked screen, and finally dissolved into devastation when I learned the man pulled it from a puddle, dead. *Bricked*, as my son, Gabe would say. No amount of uncooked rice would ever be enough to reverse that tragedy.

I stumbled to a squat on the curb and wiggled my pruning painted toes in the stream of rainwater flowing toward the sewer grate yards farther down the street. Over my shoulder, I took in the rising sun as it lit the nightmare scene, then snorted skyward.

"Fine," I called out to no one in particular. A hint of Long Island seeped into the remark. "I'll go to the summer house. *Jeez.*"

Never in my life have I applauded my laziness like I did on that disastrous June morning. The day before had been *laundry day*, but when I got caught up in the latest thriller by my favorite writer, I neglected to bring my cleaned clothes up from the basement.

Two loads I should have folded or hung and put away in my upstairs bedroom sat in the dryer and a laundry basket, a jumbled, wrinkled, albeit clean heap of both lights and darks. Another of Westchester's finest risked his way to the unfinished basement to rescue a significant portion of my wardrobe. I heaved the apparel into the station wagon before heading to the Hamptons, still in my wet nightgown and raincoat, plus sneakers I'd thoughtlessly kicked off at the kitchen door the day before. When one opts to take a break from the domestic goddess routine, timing *really* is everything.

A beyond-blunt police officer allowed me to use his phone to call my insurance agent, but I couldn't remember his name or the name of my carrier. After a few rounds of "I think the logo is red and white" and "his name sounds like some kind of bird, I think," we finally zeroed in on Geoff Larkin, insurance agent extraordinaire. We arranged for Mr. Larkin to come do whatever it is people in his profession do when trees fall through houses and then had him call my ex-husband to discuss the next steps. I'd be unreachable.

Two hours later, I pulled into the pea gravel driveway of the Durand summer home. Situated close to the road, the grand house welcomed visitors with a cobblestone walkway to a covered front porch. Weather-worn shake shingles oozed charm, softened by a lush landscape my ex-husband's lover took great pains to care for. Yes, sometimes life gets complicated.

Down the long drive, the detached garage borders the backend of the property. I parked inside it and crossed the massive lawn to a side entrance leading to a slate-tiled mudroom, my arms full of the overflowing laundry basket. My foot nudged over a faux rock, double-checking the spare key, but I used the one on my ring to gain access to the old house.

The stale, warm air of a house left vacant for months met me as I pushed through the heavy glass-paned door. Dropping my laundry in the entry, I hurried to power-up the air conditioning before the heat of the day made the climb to cool the house that much steeper. Typically, a cleaning service came before our seasonal visits, but my unplanned stay meant the job fell to me. That didn't bother me in the least. As a matter of fact, I found myself eager to do it. You choose your therapy, I'll choose mine.

It was barely nine a.m., and with the adrenaline still working its sorcery, I had all day to whip the house into shape. A large, beveled mirror hanging above the dining room sideboard offered a sad glimpse of my soggy self, bedhead curls dried in unflattering clumps around my head. A change of clothes and a ponytail would be the first order of business.

4

Asher

IT WAS NO JOKE when I told Laney I didn't know what was going on with my writing, but I sure as hell knew what *wasn't* happening. Words weren't hitting the page. I'm a straight shooter, not one to mince words, so when I said there was no flow, I meant there was *no flow*. It's not like I'm finicky about the words or the pace with which I click them out on the keyboard. That's what drafting is. You vomit the story out and then fix it in revision. But now I had no plot, no characters, not an inkling of a time or a place, and in the twenty-plus years I've hustled the best gig of all gigs, this had never happened to me. Were writers allotted a finite number of these things? Had I used up the last of mine? Was this a midlife crisis? Wait, *midlife*? *Huh, wow.*

Spilling my guts to my lit agent brought me momentary relief but in no time angst flooded back. Laney's suggestion to ditch the city to find a change of scenery sounded good at the time. A day later, as I threw a duffle stuffed with clothes and two laptops (just in case) in the passenger seat, doubts bouldered in the back of my mind. Then again, what could it hurt? Still recuperating from that impromptu morning cocktail party, I cleared my calendar, tied up some loose ends, and readied myself to skip town for the foreseeable future. Some ocean air or green grass, and an unobstructed view of sky might be the mystical combination to break the curse. Desperate enough, I could believe in magic.

I rarely drive, so owning a car borders on ridiculous. Double that, since I live in Manhattan. To that end, when a buddy of mine convinced me to buy a 1978 Tahiti blue MG MGB because it seemed the quirky automobile a well-off writer should drive, the purchase grew that much more absurd. MGs, vintage or otherwise, were not built for men over six feet tall to travel any real distance. In hindsight, the foolish purchase likely indicated the impending midlife crisis I wallowed in now. The start of the downward spiral. That was five years ago, but I missed the signal. So, there I sat, after dicking around, debating whether to take Laney up on her offer, squeezed into the tin can I hadn't driven in a year. To add to my resume of questionable choices, I'd stalled long enough that the sun sat low in the sky. Too low. In little more than an hour, I'd be finding my way in the dark.

5

Jocelyn

I PLOPPED MY FEET onto the whitewashed chest that served as a coffee table in the living room. Three walls of tall windows and French doors brought the verdant landscape inside, and the ceiling fan swirled a breeze while the air conditioner tried to beat the heat. Late season peonies cut from the yard perfumed the house atop the light Meyer lemon scent from the cleanser I scrubbed with earlier. A glass of iced tea sweated in my hand as I relaxed on the crisp, white sailcloth covered sofa.

With nothing but the rhythmic *tink* of the overhead fan's pull-chain striking the glass of its light fixture, I enjoyed the quiet when it occurred to me. No one knew where to find me. And until Raphe's groundskeeper showed up, no one would likely find out for a couple of days. Sure, I would feel bad if anyone went looking for me. But with Gabe interning on the Carolina Coast, Gigi and Laney handling Hollywood on the Pacific Coast, Will busy with summertime art shows, and the house with the tree crashed through it, no one would miss little ol' me. Check that. No one would think of me at all. I sighed, oddly contented at the thought.

The house freshened and furniture freed from ghostly dust sheets, grocery shopping sat last on my to-do list. That chore would wait until after my shower, and that shower would wait until I finished my iced tea. I gasped at the first firefly spark and took another sip, watching the backyard as the vivid colors of daytime eased into the duskier hues of eventide. Alone in the quiet, a long-ago memory rushed me, and for once, it wasn't a garbled nightmare. The *magic hour* had begun when the tree frogs kept almost musical time while fairies danced between the low-lying greenery edging the property, and the sky turned pink to signal the start of the show.

The groceries would wait.

By nine o'clock with the refrigerator and pantry stocked and the sky nearly full dark, my weary body ached for sleep. My day had been busy with a catastrophic pre-dawn start. I'd earned my early bedtime. With doors locked and the downstairs lights turned off, I shuffled up the old wooden steps to fall into bed.

As the most frequent visitor, I unabashedly claimed the main bedroom, dating back to the days when Will, Gabe, and I moved in for extended summer stays. Of course, Will slept down the hall these days if he stayed here at all, while Gigi held the place in such inexplicable contempt she hadn't visited since Gabe's pre-teen years. The largest sleeping quarters with a king-sized bed included a fireplace, and a recently gutted attached bathroom in smooth Carrera, sparkling crystal, and chrome.

The old inland Hamptons house stood rather average for the area, though still sprawling, particularly for one person. But if a crowd came, everyone had plenty of space. Another slightly less grand bedroom, beautifully decorated, had its own ensuite. The bedrooms Gigi and I slept in when we were young shared an enormous Jack and Jill bath between them. A sun porch on the second floor offered a daybed for overflow, plus the finished basement housed another bed and bath, a great room for group entertainment, and a media room outfitted with a big screen and ceiling projector for movie night fun. To say I had gone above and beyond to remake the less than happy house of my youth might be an understatement. Modern-day found it a lovely home full of more recent cherished memories, memories I meant to smother any lurking thoughts of sadder, scarier times. Success. I hardly thought about the Monsters from the early days. Hardly at all.

In a fresh nightgown, I slipped between the cool, clean sheets of the king bed, disappointed that the book I'd been reading the day before sat on my other bedside. The waterlogged one. Tentacle-like visions of the Westchester house, with its new nature-inspired skylight and two-hundred-year-old tree branches poking through the fallen plaster, infested my brain. The buckled hardwood and soaked carpet tightened my insides. Images flashed in my mind as I remembered a disgusting *Bill Nye the Science Guy* episode about the speed with which mold can take root and spread after a natural disaster strikes a house. What a mother will endure for her child.

I quickly rerouted my thinking. One of my best skills. The reality, despite the disastrous circumstances, could have been much worse. And while I like to think of myself as a glass-half-full kinda gal, I had to smile at my remarkable level-headedness, all things considered. Everything would work out in the end. The people closest to me would ensure it. They always had.

My smile grew into a snicker when I recalled the wide-eyes of the twenty-something fireman gawking as I stood in the high-beams of the ladder truck, wearing only my clinging, rain-soaked nightie. A yelp escaped me when I thought surely those weren't the only high-beams on at that moment. In the dark, a blush heated my cheeks at the suggestive joke, and I could imagine Gigi's sultry laugh coupled with Laney's raucous honk. The two would have gotten a kick out of it. Not the joke itself, probably, but the fact *I* made it.

I appreciated the hint of the young man's flattering grin as he'd rushed to cloak me in a spare jacket from the onboard bunker gear. It wasn't a look I've noticed many times in my life, but we women know it when we see it. If we pay attention. But the satisfaction of the recent memory vanished the instant the *snap, crackle,* and *pop* of the pea gravel driveway and the beams of another set of headlights shone through the plantation shutters and traveled across my bedroom wall. An unexpected visitor made a late-night arrival.

I scurried to the window to see who came to check on me—the off-the-grid, unreachable-by-phone, tree-vs-house survivor. The vehicle, a ridiculous-looking toy car, wasn't one I recognized. Shrinking from my spy spot, I glimpsed a giant man as he unfolded from the tiny driver's side and looked up at the house in the dim streetlamp light.

"Who the heck are you?" I whispered, sneaking another peek as the trespasser flung a duffle over his broad shoulders and closed the car door with a quiet shove. He sauntered toward the side entrance.

For the second time in one day, I flew out of a bedroom and hurried down the stairs, barefoot, in nothing but my nightgown, but skidded to a stop in the foyer at the front door, realizing the situation warranted some means of defense. A tall decorative canister housed a golf umbrella, a fly swatter, and a pair of badminton rackets. "Seriously," I grumbled. "It couldn't be a Big Bertha, or Louisville Slugger, a full-sized Wilson racket, even?" I halted my chatter when keys jangled outside the mudroom door. The intruder had found the keys in the flowerbed's fake rock. Had I left them unhidden? I may have cursed under my breath. With a badminton racket pulled from the brass cylinder, I crept through the kitchen to the mudroom door, surprised by the pitch dark at the backside of the house.

The heavy door creaked open, and as the man stepped across the threshold, I yelled, "*Stop!*" and swung my weapon. The tight plastic webbing bounced off his head with such force that the lightweight racket sprang from my grip and flew over my head, clattering in the hall to the kitchen behind me.

"Ouch?" The intruder's lackluster reaction sounded more like a question than any real exclamation of shock or pain.

"Ya *betta* leave now. I've *cawlled* the *POE-leese.*" I shouted the lie, wishing I could remember anything from the two-hour self-defense class the Junior League sponsored six years ago. Anything other than 'speak with authority' because, for some reason, my addled brain thought that meant using my long-absent Long Island accent.

6

Asher

"WELL, YOU'LL NEED TO call them back then, because I'm an invited guest." I dropped my bag, rubbing the crown of my head, unsure what had rebounded off it. Whatever it was, didn't help my lingering hangover. In the dark, the figure of a woman in a light-colored dress of sorts standing her ground came into view.

"Invited? I don't think so. It's my *howse*." From the inflection, she could have been Carmela Soprano.

"Lady, I swear to God, I'm supposed to be here."

"Prove it," she scoffed.

"Prove it?"

"Did I *stutta*?" Her quick reply sounded like a lousy script. Crappy dialogue from one of my novels. Back when I remembered how to write.

I couldn't help but chuckle, reaching for the phone in my back pocket.

"Whoa. Nice and easy, *Mista*."

"Just getting my phone to show the texts from my agent, giving me directions and telling me where to find the spare key. Scout's honor, this is all a misunderstanding." I spoke calmly in the hopes the hothead hidden in the nighttime wouldn't go off half-cocked and do something rash.

"Wait, your agent?" Something in the air changed. Tension eased, and it seemed my assailant had lost her accent. I pulled up my recent chat with Laney and handed my phone toward the outline of the woman.

Helped by the bright white light of the screen, a pretty face surrounded by blonde curls appeared. The stranger's dark eyes scanned the messages, her thumb scrolling the touchscreen. She cleared her throat and licked her lips in a way it surprised me to notice. I gave my head a subtle shake and focused on the situation at hand as she returned my phone. After a few seconds of nothing but the distant screech of tree frogs, I cleared my throat, too. "Any chance we could turn on a light?"

"*Uh*, wait." She moved toward me out of the shadows, and I flinched, stepping back from her as she reached out her hand. "Just grabbing a sweater from the hook in the cubby behind you. I was in bed, and I've already shown off in one nightie today."

"Excuse me?"

"Never mind." She dismissed the question and slipped on an oversized cardigan before she flipped a light switch. We both winced at the sudden brightness, but I smiled at the woman, barefoot with arms crossed and the giant sweater twisted around her, hiding all but the ruffled hem of her knee-length nightgown. I gave a meek wave, then took her hand when she offered a handshake and said, "Ash."

"That's weird. My name is Ash, too." My smile grew as the curls on my new acquaintance's head jiggled while she snickered into the fingers she brought under her nose.

"No. Sorry for the confusion. I saw Laney referred to you as Ash in the texts. My name is Jocelyn."

"Right. The texts." I felt heat rise in my cheeks, strangely self-conscious from the misunderstanding. "You know Laney then?"

"Oh, yes. Laney and I go way back."

"I see." My brows raised by reflex, and I feared a hint of disappointment colored my remark.

Jocelyn laughed again, louder this time. "Not like that. She's married to my sister."

"Oh, Genevieve." I couldn't help but voice my relief at that news. Relief? Is that what I felt? Hold up. If this woman was Genevieve's sister, that would make her... Jocelyn wrapped her arms around herself again and eyed her toes. Afraid my thoughts wandered too far for too long, I scrambled for another topic of conversation. "So, you wanna call off the cops?"

"*Hm*?" She kept her gaze on the slate floor, indicative of deceit.

"Did I stutter?" I didn't mean my teasing to make her uncomfortable, but she fidgeted in her spot and the quiet hung heavy. "That was some tough talk."

"Liked that, did you? Sorry." With the look she gave me through her down-turned lashes, I'd have forgiven her anything, least of all a white lie and a horrible accent.

"I don't think anyone knew you were out here. In this house, I mean."

"No, they didn't—*don't*. So, maybe we could keep that between us? I mean, for now."

"O-kay." It was nothing to me, but one more sign this trip was a colossal waste of time.

"I'm not asking you to lie, but maybe not be too forthcoming with any knowledge you may have of my whereabouts—you know, should anyone ask."

"And who would ask me?" My question came with a bit of a smirk.

"Well, no one, probably. I'm sure it won't be an issue." She bit her bottom lip in a way that made me swallow hard.

Flustered again, I reached for my duffle. "Your secret is— safe with me, Jocelyn. Now I'll be getting out of your way. Nice to have met you."

"Where are you going? It must be nearly ten o'clock." Her

questioning eyes hinted at a sadness I didn't imagine had anything to do with me.

"This time of night, I bet I'm back at my place in the city before midnight."

"Don't be silly. I can't kick you out, not at this hour. Besides, someone invited you, apparently, plus I beat you over the head with a badminton racket."

"Is that what that was?" I rubbed my head again.

Jocelyn glanced over her shoulder and then back at me, biting that lip again. She was going to have to stop that. "Yeah. I know I've apologized twice already, but I'm *really* sorry about that part." She turned on her bare heel, headed toward the kitchen to pick up the would-be weapon that had landed down the short hall. "It's a big house. Let's find you a place to sleep, and tomorrow you can decide if you want to stay longer. Since we're in cahoots and all."

"*Cahoots*? Great word."

"*Right*?" In what appeared to be genuine excitement, she let go of the wrapped around sweater and placed her fists on her hips. "Doing my part to make it more everyday lexicon."

"Noble pursuit." I clenched my jaw and fought to give her childlike enthusiasm and very adult vocabulary a solemn nod.

She beamed with pride and cocked her head. "Well, come on," she urged, pointing to the second story with the racket and trotting through the kitchen.

I shored up my bag and tripped a step in her direction.

"*Whoops.* Careful, now. Oh, and I should tell you. The house?" She whispered, "It's magic," then scampered up the stairs.

The fact she used that particular word jerked me upright, but with nothing but her shapely bare legs in view, I had no doubt. "Jesus, Ash, get it together, man," I muttered and followed my unexpected host.

7

Jocelyn

I CLOSED THE SOLID Shaker door to my bedroom with a quiet click and rested my forehead against it. This would definitely go down as one of the strangest days of my life. Tiptoeing across the oriental rug to climb into the raised bed, I stopped with one knee on the mattress. Thinking better of it, I crept back to the door and slowly turned the latch, hoping to lock it without the bolt *clunk* echoing down the hall where my surprise houseguest stayed. I hurried back to my bed and hopped in like a giddy teenager.

Asher Cray was at my house. *The* Asher Cray. My favorite writer—sleeping at the end of the hall. *My* hall. I pulled a pillow over my face and squealed. After returning the spare pillow back to its side of the bed, I stared at the vaulted wood-planked ceiling and the chandelier hanging from it. As soon as the light went on downstairs, I'd recognized him. His PR photo on his book jackets did him justice, but what the heck was he doing here? Of all the times to be without a phone or laptop... I smoothed the neatly folded bedding across my midsection, then grabbed the pillow again for another squeal.

"Jocelyn Mae, you're ridiculous," I whispered, squeezing the down-filled linen tight. "Get some sleep so you can fangirl tomorrow without dark circles under your eyes." I twisted the lamp switch, plunging the room into semi-darkness with only a single streetlamp's glow seeping through the shuttered windows. I fell fast asleep.

Summertime meant early light, with the sun breaking the horizon before five-thirty, so it wasn't long after I found myself ready to begin my day too. Truthfully, I loved the cool, damp air of the seaside mornings and wouldn't want to miss that early sky. Just after six, wearing a sundress and my curls swept into a messy bun, I snuck downstairs, careful not to disturb the man sleeping down the hall.

Just before sleep took over, I'd planned to bake blueberry muffins in the morning. It had been a while since I had someone to cook for, and I was eager to dust off my Martha skills. Muffins and coffee would be an unpretentious, though hospitable, offering to the celebrity guest inhabiting the spare room.

Muffins baking, I poured a cup of coffee to enjoy on the patio outside the living room French doors. The familiar hiss of the in-ground sprinklers accompanied the daybreak back-and-forth of mourning doves hidden in the trees. With the heat of the day coming on fast, I was happy to see the pool service had visited to open ours. A swim would feel good later in the day, and my limbs longed for the exercise. My summer house stash of old swimwear would come in handy.

I crossed the dewy lawn to explore. Beyond the oblong pool stood what we called the barn. Not really for penning livestock, it provided another airy lounge space we also used to store lawn furniture and yard tools. A half bath, bar sink, and small refrigerator made for relaxed poolside socializing.

I sat, dangling my feet in the clear, cool water. It invigorated me now, but by August, it would feel like bathwater after suffering under the summer sun for weeks on end. I flicked small splashes with my painted toes as I leaned back on my palms, enjoying the summer morning solitude. But out of the corner of my eye, I caught the movement of shadow and clambered to my feet to face the source of the motion. The low sun in my eyes, the outline of a man in shorts and a t-shirt approached, but the bright light beaming behind him obscured his facial features. I raised my arm to shield my eyes and took a half step back. Sliding off the edge of the concrete, my arms flailed skyward as I splashed rear-end first into the pool. By the time I resurfaced, Asher Cray stood where I had before my not-so-graceful Nestea plunge.

"Jocelyn, you all right?" Unable to make out his face as I looked up from the eight-foot-deep end of the pool, I *heard* the smile on it.

"Me? Yep. Why do you ask?" I treaded water, a bit dazed, with my sundress billowing up around my shoulders.

"You, *uh*, fell in the pool there?"

I swept hair out of my eyes and instinctively reached up for the hand he offered. With a noteworthy show of strength, he pulled me up with enough force that I crashed into his sweat-soaked chest.

"*Oh, no*. Close your eyes," I half-shouted.

"What?"

"Look away. My dress is—stuck to me. Look away," I insisted. Two mornings in a row, the Jocelyn-wet-and-dressed routine was growing old. Asher craned his neck, looking straight up while I tugged at my sundress with the unappealing sucking sound of fabric peeling off my skin. I tried to cover the noise with banter. "Well, I know why I'm wet. Why are you?" I asked, noting his soaked t-shirt.

"I woke early and ran to the beach and back."

"Oh, has the Zombie Apocalypse started?"

"Nooo?" He gave me a baffled look.

"See, because that's the only reason *I* would ever run— Forget it. This is just not my week." I bypassed the man and tromped toward the house, still trying to un-suction the garb from my body. "Hungry?"

"I could eat." Asher walked alongside me, careful to keep eyes front.

"Muffins will be ready any minute. And there's coffee. Cream and sugar are on the counter. Help yourself. I'll be down in five." I wrung out the skirt of my dress before hurrying inside to find dry clothes.

8

Asher

THE BANISTER SQUEAK ANNOUNCED Jocelyn headed my way, but I kept my eyes on the article I pretended to read on my phone, casually sipping coffee. While she dressed upstairs, the oven buzzer alerted me that the muffins were done, and I scrounged up oven mitts to pull out the pan. I left them on the stovetop and waited for the baker to return, not sure I could remember the last time I smelled anything so good or felt so domestic.

Jocelyn floated in wearing another sundress and a bright smile like the earlier incident hadn't happened. I fought to flatten my grin, provoked by a mind's eye replay of her flapping arms and shocked expression as she tumbled backward to an underwater landing.

My host took a mulligan for our day's greeting. "Good morning, Ash. Sleep well?" She tied an apron at her waist while I watched from my post at the large island. I realized who she was the night before, as soon as she admitted being Genevieve's sister, but the woman who stood before me looked nothing like the picture on my well-worn copy of her book. Full disclosure, I owned more than a few. And if we've ever spoken for more than fifteen minutes, it's likely I recommended you read it. *Insisted*, even. I dug in for some surreptitious recon, a verbal poking around to find out more about this woman's story. This woman I'd idolized since my grad school days.

"I did, thanks. Very well, which is weird because it's so damn quiet out here. Must be part of the magic."

She sucked in a huff of air and smiled. "I figured you'd feel it. The magic, that is."

"I do, *uh*, I did." No question something had cast a spell of sorts, and the effects were fast-acting and overwhelming. "In all the chaos, I don't think I properly introduced myself." I stood.

"Oh, I know who you are, Asher Cray," Jocelyn interjected but kept moving about the kitchen, gathering plates, silverware, and napkins. "More coffee?" She turned, offering me the stainless carafe.

"Please." I slid my mug across the quartz. "Big fan, are you?" I was glad she paid attention to her pouring rather than my face when I asked the pompous question. *Was that supposed to be charming? Don't be an ass, Ash.*

She shrugged. "I mean, I've read some." Her reply rang noncommittal, a not-so-subtle gut punch, but I took the opposite approach.

"I know who you are too, Jocelyn Atwater." I gulped more fresh coffee, again relieved she had turned her back to me as I shuddered from the scalding swallow.

"What's that mean?" Her cautious tone caught me off-guard. I tried to allay her suspicion.

"It means I've read your book. Like—a dozen times. More, probably. I'm a *huge* fan." *And so much for cunning stealth, Asher.* Jocelyn didn't respond, but stood motionless, mesmerized by something out the window over the kitchen sink. Could I have gotten it wrong? The picture didn't correlate, but the photograph was from twenty years ago. Still, I knew Jocelyn Atwater was Genevieve Durand's sister. But I also struggled to believe this light-hearted, welcoming woman created such a dark and vicious modern day fairy tale. Had I somehow connected the wrong dots?

With a quick jerk, she spun around and leaned back on the

counter. Tucking a wayward curl behind her ear, she cleared her throat. "I go by Durand now. Atwater was my married name."

Ah-ha, I thought. That's good intel. Married. Past tense. Promising, but I couldn't decipher the expression on the woman's face.

"Sorry. I rarely get recognized. Like ever. You surprised me." She held a dishtowel, but now folded and refolded it while gnawing her bottom lip. A tell I now knew let slip her unease, a wariness of her situation. Before I could placate her, she continued, "I wrote the book while on mandatory bed rest, pregnant with my son. They took the photo shortly afterward, and I had gained eighty pounds. Eighty-seven, really. I don't know why I say eighty when it was really eighty-seven, like eighty sounds fine, but claiming the full eighty-seven should be embarrassing. It's not, by the way. Embarrassing. I'm not embarrassed." She growled another throat clearing. "Anyway. Totally worth it, though. Got a great kid out of it and a book, so—"

"A *great* book, really," I jumped in to say. "And *you* look great now. I mean, good, *uh*, attractive even. No that you weren't before, but you must have been tired—" *Ugh, Jesus. Shut up, Ash.* I took another swig of coffee, unsure why this woman made my head spin. The spell, that's right. I remembered.

Jocelyn placed a plated muffin in front of me and leaned across the island, elbow bent, her chin resting on her palm. "Please go on, Mr. Cray. Tell me more about how you love my book and find me attractive." Her impish grin made my stomach rise and fall, and I couldn't help but return the look. But hers vanished as soon as mine appeared.

9

Jocelyn

"I'M KIDDING, OF COURSE, Asher." I twisted around, rolling my eyes at my uncharacteristic behavior. Why did this man have me so off-balance, in more ways than one? Tendrils of my still damp hair fell from the hurried updo. I twitched at the tickle on my neck, or maybe I shuddered at my lame attempt at flirting. Since when was I so forward? And since when do I feign indifference about this rock star's writing. I didn't know if I was coming or going, but certainly he saw through the bravado to the nerd-girl superfan.

Getting recognized startled me. It had been a while since I had to rehash the monstrous fairy tale, and I had no desire to go back to the story. No good would come from that, but in the meantime, let me remind everyone about my puffy postpartum days to distract from questions about my one-hit-wonder. How many more embarrassing things could I say and do in front of this worldwide bestselling author, the well-publicized Casanova sitting in my kitchen, downing hot coffee like it was cold beer?

"Hey, don't suppose I could borrow your phone?" I hoped an abrupt change in subject would save me.

"Sure." Asher hurried to hand it to me. "Something wrong with yours?"

"I left it at home, actually. My other home. Hasty departure under unusual circumstances." I avoided his eye and shrugged off the question with one of my own. "Remember when telephones hung on the wall in every kitchen? The good old days."

"You aren't going to ask me for an alibi next, are you?" His joking suspicion made me defensive. Another example of the teasing he hadn't stopped since the lights came on last night. We could delve into that symbolism another time. His attitude likely meant to make me, the silly wannabe writer, feel a little less awkward. As that realization sank in, I only bristled further.

"Like some dime-a-dozen, clichéd thriller?" *Whoa, where did that come from, Jocelyn Mae?* "No offense."

Asher blinked at that remark. "N-none taken." He shoved a bite of muffin into his mouth.

Stunned by my own words, I spit out, "I don't know why I said that."

Mouth full, he simply shook his head in a way that said *no worries.*

"No. Seriously, Asher. I don't know where that came from." The sudden guilt and my embarrassment overwhelmed my senses, compelling me to admit my nerd-girl fan status. "Truth be told, I *am*— a big fan. I've read every one. Well, I'm reading your latest right now. Or I was before I left home. I didn't bring it with me, but the day before I left, I read pretty much all day." My confession came with a growing hum in my ears and the curious compulsion to keep speaking. "I laid around with that book clutched in my hands, unwilling to put it down. I woke up with it pressed to my chest."

"Lucky book," he coughed on his muffin bite with a coffee sip.

"What?"

"*Hm*? Nothing." He rattled his head.

The hum grew to a dull roar, impairing my hearing and good judgment. I continued to share. "If it weren't for you, I'd be standing here without a stitch of clothing on. I mean, I have you to thank I'm dressed at all." *Wait, what did I just say?*

"Lucky me," he muttered.

"What?"

Again, he shook his head.

Desperate to right the ship, I stopped to breathe, trying to gather myself. "I apologize. They say you should never meet your heroes. I didn't realize it was because I'd be a garrulous fool if it ever happened. Guess now we know." The next part didn't include eye contact. "I get you've been playing nice to the lonely Hamptons divorcee, a little pity for your agent's sister-in-law. I'm not stupid, and let's face it, you've got a reputation, though I haven't really picked up on the *prick* vibe—" I gasped. "*Uh, jeez*, sorry." I shut up at the sight of Asher's wide eyes and slack jaw.

Where was the do-over button when I needed it? *Back to hostess duties, Jocelyn.* I walked down the hall to the side entry and returned with a key ring and garage door opener.

"I also imagine you're here for a reason. Laney sent you here for some purpose, and none of that is my business, but she's one of the smartest lit agents around, and more importantly, no one I'd want to go against, so you are welcome here as long as you wish to stay. Here's a key and access to the garage, so you can park your car out of sight. Help yourself to food and drink. Both the living room and the basement have well-stocked bars. You'll find bath towels in the upstairs hall, pool towels in the barn, lounge chairs and floaties too, if you need them. I will be here for a while also. Kinda got no place else to go, but I will stay *way* out of your way. You won't even know I'm here."

I took another long, slow breath. The truth was, I knew *one* phone number, and I should have used it long before now. I texted my ex-husband Will.

212-555-3815: Will, Jocelyn here. I'm all right. At the summer house, but no phone or computer. You can use this number if it's an emergency, but ONLY if it's an emergency. I assume Geoff Larkin got in touch. I'm going to need you to fix this. I don't have it in me right now, but I trust you completely. Love you.

I returned the phone to the handsome man sitting stone-faced opposite me. He hadn't found a way to respond to my rudeness, opting to take the high road with silence, I guessed. I should have been thankful. I set my coffee cup in the sink and slunk off to the sanctuary of my bedroom. Not only was I embarrassed again, but ashamed, finally realizing the extent of the impact of a two-hundred-year-old white oak tree, some twenty-seven hours after the fact. These things tend to spew out one way or another. So much for glass half-full.

A half-hour later, a light knock tapped on my door. Asher, with his face softened, stood in the hall. One hand holding his phone, the other behind his back.

"You got a text. Sorry, I read it before I realized it was for you." He handed me his device.

"I told him emergencies only."

"I don't mind."

212-555-2704: Glad to hear you're ok. I've got it taken care of. It will take time, but it will be better than before. Promise, Love. Should I come to you? I could be there tonight.

212-555-3815: No but thank you. Sweet to offer. And seriously, this is only for emergencies.

I hit send and handed the phone back to Asher, patiently waiting.

"Thank you. He shouldn't bother you again."

"No bother. Besides, it gave me an excuse to knock and give you this." He handed me a copy of his latest book. "Now you don't have to wait until you go home to finish it." Little did he know *that* copy was probably unreadable by now. Bill Nye said as much.

"You carry your own books when you travel?" I asked as he

backed down the hall.

"Yeah," he shrugged, "I guess I really *am* a prick," and closed his door with a gentle thump.

I winced hearing my words come back at me, then closed my door too. My thumb stroked the black and white headshot on the back cover. I was mistaken to think the photo did Asher justice. It didn't. The real man wasn't nearly as self-assured as the two-dimensional version, at least not these days, and certainly not after my abhorrent behavior. I hopped on the high mattress, eager to escape the morning's unpleasantness and get back to the story. When I opened the book, a piece of fine linen stationery fell from it. It read:

FROM THE DESK OF ASHER CRAY

Dear Jocelyn,

I apologize for the dreadful start the two of us shared. An unfortunate series of events, likely on both our parts, found us in this spot, and I don't suppose we can go back now. Please know when I said I was a fan, I meant it as sincere praise. Your novel has been an inspiration to me over the years and to think I somehow squandered an opportunity to discuss it with the genius behind the story will be one of the biggest regrets of my writer-life. And on a more personal note, while many adjectives have run through my head to describe you, (and there have been a surprising number in the less than ten hours since I made your acquaintance) 'stupid' or 'in need of pity' were not among them. Not by a longshot. Not even close.

I understand the desire to be alone, to avoid people. It's common in our vocation, but don't stay out of my way on my account. I would welcome the company. Your company, anyway.

-Ash

Well, goodness. The man could write.

10

Asher

LANEY HAD ME COME to East Hampton to get out of my head. Well, that may have happened, but dammit if someone else hadn't taken up residence. And how did it run off the rails so quickly? From stinging barb to effusive flattery, Jocelyn had me flummoxed, a little whiplashed, too. Somehow I left her thinking I was blowing smoke when nothing could be further from the truth. What would make a woman, a funny, smart, talented—*beautiful*—woman assume malfeasance as the default position? Divorced. Right. Some jackass must have done her wrong. And what about the text message? A friend? Something more? Not necessarily. The beautifully *feminine* name *Wil*helmina has long begged for a comeback. And one should never assume...*Oh, shut up, Asher...*

How disappointing my jotted note didn't coax Jocelyn from her room. Maybe it needed another draft. Revision is a writer's best friend, after all.

I love revision, all those words to play with, sentences to rearrange, paragraphs to rework. It's the blank page I can't handle. The thing that wakes me in a cold sweat or keeps me from sleeping in the first place. The blank page is the devil, and it taunts this writer. Cruel torment. And that is how I spent my day, staring at a screen. A *blank* screen.

I'd brought a copy of my last book with me for inspiration. Maybe not the words on the pages, but an example of a finished novel. A "see, here's proof-positive, you can do this, Asher Cray."

But I gave the book away in an attempt to be a nice guy. Double-crossed, the well-meant gesture made me look like the *prick* media has conspired to make me out to be.

That particular tactic, an *intentional* marketing strategy, has proven to work. Spectacularly. Jocelyn spoke the truth when she said Laney Li ranked as one of the smartest agents in the biz, and she successfully molds talented wordsmiths into public figures people wanted to know. This included one client whose real name or face, until this past year, no one knew. The writer remained a ghost for over two decades, and that ghost's fandom pursued her identity, not to mention bought millions of books. *Millions.* A clever ploy, whatever the reasons behind it.

My persona is less complicated: a bit of a suave playboy who writes urbane, sexy thrillers with an above-average vocabulary. They are not Great American novels or praise or prize-worthy literature. They aren't the caliber of Jocelyn Atwater-now-Durand. Anyway, the ruse, Laney Li's ruse, never really bothered me, until now.

Early in the evening, I stepped from my guestroom and found Jocelyn's bedroom door closed as it had been all day. I had showered and changed, and my growling stomach said I needed an outing. I'm the kind of introvert who likes to be alone in a crowd.

My first stop? The well-stocked bar in the living room. The supply included a top-shelf Scotch I recognized from many nights of trying to keep up with Laney. Keeping pace with the five-foot-nothing badass proved an impossible feat no one should ever attempt. My agent was a force of nature with a superhuman liver.

I tipped a generous pour on the rocks and found some shade on the patio to enjoy the drink, but bounded to my feet again when Jocelyn, barefoot and sleepy-eyed, exited the French doors, clutching my book to her chest.

"It's the best one yet," she gushed with a genuine smile, wearing her wrinkled dress and wild curls half-fallen out of their pinned-up do. "Of course, I say that after every one of them. I don't know how you do it, get better and better. It's my new favorite." She squeezed it, then handed me the novel.

"Well, you're *my* new favorite." Clumsily, I returned the compliment, taken aback by the lavish approval, fumbling with the book in the exchange.

"*Aww*, I bet you say that to all the girls, Asher Cray," she chortled with a flush in her cheeks. Or was that the evening light?

"I don't, really. Not at all if you want the truth." The extent to which I needed her to know that fact surprised me, and I made sure to look her dead-on as I said it despite the warmth billowing under my collar. The slug of Scotch didn't help matters.

"I'll always want the truth, Asher. Always. No matter what."

"Then you'll have it, Jocelyn. No matter what."

We stared a beat, then with a sharp inhale, Jocelyn sped forward. "You found Laney's Scotch. It's good, right? And you're all spiffed up. Going out? Lots of places to wine and dine, within walking distance even."

"I thought I might. You wouldn't— care to join me, would you?"

"Thank you, but not tonight. Ask again, though, another time. Tonight, I think I'm gonna wear myself out in the pool. Swim laps until my thighs shake, and I can't feel my arms. After this decadent, lazy day, I need a hard workout." Jocelyn had a talent for saying one thing while making me hear something else entirely, a skill I guessed she had no clue she possessed. I only nodded, accepting the rejection while clinging to the possibility that accompanied it.

11

Jocelyn

A MIX OF RELIEF and disappointment came over me when Asher went out for the evening. And you could throw a little immature silliness into the stew. I'm sure his interest in dinner with me was purely professional. A writer sharing a meal with another writer. His kind note expressed as much. Flattering in its own right. But if one read between the lines, an activity no one should take part in, there *could* be indications his attention *might* indicate a more personal pursuit. Don't misunderstand me, I'm well aware of the author's reputation, his public persona of a womanizing rake. Then again, other than some good-natured teasing—warranted considering my exploits since his arrival—I hadn't felt uncomfortable in his presence. Not because of *his* behavior, anyway. His advertised Casanova routine had yet to show itself. Not a hint of a suggestive or even admiring leer.

I know I said earlier, "a woman knows," but I may have overshot with that declaration. I'm not a stellar judge. *Uh*, hello, I married a gay man. The reality is, I'm as likely to notice things that aren't there as I am to miss something staring me in the face. Which brings us back to the more likely scenario. He intended to discuss writing, process, craft, as colleagues, nothing more.

Now to circle around to the disappointment portion of the evening's emotional soup. Asher Cray was an incredibly attractive man, ruggedly handsome, tall, fit, with salt-and-pepper hair and head-turning light blue eyes. His smile, more than likely, has convinced typically resolute women to do things they might not have otherwise. So, his willingness to search out an environment *without* me in it was—not great. A disappointment. But let's be realistic. There is no way I could even think about navigating that. Him—a jet-setting Playboy? Me? A woman in her waning forties whose one-and-only came out of the closet twenty-four years into the marriage. *Ha!* There is nothing this ol' gal could offer that beautiful man—well—anyway...

Of course, it was his mind I found most appealing. Yes, *really*. His fantastically creative brain fashioned worlds and wove stories, putting words in the mouths of compelling characters while building tension with provocative prose in a blood-pumping way like no other. Which delivers us, finally, to my relief. My head, heart, stomach, and dare I say, loins needed a break from being in the presence of all that imaginative brilliance. Fan-girling is exhausting. Seriously. Because what if something more—no. Never mind.

In the pool, it felt good to stretch and glide, kick and stroke, flip and push off the gunite wall to do it all again. I relaxed into slow laps, enjoying the cool water on my skin, buoyed in the saltwater, near-weightless. But before long, I thrashed harder, pumping my limbs until my joints ached and lungs burned. Back and forth, I alternated between smooth, gentle motion and bursts of intensity.

When I hoisted myself onto dry land, I sucked in air, then spewed droplets that clung to my lips when I exhaled. The night chill on my wet body provoked gooseflesh that glistened in the dusky light. With a slight sting in my eyes, I tasted salt as I inhaled, trying to slow my breath. The exercise provided precisely what my body and mind needed, but it wasn't my only plan for the evening.

I traipsed across the yard, wrapped in a colorful bath sheet. After a quick drying-off at the side door, I took a moment to notice the hideaway key back in the flowerbed's fake rock. I turned on the porch light to welcome my houseguest back after his dinner jaunt and locked the door behind me, since Asher had his own key whenever he returned. Barely stopping on my way through, I grabbed a chilled half bottle of white wine and a glass. This would constitute dinner, and I would drink it in my bathtub and then in my bed, if any remained. Don't judge me.

When I climbed up into my bed, I smiled at my full-body fatigue. But part of me wished I hadn't been so quick to return Asher's novel because I would have enjoyed rereading some passages, if not starting from page one and devouring it all again. Flipping through the New Yorker, it became apparent my "dinner," on top of the lap swim, would not allow me that level of focus, anyway. After downing a large tumbler of water to ward off any adverse effects of my Sauvignon Blanc supper, I turned out my light, only mildly curious as to the whereabouts of the visiting novelist, then closed my eyes and dropped off to sleep.

The distant popping of pea gravel woke me, initially. Earlier, when I hadn't seen the little blue convertible in the driveway, I assumed Asher parked it in the garage with my Volvo. To drive to dinner seemed unnecessary, particularly for such a city dweller. With no idea of the time, I rolled over, back to my tipsy slumber.

Roused again, giggling lured me out of a pleasant fantasy. A quiet, somewhat muffled giggle that, at first, made me smile. Soon, any sense of my own dreamy enjoyment quickly dissipated, and a nightmare began. The hushed laughter morphed into a still low volume but decidedly appreciative—moan. Two distinct pitches of moans to be more accurate. The sounds overlapped, rose, and fell, punctuated by the occasional whimper and gasp. When the unmistakable squeaks and creaks of antique furniture being put through its paces began, I thought I'd die. Check that. I wished I *was* dead. Officially sober, I wondered what one is supposed to do in this situation. Waves of feelings crashed through me. Shock, humiliation, anger, maybe, and... and... what's that? Jealousy? Seriously though, what kind of man brings a one-night-stand, a no-strings-attached and probably booze-fueled hook-up to someone else's home? A *prick*, that's who.

I wrapped my head in the down-filled linen to drown out the already muted sighs of two people in the throes of—I didn't want to think about it. I tried not to let any images come to mind, desperate not to conjure up those light blue eyes or salt and pepper hair, but too late. Squeezing my eyes tight, I hummed through nursery rhymes, finally settling on the complete verse of "Row, Row, Row Your Boat" one hundred times under my pillow. The carnal commotion had gone on for several minutes before I started my poetic distraction. Imagine my surprise when, after the one hundred choruses, the tryst down the hall was still rocking the boat. I suppose you had to give the man props for stamina.

12

Asher

THE OBVIOUS QUESTION IS, why didn't I pack up and leave as soon as I realized the situation? It's a fair one and believe me when I tell you I wished I had. Many times. But I couldn't collect my things without taking my fingers out of my ears, and that sure as hell wasn't happening. Aside from this incident, I could count on two fingers the number of times I'd woken to the sounds of—coupling. *Come on, Asher. Be a man and use the proper vocabulary.* Sex. There, I said it. Don't think me a prude. I'm not. But some connections to sex I'd rather not make. My parents, of course, my rabbi, and my third-grade teacher who reeked of cigarettes, had a hairy mole on her chin, and a genuinely disconcerting love for bats. Now, Jocelyn Atwater joined that list. Okay, that wasn't one hundred percent true, but I didn't care to dwell on it any longer, not outside the privacy of my own thoughts. Anyway, both episodes occurred when I was in college, and one of them turned out to be my roommate, watching porn—alone.

I'd enjoyed my evening outing at a little bistro a short walk from the house. The service was fine, the food good, and no one bothered me. Again, not one hundred percent true. Jocelyn bothered me, but not in a way I minded very much. I wished she had joined me, but I thought our last interaction signaled a change, a new direction. The tension that bubbled up in the morning had eased, and I saw a path to getting to know the woman I admit captivated me at once. Her smooth tanned skin, gentle blonde curls, and sad brown eyes under impossibly long lashes... well, never mind. She had a brain, too, and talent.

It was no exaggeration when I admitted Jocelyn's book had influenced my life. The first time I read it, I was between terms in grad school. It scared the crap out of me. Not because it was a scary story, though it was (and to this day, I am so curious as to the inspiration for the tale), but because it forced me to rethink the entire trajectory of my life. Simply put, I would not be the writer I am today had I not picked up the novel when I did. Almost done with my master's thesis, I was *this* close to moving forward with a PhD program. Had it not been for Jocelyn Atwater, I'd likely be back at my alma mater as Northwestern's favorite poli-sci professor or some stuffed shirt at a D.C. think-tank, and most definitely an unhappy man with questionable taste in Scotch. No, it would not be hyperbolic to say the woman saved my life.

The fact Jocelyn never wrote another book, or at least never published one, rattled me considering the situation I have found myself in this last year. Had she not written by choice or maybe some other impediment barred her way? Regardless, I wanted to change it. Encourage her. Help her, if possible. Jocelyn's words made the world a better place, and I couldn't imagine *my* world had she never given them to the universe in the first place. It stood to reason; life would be better, that much sweeter if she gave us more.

Suffice it to say, I ambled back to the house with renewed optimism. She had retired to her room for the night, and I thought I heard water running, the noisy rush of a spigot filling a bathtub, but no good would come from dwelling on that idea. I knew, come morning, I would make every effort to engage with my fascinating host. On my stroll from dinner, I already felt lighter at the prospect. Sure, it might all be a distraction from my writerly issues, the reason for this seaside escape. Who knew what might become of it? Besides, what was writing anyhow, if not finding yourself in the exploration of others?

All that hope and promise crumbled when I woke from a sound sleep and pleasant dream to the unmistakable sounds of—sex. It didn't take me long to decipher the noises or to recognize they came from down the hall. At first, I tried to convince myself the scene was not as it sounded. I mean, the giggles and moans didn't even sound like Jocelyn (all twenty-four hours I knew of her), but the doors were solid, and she slept in a room several yards down the hall, and something in the subsequent sensual sighs and gasps said it *could* have been her. By then, all I could imagine was her.

Whoever had joined Jocelyn—the Will, of *emergencies-only* text fame I ventured—must have been a younger man. More than once, I thought the dynamic duo had to be done. I waited a while longer, hoping they would fall asleep so I could make my escape. I would throw my things in the duffle, creep downstairs, and hightail it back to the city. But each time I thought my getaway moment arrived, they began again. Yeah, Will had to be a *much* younger man.

I had read his texted offer to come here, but Jocelyn said no. Evidently, someone reconsidered, and in Will's defense, if I had been in his shoes, I'd have moved heaven and earth to get here. Now, I thought I'd sell my soul to not be here at all.

Did my reaction to the whole affair surprise me? I don't mind saying it did. I'm not a sentimental guy, and I, by no means, had any claim on or expectations of the woman. Still, the last twenty-four hours had left me a bit awestruck, and now I had an unfamiliar ache in my chest I hoped stemmed from my dinner and not the surreal episode that I could now count on an unfortunate third finger.

13

Jocelyn

By sunup, while no one had gotten much sleep... at all... I had no plans to lie in my bed another minute longer. I imagined it would be some time before the tawdry twosome showed their faces, but I didn't want to take the chance of missing them. No, I had every intention of forcing a confrontation of some sort. Shameful or cocky, I wanted to see Mr. Cray's face, now he'd shown his true colors. Deep down, my anger pointed inward, and it came from the foolishness I allowed myself to be swayed by and in so little time.

I stewed at the kitchen island, staring at a lukewarm cup of coffee. The telltale creak of the nearly one-hundred-year-old stairs gave away someone's descent. By the careful yet hefty sound of it, Asher was on the move. Immediately, I regretted my scheme to coerce a tête-à-tête. Those blue eyes were the last things I wanted to see. I considered hiding in the pantry, but the time for that had come and gone, and besides, I was a grown-up.

Try as he might, Asher's six-foot whatever frame couldn't move silently down the stairs, but it seemed it was his intention. When he rounded the corner, our eyes met, and I couldn't help but smile. Shame. That was the look, and I took some solace in it. It surprised me to see him carrying his bag. The short-term resident writer apparently planned to sneak out. And what of his partner in crime? Had he kicked her to the curb before sunrise or left her to face my wrath alone?

"Good morning," I squinted over the rim of my mug.

"Morning." Asher failed to fake chipper, but who could blame him? He must have been exhausted.

"Change in plans you neglected to tell me about?" I eyed his luggage. "Or maybe you left me another well-written missive somewhere. Surely, you'll want a cup of coffee before you hit the road. Or is time a factor?" I pointed toward the stairs, implying his attempt at a quick getaway.

Asher glanced over his shoulder, then at me. His expression read confused, but it seemed his attitude built steam. He cleared his throat. "I, *um*, I thought maybe this big old house was getting a little crowded."

"Whose fault is that, Asher?"

"*Huh*?" His defiant mien infuriated me, but I lifted my mug and continued with my forced grin. Cold enough now, the coffee was barely palatable, but it helped my act, the casual vibe I aimed to convey. He continued, undeterred. "Look, I was unexpected. I get that, and this is your house. Far be it for me to get in the way of you—living your best life." Asher set down his bag and took a haughty stance, hands at his hips. "But I don't think you need an audience, then again—"

I detected more than a hint of disdain, and I met it in kind. "*Best life*? This coming from the man who asked me to 'dinner,'" I used the air quotes, "and then getting *rejected* goes off and—"

"Whoa, for your information, my invitation to dinner was just that: dinner. This may be news to you, but you and I are not the only yarn-spinners in our mutual circle. Your sister-in-law has made more than a little fiction fly, and plenty of it has had to do with me. Believe what you want, but I'm not the player Laney Li would have the world believe. And frankly, what the hell does any of that have to do with your 'workout' last night?" The man had the gall to air quote *back* at me, and my head swirled as our volume climbed.

"My *workout*?" Unable to keep up with his smooth talk and confounding slight, I resorted to repeating him instead.

"I understand you have been out of the writing game for a while, but your euphemism ran a little wordy. All that 'shaky thigh' and 'until I can't feel my arms' crap? Vivid imagery, excruciating really, and while I'm sure your *emergencies only* text buddy gets off on it, it was a bit over-the-top. Brevity, Jocelyn—you should try it."

"That's rich. *You* giving a lesson in brevity?" That jab landed on his long-winded diatribe *and* his bedroom antics. Yes, in immediate hindsight, that last bit wasn't really an insult, and obviously, I was outmatched here. "I can't believe it ever crossed my mind that something was happening here—"

"Well, hold on to that memory, lady, because—"

"Yo! What's with all the racket down there?"

An unseen man barked from the top of the stairs that neither Asher nor I could see from our spot in the kitchen cut short Asher's interruption.

"*Oops*. Guess we woke Will." Asher frowned.

"What? Will? That's not—" I leaned toward the stairs, eyes up. "Hey, you," I called. "Get down here. Now, please." My unusual bellow met a stunning silence, followed by slow footfalls on the old stairs. Sleepy eyes met us while rangy muscular arms stretched over the young man's head of wild blonde curls that echoed mine. My stomach tightened, and not only because of his navy-blue boxer briefs that highlighted more than I cared to see so early in the morning. "Asher Cray, meet Gabriel Atwater. My son."

14

Asher

THE KID'S BLONDE CURLS and brown eyes definitely suggested he belonged to Jocelyn, but when he smiled, I knew it for sure. *Kid* is probably not an accurate term, especially when you factor in his bedroom skill set. He might have been old enough to buy beer, but barely.

"Asher Cray? Hey, you're like my mom's favorite writer—"

"Gabe—" Jocelyn tried to intervene.

"No, I mean, *favorite* writer. Like if she's reading you, don't even bother trying to talk to her, and oh, by the way, you're having cereal for supper."

"*Gabe*," she tried again with a louder plea.

"Oh man, I hope she didn't do anything creepy to lure you here because it wouldn't surprise—"

"Gabriel James Atwater!" Her pink cheeks and wild eyes were too much.

I stifled a laugh with a cough in my fist.

"Go put some clothes on, young man. You and I are gonna have a little chat."

"Right." Gabe pointed and spun his lanky body toward the front hall. He called over his shoulder, "If you're trying to make your escape, Mr. Cray, she's good and flustered, so now's probably the time. If you're gone when I come back, nice meeting you."

Jocelyn and I stood in the kitchen, listening to the young Mr. Atwater stomp up the stairs. When the latch of his door clicked closed, I waited, unsure how to proceed. Finally, I broke the quiet. "Nice kid." I grinned as those brown eyes lifted in her down-turned head while she rearranged lemons and limes in a crystal bowl on the counter.

"What are you *smiling* at?" she hissed.

"Oh, Jocelyn, many things. *So many* things," I chuckled.

"Like what? What could you possibly find to smile about?"

"Let's see. The sun is shining," I started.

"Okay."

"I think I heard some birds chirping."

"Fine." She shook her head.

"Apparently, you really *are* a fan."

"Ha-*ha* All right." She met my eyes again and then rolled her own.

"No, like a *big* fan." I gestured with widespread hands. "The pre-order, hardcover, shirk-your-motherly-duties kinda fan."

"Hush. It was *one* time. Maybe twice. Three tops." She relented to her smile but tried to cover it.

"That's the trifecta, right there."

"*Stop*." Her bitten lip compelled me to obey.

"But I'm actually smiling because—everything I *thought* happened last night—*all night*— did not."

She reverted to a whisper. "Right? *All night*. I mean—"

"God, to be twenty again," I sighed while she tried to disguise a shocked innocence. The pink in her cheeks deepened, and I wanted to feel the heat I knew radiated off them. "Also, in our earlier—*uh*, discussion, I guess we'll call it—I thought I heard you say something—maybe— crossed your mind—"

"Yeah, about that, Asher."

"No," I raised my hands again, this time to stop her speaking. "Let me smile about that a little while longer, 'kay? I know it's early, in every sense of the word, but that's made my day, my week—*month*, even." Picking up my duffle, I hoisted it over my shoulder. "Think I'm gonna— go unpack if that's all right?" I waited a beat for some reply. She gave a shy smile, more pink cheeks, and a definitive nod.

15

Jocelyn

His bag resting across his broad back, Asher strode away, surprisingly light on his feet. He met Gabe at the foot of the stairs.

"This isn't a Stockholm thing, is it, Mr. Cray? Blink three times if you're being held hostage—"

"Gabriel James, get in here," I called from my stool at the kitchen island.

"It's Asher, or Ash is fine. Nice to meet you, Gabe. Good luck in there. Go Bears." Asher bounded up the stairs.

Gabe wore gym shorts and a Brown University t-shirt, beelining to kiss my cheek. "Hi, Mom." He went in search of juice. "Whatcha doin' here? Could have sworn you said you wouldn't be."

"What am I— what are *you* doing here?"

"I had a few days before my check-in in Wilmington."

"I thought you were going to North Carolina?"

"Yes, Mom. Wilmington, NC."

"Oh, and who's your— guest?"

"Frannie. Her name is Frannie."

"And Frannie is...?"

"Fun." His grin grew broad. Too broad.

"That I already knew, Gabe. That I knew."

"She's smart and nice and fun, and don't make a big deal out of this, okay?"

"Who's making a big deal? I can't even ask?"

Gabe shrugged.

"How long are you staying?"

"We planned to leave Saturday, drive to Richmond, then the rest of the way Sunday, but if we're intruding on something here...?"

"Huh? What do you—? Oh, stop. I didn't plan to be here, and I had no idea he would be here. It just worked out that way."

"Meant to be, huh?"

"Don't be silly, Gabe. I don't even know the man."

"Well, that's not true. Your fan-girl obsession aside, clearly something is going on here. That little *discussion* I interrupted?"

"What about it? A misunderstanding. Nothing to be concerned about."

"Never fought like that with Dad? Like ever."

"Your father and I never fought. *Like ever,*" I mimicked my son.

"Why is that?"

"What's with all the questions? I don't enjoy fighting, and you know it."

"Oh, I know. Happy voices, quiet doors. House rules. Always have been."

"Yep." I dumped my cold coffee in the sink.

"And this morning?" Gabe had a talent for raising one brow, a pronounced arch. He did it now.

"What about it? A misunderstanding. I told you."

"A misunderstanding? A fight? Potato, Pot*ah*to, as Aunt Laney says. You liked it."

I took out a plate, two napkins, and two leftover muffins. "I don't know what you are talking about. You should see to your guest, Gabe." I handed him the breakfast.

"And you should see to yours." He gave an exaggerated wink and backed out of the kitchen.

The flush I felt earlier returned. It climbed my neck and settled on my cheeks. I couldn't help but wonder what Gabe knew that I didn't. I feared the answer was—*a lot*. Rather than dwelling on my inadequacies, I poured a fresh cup and went to visit the backyard peonies.

Peonies are my favorite, and I had them planted all around the yard. Their bloom time was far too short, but I got lucky, catching the tail-end of their annual appearance. I love the cut flowers and how they perfume the yard and the house. There was a time when this place carried different smells. Chlorine, quaggy heat that hung on everything, and the patent but indescribable stink of fear. I had purged all of that with saltwater, air conditioning, and happy memories. Still, to my mind, more is more when it comes to these June bloomers. A new bed Raphe planted a few feet from the pool hadn't done well. Almost zero blooms on those struggling stems. Disappointed, I chalked it up to the first growing season stress, or that pesky acidic Long Island soil. I'd talk to my gardener about it whenever he came around next.

16

Asher

I smiled all the way up the stairs and into the guest quarters down the hall. Things changed on a dime. *Of course,* the shenanigans of the night before had involved a couple of college kids. Laughable to think anything else, except both Jocelyn and I *had* thought something else, and neither of us liked it. Significant? The researcher in me wanted to delve into that revelation, "unpack" it, as they say. Seemed to me that *packing crate* measured rather small. What other explanation could there be other than, at the very least, something was brewing between Jocelyn and me that's worth exploring? I planned to keep my duffle empty until I studied the situation further.

I stepped from my bedroom and onto a sun porch at the end of the hallway. The narrow but long room stretched the width of the old house. Windows on three sides ran consecutively from waist high to crown molding at a ten-foot ceiling. Arranged like a small library with a daybed, I figured it served as surplus if ever there was a crowd. Laney told me she had been here a few times, and though she enjoyed it, they never stayed long, never overnight. Her favorite times had been when Gabe visited, too. My agent didn't have many soft spots, but she had one for her nephew Gabriel Atwater, and I could see why. In our brief meeting, Gabe showed himself to be a whip-smart guy with a dry sense of humor and adoring eyes for his mother. Coincidentally, I shared more than one of those traits.

Laney also indicated the summer house was *not* a favorite of her wife's, but Laney had learned to let the subject lie. By her fourth drink at our impulsive eight a.m. cocktail party earlier in the week, she confided the summer house made Genevieve sad in a way she couldn't bear, so for both their sakes, the topic remained off-limits. It represented the only ding on an otherwise enviable relationship, but then who was I to have an opinion of marriage?

The conversation reminded me how fierce a partner Laney Li is to those closest to her. A protector who would go balls-to-the-wall for you if you are lucky enough to break through the rock-hard exterior and allowed to live in her gooey center. But don't tell her I said that. I'll deny it.

The details—such as they were—of Genevieve's opinion of this place didn't amount to what I saw as Jocelyn's take on the property. Someone had meticulously cared for the home. Decorated it beautifully, with high-end finishings and a discerning eye for detail. Despite the age of the place, it gleamed like new, as if they had meant to scrub away any hint of another time, eradicate it even. So, when viewed under that lens, something troubling seemed to lurk beneath the surface, or at least, something almost unnaturally clean blanketed it. Add Jocelyn's talk of magic and her eagerness to show hospitality, a hazy picture grew even harder to discern. Flashes from my favorite novel sparked in the back of my mind. Exquisitely haunting passages that blurred the lines between real and imagined, splendor and fear. An inexplicable shiver hit me in the rising heat of the glassed-in room.

The muffled voices of Gabe and his guest pulled me from my thoughts just as I spied Jocelyn on the shaded back patio. She held a coffee cup and smelled the large pale pink blooms I'd also noticed in vases dotting the inside of the house. Their sweet scent permeated the home, powerful but appealing. Uninterested in hearing any more of Gabe and his company, regardless of the sort of communicating, I felt a sudden desire to smell that floral freshness and headed downstairs to do just that.

I stepped onto the patio, one hand holding my coffee cup and the other the stainless carafe, still half full, intending to offer a warm-up to Jocelyn. Nudging the French door with my foot as I passed, a breeze gusted, helping the heavy door to a decisive close. A starter pistol-like *bang* erupted, followed by the sharp crash of a ceramic mug shattering on the stone patio. My head whipped from the slammed door to a wide-eyed Jocelyn, stunned in an acute panic. We froze.

"Don't move, Jocelyn. You're barefoot." The shout felt necessary and yet wildly excessive as I hurried to empty my hands on a bistro table before taking quick strides to reach my shaken host, splattered coffee and shards of stoneware at her feet. I held her by the shoulders, directing her backward to avoid the mess in her path when the offending door flew open, this time with Gabriel pushing through it in a freak-out of his own.

"Take your hands off my mother, Asher," Gabe growled the demand. A *not*-so-affable college kid arrived on the scene.

"Gabe," Jocelyn murmured, blocked from her son's view by my broad frame.

"I'm trying to keep her from cutting—" I tried to explain.

"Let go of her now." By then, Gabe had crossed the terrace and gripped my arm with impressive strength.

"I'm not—" I yanked from Gabe's grasp.

Two women, in stereo, exclaimed, "*Gabriel.*"

With Jocelyn's trance broken, she leaned, reaching for her son's hand. "He didn't do anything, Gabe. Asher didn't do anything. He was trying to help."

"Watch your feet, both of you," I managed to say as I spun out of the settling fray. I caught the shocked face of a brunette perched in the doorway to the living room. The young woman wore another Brown University t-shirt and a look of alarm.

"You okay, Mom?" Gabe's gentle tenor had returned as his hand skimmed over her matching curls, then lifted her chin so their eyes met.

"Yes, I'm fine, and Asher did nothing wrong. Breathe." Jocelyn cupped her son's cheek and forced a smile as she repeated my defense.

"I heard the slam, and then you were—" Gabe spoke quietly, words meant only for his mother.

"I am okay."

"Hey, sorry, Asher. I didn't mean to—"

"No problem, kid. You were just looking out for your mom." I stood with my hands on my hip, trying to take Jocelyn's breathing suggestion, baffled by the commotion. "Why don't you two step around there. Careful. I'll get the broken bits."

Mother and son headed inside. The young coed, in flip-flops, came from behind with a broom and dustpan to help with the clean-up.

"You sweep, I'll hold," she said, handing me the broom. We completed the task in less than a minute. "I'm Frannie, by the way." She stood and offered her hand in a business-like shake. "Honor to meet you, Mr. Cray."

"Mr. Cray? Asher, please."

"Exciting start to the day, huh, Asher?"

"Do you know—?"

"Nope. Never met her before and *never* seen Gabe act like that. Ever." She beckoned for the broom, and the *slap-slap* of flip flops faded toward the house with the remnants of the morning's second disturbance.

It looked like I had found a larger box to "unpack" after all. More highlights of my favorite book ricocheted in my brain. *A door slams and liquid heat, fresh but dark, drips down walls that hide everything and nothing.* Rusty second-guessing gears ground to a start, unsure whether I *wanted* to know the genesis of Jocelyn's novel anymore, but now I knew I *had* to know.

17

Jocelyn

Determined to brush past the patio incident, I went full-on Martha. "Who wants pancakes?"

"Pancakes? Mom, that's not necessary."

"But I'd like to. You know the ones, sweet and fluffy. What was it you used to say they tasted like?" I practically skipped to the pantry for the ingredients.

"*Uh*, rainbows. I said they tasted like rainbows." Gabe dropped his chin in embarrassment while Frannie giggled.

"That's right," I said, as if I hadn't remembered. But who could forget?

Asher entered from the living room.

"I'm going to make pancakes, Asher, and they're going to taste like rainbows. Say you'll join us." My voice held a tinge of desperation. I wished it hadn't, and a chanced look caught a flicker of concern in those light blue eyes.

"How could I say no to that?" His new look included a smile and somehow telegraphed that everything was fine.

I took a deep inhale of relief and sent back my thanks with a nod. In all the speechless communication, I had no doubt we both understood. Our ability to do it left me awed and a little nervous.

In the dining room, we chatted over rainbow pancakes about Providence and Gabe's summer internship on the Carolina coast, all acting as though the awkwardness of the night before, the misunderstanding, and the door slamming panic of this morning never happened. Conversation flowed, and laughter came easily as a friend, family, and a stranger got to know one another. With everyone done eating, I brought the stainless carafe full of a fresh brew from the kitchen to offer refills. I casually placed my hand on Asher's shoulder in a surprisingly forward gesture I hadn't intended and quickly tried to recant. He promptly took a brief hold of my hand with a simple squeeze before I pulled away to fill Frannie's outstretched mug. The whole interaction took a second, maybe two, yet I'd swear time stood still and sped forward in the subtle intimacy. Nerves assumed the momentary calm when I realized the change. Something new sparked between us and we couldn't ignore it. And while the thought of exploring it prompted a grin, I doubted my ability to navigate the new dynamic.

Lingering over coffee, Gabe announced his plan to show Frannie around our little hamlet on some bicycles we kept in the barn. I thought it was an excellent idea until I realized it meant Asher and I would no longer have the buffer of company. No buffer meant there could be questions or more touching, and I wasn't sure which concerned me more. Plus, some attention would need to be paid to our mutual misunderstanding about last night and our heated response to it. Those college kids provided a bulwark to a minefield we adults wouldn't be able to avoid if I let them out of my sight, but I couldn't find justification for grounding them or tethering them to my hip. I don't think I had grounded Gabe since he was fifteen, so the warrantless punishment of a twenty-one-year-old didn't seem a viable option. A different tack would need to be employed as soon as the two budding marine biologists made for the barn and bikes.

"I refuse to accept any help with the dishes, so don't even bother." My swift offensive ploy caught my guest unprepared.

"I—I was just going to insist you let me do it all, not just help."

"Oh, yes, I detected the look of an eager helper from across the room, and the answer is no. Besides, Laney will have my head if I take up any more of your time. Surely she is going to check in at some point, and I will not be your excuse for not getting any work done, whatever that work is. The text from her you shared was—emphatic." I took our plates to the kitchen. In one of the old house's many renovation projects, I'd widened the kitchen entry for a more modern open-concept space. Part of me regretted that design choice now. Nowhere to hide.

"Laney is nothing if not categorical, but how could you possibly be my excuse when you aren't even here?" Asher raised his brow in the way Gabe could when I eyed him with my own questioning look. "We're in *cahoots*, don't forget," he reminded.

"Cahoots. Yes. You and I."

"You and I, what?" That single brow remained unnaturally high.

"What?" I put the dishes in the sink, desperate for an escape hatch.

"You said, 'you and I,' and I'm asking, you and I, *what*?"

I cleared my throat and kept a steady gaze out the kitchen sink window. In a moment, Asher stood at my side.

"Jocelyn?"

"*Hm?*"

"Can you look at me?" He placed his hand on mine at the sink's edge.

"Hey, Mom?" Gabe barreled through the side door. "Do we have water bottles somewhere?"

Asher slid his hand off mine as I rotated headlong into his chest, scrambling toward the overhead refrigerator cabinet where we stored reusable sports bottles.

"Oh, sorry." My hands landed on either side of his waist.

"Let me, *uh*..." He raised both hands and spun to let me by. The huge kitchen had the sudden feel of tight quarters, and our awkward dance rattled us both, earning a chuckle from Gabe.

Adequately supplied with two icewaters, Gabe repeated his goodbyes. "We'll be riding around for a while. Think I'll take Fran to Scoop Du Jour afterward, so we'll be gone—for *hours*. So, kay, bye." His blonde curls bounced as he jogged out the door.

Asher had made his way to the other side of the kitchen island, reading the labels of wine bottles set at slants in an antique wooden wall-hung rack. "I see the Durands have excellent taste in wine." Asher's inflection told me his comment was genuine, and I happily moved on from our poorly executed sink Mambo.

"Well, you are welcome to any of it, and I can't take credit. That's all my husband's doing—*ex*-husband. Will. Will Atwater." It felt like the right way to tell Asher who the *Will* of the text messages was to me.

"Will, as in—?"

"My emergencies-only text-buddy? Yes." I nodded, folding and refolding a dishtowel. Reminding myself not to bite my bottom lip as we waded into this quagmire.

"That's funny." Asher eyed the wine again. "I know a *William* Atwater. I've had some dealings in art with him. First, it was research for *High Art Heist,* and then he helped me invest in some paintings. Great guy, really knows his stuff, found me some wonderful pieces. Of course, he couldn't *possibly* be your ex-husband."

Well aware the two men had business dealings, I watched Asher continue his winemaker survey for a moment without comment before forging ahead. "Laney Li set that up for you, did she? The research and investment advice? With *William* Atwater?"

Asher kept on with his label exploration. "She did. She's a hell of an agent."

"Also, a heck of a sister-in-law—and *ex*-sister-in-law." I smiled, waiting for Asher to do the calculus. Three, two, one...

Asher swiveled to face me. "Oh my God, William *is* your ex-husband. Will who texted you. You were married to him. The very—"

"The very one," I interrupted. "Twenty-four years. College sweethearts, the only man I've ever—well, that's not important. He'll always be Will to me, but he insists everyone else calls him William. I mean, *everyone*. I've been given special dispensation, I guess you'd say."

"*Earned* it, I'd say." Asher gawked longer than I liked.

"Will and I are great. Very close. He's a great dad, a great friend, and his partner Raphe is—fantastic. It's all very tidy."

"So—with Laney and Genevieve—and Will—William and Raphe—?"

"Yes, it's one big game of *Which of These Doesn't Belong Here?*" I smiled while Asher laughed. "So. You and me."

He quieted and grew serious with both brows raised this time. "Yeah?"

"I wash. You dry?" I tossed him the towel across the island.

Asher nodded. "I thought you'd never ask."

18

Asher

WHETHER OR NOT SHE meant to, Jocelyn was the distraction keeping me from my work. And while Laney had hinted at another possible solution for what she considered the more urgent and likely related issue, I'd guess she didn't have her sister-in-law in mind when she brought it up—*Jesus, Asher.* I closed the laptop on a still blank page.

The blogosphere painted a womanizing picture of yours truly, and my recent inner dialogue hadn't helped dispel the image, but I was not some great seducer of women. In fact, the truth couldn't be further from that rumor, and that concocted tale has meant the demise of the few relationships I've ever given much thought. The fact is, my lonely existence, until recently anyway, has satisfied me, and I'd hardly ever thought back on the one that got away. I do owe Facebook a big thank you very much for the update that her twins recently graduated from high school. So, *Thanks, Facebook.* But I'm pretty sure marriage is overrated. Yeah, pretty sure.

Anyway, it would take an extraordinary woman to break through the years of my solitary lifestyle. A timid knock at my door nailed its cue. I rushed to open it, convinced I'd find my host on the other side.

"Sorry to disturb you."

"You didn't—aren't—I mean, nothing going on in here." My insistence felt a bit forced.

"I'm headed over to a Farmer's Market up the street and

wondered if you might have any requests. Favorite fruit or—"

"I do," I jumped to interrupt.

"What's that?"

"Take me with you? Please. You'd be doing a fellow writer a solid. Save me from the blank screen. I'll beg if you like."

"I'll take the company. We'll be walking, so I could use the extra set of hands, but I'll beg of you not to refer to me as a fellow writer, Asher. I hardly qualify."

"We can explore your qualifications later. Consider me your pack mule."

The pink in her cheeks sprang up again, this time extending to her ears.

"What was that? What thought skittered across your mind that made you blush?" I smiled at Jocelyn as the color deepened, and she remained mum. "*Come on*, tell me," I pushed.

Jocelyn cleared her throat to find her nerve. "When Will hires help to schlep heavy art around town, he calls them—*beefcake*." She only had eyes for her toes.

"Beefcake, *huh*? I'm your beefcake, then?"

She spun on her heel, heading for the stairs before shrugging. "Well, we can explore your qualifications later."

It may have been another example of her saying one thing while I heard another, but something in the way Jocelyn's brow twitched made me wonder if I hadn't heard precisely right that time.

The market had a year-round set-up with both indoor and outdoor space for vendors. Fresh fruits and vegetables lined the aisles, as well as meats, cheeses, and eggs of many varieties, plus smelly herbal soaps, local honey, artisan bread, and macramé crafts. A who's who in local color, Jocelyn greeted each seller like she knew them, and I think she actually did. I watched her examine greens, smell peaches, lift watermelons, gauging weight versus size, and finding the right buttery yellow ground spot before choosing her purchase.

"How do you know which to choose? All the different techniques for finding the right pick?" I followed close behind, ready to carry whenever Jocelyn decided.

"Practice, I guess. I have been shopping in markets like this all over the world. Right after high school, I spent the summer in France with family I didn't know, and when Will and I were young, we traveled a lot. Every country has its own version of this." She gestured to our surroundings with a kind of affection. "Some places, you never touch the produce. You only point, and the merchant chooses for you. While that might be off-putting at first, it shouldn't be. They are vehemently proud of their wares and want the customer to be in awe of them too. They always pick the best available. The difference between home and abroad. One difference, anyway. One of many."

Her smile turned shy, like she had forgotten we were still new to one another but now remembered. The shift back to mere acquaintance status might have gutted me. Lost ground simply because of some societal norm that dictates how long you have to know a person before you can really get to *know* a person. But then she kept speaking.

"Don't think I'm some expert. I'm not. I have made poor choices in the past, allowed the heft of a thing to take me in, only to find out it wasn't as sweet as I thought it would be. But then you make do with what you bought. Buyer beware." Jocelyn sped up, moving to another seller's booth. Again, she spoke about produce, but I heard something else.

We made our purchases along the way, and Jocelyn strategically kept me loaded down, unable to reach for my wallet. She refused any compensation from me, insisting I earned my meals via my beefcake duties. It had never been my intention to be waited upon, so I would need to find some way to reimburse my host, repay her kindness.

"May I ask why you're here? I mean, I know it's your home, your summer home, but why are you here now with all the secrecy? Obviously, Gabe didn't know you were here either." We were headed back toward the house, I thought, but we took a slower, meandering route. "I don't mean to pry."

"Well, there was this two-hundred-year-old white oak tree, and she crashed right through my house, my other house, before dawn two days ago... three days ago? What day is it?" Jocelyn shook her head with a shrug.

I chuckled. "There you go again."

"There I go again, what?" She turned around, eyeing me as she walked backward.

"Being a little wordy with your euphemisms and I don't get this one."

"Asher Cray, you should know by now I am not euphemistically-inclined. Is that a thing? My workout was just that, and in retrospect, I can see how you may have gleaned otherwise, but honestly—that's on you. And when I say a two-hundred-year-old white oak tree crashed through my house, I mean a two-hundred-year-old white oak tree crashed through my house."

"Oh my God. Were you hurt?" Stunned, I stopped on the sidewalk.

"I'm better than the house, that's for sure."

"So, your hasty getaway without a phone? And Will texting it will all be better than before? A tree fell on your house?"

"In a storm. In the middle of the night. Pretty much. But not a scratch on me, so—"

"Still. I suppose a catastrophe like that warrants some jumpiness."

"Jumpiness? Oh, no. That's not—" Something in her look

troubled me, something that said I had it all wrong, but then we were done with that topic. "Anyway, no one got hurt. It's just stuff, and we are well-insured." She continued a few steps down the street. "So, does Asher Cray cook?"

"I cannot tell a lie, I do not, but I am a quick study and eager to learn. Besides, I need to earn my keep. Other than—" I hoisted the reusable woven bags like a weightlifter.

Stopping again, she squinted at me. "Careful, Asher. I might put you to work, and once I get started—" Jocelyn didn't finish that thought. A thought I was eager to hear about in detail. "Sorry, I shouldn't—"

"Write checks you can't cash?"

Jocelyn let go a gasping laugh. Her blonde curls almost danced, and for a moment, the ever-present sadness that lived in her honey brown eyes vanished. It was the moment I decided to seek out more opportunities to make that magic act happen again.

"I'm just saying I can do more than the heavy lifting, Jocelyn. I take instructions well." We walked through a neighborhood with nothing but distant traffic sounds and the rustle of the bags we carried. I could see the Durand home half a block away, but I wasn't ready for our field trip to be over.

"Thank you for your help this afternoon. Obviously, I couldn't have done it without you. Not on foot, anyway."

"My pleasure. Really, there is no other way I would have rather spent the time." I walked a stride and half behind her, but she stopped before turning into the driveway of small brown pebbles.

She pivoted to face me, a slow turn, allowing me to catch the tail-end of a bottom lip nibble. A fleeting look said she chided herself for doing it. With a deep breath, she lifted her chin before she spoke. "I—I meant what I said before, about not being euphemistically-inclined." She almost bit her lip again, but this time I saw her tell herself *no*, and I tried not to smile at her inner-struggle. She cleared her throat; another tell that gave away her search for courage. "So, as far as my first bit of instruction? I'm going to need you to speak plainly and—maybe more importantly—go slowly." With a single, decisive nod, Jocelyn hurried down the driveway to the side door, and as soon as I found my breath, I followed her.

19

Jocelyn

WALK. DON'T RUN, JOCELYN. I said this on repeat until I made it to the side door, fumbling to get my key. Help appeared in the form of a red-cheeked Frannie.

"You've quite an armload, Ms. Durand. Let me help."

"Thank you, Frannie, but I'm Jocelyn, please. Did you have a good bike tour?" I hurried in to set my farmers' market goodies on the kitchen island.

"We did. Worked up a sweat too. We're about to jump in the pool."

That's when I noticed Frannie wore a conservative, red and white, one-piece swimsuit. "Are you a lifeguard?"

"I am. Summers in Ocean City, well, until this summer."

"Ocean City, MD? That's a big beach. Real waves hit that stretch. Not an easy job." Asher had caught up and came through the door to join the conversation.

"Yes, sir," came Frannie's serious reply.

"Enough of the *sir* talk. I bet you have some stories to tell." While Asher spoke to Frannie, he only had eyes for me, and my flight response hit hard until I registered Frannie's cryptic reply.

"The stories you'd *want* to hear I'd really rather not share." Frannie gave a slight neck stretch, like she tried to release a sudden tension in her shoulders.

"Did you get ice cream? Scoop Du Jour is my favorite. Well, it's gelato actually. Better than ice cream, in my opinion." My attempt to divert the discussion failed.

"People think they want to hear the harrowing details," Frannie continued, "but they don't. Not really. Not when they realize the stories are fact, not fiction. People live for the fiction."

"Well, let's not spit in the eye of fiction fans. They are my bread and butter." Asher helped me unload our bags full of fresh food but missed my cues to veer from the topic.

"And that's all well and good, but how much bread and butter has Disney made re-fictionalizing the darker tales of society's early make-believe stories? The mermaid gets her Prince, the Ice Queen has a snowman sidekick, and Cinderella's step-sisters keep their feet intact. I mean, what's that about?"

I didn't know or care, but I also didn't have a good feeling about the course of the conversation. Familiar with the hungry look of a college student eager to prove her critical thinking skills, I had no interest in being Frannie's fodder so she could impress the ruggedly handsome novelist in our midst. How did we get here? And where was Gabe?

"And here I thought you were a budding marine biologist like Gabe. Where is Ga—?"

"Nope. Dual concentration, actually. Cognitive Neuroscience and Comparative Literature."

That'll teach me to ask questions. Wait, I didn't. "*Ha.* Did you hear that, Asher? That can't possibly be a thing, right? Remember when we just had Psych and English, and you only picked one?" Was I the only one hearing the warning bells?

"Let's take your novel, Ms.—Jocelyn."

"Oh, Frannie, let's not. Where's Gabe? Thought you were going for a swim?" I kept my tone upbeat, my hands busy with the produce.

"Have you read it, Asher?" Frannie pushed on like I hadn't said a word.

"I have. More than once, I don't mind saying." He leaned in on the kitchen island, intrigued by where the young woman headed. But while the route proved unique, I recognized her destination from a good distance. This wouldn't end well.

"Well, whether there is any—*basis* for it—and I'm not saying there is—but surely it must have crossed your mind. Certainly, in academic lecture halls and coffee klatches and wine-infused book club meetings, people wonder, ask the question. What makes a brain capable of, I mean, what kind of shitshow upbringing could have conjured a story like—"

"Frannie," Asher snapped.

Stoic, I poured a glass of water, waiting for the inevitable to come to pass. Frannie joined in the unpacking with her mouth moving faster than her hands, and evidently her brain. "No, I'm not saying there's truth to it. The opposite, actually. Those thoughts are fleeting. No one would want to dwell on the notion." She homed in on me. "But who could blame you, Jocelyn, for staying out of the limelight, actively avoiding it by never writing another book. I'm sure the Grimm brothers and Hans Christian Andersen wouldn't have held up to the scrutiny. Why would you put yourself in the position to endure an incessant indictment, or worse yet, admit to it?"

"Francesca!" Gabe, fresh on the scene, barked.

"What?" Frannie spun to face three sets of wide eyes.

"Outside. Now. Please." Gabe's punctuated speech wasn't loud, but everyone knew he meant for the young woman to move and quickly.

"What did I—say?" Her gaze bounced to meet each of ours. I don't believe she meant any harm, but the two guard dogs in the room had chosen a side, and it wasn't hers. I opted not to come to Frannie's defense. Extricating myself from the equation felt like a prudent move.

"I'm sorry. Excuse me. I'm a little sticky from the walk. Think I'll go change. Would you—?" I waved my hands at the remaining shopping strewn across the kitchen island, speaking to no one in particular. As I climbed the stairs, my head pounded in time with each step and the mighty thud of my heart. I leaned against my door, and the short snort of a suppressed laugh oinked its way out. "Well, that'll slow him down," I sighed. Check that. That'd stop the fast and loose writing Lothario *dead* in his tracks.

20

Asher

With the last of the shopping put away, the obviously torn Gabe pointed to both the patio and the upstairs.

"Your call, kid."

He directed me to the patio, where the mouthy Francesca had been banished, and turned toward the front hall to head upstairs to speak to his mother. I had my marching orders. But once he'd traveled the hall and up two steps, he called out, "Wait. Switch." Gabe jogged back through the kitchen to head outside to Frannie. The choice belonged to him, and I planned to let him make it. Each had its pros and cons, but I believe, at that moment, he made the right call. The right call for me anyhow.

I started toward the stairs, then backtracked to the well-stocked bar in the living room, followed by the kitchen freezer. If I was going in, I was going in armed. Two lowball glasses with ice and a nearly full bottle of very good Scotch, and may the odds be in my favor.

Now, this was not a conquest. I knew my boundaries and had no plans to cross any of them without sober consent. But I also figured my next stop included some hurt, so bringing along a numbing agent felt like wisdom. But what the hell did I know? In the back of my mind, something said I should have some trepidation about knocking on the door, but foolish or not, I had none.

"Come in?" Jocelyn's reply sounded more like a question, but my hands were full, so I couldn't open the door.

"Jocelyn, it's Ash. Could you open the door?"

When she did, her sparkling brown eyes landed on mine and then the booze. With the sudden realization that this scene likely translated as the *opposite* of "go slowly," I feared the error doomed me.

"Oh, thank goodness." Jocelyn reached across the threshold, snatching the bottle from my grasp. "Come in, come in, and close the door." She trotted to the opposite side of the unusually high bed and hopped on it, sitting in a puddle of her own dress. Her hands reached toward the glasses I held in mine. This was going better than I had dared to dream. Then Jocelyn gasped, and I figured the woman had come to her senses.

"What?" I asked, keeping to my side of the room. *My side,* as if the whole place didn't smell of her. Was it her soap, her shampoo, perfume she wore? The combination proved powerful, and I wondered why the world needed Scotch at all. I could have drunk that scent all day and night, and the mere thought of it made the aroma-filled room tilt.

"Is it after five o'clock?" Jocelyn asked from her knees on the bed, and while I'm not a religious man, I said a little prayer for time to be in my favor.

With a little gasp of my own, I pointed to the bedside clock. "Four-fifty-eight."

"Oh, then I'll pour slowly. I'm a lady, after all." She gave a cheeky grin and reached out again for me to offer her the glasses. I couldn't move fast enough, thrusting the short tumblers toward her. With the deftness of a seasoned bartender, Jocelyn poured two fingers for each of us, then placed the bottle on the bedside chest behind her. She patted the mattress as an invitation to "climb aboard."

My eyebrow had an annoying habit of giving a questioning look when questions probably shouldn't be asked, and yet, there I stood—with an inquisitive eye. *Chump.*

"*Ah-ha*," Jocelyn said and looked at her hands resting in her lap.

"Ah-ha?" I asked, stock-still with a Scotch on the rocks in each hand.

"I have heard of these moments, these moments that seem to send confusing messages to men, and I—in the past—have wondered how these moments of confusion manifest themselves, but now here I am, in one of those moments."

"*Huh*?" I'm eloquent when I need to be.

"I can see how this whole scenario is running counter to what I said before about going slowly, and I *meant* that, but right now I need a drink, but there's a feisty twenty-one-year-old lurking downstairs that I'd rather avoid, so if we could make this about *that* and not about *us*—for a moment anyway, that would be great. I'm looking for solidarity here, Asher."

From the edge of the bed, I offered Jocelyn a drink she had poured. "Kids. Am I right?" I asked and raised a glass in a toast. Jocelyn laughed, and we each took a sip. In a minute, we had each settled against the headboard, legs outstretched, crossed at the ankles on our respective sides of the king bed, clutching our good Scotch.

"Do you have kids? I mean, that you know of?" Jocelyn asked the questions and quickly took another taste of her drink.

My chin hit my chest.

"I'm kidding, *kidding*. Sorry," she followed with a snicker.

"I don't." I swirled the dark liquor in my glass, the ice clinked. "I'm pretty sure I'd know."

"What was that? Frannie, I mean?"

I shrugged. "College kid in the company of literary greatness trying to look smart, maybe?"

"Woke," she interjected. "I think that's the term. And literary greatness? Jeez, Asher, I know your sales are good and all, but—"

I nearly choked on my sip with a laugh. How did she do it?

In a moment of being called to account in a way she had no responsibility to answer and in front of her own kid no less, and she made jokes. Funny jokes. "You know I meant you."

"Shut up, Asher Cray. You are practically lying in my bed, feeding me Scotch, and now calling me a literary great. Not exactly playing fair."

The speed with which I leaped to my feet surprised me. It made an impression on my drinking companion too. "This is not that, Jocelyn. If you know anything, in all of this, please know that." I set my glass on the bedside chest near me. I had only drunk two swallows, but it was the proximity to her that intoxicated me, and yet her stunned face said she didn't know it could be true. How long had it been since someone told her how amazing she was?

"I'm sorry, Asher." She rolled to her knees again.

"And you should stop that." That boomed louder than I intended.

"Stop what?"

"Stop *apologizing*." I'd brought the sadness back to those brown eyes. "I break into your house, you apologize. A young woman questions your upbringing, you apologize. I try to tell you that you're an extraordinarily talented woman, funny and smart and down-to-earth and so incredibly beautiful that makes it hard for me to *breathe*, and you— apologize."

"Stop, please. Just stop talking." Her hushed plea nearly broke my heart. "Can we just sit here and enjoy the Scotch and the quiet company? Can you just sit here with me, so I don't feel alone, for a minute? Two, maybe?"

On the edge of the bed, I faced away from her, running my fingers through my hair, startled by her request and my loose tongue.

I stiffened when her hand touched my back. It was an intimate gesture in an intimate space, and I had brought the booze. I stood.

"Guess it's my turn to apologize." I wasn't sure looking at her was the smart play.

"Why? Did you say something you didn't mean?"

"No. I promised you the truth, Jocelyn. Always."

"Then why apologize?"

"I don't know how to—" My legs needed to move. I paced.

"You don't know how to—what?" She sat curled up on that high bed, still not understanding.

"When was the last time you—" I couldn't get the question out. The thought of it physically hurt, but my head-bobbing filled in the blank. But she went further than I meant.

"Jeez, Asher. Okay. Yeah, it's been a while." She pulled in tighter.

"No, I'm not asking that," I sputtered to allay her concerns, but the truth of the matter was worse than she knew. And when I saw relief flicker in her eyes, guilt flooded my chest.

"What then?" Her concerned look for me was so out of place, yet I wouldn't have expected anything other than her bitten lip. She didn't disappoint. She couldn't help herself.

"When was—the last time—someone *kissed* you?"

"Oh." She set her glass on the bedside table.

"No, I mean, when was the last time someone kissed you—who *wanted* to kiss you?"

"*Oh.*" Those brown eyes met mine, and with them the realization that every time I ever thought I'd known what heartbreak looked like, I'd been wrong. It stared me in the face now, and I didn't know what to do. Every instinct said to go to her, comfort her, take her in my arms, but in reality, those acts were no solution, and even if they were, I wasn't the man for the job.

An aching silence loomed. "Jocelyn."

"Sorry. *Uh*, never."

"What?"

"*Oops.* The apology was for taking so long to reply, but in my defense, the answer is nothing short of embarrassing. The answer being: never. I have never been kissed by someone who actually wanted to kiss me. *Oh my God.* I am forty-six years old, and no one has ever wanted to kiss me." She clutched at the fabric of her dress. Both fists white-knuckle tight.

"No, that's not true. I promise you that is not true."

"Oh, sure. No one put a gun to Will's head but—"

"No. Other than Will—I'm sure others wanted to, but couldn't because you—"

"Right. I see what you're saying. Not that no one wanted to, just that no one ever— has. That's better, right?" She started rocking back and forth. She had released the grip of her dress but held tight to her shins. Swaying.

"Jocelyn, please."

"Oh, no, Asher. I feel the pity acutely now. Please don't make this worse. Because if it can get worse, I really don't want to know what that feels like."

"Whoa, wait. If I could come over there now and kiss you, I would. But—you said, 'slowly' and I'm not rushing anything, and under the circumstances, slow is definitely the right call. No question."

"To be fair, that was before someone brought it to my attention that I've never been touched by a man that actually wanted to. You'll excuse me if now I'm feeling some urgency in the matter."

I almost pounced but stopped myself. Everywhere I looked, I saw danger signs. Did she want this? Was I up for *the* kiss, the first *real* kiss? And how much Scotch did we drink? I eyed both our glasses.

"What's wrong?" She crawled back to her knees, biting that lip again. I reached for my glass and downed the contents. An ice chunk stuck in my gullet, and I walked out of her room straight to mine, wishing I had brought the bottle, too.

21

Jocelyn

ASHER DIDN'T EVEN HAVE the decency to close the door behind him when he left me alone, staring at my drink—a reminder of the first time I met Laney Li.

I knew it was a big deal. Gigi had been out of law school a year, toiling away at a top New York City firm, miserable. Will and I were in our last year at NYU, about to run off to Europe to drink wine and look at art.

Our parents, Hugo and Juliette Durand, made education a priority. They were French and proud and provided for their daughters to go to college, even from the grave. But four years marked the limit of their generosity, thus when Gigi went to law school, Yale no less, she finished under a mountain of debt, so she put her nose to the proverbial grindstone, whereas I freely gallivanted around Europe.

A few years older than my sister, Laney and Gigi missed each other during their Yalie years, but an alumni networking event put them in the same room one night, and they have been together ever since. Not long after, Laney got Gigi a job deciphering contracts at a literary agency, and then the two struck out on their own to set up their own shop. But our first meeting took place in a dark, smoky bar near the Meatpacking District that had barely begun its upward trend. I was dubious. More so when Gigi arrived late to join us. Laney had planned it that way.

"Do you drink Scotch, Jojo?" Laney casually signaled the

bartender with two fingers while asking me the question.

"Only Gigi calls me Jojo. Jocelyn will do, and no, I drink wine."
When she brought her gaze to me, I met it, careful not to blink.

Laney's loud honk of a laugh surprised me. "Not here, you
don't. I like you, kid. We're gonna do fine."

My drink arrived.

"What does Scotch taste like?" I asked with a curled lip and
flared nostrils.

"Rubber, wood, fire, some leather, dirt, but in a good way." She
slid a heavy-bottomed glass with a healthy serving of amber liquor
in it, neat. "Good to meet you, Jocelyn. *L'chaim.*"

It was the first and last time I *gulped* Scotch, or so I vowed at
the time. I'm not sure about the rest of it, but I definitely tasted
the fire. Felt it too, all over as Laney let her raucous guffaw bellow
again.

I taste all of it nowadays. The rubber, wood, leather, even the
dirt, and I like it. To be honest, I prefer it neat, but when Asher
Cray stands in your bedroom offering Scotch rocks, you drink
Scotch rocks.

But Asher no longer stood in my bedroom. He dropped a
bombshell observation and bolted. Coward. Turned out the
internet didn't always get it right, and it certainly got that guy
wrong. I took another sip, letting the liquor swim through me with
nothing to slow it on its way to my brain. I hadn't eaten since the
rainbow pancakes, and even then, I hadn't eaten much.

Stretched out on my bed, I pointed and flexed my feet as I stared
at my open door. Slow steps trudged up the stairs.

Gabe stood in my doorway; brow arched. It really was a neat
trick. "Where's...?" he asked.

I pointed behind him, indicating the guest room down the hall.
"Where's...?" Our verbal shorthand communicated all we needed.

"Outside." Gabe leaned on the doorframe.

"Hope you weren't too tough on her. Some smart people let their mouths get them in trouble. They can't help themselves, poor things."

"That's why I've always aimed for middle-of-the-road." He frowned with a raised shoulder.

"*Aw*, come on, Gabe. You're just a smidge above average. Don't sell yourself short." I tried to keep a straight face.

"Seriously, Mom. You okay? Dad just called and told me about the house. Why didn't you tell me?"

"Gee, Honey, I don't know. Not your problem, not a good time, been a little preoccupied. It'll be fine. I'll stay here until it's fixed. I didn't count on it being so crowded, but I guess that won't last long. Since we've been such welcoming hosts," I joked.

"Speaking of—" Gabe tilted his head, a signal someone headed our way. "Hey, Asher. What's going on?" Gabe crossed inside the door to my room. Asher had his hands in his pockets and a serious expression.

"Asher here was thinking about kissing me," I offered, then took another taste of Scotch.

"Jesus, Jocelyn," Asher muttered behind a dumbfounded smile he tried to hide.

"That right, Asher?" My son gave an approving nod. "And what were my Mom's thoughts on the matter?"

"Oh, I was definitely *pro* at first, to be sure, but then Asher made some points that have me going the other way now. It's a toss-up, really."

Gabe took hold of Asher's shoulder in consolation. "Imagine what it was like growing up with her. On the plus side, you never have to guess what she's thinking. What you see is what you get. I got spoiled. Between her and my aunts, I assumed all women tell it like it is. Not so, it turns out. Not so at all. Of course, then my Dad—well, I guess that's a whole other story, huh?"

"For the record, I'm done defending my ex-husband for today. Met my quota."

"Good," Gabe and Asher stated in absolute and simultaneous agreement.

"Now who's in cahoots?" I asked. Asher chuckled, and Gabe cocked his head like he might ask, but he didn't.

"Frannie and I are moving downstairs. That's for us, not for you."

"You give candid, you get candid in return. Reap what you sow." I raised my glass at both men, shaking my head in mock-exasperation.

Gabe continued. "And I've already lit the grill to throw on my signature chicken, make a salad, and I think we should have a movie night—just maybe no Disney. We, Frannie and I, hope you both will join us for any or all of it. Good luck, Asher." Gabe gave Asher a friendly thump in the arm and left.

"Your kid's pretty great."

"I *know*," I mouthed for dramatic effect. "Meh, Gabe's all right," I said louder than necessary.

"Love you too, Mom," Gabe shouted from partway down the stairs.

I didn't move from my spot, reclining but propped with a pillow, ankles crossed. I smoothed out the skirt of my madras sundress in patchwork shades of pink. Asher remained in the hall, inches from my bedroom's threshold. The symbolism bordered on ridiculous.

"Are you leaving?" When it seemed he would not talk, I dove in with the obvious question. "Are you going? Whatever your plan, your agent's plan, it didn't include this circus, so I get it if you need to go."

"Would you prefer I go?"

"Surely, I would have said so if I wanted you gone. Haven't we figured out that much?"

"Does that mean—?"

"It means I want you to stay." I liked that we were both speaking plainly now. "Also, I remembered something. Some*one*."

"What's that?"

"Senior year. High school. Prom, actually. My parents died a few weeks before. Car wreck if you didn't know. Anyway, I still planned to go to prom, because I was seventeen and lost, so why not put on a pretty dress and go to a dance, right? Gigi had graduated from Columbia, she's the brains, and was home before moving to New Haven for law school. My parents planned for me to spend the summer in France. Distant relatives. While I traveled, Gigi sold our house. Our Bayborough house. We kept this one, so I could be here or in her apartment in Connecticut on school breaks. Of course, it wasn't long before I went to the Atwaters' home in New Canaan, mostly. Anyway, Darren Kolchek—a classmate of mine."

Asher had made himself comfortable, leaning in the doorway, arms crossed, listening to me ramble. He had a look of genuine interest, and as long as he gave it, I wanted to feed it.

"Darren Kolchek?" Asher asked because I had stopped my long-winded over-share. "Sounds like a hockey player."

"Soccer, I think. Anyway, Darren kissed me. He wanted to, and he did. Prom night. Right out in the backyard. I haven't thought of him since. Two days later, I took off for Èze on graduation night. Huh. Funny the things you forget—"

"Well, see? Told you."

"Just didn't want you to think you were alone. Some weirdo outlier if you're still contemplating kissing me."

"I am, since candor appears to be the theme of the evening. Can't stop thinking about it if I'm honest—and I am."

A bubbly wave crested inside me but then Asher kept talking.

"But now I've learned of Darren Kolchek, so the urgency you spoke of earlier has waned. No reason to rush it given this new information. Though hearing you're on the fence is kind of a bummer. Sure hope things go my way—eventually. In the meantime, I'm gonna get cleaned up for dinner and movie night. Meet you downstairs?"

I cursed both the long-forgotten Darren Kolchek and my big mouth, nodding after the sexily smug Asher Cray.

22

Asher

JOCELYN BEAT ME DOWNSTAIRS, and I found the first-floor buzzing with activity. She whisked a homemade dressing for a colorful salad full of fruits and vegetables from our earlier field trip. Gabe sliced cucumbers, and Frannie set the table for four while eighties music played in the background. Such a foreign environment for me and yet I felt completely at ease, aside from the desire to kiss the blonde subtly bouncing to the beat of Echo and the Bunnyman's *Lips Like Sugar*. That couldn't be a coincidence, could it?

So, what you see is what you get, huh? Well, it was unlike anything I had ever encountered. The mile-a-minute brain, the frankness, the unabashed adoration for the ones closest to her, and a resolve to get back up, with a luminous smile, no less, when someone knocks her down and hard. Her tenacity inspired a lesson this aging author needed to learn.

"Give me a hand at the grill, Ash?" Gabe skidded by on his way to the patio.

"Sure," I replied, but the kid hadn't checked up. I stole a quick look at Jocelyn, but she bobbed her head, lost in the Psychedelic Furs and leafy greens. *Pretty in Pink. Isn't she?*

I stepped out to find a mostly shaded patio and the mild, earthy aroma of real wood charcoal. The grill fire only added to the oppressive late day heat. Gabe mopped chicken with a golden infusion of fresh herbs and lemon. It sizzled when it dripped off the meat, while little bursts of flame flew up and died down just as quickly. It smelled delicious.

"Beer?" Gabe pointed his basting brush to a cooler.

"No thanks. I'm good. What's in the—"

"Why not have a beer, Asher?"

I eyed the young man with some skepticism, then realized what was happening. The heat radiating from the stainless cooker and coupling with the evening's stagnant, humid air seemed intentional. An interrogation tactic even.

"It's just when I ran through this in my head we were drinking beer, is all. Forget it." Gabe shrugged, keeping his eye on the grilling task.

"What's on your mind, Gabe?"

"My mom, I guess."

"That affliction is going around," I joked.

"Affliction? Like a sickness? *Hm*, this isn't going well." The young man pushed back, and I appreciated it.

"Well, she is discombobulating."

Gabe grinned at that descriptor, and we nudged back into friendlier territory. "She is that," he agreed, then stayed quiet for a while, finishing his saucing of the meat before closing the heavy lid. "This is weird, man. Just be nice to her. She's been alone for a long time, and even before, well, you gotta figure—right?"

I wasn't *exactly* clear what he meant, but I nodded anyway because I had a pretty good idea, and I didn't want further explanation. Anything but that.

"I don't want you to think I'm a pushover in this department, but I know my aunts like you, so I'm giving you the easy pass. For now."

"Do this a lot? Vet your mom's suitors?" I kidded again.

"First time," he replied.

"Well, you're doing fine. And don't worry. If I do anything

wrong, your aunts will have my nuts in a—"

"How's it going out here, fellas?" Jocelyn's head poked out the French doors.

"I think we're ready to pull the chicken, Mom. It'll need to rest for a few minutes, but it's ready."

"Great. Hey, this music—did you make this playlist? It's like high school all over again."

"Frannie and I did, just a bit ago. She's good at it, right?" He smiled at his mother's head-bopping as she closed the door.

"The music is you?" I asked, squinting in disbelief.

"Yeah, thought maybe you could use a little nudge. Bit over-the-top, but Mom's clueless. She really has no notion of guile. It's pretty refreshing. But— it does make her vulnerable, so, for the record, you have more than my aunts to worry about. And I have access to fishing boats, so they'll never find the body." Gabe's nonchalance as he pulled the last piece of chicken from the grill surprised me. Holding the platter piled high, his broad grin appeared. "Wish you'd taken the beer, huh? Go ahead, grab one now."

I did.

By the time we finished eating, and the polite after-dinner chit chat wound down, the last light of the day faded. Jocelyn gave no indication of a grudge, but Frannie spoke little, avoiding any sort of controversy. Shooed from the kitchen, all attempts to help with the clean-up thwarted, I stuck nearby in the hopes that Jocelyn and I could have another she'd-wash-I'd-dry moment.

I stood in the living room, watching the backyard greenery turn to shades of purple in the nighttime light while the first fireflies lit up their tails. More and more followed until they were everywhere, flickering their goodbyes to the dwindling day.

"I told you." Jocelyn appeared beside me in the dim room. The sounds of the sink, jangling silverware, and clattering dishes settled in the background.

"The magic, you mean?" It took all my strength to keep my eyes on the twinkling light show rather than look at her. But I caught moments of her reflection in the paneled glass doors in front of us.

"The magic," she echoed.

"When did it start? The magic?"

"*Huh*. Don't know." She only had eyes for the outdoors. "Funny how we tend not to take notice of the start of a thing but always recollect the end of one. Why are *beginnings* less noteworthy? Why do we glide by them, but etch the *end* in our minds— in stone? In legal paperwork?"

"Probably because not every beginning *is* noteworthy. Some things look like a beginning, but they're over before they really get started. Never achieve lift-off. You don't know a noteworthy beginning was worth noting until you're a good bit into the thing, right? Beginnings are in the rearview, whereas endings come barreling at you head-on. Couldn't avoid them even if you wanted to. But I think you find, once the dust settles, it was over *long* before the paperwork."

We stood in the dark. The kitchen had gone quiet, but the outside noises of the nocturnal creatures crept in to fill the stillness.

"Asher Cray. I don't recommend making the genre switch to romance any time soon. Jeez. And not for nothing, but sometimes endings come flying at you from outta nowhere."

"Yeah. Guess so. Sometimes beginnings do too. Like a badminton racquet out of the shadows." I rubbed my head with the recollection, rather than cave to my desire to touch her.

"Well, I hope it inspires you to *begin* something. That something here stirs you to—*write*."

"Write? Yes, of course. That's why I'm here." Obviously, I needed a reminder. "I told Laney the other day I have never had a problem doing two things, and the second one is writing." The proverbial crickets chirped in earnest, and it was the only sound other than the *thud* of my joke.

After far too long, Jocelyn asked, "What's the first one, then?"

"Never mind." I chuckled at her naivete.

"Wait, it was a joke, right? And I missed it."

"Don't worry about it. It wasn't very funny."

"No, I bet it was. Did Laney *honk* at it?" Jocelyn's sweet sincerity and her mention of Laney's goose-like laugh made me chuckle.

"She did—*honk*, yes."

"And I thought you came here because you *were* having trouble writing."

"Oh, I am having trouble writing. Lots of trouble."

"Then maybe you should do the other thing." She gave my arm a reassuring poke.

"The other thing?"

"The other thing you don't have a problem doing. The thing you just joked about. Maybe if you do that thing, the words will start to flow."

I tilted up at the coffered ceiling, pushing the palms of my hands into my eyes with a laughing sigh. "I'm trying, Jocelyn, I'm trying."

"*Knock, knock*. Am I interrupting?" Gabe knocked on the doorframe, his silhouette highlighted by the kitchen's glow. He flipped the light switch.

"Just talking, Gabe. What's up?"

"You wanna watch that movie now?"

"Which movie?"

"I picked your favorite, Mom."

"*Jaws?*"

"No."

"*Singing in the Rain?*"

"No."

My laugh interrupted the guessing game. "This is a rather

eclectic favorites list. How many favorites do you have, Jocelyn?"

"Too many, Asher. Too many." She took my hand and pulled me toward the door, only to let go. I reached to grab hold of hers again. Her quick glance and squeeze said progress.

I found myself in the finished basement level of the house. Unexplored territory for me. The space was as well-renovated as the rest of the house, high-end and comfortable with details to make guests feel at home and every need seen to.

Off the main room, a windowless theater included reclining leather loveseats with a large screen and a projector hanging from the ceiling. Light sconces and speakers lined the walls, and the smell of popcorn filled the air. The Durands did movie night right.

What movie? An eighties classic, another of Jocelyn's "favorites," with all the hallmarks worthy of its cult following. A pirate, a giant, and mustachioed swordsman. Plus, there was Peter Falk. Everyone loves Peter Falk.

Captivated by the look of the young woman in the film, my mind wandered. She could have been Jocelyn twenty-five years ago, and I couldn't help but wonder how close the comparison was in real life and where I could find a picture for proof. A yearbook? A snapshot from a trip abroad? A wedding photo? I would hunt for that later.

I tried to pay attention, I really did, but Jocelyn sat so close and let me hold her hand. As with the earlier music, it was like high school all over again. We sat in the dark, and I knew she liked me, was pretty sure she *liked me,* liked me, but there were chaperones in the room, and well—I chickened out. Her constant smile beamed, incredible to witness, and distracting as hell. And have I mentioned her scent? When she rested her head on my shoulder, you'd have thought I scored the winning basket at the buzzer.

As the movie ended, the heroes rode off into the sunset,

on horseback, no less. My issue? The bad guy didn't get his comeuppance. The good guy, rumored to be a villain but wasn't, let him go. Oh well. Sometimes that's real life, I guess. Anyway, it was late, and no one had gotten much sleep the night before. My companion sighed and grinned at me with drowsy eyes and wayward curls as the rolling movie credits reflected on her face. I should have kissed her right there.

Then with a quick, "Goodnight, all," she took off, practically running from the room.

With Jocelyn's hasty exit after the movie, I assumed she got cold feet, was tired, or pumping the brakes. Somehow I missed a sign. Hindsight rarely helps at all. I stayed downstairs and chatted with Gabe while Frannie fell asleep in his lap. He slid out from under her and walked me to the main room. I asked about old photos under the guise of an interest in the architectural changes of the house. I hit pay dirt.

Gabe pulled out a stack of photo albums. Most of the snapshots detailed times spent here at the Durand summer home, lots of them. The house was old even then, and I easily rifled through the photographs with detachment because I didn't recognize anyone in them. Someone lovingly cared for the pictures, labeling them with names, dates, and locations. But the photos all but stopped with one summer. From those last photos, I guessed Jocelyn with her missing front teeth would have been six years old or so, making Genevieve ten. A final album had random photos through later years but nothing like the earlier collections.

When Gabe opened another drawer, he pulled out a box of thumb drives. "This is me," Gabe announced with pride. "First kid, only kid. Don't worry. They'll keep—until tomorrow." He winked. "I'm beat."

"Me too, kid. I'll turn out the lights on my way up."

"G'night, then." Gabe disappeared into the theater, then

reappeared carrying a sleeping Frannie to their downstairs bed, closing the door with his foot.

I returned to the pictures marked that long-ago July, the last organized pictures taken here in Amagansett. I zeroed in on the eyes of the people in the photos. The eyes tell the tale. Intentional or not. Then again, some have the talent to hide, even in plain sight. Add squinting in the sun or sunglasses and the science falls apart. But something was off. One more underlying whisper of sadness or fear or—maybe sometimes writers let their imaginations get the better of them.

My own eyes couldn't focus any longer, and Gabe and Frannie had gotten their second wind. Ah, youth. When I switched off the light to head up to bed, I heard a grinding, popping sound outside. A car pulled into the driveway.

23

Jocelyn

Was I tired? Yes, bone-tired, but I couldn't justify why until I heard Frannie giggle, and it all flooded back. I couldn't get out of the room fast enough. "Goodnight, all."

In hindsight, bolting like that may have sent the wrong message to the handsome man who held my hand, sitting shoulder to shoulder with me throughout the film. He acted like a complete gentleman, and I was learning not to be surprised. Laney had done a number on this man's reputation, and the rumors couldn't be further from the truth... and that conjured a mix of disappointment and relief.

Stalling on the main floor, I set up coffee for the next morning, wiping down already spotless kitchen counters, checking and rechecking, making certain I'd locked all the doors. Surely, I had been clear with the forward talk earlier. My candor, as he put it. The hand holding. I laid my head on his shoulder, for goodness' sake. Was the earlier teasing "toss-up" quip the culprit? Could he possibly think I was still on the fence? What was he waiting for? *Time to take it to the next level, Jocelyn Mae.* Consent is the new sexy. I read that somewhere.

I hopped up on the kitchen island, adjusted my sundress around me, and simultaneously fluffed and flattened my curls that always went haywire at nightfall. Feeling the sway of sleepiness, I moved to the tufted bench under the wine wall rack. He would come upstairs eventually, and I would wait until he did. I only hoped I would be awake when it happened.

No such luck.

I sat upright; my head propped in a corner. When I did wake—or partially wake—it happened quickly. Gentle fingers brushed aside my curls, and I lifted my chin and pressed my lips to his. Eyes closed, I held him by his face, my hands pulling at his cheeks, when I felt him hesitate. I pushed in for more, making my permission clear. It was very brief, not at all what I imagined, and yet oddly familiar. For a drowsy moment, I tried to take some comfort in that, but confusion hit with two voices in stereo.

"Uh, sorry," one began.

"Hey, old girl," the other chortled.

"Didn't mean to interrupt. I heard a car. I'm just heading up to bed." Asher's voice, seemingly far away, compounded the mess.

I pulled from the passionless kiss with a grunty, "Huh?" and gave a healthy two-handed shove to the man kneeling in front of me.

"Just like the old days, right?" Will snickered and patted my thigh.

"Will?!" I wiped the back of my hand across my lips. "What are you doing?"

"Just trying to wake you, Love. You were the one with the grabby hands and the eager mouth. Softer than I remember, not like you at all, come to think of it. Have you been kissing someone else lately?"

"No." The disappointment and frustration oozing from that one-word sentence amounted to a lot. My head jerked in surprise when I registered motion across the room. "Asher." His light blue eyes read a little darker, hurt maybe, and a current of sickness rippled in my stomach. "I thought—I waited—where have you—?"

"Asher?" Will stood. "Asher Cray? *The* Asher Cray? It *is* you. Well, if I didn't know better, I'd think I'd come upon a hostage situation." He eyed me. "It's not, is it? Tell me you haven't gone off and done something nutty now have you, Love?"

"Shut up, Will."

"Being a fan is one thing, but there are lines, dear heart."

"Shut. Up. Will." I wiped my mouth again.

Asher made his reluctant way to where my ex-husband stood, hand outstretched to shake a former colleague's. "Good to—see you again, William."

"Is it? My, my, this is—unexpected. You little minx." He tapped his finger on the end of my nose while I remained perched on the bench, cringing at his touch.

"Settle down, William. I came here to work. Laney and Genevieve sent me. Jocelyn being here was unplanned. You know that by now. I'm working."

"Really? Do tell. What's the next bestseller? Seaside caper? Beautiful, lovelorn divorcee dupes hot, bestselling author into captivity? A victimless crime, obviously."

"*Hm.* Sounds promising." Asher grew impish, nodding like he considered the premise.

"Does it now?" I asked, standing to intervene in the banter of what I feared might be a budding bromance. "That would definitely take some work."

"Hard work never scared me."

Sleepy, while simultaneously stunned at the sight of these two worlds colliding, I couldn't keep up with all the innuendo swirling around my kitchen. Will disappeared from my periphery as heat crept up my neck.

"Then again, sometimes it's just about showing up." I gave another verbal jab and frowned. How long had I dozed on that bench?

"Something tells me it will take more than that to get inside a beautiful, lovelorn divorcee. *Uh*, in-inside her *head*, I mean." Asher may have lost his nerve with that last parry, clarifying his remark.

"Hey, you old goat. That's my wife you're talking to."

"Ex-wife," Asher and I corrected at once.

"You okay, Love? You look a bit—splotchy." Will gestured to my mottled chest.

Exasperated and determined to end the uncomfortable scene, I took on the role of the innkeeper. "Gabe and his—Frannie are staying downstairs; you'll want to avoid hearing that. I'm in our—*my* room, and Asher is in the second guest suite. The kids had their way in my old room last night, so Gigi's is the only clean bed I can offer you. Or the sunroom, your pick."

"That's it? We all go to bed? I brought wine!" Will pouted at the kitchen sink, pointing at a case on the counter.

"It's late, Will." I trudged toward the front hall.

"Very late, William." Asher grumbled, following me.

"Party poopers."

Asher and I lumbered up the stairs, my footfalls synced with his a few risers behind me. As I headed to my room, he took my hand over the banister, looking up at me in the dark from his spot still steps below. He stroked my fingers with his thumb as Will clinked bottles, unpacking his wine haul in the kitchen.

"I didn't know you were waiting," Asher whispered.

I exhaled with a relief of sorts. "Good to hear." I tried to smile.

"Is it too late to—?"

"It is, Asher." The fingers of my other hand reflexively touched my lips. I couldn't shake where they had just been. One more undesired kiss to add to my romance résumé while my tidy life grew decidedly less so. I didn't like it. Tomorrow called for cleaning.

24

Asher

I HADN'T REALIZED MY exhaustion until my head hit the pillow and thank God for it. What a fiasco, and does anyone show up at this place in the daylight hours? What's with all the late-night arrivals? My own included.

In my mind, I flipped through that last photo album as I drifted off to sleep. The mental slideshow served as a distraction from thinking about William Atwater's arrival, and the new dynamic his presence promised to affect. No use mulling over that inevitability.

Only one sparsely filled album held photographs of the Durand sisters' teen years, with a significant time leap from pictures of Genevieve graduating high school to two stray pictures, the last in the book. The sudden gap struck me as strange, the final two in particular. One showed Jocelyn on prom night. Only one photo marked the occasion. She was a pretty teen, the kind who didn't know it, but it surprised me to see her sad brown eyes weren't on display. For a young woman whose parents had recently died, she looked remarkably happy. The quality of the photo and the label told me the photo's date, but it could have been from 1950. Her dress had a vintage look with a full skirt falling below the knee and a fitted, sleeveless bodice. It wasn't the first time I had seen Jocelyn pretty in pink. But another oddity? Jocelyn had a cast on her left arm, from her shoulder to her hand, the limb held by a sling. How had that happened? And where was her date? The lucky bastard Darren Kolchek?

The last photo showed Jocelyn in cap and gown, her arm still in a cast, but this one differed from the white version she wore in the prom picture. The graduation regalia covered most of the arm, but the lower part showed a cast decorated in coordinating colors of blue and gray like the cap and gown and mortarboard tassel. School spirit, I supposed. That's where the photos stopped. I fell asleep with more questions than answers knocking around in my skull.

Sunlight streamed through the shutter cracks and into my eyes at an ungodly hour. I'm a city guy with a city apartment that includes lots of windows, but dammit if I don't have blackout shades. I needed to hit the sheets earlier or get out of this Rockwellian town altogether if I wanted to get a decent night's sleep. But when last night's events eased in through my brain's morning fog, I smiled, knowing I planned to stay put.

I rolled out of bed to face a mirror. The reflection wasn't bad, good even, but I wondered if it was time to join a gym. William evidently had. *Come on, Ash. William is not the competition. But you should go for a run.*

Heeding my advice, I threw on shorts and a t-shirt and laced up my running shoes.

All the bedroom doors stood closed, but I crept to the kitchen to find coffee brewed. A quick survey did not indicate who made it, but another round with William the Art Dealer didn't appeal to me, so my best bet was to leave quietly and hit the pavement straight to the beach. When I stepped out the side door, the gentle, rhythmic splashes of a slow and easy swimming stroke came from the backyard pool.

The sun hadn't made its way over the house yet. The resulting shade made a considerable difference in the feel of the morning air. Cool and damp. The balmy temperature wouldn't last but the ever-present moisture would cling to everything through the end of the wretched dog days of summer.

Jocelyn was a gorgeous swimmer. No surprise there. Gliding in the water, her graceful hands cut through it with ease, taking a breath every other stroke. Before reaching the end, she flipped, turned, and pushed off the wall with a powerful thrust to coast, arms and legs stretched straight and long. She made several passes but then her rhythm sped up, the splashes grew, and she took fewer breaths. She still flipped and turned but barely drifted, roaring out of the water into a faster, more forceful stroke. There was nothing easy about these laps. No peace or calm. The workout swelled into a brutal exercise— almost violent. She pushed her body harder. Thrashing from end to end, again and again until, with a sudden, sharp gasp, she reached the pool's edge and hoisted herself onto the concrete surround with a throaty, bestial cry. Skidding forward with her own momentum, her beautifully sculpted body heaved and coughed on all fours. Desperate for air, she choked like a drowning victim plucked to safety until her lungs got what they needed. She stayed on her hands and knees, waiting for her frantic breath to slow.

Instinct told me I had just invaded Jocelyn's privacy. Witnessed something I shouldn't have, but I couldn't deny seeing the harrowing scene. Whatever it was. My impulse was to step in, offer help. But how do you intervene in a wrestling match with only one contender? Some battles have to be fought solo.

Jocelyn got to her feet, back still to me, taking long, deep inhalations with the occasional sputtering cough. Worried I would spook her, I cleared my throat too and offered her a swim towel—the only aid that seemed appropriate. With a jerk, she faced me, droplets flying from her curls with the sudden head turn.

I smiled until the bright red and watered-down pink streaking down her shins startled me. "Jocelyn, you're bleeding."

"*Hm*. I thought I felt a sting." She reached down and wiped both knees like it was nothing. "Fouled the dismount. Scraped my knees. No big deal." She stood with her hands on her hips, regaining her breath, then beckoned for the towel. "You just gonna stare, Mr. Cray?"

I handed her the plush Egyptian cotton. "I could, Ms. Durand. If I'm honest—"

"And you are." She wiped her face and dabbed at her hair before wrapping the towel around her body, under her arms. "You're also up early. Going to run?"

"Thought I would, but—you really are bleeding, Joce—"

She looked down to see the beads of water and blood breaking off like tributaries, puddling on the tops of her feet. "I've seen blood. This is nothing."

My neck wrenched at her comment. "What's that mean?"

"It means I raised a boy. A sports-playing, tree-climbing, scooter-riding daredevil of a son. Why the face? You squeamish about blood?"

"Blood on you? Yeah. I guess I am."

She walked toward me, raised on her tip-toes to kiss my cheek. Too mystified by the swim-fury and troubled by her scraped knees, I missed the opportunity to take part or even enjoy it.

"Would you go on a date with me?" The question blurted out of me. I had no plan.

"A date?"

"A walk? Drinks? Dinner? Coffee and dessert, if you like?"

"I have to pick one?"

"For you? I offer it all. The whole deal. Go all the way."

"Oh, I wouldn't bank on that, Mr. Cray. Not on a first date."

I stood eyeing her straight face and dripping curls. "Jocelyn, you just made a joke. A *dirty* joke."

"Dirty? That can't be. I'd never—"

"Oh, never say never. But please say yes to the date."

"When?"

"Soon?"

"Tonight then. Pick me up at seven-thirty?"

"It's a date."

Smiling, she moved past me toward the house but then stopped. She didn't face me when she spoke in a humorless tone. "It's been a long time. I'm not sure I remember how to do it. Come to think of it, I'm not sure I ever did it right."

"Dating is easy. You'll do fine," I assured her as she kept her back to me.

With a slight head tilt, her shoulders dropped a few inches. "Yeah—that too." She walked across the dew-sparkling grass into the morning sunlight that had shifted enough to reach the pool.

On the return from my hour-long run, I pushed myself harder for the last quarter mile, hoping for some insight into Jocelyn's last laps. I yearned for some epiphany, a release of some sort, something that would leave me better off than when I started. I didn't get it. Maybe I hadn't pushed hard enough.

Breathing labored and sweating, I paced the patio instead of walking into the breakfast party ratcheting up inside the kitchen. The clank of dishes and jangle of silverware collided with a mix of laughter and atop it all, the unmistakable noise of William

Atwater holding forth. The ruckus got momentarily louder when the French doors opened behind me.

Jocelyn, dressed in short pants and a long tank-top, offered a tray with a glass of water, two cups of coffee, and a hand towel.

I took the cloth first. "You think of everything. Thank you." I wiped my brow and reached for the water.

Jocelyn set down the tray and held the coffee next while I drained the water glass. "If I'd thought of everything, I'd have brought the Scotch—and maybe car keys." She looked over her shoulder as another boisterous howl erupted indoors. She sighed. "I think he'll settle down soon. Last night might have knocked him off-kilter a bit."

"He stole my kiss. I'm not feeling particularly gracious toward the man."

"What can I say? He beat you to it."

"I don't plan on losing out to him again."

"I see you're serious. You've upped the cardio just to be sure."

My breathing eased despite Jocelyn catching my flex in some non-existent contest with her ex-husband. "Oh yeah, I'm serious." Quiet settled in around us as we sipped our coffee. The resident mourning doves I'd noticed earlier in the week began a low melancholy call back and forth.

"I think they follow me." Her finger traced the rim of her cup. "The birds. I hear them at home too. My *other* home."

"That's a good sign, you know. The cry symbolizes optimism. It means hope, renewal, peace." I took another swallow of my coffee while Jocelyn gave me a doubtful look. "It might surprise you all the things I learn when researching a book. So much useless knowledge up here." I tapped my temple.

"Useless? I think it's just what I needed to hear. Tell me something else. Something weird and wonderful."

"Let's see. Butterflies taste with their hind feet."

"Do they?"

I nodded. "Donkeys will sink in quicksand, but a mule won't."

"That can't be true."

"Don't doubt me. Look it up." I shrugged.

"Count on it, sir."

Chuckling at our back-and-forth, I continued. "A gathering of ravens is called an *unkindness* and a group of crows is called a—"

"*Murder.*" Jocelyn finished my factoid with a wicked grin. "But speaking of research, you have the perfect excuse to avoid *The Will Show*. No one will think twice if you barricade yourself in your room for the day. If I had a computer, I might give it a go." Her snort said the idea was silly, but I thought it was anything but. I also had a solution for her and couldn't move fast enough to deliver it.

"I'll be down for breakfast. Ten minutes. Quick shower." I stopped short at her side and placed a gentle kiss on her cheek. Her mini-gasp in surprise caught my breath too. "It's going to be a great day, Ms. Durand," I whispered and hurried inside.

25

Jocelyn

THE EARTHY SMELL OF his sweat and the scuff of his morning
beard hung with me after Asher closed the door between us, and
I casually took another swallow of coffee. His whispered words
stayed with me, too, tickling my ear in the aftermath. I relished
the bird song in its new light, giving myself time to be sure the
confluence of Asher's smell and touch and sound wouldn't leave
me in a puddle. Steadied again, I rejoined the merriment in the
kitchen.

"Did you run the man off, Love? Insist he go shower off his
stench?" Will poured batter into a waffle-maker.

"One man's stench is another's allure. Surely, Raphe would
agree. Speaking of, where is my favorite landscape architect?"

"Sweating somewhere, I'm sure," Will spoke with more snarl
than usual. "Who wants a waffle?"

Gabe and Frannie traded knowing looks and hurried to escape
to the dining room, their full plates in hand.

"Will?" I gave a cock-eyed look of concern.

"It's fine, Love. Everything's fine."

"If you wanna talk about it—"

"Yes, let's. Your house is a pile of rubble, but we should talk
about my *boy* troubles. If that isn't indicative of our current *modus
vivendi*—"

"I'm here if you need me. Anytime."

"Except tonight," Asher entered from the front hall, showered, but unshaven.

"What's that, old boy?"

"Come on now, William. I'm pretty sure we're the same age. And Jocelyn is unavailable tonight. She has plans. Is there more coffee?" He crossed toward the carafe.

Will gave *me* a cock-eyed look now and pursed his lips. "With you, Asher Cray? Does my wife have plans with you?"

"Ex-wife," Asher and I said together.

"You know what they say, if three's a crowd, five's a party." Will pantomimed counting. "Where are we all off to then?"

"Yes, let's," I chirped, "because I'd like to have a quiet dinner for two, but you want to turn it into a big social occasion. If that isn't indicative of our *former modus vivendi*—"

"Well, Jocelyn Atwa—*Durand*. You grew some *sass*. Fix your own damn waffle." Will huffed before snatching his plate to join Gabe and Frannie in the dining room.

"Sorry, Asher," I whispered.

"What have I told you about the apologies? And I hope this doesn't sound out of line, but—I like your sass, and I look forward to seeing more of it. As a matter of fact, feel free to show your sass to me anytime, anywhere, and definitely at our quiet dinner for two tonight which I'm also looking forward to. I mean, I was before, but now I know sass might play a part, I'm *really* excited about it," Asher teased.

I stole a glance at the dining room, and the threesome seemed involved in their own chit chat. I reached for Asher's hand and mouthed, "Thank you."

"You're welcome," he murmured his reply. "Oh, and I left something at your bedroom door. It's yours as long as you need it."

I squinted, then scurried around him to the front hall stairs, eager to see what he left for me. Propped against my bedroom door was a silver laptop with an accompanying charging cord. Familiar fine linen stationery was sandwiched inside.

FROM THE DESK OF ASHER CRAY

Dear Jocelyn:

Now you have no excuses not to hide away in your room and write all day. Well, not all day because I'd miss your face, but you could try. Be brave. Take a chance. Regardless, I'll see you at seven-thirty for our date. Meet on the patio? I'll be the eager gent who shows up early. I know I said it was going to be a great day, but now I think it might be agonizingly long.

Impatiently, Ash

When I learned Frannie and Gabe had beach plans with visiting friends for the upcoming July Fourth holiday, I felt free to do as I wished. Asher closed himself off to write, and Will could fend for himself. I had housekeeping to attend to.

The satisfaction of clean sheets and towels was the most potent panacea I knew. I also baked some scones with the left-over blueberries and mixed a big salad, undressed with sliced chicken leftovers. If anyone found themselves peckish, food would be available. It was my ideal kind of day, and Martha would be proud. And someday I would drive the five miles down the road to knock on her door to ask just to be sure, but not today.

26

Asher

I KNOW. YOU THINK there is *absolutely* no way I could sit down and write after the night and morning I'd had. Hell, the night and morning before that, too. But you'd be wrong. So wrong. I sat, looked at the screen, and boom. You wanna talk magic? It was magic. *I* was magic. Or maybe the house really was magic. I didn't know, and I didn't care. I wrote again.

When Laney texted:

Badass: We need to talk.

I ignored it. I knew she'd understand, eventually.

That said, any other day, in ordinary circumstances, nothing could pull me from the keyboard. Akin to the old chestnut, "Never wake a sleeping baby," never interrupt a writing writer, particularly one who hasn't written in almost a year. But the clock read six-thirty p.m., and I had a date in one hour, and wasn't it just like the writing gods to hassle me in this way? I closed my laptop. Not today, writing gods. Not. Today.

"Asher Cray." Will's chortle startled me. I purposely scoped out the back patio in the hope I'd avoid a run-in with the man. He crept out from the side of the house, a wine glass in one hand while he tried to zip his fly with the other.

"Jesus, William. Was the bathroom really too far?"

He brushed off my disapproval. "Don't you look dapper this evening? Fit in just right out here. Very chic with your $300 t-shirt and $900 loafers. Throw on the navy Brooks Brothers dinner jacket, and you are just nautical enough to—"

"Hey William, I'm gonna stop you before you say something to embarrass me now and yourself in the morning. And maybe sober up? Last I checked, you're a guest in this house—an uninvited one at that—and your son is around with his own guest. Maybe *piss-drunk jerk* isn't the best look in this situation."

"Aww, I like you, Asher. Always have." William tumbled into a seat to keep from falling down. "Straight shooter. A little too straight for my taste, but I think you're a good guy."

"Thank you?" I sat too, waiting for the inevitable jab.

"So, how long have you and my wife been—"

"She's your ex-wife, William, and anything she wants you to know, she can tell you herself." I looked at my watch, wondering if I could somehow get William out of sight before Jocelyn arrived. Hard to imagine a boozy send-off by my date's ex-husband would bode well for the rest of the evening. And yet, I didn't see any solution other than a direct plea. "William, could I ask a favor?"

"Asher, I don't kiss and tell. You're on your own, old boy."

"Wow, you're a real piece of—"

"Hey, I played a fine husband." Playtime ended and any guise of light-hearted ribbing went with it. "I loved her the best I could, under the circumstances, and Lord knows she could have done worse. Hell, she saw worse, much worse. Lived it up close, and personal. A fucking *horror* show. But she's resilient. Tough, smart, and the best friend I've ever had. But it wouldn't surprise me if that demon lives inside her, too. Just somehow she's figured out how to keep it locked in there. Mostly anyway. But one loud—" William stopped talking, mesmerized by something at the bottom of his wine glass, or entranced by some memory. His use of the word *demon* rattled me as the sound of Jocelyn's earlier savage yawp as she tore out of the pool echoed in my ears.

"There she is. You look beautiful tonight. My Greek goddess in white and blue. Stunning, Love. Really." William and I were both on our feet—one steadier than the other. Jocelyn radiated beauty in a sleeveless, long, white linen dress with brilliant cerulean stitch detail at the hem and squared neckline. "Was that dress here? We picked it up for a song in a market in Greece. What was the name of that village? Oh, it doesn't matter. Jocelyn loved those markets." It didn't go unnoticed that William possessed unusually doting eyes for his ex-wife. Not by me, anyway.

Jocelyn smiled at me, a silent reiteration of her affection for village markets. "It was here. In the cedar closet. Lucky me."

"Lucky *Asher*." William swung a brotherly punch to my arm. "I was just telling Ash, old boy, what a lucky guy he is. She's the best girl I know. Now you kids have fun tonight." He ushered us to the side yard gate. "Home at a reasonable hour—kidding, of course—sort of. Kisses, but just on the cheek this time, okay, Love?"

Jocelyn rolled her eyes with a peck on William's cheek as she grabbed for my hand, encouraging us to make our getaway. The arched white gate closed behind us as William called, "Toodle-oo," through the wooden fretwork.

At a fast clip, Jocelyn pulled me several yards down the pebbled driveway. The hurried departure came to an abrupt stop when she pivoted back around, boomerang-like, releasing my hand to put her mouth on mine. A brusque kiss, rated-PG, first date material. That it occurred at the top of the date was a new one to me, but I believe a change in the program tends to make things interesting. She pulled away far too soon, particularly when I missed the start of it for the surprise of it all.

"I was going to be thinking about that all evening, so I figured I would get that first awful kiss out of the way early. That way, we have it done with and can enjoy the rest of the night, knowing the next one will be better. The next kiss, I mean." She held me around the neck but leaned back to speak to me. My hands found a respectable place at each of her hips, and I tried not to laugh while she explained her logic for the sneak attack.

"First, this is the weirdest date. Second, I am one hundred percent here for the whole out-of-the-blue kissing thing, and third, it wasn't an awful kiss."

"I can do better," she declared with a furrowed brow.

"Well, it's kind of a team effort sort of thing, and I've got all night." I gave her hips a reassuring squeeze and watched her brown eyes dart back and forth, looking into mine. Our spot in the driveway, dappled by the sinking sun beyond the backyard trees, allowed flickers of late sunshine to highlight the golden hue in her eyes. The sadness vanishing act happened again, and I hoped I played a part in it, but William's cryptic, drunken disclosure in the harshest language regarding Jocelyn's past already weighed down the evening. *Horror show.*

She leaned up again. This kiss was softer, still Jocelyn-led, and definitely still rated-PG. Letting her find her way seemed the right course, but my distraction persisted. Jocelyn gave a questioning look when our lips parted.

Come on, Ash. Focus. Reasonable odds, my smile looked as forced as it felt.

27

Jocelyn

WHERE WE DINED DIDN'T matter to me, but Asher chose a great locavores' spot run by a nearby Sagaponack winery. We strolled a quarter-mile down the main drag. Car congestion grew with the upcoming holiday, but sidewalks on the shaded side of the street made it an easy trip. On the downside, noise from the increased traffic kept conversation virtually non-existent.

Tension strained the air between us, and I couldn't make out the cause. Asher's tight smile and raised shoulders told me something weighed on him, and I had my suspicions. *What did you do, Will?* Seated immediately, I reached for my just-filled water glass and nodded thanks to our hostess. Chugging the water helped me swallow the nerves threatening to bubble out of me.

I insisted Asher order the wine. If it was wet, I'd drink it, so the vintage made no difference.

The steward serving the bottle started in with polite chit-chat. "Special occasion this evening?"

"It's a date. A first date," I explained with a giddiness that belied my age, not that I cared.

"That *is* special." Came the banal reply as he showed off his wine tool skills, a quick slice with his foil blade and speedy twists of a carbon fiber corkscrew.

"I'm a little excited," I continued. "Do you know who this is?" I asked the man as he poured a splash of a local claret for Asher to taste.

"I do." He nodded as Asher gave a thumbs up to the sample. The server poured the red wine into my glass.

"And do you know who this is?" Asher asked the waiter with a gesture to me as I rolled my eyes.

"I do," the aloof man repeated himself as he filled Asher's goblet. "Please enjoy." He left the bottle and cork and stepped away from the table.

"He doesn't know me the way you think he does." I leaned in to whisper. "I'm far more infamous for being the longtime seasonal resident with the fabulous landscape because my husband ran off with the gardener."

"Ex-husband," Asher interjected. "How about no more William talk for tonight?"

"*Uh oh*, he *did* say something, didn't he? What?"

"He'd had a few. He said some stuff. But enough of that. I want to know about you." He leaned toward me with an eagerness I couldn't decipher. Was it about learning about me or moving on from mentions of Will?

"Ask away," I encouraged with open arms.

"All right. Rapid fire. No thinking. Favorite color?"

"Pink."

"Favorite place?"

"Ooh, for the people, Italy, maybe Greece. For the city, Manhattan, hands down."

"Ever jumped out of a plane?"

I snickered. "No. Why would I do that?"

Asher shrugged with a smile. "Do you have any tattoos?"

"Nope, but the night is young."

He chuckled. "Been arrested?"

"No, but to be fair, that's only because no one's ever caught me." I punctuated my joke with a wink.

With the slightest head tick, he paused before asking, "*O*-kay.

Ever broken a bone?"

The room fell silent, at least to my ears. "*Uh*—yes." Fidgeting with my silverware, I glanced around unnerved, wishing I hadn't gulped down all the water.

"Details," he prodded, apparently oblivious.

After a shaky sip of wine, I continued. "My arm. Senior year of high school. Car wreck. My parents died. Next." I wiped my palms on the napkin draped in my lap.

"*Shit*," Asher muttered. "I didn't realize you were in the car—"

"Nope, how 'bout my turn?" I straightened for a breath.

"Jocelyn—"

"My turn. Cake or pie?"

"Joce—"

"*Cake*. Or. Pie?"

"Pie."

"Beach or Mountains?"

"Five-star high-rise, the highest floor, twenty-four-hour room service—with pie."

I recognized his effort to lighten the mood, but I chose a different route.

"Your last kiss?"

"You."

I thwarted his attempt to touch my hand. "Before me and not who, but when?"

"You mean a *kiss* kiss, a romantic kiss?"

"Yes, if it *was* romantic." My head swirled with the realization I didn't really know the difference.

"It wasn't," he delivered that part of the answer with emphatic speed, "and over a year ago."

"Really? If it wasn't romantic, what was—? Never mind. Worst date experience?"

"I'm pretty sure I'm living it right now, Jocelyn." He reached for his wine, but I grabbed his hand instead.

"What do you want, Asher?"

"What do I want?"

"World peace, a Pulitzer, me?"

"I can only choose one?"

That elicited a short laugh, and the tension eased for a moment.

"What do you want, Jocelyn?"

"To get out of here." I emptied my wineglass in three unladylike gulps.

Asher raised his hand. "Check, please."

Asher carried the re-corked wine in a brown paper sack and held my hand as we walked in silence. I directed us to a quieter, tree-lined, two-lane road that offered a paved path on one side. The street's narrow shoulders were sandy, and the stately homes sat well off the road down long driveways hidden behind lush maritime landscapes. Crashing waves roared louder the farther we traveled from the main thoroughfare until our way dead-ended at a sparsely occupied parking lot. Dunes rose, divided by a pathway to the beach. Squawking gulls swooped to scavenge the brimming trash cans full of discarded picnics and summertime snacks left behind by the day's visitors. A veritable feast.

The sand had long since lost the heat of the day, cooling my bare feet. Asher didn't hesitate to kick off his shoes and followed me on the narrow trail through protective banks that sprouted tall wisps of beach grass in shades of green and brown. Beyond the natural barricade, a few small gatherings dotted the vast stretch of low tide around newly lit fire pits just beginning to spark and smoke. The descending nighttime meant bonfires, stargazing, and canoodling couples sneaking more kisses the darker it got. It always surprised me how the evening sea breeze blew milder than the warmer air a mere few blocks inland. Clouds rolled along the horizon. Nothing looked too troublesome, but my achy arm hinted otherwise.

It had been ten minutes or more, so I felt compelled to end the quiet. "Worst date ever, huh?" I watched Asher scrutinize the waves.

Asher sighed but kept his stern gaze and the jut of his clenched jaw to the water. "That is not what I meant, and you know it, Jocelyn."

"Well, you said *weirdest*."

"Between your ex pissing in the side yard and his drunken implication that I was looking for sex tips, and you pouncing on me in the front driveway, you now—to get it over with, yeah—I'll stick with weirdest."

I yanked the brown bag from Asher's grip, pulled the cork with my teeth, spitting it onto the sand. I took a healthy swig before offering it to my date. He followed my lead.

"Should we cut bait? Order an UBER? Call time of death?"

"I'm no quitter, Jocelyn. You don't strike me as one either." He handed me the wine and stared as I took another long draw. "You are beautiful, though. William beat me to it—*again*."

I swallowed, keeping my eye on the ocean, a little stunned. "No, he didn't. He said I *looked* beautiful *tonight*. You said I'm beautiful. For a man whose world is words, you ought to know there's a difference." I met Asher's eye as a rush of wind off the water gusted hair across my face.

Asher dropped his shoes and tucked the breeze-blown curls behind my ear, then lifted my chin. "Is it okay if this happens now?" His lips were almost touching mine.

"If what happens now?"

"I'm going to kiss you now. If it's okay."

"It is, but it'll be for the third time." I scrunched up my face in confusion.

He smiled. "No. For the first time."

"How—"

Asher cut short my question. Cupping my face in his hands, he delicately brushed his lips against mine. It tickled at first, but that part didn't last long. The tender touch grew stronger. He pushed in with an urgency still blanketed with a softness I couldn't quite comprehend. Dizziness hit, and I dropped my sandals and the wine bottle. Holding firmer still, his lips parted, and his tongue gently met mine. A lusty sensation startled me upright. My arms landed on his shoulders as my knees buckled. He caught me, pulling tighter as I gasped at another sweet caress, letting slip my eagerness for more. I pulled at his neck as he gave one last slow promise that more would come. Ending it, he pressed his lips against mine, released, then did it again, ever so lightly.

I held onto the lapel of his jacket, breathing into his chest; his grasp around me didn't let up.

28

Asher

IT IS NOT WITHOUT some concern of having my man-card revoked that I tell you about that first kiss. It was—well, it was extraordinary. Sure, the scenery was ideal: on a beach, crashing waves, a late twilight sky, not to mention (though I will) the breathtaking beauty of the woman in my arms. A woman so intriguing she drew me in the first time I saw her bite her bottom lip. And now, having tasted that lip, pulling away from the kiss felt both foolish and necessary at once. *Her* reaction to the thing overwhelmed me, like she couldn't comprehend what was taking place at the start. Her *oh-this-is-happening* realization led to a jolt of surprise followed by our near-collapse into the pleasure of it. I held tight for my sake as much as hers, but that riled her enthusiasm in such a way I had to end it before I lost my composure. Yeah, it was a *good* kiss.

Jocelyn leaned into me, but I think we braced each other in the less than solid sand under our bare feet. With her head cradled against my shoulder, she stood motionless except for her warm, ragged breath on my skin. But after a moment, doubt flooded my whole interpretation of the event. She held me at the waist, under my dinner jacket, and I was relieved when she came alive with a gentle squeeze to my sides. One hand traveled to my stomach, then firmly slid up my chest. Fingers grazed my neck, traced my jawline, coming to a tentative stop on my lips. I kissed the thumb she brushed across my mouth, then smiled at the tickle.

Her sighing laugh floated on the wind, and she patted my chest before taking me about the waist again. I couldn't recall a time my body entwined with another and felt exactly right. Hands, arms, head, legs, each had its spot, and each fit perfectly into it. Spaces finally filled where before they lived empty. The cold places were warm now, and it all came from her touch.

Without warning, she wrenched away with a gasp, "I dropped the wine."

Miraculously, the bottle rested in a divot at an angle, but upright enough that the remaining wine hadn't spilled. We both bent, nearly knocking heads to retrieve it. I reached the bottleneck first and handed it to her. The stiff breeze had its way with her curls again, masking the eyes I didn't want to lose sight of. Our hands met when we both moved to sweep away the out-of-place locks.

Her eyes widened, startled. "Are you going to do that again?"

"Do what? Kiss you?"

"Yes."

"Right now—or ever?"

"It's just brushing my hair aside is how it started last time, and I'm gonna need some warning, a heads up, an *'incoming'* because before, I had trouble keeping on my feet, so—"

I brought her hand to my lips to kiss it and stifle my laugh. With my best serious face, I assured her, "I definitely plan to do that again, but I will make an effort to give you notice so you can prepare yourself, taking the necessary steps to prevent collapse. Fall hazards at our age get much more serious—"

She gave no warning but took me by the back of the neck with one hand while keeping a firm grip on the wine bottle with the other. This Jocelyn-led kiss was *not* rated-PG but rather a staggering mix of rough and tender that surprised me. But when my groping fingers tugged at the roots of her hair, she emitted a low moan, a hum of pleasure, then shoved my chest, prying us apart with her free hand. A couple of backward strides away from me, she wagged a finger that signaled, *don't take a step.* I stopped short, afraid I had crossed a line, but her upturned mouth told a different story. She wobbled in the deep sand, taking a prolonged swig on the wine bottle with a hard swallow, her finger still holding me at bay.

"Well, I know how to shut you up now." She snickered and cleared her throat.

"And I know how to get you to make noise." I composed myself with a deep breath.

Jocelyn's mouth fell open, and her eyes narrowed at my remark. While it grew challenging to tell in the dimming evening, I was sure her cheeks had turned her favorite color. I grew fond of it too.

"Was that a suggestive joke, Mr. Cray?" She feigned a scowl.

"No, ma'am. To be a *suggestive* joke, I would need to be joking, and I promise you, I wasn't. Now, give me some wine."

Arm outstretched, offering the bottle, my date meant to keep her distance. My swift lunge in Jocelyn's direction sent her scampering across the beach, laughing into the thickening night air. She spun around, moving faster on the hard sand packed down by the rolling surf, her white dress reflected in the flickering glow of now blazing bonfires. I hung back as she approached a crowd, swaying to music I barely heard over the surf from my spot several yards away. A boom of laughter erupted from the gathering, and I knew she had them entertained. Muffins or fancy towels or a quick funny quip, Jocelyn Durand was the consummate hostess, even if it wasn't her party.

Over the rhythmic roar of the tide, I heard her say goodbye as she skipped my way, and I sped up to shorten the distance between us. Directly behind her, a jagged lightning bolt lit up the far horizon, a flash of electricity that raised the hair on my arms. Distant thunder came well after, adding a low rumble to the beach soundtrack.

When she reached me, I got a simple kiss, short but sweet with the offer of wine. I took the bottle but didn't need the drink, naturally lightheaded with infatuation, curiosity, and desire, like it was the first time all over again. Teenage-like marvel. A whirlwind of sensation spiraled, new and fresh, a slightly messy thrill-ride, clumsy with our fumbling, exhilarating in the unknown possibilities, and no comparison to past experiences. It surpassed any memory. For a moment, she curled into that spot where all the parts fit just so, and I kissed the top of her head.

"Let's go home," she said with a contented sigh I could have listened to for the rest of my days.

My man card? Here. Take it.

29

Jocelyn

OFF THE BEACH WITH feet cleaned the best we could, I asked Asher if he wanted to risk the rain to walk the mile to home.

"You think it's gonna rain?" He looked skyward with a shrug.

"I *know* it is. And soon."

"How's that?"

Revisiting the broken arm felt like a step backward when things were going so well. I deflected.

"It's my superpower. Sure, some people fly, others go at super-speed, but me? Weather prediction, though only rain, so not really the most super of superpowers." The sky had dimmed beyond dusk to dark, but we stood under a fluorescent-lit parking lot utility pole. The harsh white glare showed Asher's skeptical face as he offered me the last of the wine. I declined, and he added the bottle and sack to the overflowing trash can.

Doubt in my ability to stymie uncomfortable conversation with a wisecrack crept in—doubt at least when it came to Asher Cray. I thought Asher saw through it, and the prospect of being seen both elated and terrified me. I cleared my throat to confess. "My arm aches when rain is coming. Nothing bad, but it happens. Every time, without fail. One perk of a decades-old proximal humerus fracture." I lifted my left elbow to show the faded scar that ran the length of the underside of my upper arm. No one would notice it unless I meant them to. Asher reached to touch it but hesitated. I didn't move, inviting him to continue. His fingers gently traced the hardly-visible remnant of the old injury. I shivered at an uptick in the breeze.

"Take my jacket." Asher removed his coat.

"Oh, I don't need it."

"Please. I insist. It's the most gentlemanly thing I've done in a while."

"I'll say." And heat rose from my body again, making the coat unnecessary.

He chuckled, draping the linen blazer around my shoulders. His warmth and smell surrounded me. An intoxicant—fast-acting, and no doubt addictive. I slipped my arms through the sleeves. "Thank you. We should hurry." I pointed us in a new direction.

Out of the parking lot's single pool of light, we walked through the dark. This far off the main street, at this time of night, no traffic helped or hindered our trek, but the cloudy skies robbed us of moon and starlight. Except for the occasional distant porch lantern, we felt our way in near pitch-dark conditions. Close, side-by-side on the narrow sidewalk, we kept a brisk pace along beach plum shrubs and fragrant swamp rose at the peak of their bloom season. I slowed to take a deep sniff of the pink flowers when the first raindrop hit me.

"*Uh-oh.*" I could make out Asher's shaking head.

"I will never doubt your precipitation prognostication again. We're gonna get soaked, aren't we?"

"Third time this week for me. And in a white dress, no less. Thank goodness it's darker than dark out here."

"Yes, thank goodness." His blatant sarcasm won him a swat. "Do we run for it?"

"The turn is probably another couple hundred yards and then another quarter mile straight shot from there." I pointed to oblivion.

"I know that last quarter mile, but I'm not exactly in my running shoes." We looked at what I imagined were expensive Italian leather loafers, invisible in the night.

"Your shoes."

"Nothing to be done about that. I'm more concerned about the zombies."

"The zombies?"

"The lack of them, actually. Am I gonna get you to run after all?" With that, the nighttime sky opened and poured rain. Sheets of water slanted down on us, hitting the pavement and viciously splashing back up, like it came from every which way.

Letting it shower my face, I squealed and shouted over the roar, "It's practically swimming. Let's go." Hand in hand, we took off down a sidewalk we couldn't see, the patter of rain deafening in the force of its fall. Muddy sand seeped between my toes, my sandals offering no protection from Mother Nature's muck, and Asher's coat swelled, absorbing the soaking torrent. The weight of it dragged me down as Asher pulled me forward. Not wanting to slow him, I tried to release his hand to signal him to go ahead. He wouldn't let go. And just when I thought I'd have to stop, the rain hammered down harder, lashed at us from all directions, it seemed, so I took a deep watery breath and redoubled my efforts too. The scene hit max absurdity, and I couldn't help but laugh. "Can you see it?" I tried shouting over the torrential downpour.

"What?"

"Can you—" My laughter bubbled louder as the rain fell harsher still.

"Are you okay?" He'd stopped, but I could tell he breathed easily. His other hand reached for my cheek, but between the water in my eyes and the dark, I couldn't see much, and the noise of it all made communicating difficult. "Jocelyn?"

"I'm okay. I'm laughing."

"Laughing?"

"Let's go. It has to be close by now." I squawked again, taking off for what I knew couldn't be much farther to the house. It wasn't. We hopped up on the curb, crossed the wide strip of soggy grass to the slick walkway leading to the front porch. No lights were on out front, but a dim glow traveled from the back of the house through the front windows, scarcely enough to decipher the outlines of porch furniture and our soaked bodies. Shelter from the pummeling brought relief, but the racket grew louder as the metal roof took a beating, and a mist blew toward us when the wind gusted. Asher released my hand and cupped my face toward the faint light. Raindrops hung on my lashes, and I tried to blink them free and slow my breathing as Asher hardly panted at all.

"Jocelyn?"

"Yes?"

"*In—coming.*" He waited for a beat before kissing my smile. Our lips were wet, everything drenched, but his mouth was soft and warm, and I pulled at his clinging t-shirt to get closer. The weight of his blazer hung on my frame, and I tugged, trying to wriggle free of the hefty garment without losing Asher's sweet kiss. His hands joined in to help me out of the coat, and it landed at my ankles with a sopping thud. I tripped over it, stepping back, but he caught my arms to steady me, then kicked the waterlogged jacket out of his path in a smooth move that found me up against the swath of cedar-shake between the foyer window and the front door.

Something changed. Asher's hands caught me at the elbows but slid to my wrists he held at shoulder height, pressed against the house. Pinned to the jagged wood, I lifted my chin when he released my lips, trying to find my way back to his. Instead, he assailed my exposed neck, and I gasped at the thrill of his tongue just above my collarbone. Wrenching my arms, I wanted to touch him, hold him, but he gripped too tightly. I wheezed another sound, a whimper, but from pain juddering down my left arm. He must have misconstrued the groan because he only pushed harder. His lips back on mine, I tried to relax, enjoying the taste of him, his needy nip of my lip. The encounter was unlike any I knew, but he kept me restrained. Overwhelmed, my body responded to each new sensation. Twisting my old injury sent another shooting pain from my shoulder to my trapped wrist. I hissed with another agonizing shot. "Asher," I gritted his name through a clenched jaw, my body rigid. I repeated his name, louder.

As he kissed my cheek moving to my ear, he whispered, "Jocelyn," the tone, a mix of affection and desire, combined with my distress, made me dizzy.

"Asher, you— you're *hurting* me." My pain made it louder than I meant.

He let go at once, retreating to the porch rail with his hands in the air and the whites of his eyes huge. I lunged to keep him close but then grabbed my arm as another searing jolt radiated down my limb, yelping in the shock of it at the same moment the front door flew open.

"Jesus H. Christ. Asher Cray, make one move toward my sister-in-law, and I swear to God you will *not* live to regret it."

Laney bent at my side, doubled over in the momentum of reaching for Asher, then grabbing my hurt arm. "No, Laney," I force a grunt in agony.

But Asher did move, reaching for my down-turned face, two hands lifting my chin to look me in the eye. "Jocelyn. I am sorry, I didn't—"

"I know. I know, Asher. I'm fine."

"Back off, Ash," Laney snapped.

"Laney, I'm okay."

Blocking the perceived threat with her small frame, Laney eased me to a wicker settee on the other side of the porch. "My God, you're soaked."

I stretched my neck and hugged my arm, waiting for the burning ache to subside. Mud splattered a foot or higher around the bottom edge of my white dress. I lifted the hem, snorting at the mess while also exposing my scraped knees from my early morning swim. Wet and mucky in the murky light, the wounds looked fresh.

"Jocelyn, your knees. Did you fall?" Before I could reply, Laney beelined to Asher, fist at the ready. "You son-of-a—"

"Laney?" Gigi's sultry tone came from the doorway. "What the hell is going on out here?"

"Gigi?"

"Jojo?" She stepped from the door to see me sitting in the semi-darkness, then reached to flick on the porch light. We all flinched at the glare of it. "What are you doing here? Good Lord, look at you. Are you all right?"

"Yes, *everyone*, I'm *fine*." Finally, I found my bearings and stood. The cold of the soaked clothing stuck to my skin, and the mud oozed out of my sandals. A hot shower could not happen soon enough. I kissed Gigi's cheek. "Good to see you, Gi. I can't believe you're here."

The next kiss was for Laney. "Thank you, Laney. You can dial it back now. You know Asher. Don't believe your own hype."

Then I crossed to Asher, who stood stiffly, drenched, hands on his hips, wide-eyed with concern. I held him at his soaked waist but winced when I tried to raise my arm to stroke his cheek. He grimaced too.

"Breathe," I demanded in a whisper, noticing in all the commotion, the rain had at last eased to a light shower. "Everything is fine. We will talk about it, but after we've gotten clean and dry, okay?"

He nodded, but dread-filled eyes said he wasn't sure.

"*In-coming*," I mouthed the playful warning, and he rewarded

me with an airy start to something like a laugh. I rose on tiptoes to
kiss him gently on the mouth in a suitable manner for the mixed
company but with enough promise for more to come.

"Well, I'll be damned," Laney remarked in disbelief, then let go
her loud honk of a laugh.

30

Asher

THE HOT SHOWER STREAM pelted me for a long time. My brain reeled from the evening's events, a goddamn roller coaster with a watery crash at the end. Jocelyn's words echoed on repeat. *Asher, you're hurting me.* Jesus. I rubbed my face and vigorously kneaded my scalp, trying to clear my head. I couldn't get the return of her sad eyes out of my mind, and I knew I bore the responsibility for their reappearing act. Still, her last kiss burned my lips, and I didn't know what my next move should be.

I dialed the shower to its coldest setting and forced myself to endure it.

In shorts and a t-shirt, I opened my door to find Jocelyn's room open and empty, with voices drifting from the first floor. More unexpected guests arriving in the dark. All I wanted was to speak with Jocelyn, make things right, but hiding from the rest of the suddenly very crowded house looked sheepish. I descended the stairs to face the latest invaders.

The scene included more than I had expected. Even Gabe and Frannie were there, and how William hadn't passed out hours ago, I'll never know. Jocelyn bolted vertically from her curled-up spot on the sofa when she saw me. I tried to smile, but I'm not sure it happened. William spoke first, after the brief but awkward hush at my appearance.

"Pay up, you faithless scoundrels. I told you the old boy hadn't packed his bags— yet."

"Maybe they're in the front hall. I'd have left them at the door." Frannie rubbernecked to see the foyer. Her presence surprised me, even more so her daring to offer unsolicited opinions. Gabe gave her knee a *shut-up* squeeze.

"If I'm interrupting some sort of family meeting, I can—" I pointed over my shoulder.

"Have a seat, Asher. Now," Laney insisted.

Jocelyn stood. "You must be starving. Can I—"

"Sit down, Jojo. The man has made himself at home, it seems; he can fend for himself for a snack." Genevieve and Laney were a united front and scary as hell.

"Gigi, don't." The plea in Jocelyn's tone squeezed my chest.

"Speaking of a *snack*—"

"Shut up, William," Jocelyn, Genevieve, and Laney demanded in unison.

In an ill-conceived effort to appear confident, I strode across the room to sit next to Jocelyn. She made space for me on the sofa between her and Gabe, but Gabe moved. I motioned for him to stay.

"No, man. We're cool. Fran's and my party got rained out. We shouldn't even be here tonight. We'll go throw in a movie. A loud one. We won't hear a thing. Come on, Frannie. Dad? Why don't you join us?" Clearly, Gabe held the role of diplomat, and I wondered how long he'd been negotiating the peace for the Atwater-Durand-Li family.

"Good idea," Jocelyn added with haste.

The threesome left, William at a snail's pace while belting out, *"Blame it on the rain—"*

"Shut up, William," everyone but me sighed. I busied myself trying to decide how close was too close to sit next to Jocelyn, then gave myself a silent chiding for thinking I had anything to prove to anyone other than the woman on my left. I had to admit, the three women remaining in the room made for a daunting audience, and I planned to tread lightly.

"You want to take this, Gen? Or me?" Laney took charge.

"He's your client, Lane. You go."

"He's *our* client, but you know I love Jocelyn like a sister-in-law."

"I *am* your sister-in-law." Jocelyn squinted at Laney with a head shake.

"Exactly." Laney sipped what I guessed was the *good* Scotch but didn't imagine anyone would offer me a glass anytime soon. My agent's gaze met mine. "So, what the hell is going on here, Asher Cray?" she asked in a slow, rhythmic way. Had she been stroking the head of a purring black cat, Laney might have passed for a Bond villain.

I'd known Laney a long time. We had a good relationship, better than good, and I was familiar with her tactics. More than that, I knew how she felt about me, and despite the way it seemed at the moment, I ranked well. Genevieve, on the other hand, was not someone I met with often. We didn't share a rapport. We had no shorthand or private jokes, no bared confessions over expensive liquor. Our only link was Laney and now Jocelyn. Her baby sister. A sister she protected fiercely, and an easy misinterpretation of the scene on the porch could indicate I had *hurt* her sister. *Shit.* I *had* hurt her, but—

"*Asher?*" Laney raised her brow.

"Look—Laney, Genevieve, I'm not gonna sit here and make excuses or give explanations unless Jocelyn is asking for them. We're all adults, and anything going on between Jocelyn and me is just that. Between Jocelyn and me. If she has details she wants to share, I wouldn't be fool enough to get in the middle of that. I, however, have no intention of divulging the particulars of our relationship. Whatever it may be, or what it might become. And again, unless Jocelyn says otherwise, I don't think we need any help or interference from friends, family, or business associates." My direct eye-contact shifted from Genevieve to Laney and back again. Genevieve cleared her throat, and Laney looked at her for what I guessed was a telepathic matrimonial moment. For better or worse, my nerves compelled me to continue. "I would also like to say, I realize Jocelyn and I are just getting to know one another, but I find her to be extraordinary. Smart, funny, kind, selfless, an out-of-this-world mother, and anyone who calls her friend is beyond fortunate."

"My sister's not bad to look at either." Genevieve's gravelly lilt could be both unnerving and soothing. An odd feat.

"Not bad at all, Genevieve. Not bad at all." I leaned into the overstuffed sofa cushions with a deferential grin, relieved when Jocelyn's hands found one of mine and clung to it. They were smooth and warm, and she nibbled that lip, aglow in pink.

Both Genevieve and Laney stood, and I moved to do the same. "Keep your seat, Ash." Laney barked out of habit more than anger.

"I'm glad we could get that all cleared up. Stop biting your lip, Jojo." Genevieve nodded and left with Laney following behind, but not before my agent offered me a surreptitious fist bump and a big wink to Jocelyn. "Leave them alone now, Laney," Genevieve called from the kitchen, and Laney grabbed her Scotch to exit.

"Laney? You texted we needed to talk?"

"We do, but it'll keep until morning."

"You're staying?" I eyed my Scotch-drinking pal hard.

Laney looked over her shoulder toward her already-gone wife, who didn't like to sleep under this roof. Laney shrugged. "We're staying. One night. Goodnight, you two."

31

Jocelyn

WATCHING THEIR EXCHANGE, ANYONE could see Asher and my sister-in-law were more than business associates. They shared an undeniable confidence, and clearly Asher Cray was one of the chosen few to make it beyond Laney's prickly exoskeleton. That pleased me. Relieved me. Made moving forward—should we want to—easier for all concerned. And the way he spoke to the intimidating pair? Stood up to them and shut them down? Calm but adamant. I'm not sure I'd ever seen anything sexier.

I chose not to speak but tried to nestle into a comfortable spot, like a puzzle with pieces perfectly met, meant to be—different from our time on the porch. That episode still rattled in my brain. Flashes of both pleasure and pain made it hard to breathe. And while the physical sensations still made my skin tingle, it was the *want* I found curious. The desire, his desire, was the foreign element. No one had ever wanted me like Asher did at that moment. I should have been pleased, satisfied with the experience and hopeful, eager for the opportunity for more like it. But sadness crept in, a sorrow borne from years of deceit, fraud, a sham marriage. Then I remembered the sham had also given me Gabriel, and I wouldn't trade anything for him.

My eyes stung, and I pulled away from Asher, bothered by the mere thought of unusual tears. Crying wasn't something I did. Durand women didn't cry.

"Jocelyn. You're upset." Asher reached for me, but I rose to skirt his grasp.

"I'm not."

"Obviously, you are."

"Not at you."

"Who then? I am so sorry. I can't—I don't know how else to—"

"You did nothing wrong."

"I hurt you. I *physically* hurt you. You said so. *Asher, you're hurting me*. I can't un-hear it." Asher stood with speed, like he meant to get away from something inescapable.

"Not on purpose—and it doesn't always go like that. And you stopped as soon as I said and—it *definitely* doesn't always go *that* way."

"Jesus, Jocelyn. What—? William said—"

"Will said what?" How had Will wormed his way into this? "Will said *what*?" I repeated.

"Nothing. He'd been drinking. Never mind." Arms stretched-wide, Asher gripped the fireplace mantel, not showing his face.

"Are you angry?"

He spun to face me, and I flinched. "God, no." He took quick steps in my direction, and I forced myself not to move. His hands came toward me but stopped, still out of reach. He had that pity expression about him, the *poor-Jocelyn* face.

"But you don't want to touch me."

"Don't *want* to? Jocelyn, if you—"

"You can, you know. I'm not fragile. You can't break me." I'd heard those words before. Who said them? I didn't recognize the voice.

"I don't think you're fragile."

"What then? Everyone else does." I pushed past the nagging memory.

"I think—I think your experience is unique."

"Everyone's experience is unique, Asher."

He took a long, slow inhale with a step toward me. "Earlier this week, you said to go *slowly.*"

I grumbled at the recollection.

"And I hit the gas when I should have pumped the brakes."

That imagery didn't feel appropriate, but I'd give the man a pass. "Who's euphemism-happy now?" I smirked at his grimace. "So, you wanted me, but now you don't."

"No, I didn't say that."

"Oh, so you didn't want me? *Huh*, cuz it kinda felt like you did."

"Jocelyn." The pink rose in his cheeks this time.

"Well, which is it, Asher?"

He kept mum, but the color inching up his neck said it all.

"Earlier this week, I also asked you to speak plainly. I don't want any misunderstanding. So, let me be sure I'm clear. You *did* want me. You *do* want me. But you plan to— *refrain* from having me."

"Oh my God," Asher murmured with a chuckle, his gaze squarely on the jute rug.

"Is this an indefinite plan? Is there a loophole to be found? If I were to wake in the night and find my way to your door, would it be locked? Because if you were to wake in the night and find your way to *my* door, it would *not* be locked."

"What are you doing, Jocelyn?"

"Making a point."

"And what point would that be?" Asher stroked his throat.

"My point is I am not fragile. As a matter of fact, I have never felt more powerful than I do at this moment." I don't know where my nerve came from, how I got so bold, but it was exhilarating.

"You win." Asher's hands rose in surrender.

"I do? *What* do I win?"

"I don't know, Jocelyn. All of it. Everything. Anything. You name it."

"How's about a goodnight kiss. Not just yet, but whenever we go to bed. When I go to my bed, and you go to your bed, both safely behind *locked* doors. Before that, I get a goodnight kiss. From you."

"I can arrange that." Asher's shoulders lowered with a nod.

I let nothing but the pull chain's *tink* on the spinning ceiling fan mark the time for a long moment before I spoke again. "It's strange how incredibly crowded this house has gotten this week. I thought it would be just me and then you broke in."

He cocked his head. "Someone invited me, and I used a key." He corrected me as I took him about the waist.

I drolly brushed off his version of events. "Then the kids showed up, going bump in the night."

"They bumped in the night, for sure." Asher tucked some still damp, untamed nighttime curls behind my ear.

"Will showed up in the dark." I tucked into my just-right spot with all our pieces fitting just so.

"Stealing my kiss." He held tighter. "No, I'm not over it yet."

"And then Gigi and Laney Li—"

"Hey, why are they here?" He twisted to see my face.

"Work apparently. Something to do with you. I don't ask about such things. Besides, they were too busy giving me the third-degree. But Laney said she tried to contact you today. More than once."

"I—was writing." He hesitated, but a combination of pride and relief permeated his statement.

"You were? What is it?"

"I don't know yet. But it's for my eyes only— for now."

I didn't push, knowing a writer finding his words again wasn't something to take lightly. Jinxing it was all too easy. "So, it's working? Laney's plan."

"I suppose it is. Not that we need to give her credit or anything.

But you were talking about the crowded house."

"Yes, but by my count, in three days, everyone will be gone. Except me. And I hope you."

"Hm. What will that mean?"

"You just might find your brake lines cut."

"That's sort of a *backward* euphemism there, Ms. Durand."

"Oh no, you misunderstand." I pulled from our embrace. "No euphemism at all. I will cut the brake lines on that silly car of yours so you can't drive anywhere. Lovelorn divorcee dupes *hot* bestselling author into captivity. A victimless crime."

"It sounded promising before, but the way you say it—"

"Even better, right?"

32

Asher

THINGS HAD SETTLED. WITH the tension dissipated, Jocelyn and I found the fitted spot that brought a serenity I didn't know I had missed, or needed, or wanted. At the same time, something more perked underneath it. There were things I didn't know. And why should I? That's how I tossed aside my questions, allayed my concerns. Jocelyn revealed more of herself. Slowly. Her confidence grew. It was early days; we would learn more about one another as time went on. No need to dig for details. Let her story unfold in its own time, in its own way. Plot twists made for more fun.

It got late but a buzzy excitement from the chaos of the evening's activities, plus the exhaustion from the physical and emotional exertion made for wired sleepiness. We sipped the dregs of a bottle of wine William left unfinished and picked at a salad Jocelyn prepared earlier in the day. We talked with ease, laughed, and continued our get-to-know-you game.

"Football, baseball, or basketball?" I asked.

"Uh, baseball? But that's only because of—"

"Laney," we said together and chuckled at our diehard season ticket-holding Mets fan friend.

"To be honest, I could take or leave any of it until I'm watching, then I can get a little rowdy. It's ridiculous. Uh, but never against the Mets. I'm no fool," Jocelyn admitted.

"Rowdy, huh?"

"Just saying, if we ever found ourselves on opposite sides of a game, a match of some sort, an issue even—"

"I'll never have to guess what you're thinking..."

"Well, if you find yourself unsure, you only need to ask."

There was my opening. Jocelyn's invitation to ask, ask anything, and I bailed. That was on me. Did I decline the offer because it was late? Because I didn't want to stir up trouble after we'd found some calm after the earlier storm, out of apprehension? It didn't matter. I didn't accept it, but it didn't mean I wouldn't revisit it another time.

"Right or left?" Her question came after a brief quiet.

"Excuse me?" I asked for more context.

"Do you sleep on the right or the left?" Jocelyn stood, wrapping up leftover salad and avoiding eye contact.

"*Hm.* Smack dab in the middle, I'm afraid." The daring question felt like progress until I realized she had pushed beyond her comfort zone. It ended our evening.

"*Hm.* Me too. Speaking of—I think I'll head off now. Tomorrow I have to face decisions about my house—my *other* house. And the sooner I do, the sooner Will gets out of my hair. Maybe."

"I'm all for that—sorry." My quick snark elicited her laugh.

"I guess you'll be working tomorrow?"

"Yes, it will be very official, double-teamed by agent and attorney, apparently."

"And in the evening? Maybe another—?"

"Date? Yes." Hell if I cared how eager I sounded.

"Nothing elaborate. A drink on the patio, perhaps?"

"Sounds perfect."

"Great. G'night, then." Jocelyn gave a sort of weak wave and left me sitting at the kitchen island. What happened to the goodnight kiss? I stood, considering whether I should go after it, but I was too late.

"Asher, old boy. Still up?" William slithered from the basement.

"Just heading that way now, William—"

"Quite the brouhaha you kicked up tonight." William methodically rotated the wine stored in the antique wall rack, twisting each bottle a half turn in its wooden cradle.

"A misunderstanding. Cleared up now. Goodni—"

"It seems you have gotten the seal of approval from everyone, well— not Frannie, and I *do* like her."

"Not really looking for approv—"

"Go easy, Cray." His incessant interruptions and snarl told me William pressed for a fight I was eager to deliver.

"Do we have a problem, William?"

William sighed. "No, just keep in mind, Jocelyn and I may not be married anymore, but she's still mine to protect." He withdrew to head upstairs.

"She's not," I mumbled, quietly taking his bait.

"What's that?" William spoke up, making a graceful about-face, almost gleeful that I had accepted his invitation to spar.

"She's *not*." The second time, I enunciated with volume. We stood toe to toe. "She's not yours," I continued. "She never *was* yours, and the fact you led her to believe otherwise, lied, cheated—is tantamount to abuse. A decades-long mind-fuck. It's a wonder you didn't wreck her for good."

"Watch it, Asher. You have no idea of her abuse but speaking of fucking, mind, or otherwise, I know your reputation, and if that's what you're out for, I suggest you sniff elsewhere, *dog*. She's not up for it, and her family won't tolerate it, and you have your career to think about. Best you make your excuses and get outta here before someone really gets hurt. She's had enough of that for a lifetime."

"Is *that* your worry, William, *old boy*? Really?" I countered as William's condescension got the better of me. "Your concern is for *her* welfare? How *she* feels? You're worried she's going to get *hurt*—or are you more bothered at the idea she might finally be properly fu—"

"*Asher*." Jocelyn stood in the doorway to the front hall, wide-eyed and crimson.

William snorted as he gripped my shoulder. "Not anymore, Ash. Not. Anymore."

I shrugged his hand off me before he crossed to his ex-wife and kissed her cheek. She took the gesture without taking her eyes off me, never moving a muscle.

"Goodnight, Love." William went upstairs.

"Jocelyn, that was not—that was two men—that was inappropriate, and I'm sorry. It had more to do with him than with you, but I shouldn't have—"

"Allowed him to get in your head? Under your skin? Shouldn't have sunk to his level? Tried to match wits with the most manipulative, passive-aggressive man you'll ever meet?"

Those whispered questions all felt rhetorical. *Yeah, Ash, best to keep your mouth shut.* But after a long pause with nothing but the hum of the refrigerator for distraction, I couldn't help myself.

"Why'd you come back down here, Jocelyn?"

"I—I'd forgotten something. Well, I didn't forget, I just left without it, but I don't want it now. Goodnight, Asher."

Welcome to plot twist number one, Ash. Fun, right?

33

Jocelyn

SLEEP HADN'T COME EASILY the night before, so it shouldn't have surprised me when I woke to find I missed the early morning seaside sun I liked so much. Despite a house full of guests, I slept the first daylight hours away. I scrambled from my bed, shocked by my wild hair but more the dark circles under my eyes. *Perfect.*

Dressed, with my hair tamed, I darted from my room to find all the other doors already open. I nearly crashed into Gigi, rushing into the kitchen when I glimpsed a fraction of Asher drinking coffee on the patio with Laney.

"Morning, Jojo. Lazybones. Relax. Gabe wisely suggested he should take Frannie and William to The Funky Brunch for breakfast."

I kept my eyes to the outdoors, watching what looked to be a quiet but heated talk.

"Sooo, what was your plan? Lure the unsuspecting writer to your summer home and then—"

"Yeah, I mean, *what*? No. *Stop.* You're not the first to make that joke, or even the second, and I'm not in the mood. But good morning to you too. Why are you up? Awfully early for you." I wanted to normalize Gigi being here, but without questioning the magic that made it happen. Still, most of my attention zeroed in on the patio.

"One, I don't sleep well here. Not news. Two, we gotta hop a plane back to LaLaLand. You'd think in this age of video this and digital that and everyone's concerns about carbon footprints, there'd be a better way to conduct some of this business, but it's their dime and first-class, and I get the miles so hey, what the hell? Hello. Earth to Jojo. Wow, this is happening, isn't it?"

"Probably, wait, what?" I didn't pay attention to my sister, preoccupied by her wife and—

"Asher's got you—distracted. I know this because my coffee cup is barely three-quarters-full, and you aren't rushing to fill it. It's a whole new world, and you, Jocelyn Mae, are smitten."

"Shut up. My fondness for Asher Cray is hardly a news flash—obviously." I poured a topper into Gigi's mug, still trained on the slice of the patio where heads bent in conversation.

"No, this is different. This is not you pining over a PR photo and some well-written prose. This is—you haven't—? Wait, did you—?"

"*No.*"

"But you want to. I mean, you would."

"Jeez, Gigi. Wouldn't you?" I whispered, straining on my tiptoes at an awkward angle, unable to stop looking at the man.

"Um, no."

"Well, if he were a woman you would, trust me. He kisses like—"

"Okay. I'm out. I have a six-hour flight with the man today and don't need to be thinking about his tongue talents all that time. *Aww, dammit.* Now I'm *gonna* think about it all that time. Thanks, Jojo."

"What?" I sank flat-footed.

"Now I'm going to be thinking about—"

"Not that. A flight? Today? With *Asher*?"

"That's why we're here. To get him on a plane and in front of some movie executives. They want some Asher Cray all their own. Hollywood is officially your competition, little sis. What's that look?"

The sinking feeling in my stomach must have shown on my face. Asher had conveniently found a way to take Will's suggestion to get out before anyone got hurt.

"Jojo?" Gigi waved a hand in front of my face.

"Nothing." I took a breath. "I'm glad it will quiet down here. You're right. I got a little distracted by my schoolgirl crush. It's nothing, though. Really." The neatly folded dish towels aligned on the counter needed refolding. "Besides, you know the man's reputation..."

"Know it? Come on, Jo. I helped create it. And he's *not* that guy, and by now you know that, so what's with the one-eighty?" Gigi's husky voice got lower as she leaned in with her interrogation.

I slumped across the island. "He and Will got into it, more than once, I think. Seems Will did what Will does, and now Asher Cray can't get out of here fast enough."

"God, Jojo. I hate how life has you tied to that man."

"That man is the father of my son, a dear friend, and a generous benefactor."

"Benefactor? Good lord, Jojo. It's called alimony, and you earned every dime. It was the best bit of lawyering I ever did."

"Still—"

"I get you care for one another. It is the most bizarre divorce arrangement I know, but he has no right to get in the way of your romantic life. He has his, and you deserve yours."

"I think things went south with Raphe. I haven't gotten details yet—"

"Good morning, Jocelyn." Laney entered, followed by Asher. I straightened but was glad to have the island for support. I almost bit my lip, but Gigi's dagger glare stopped me.

"Morning." I took a swig of coffee, eyes locked on his. "Asher."

"Good morn—"

"Sorry to steal your houseguest," Laney interrupted.

"Yes. It's a shame," I replied in earnest.

"He said as much—and *more*." Laney glanced at him.

"Well, I'm sure now that he's writing again, he can do it anywhere." My chipper tone fooled even me.

"Writing again?" Laney's face said she hadn't heard about Asher's breakthrough.

"For his eyes only, of course, but yes—" I continued, then wondered if I had betrayed a confidence.

"Since when? Asher? Since when do you *not* want me to read your first pages of anything?"

I *had* made a mistake. Whatever Asher was working on wasn't something he wanted to share. I mouthed, "I'm so sorry."

He gave a small head shake in frowning forgiveness.

"You've got six hours at thirty-five thousand feet to badger the man about it. We need to get going." As usual, Gigi played the law-and-order chaperone.

"What about your shoes and jacket? They're ruined." I sought any excuse to prevent the inevitable.

"Brooks Brothers and Ferragamo at JFK." Laney had an answer for everything.

Asher finally spoke. "Genevieve, Laney, I'm gonna need a minute, please." His words sounded like he hoped for permission, but the rest of his demeanor said otherwise. "Jocelyn, would you join me on the patio?"

"I should get your laptop and—"

"Patio, please."

A quick look to the other popeyed women, and they each spun to busy themselves with other things. *Pretend* things. I set my coffee cup on the island to head to the backyard. Asher held the French door open for me, allowing me to pass. His unavoidable, heady smell made my sinking feeling plunge deeper. The lawn glistened a more vibrant green after the nighttime rain as the morning humidity burned off. A distant mower revved, but not loud enough to impede the looming goodbye.

"This is not goodbye," Asher said before I even faced him. "I know this must look like I got busted saying something asinine, and William said I should leave, and now I'm doing just that. Leaving. But it's not. I'm not."

"You're not leaving?"

"No, I am, but just for a few days. I'm coming back. And I'm leaving my car and my computer and my ruined clothes and anything else I can think of, so I have to come back, and you have to let me cuz— it's my stuff. But you have to be here too when I come back because I hate the car and I can buy another laptop, and the clothes are *ruined*, so the only reason I'm coming back is you, Jocelyn Durand. I will get a motel room or an Airbnb, so we aren't living under the same roof. We can start fresh, date like normal people with normal boundaries and not with children and siblings and ex-spouses and business partners all underfoot with their noses in our—"

"Okay."

"Okay?"

"Okay. Come back. I'll be here. Waiting to be normal if that's your goal. Usual. Ordinary. It seems like we could do better, though. I mean, the potential feels like—"

"More?"

"To me, yes. But what do I know? Don't answer that. My *unique* experience or *in*experience precedes me."

"I feel the same." Asher moved toward me.

I squinted at his remark. "If we know anything, it's that you have more experience, Mr. Cray." He got my jesting, but something in it made him stop on his route to where I stood.

"About that."

"About what?" I looked at him askance.

"I'm heading to L.A. and—"

"Ah. You have someone in L.A." My gaze hit the flagstone, and my teeth found my bottom lip. *And it was going so well, Jocelyn.*

"No. Well, yes. I have several someones in L.A."

"Oh, jeez—"

"No." Asher attempted to reach for me. I evaded his touch. "What I mean is, I don't know what the two women inside have planned for me in California. But it's often something, so I wanted to warn you."

"Warn me?"

"Not warn—make it clear— if you see something or hear something, read something—nothing is as it appears. It's show biz, as they say. Smoke and mirrors. Fantasy."

"And your fantasy may involve a leggy blonde?"

"For the record, the only legs I'm fantasizing about belong to the blonde standing in front of me right this minute. The ones with the scraped knees."

"Wow, that's some pretty forward talk for us having barely started to date."

"I'm just following your instructions. Speaking plainly," Asher teased.

"Why don't you follow my fingers over here for that goodnight kiss I missed last night and the good morning kiss I've been waiting for and the *goodbye* kiss—"

"Not goodbye—"

"That *see you later* kiss you apparently owe me too."

Asher had his arms around me and with his lips an inch from making sweet contact with mine when—

"*Ahem.* We have a plane to catch, Ash." Laney's head poked out through the French door.

"Laney? Sister-in-law to sister-in-law, you know I love you, right?"

"Yes, Jocelyn?"

Still wrapped in Asher's embrace, I continued, "You may find this client here less inclined to take part in your West Coast PR shenanigans this time around. For the record, he's his own man, makes his own choices. I've given him no instructions, no ultimatums, no lists of what he can and cannot do or with whom he can or can't do those things. I know better than to get in the way of your work."

"For the record, huh? Good to know, sister-in-law. Come on, Asher, kiss her, and let's go."

He did.

34

Asher

I LOVE AIRPORTS. FLYING, not so much, but airports are fantastic. Like small cities unto themselves, aside from the greatest people-watching, they often have some of the best food and drink, shopping of all kinds, and of course, books. I like to sneak into the bookstores and autograph copies of my work on the down-low. Readers seem to get a kick out of that. You can also get your shoes shined, a neck massage, and your nails done, if that's your thing. Plus, those international airports sell liquor, perfume, expensive jewelry, fancy bags, and shoes to match. And since you are a captive audience of sorts, why not?

I had errands to take care of, and my agent, ever helpful, jumped at the chance to take part. I hadn't packed for L.A., and L.A. required a special wardrobe. Cool, but casual, nothing fancy, but it ought to be expensive. And somehow West Coast folks can spot pricey casual over inexpensive casual with precision. As a decidedly East Coast guy, I don't possess the talent, so delegating the task seemed a wise choice. Laney and Genevieve threw together the essential items and fast, too, so I could take care of my own secret mission. I wasn't super jazzed about leaving what had gotten started with Jocelyn, but it was pretty clear we were both eager for my return, and that notion left me with a stupid grin. My travel companions wouldn't stop scoffing. Let 'em.

"You really do need to knock it off, Asher." The little hand hadn't reached the twelve yet, but that didn't mean Laney couldn't nurse a Scotch in our first-class seats.

"I'm happy to switch with your wife if my good humor is too much for you to stomach."

"It's just the last time I saw you, the hole looked pretty deep. What a difference four days can make."

"And I owe it all to you, you little matchmaking pal o' mine. *Yenta* Li"

"Oy, it's *shadchan* Li, and *you* should know better. Your poor *bubbe* is rolling over in her grave. And I had nothing to do with it. Mother Nature, with her uprooting of trees, is the culprit, not me. I sent you away to write not—"

"Hold up. I believe you suggested both things, and I *am* writing again. Don't forget."

"Yeah, what's it about?"

"Give me a minute, Laney. It's just getting started."

"You never asked for a minute before, Asher. What's different?"

"Not sure, and I'm done talking about it. But if you wanna talk about Joce—"

"Nope. Seat switch," she sing-songed, pointing across the aisle where Genevieve sat, eye mask and noise-canceling headphones affixed. "You can go moon over there, Loverboy." Laney stared at her resting wife before downing the last gulp of booze. "Hey, real talk. Jocelyn is— she's my wife's kid sister, and I've known her for a long time. She's special and she's Genevieve's everything, despite what it might look like sometimes. And if she had to choose between Jocelyn and me, I'd lose every damn time. I've made my peace with that. Blood is thicker, yadda, yadda. But like I said before, there is something there—the house, I don't know—something—bad. I woke last night to find Genevieve sitting in a chair, just staring out into that backyard, like she was waiting for something to happen, someone to appear. Eerie. I don't think she slept at all." Laney watched her sleeping wife for another moment, worry etched into her brow. "Anyway. Be careful. For all our sakes."

I didn't know what to do other than nod. Laney was right. I knew something was *there*, but for now, I planned to close *my* eyes and picture those big brown ones, surrounded by blonde curls, minus the sadness. Her story would reveal itself along the way, no point forcing it. Of course, what would a few Google searches hurt? Not right now. Not today. But it might surprise you what one learns when researching a book. Never take a writer's internet search history too seriously.

35

Jocelyn

"Because I liked it the way it was. It's practically a hundred-year-old house, Will. It's a wonder they aren't telling us we have to knock it down completely." The original house plans lay spread across the dining room table marked up with some changes Will wanted me to consider.

"I don't think you're focusing on the big picture, Love. And just where that pretty little head of yours is right now, I can only imagine—"

"Nope. Not playing this game." I walked to the kitchen. "Iced tea?"

"No. Like I need more caffeine."

I returned to my seat with one glass and reached for Will's hand. "Will. William."

"Oh no, if you're calling me William, this is going to be bad. Should I pour myself a tumbler of wine first? What?"

"Will, you know I love that house. Gabe grew up in that house. We had some good times there, but it is more home than I need, particularly when I have this one too. Let's just—"

"You want to sell? Good grief, Jocelyn. Why?"

"Why keep it? I could get something small in the city. Be closer to Gigi and Laney Li. Or stay here. A small community I love, I can walk everywhere—it's easy."

Will kept his eyes to the blueprints in front of us while giving a spirited headshake. "Where is this coming from? Tell me this has nothing to do with a certain writer?"

"Yes, Will. I have made the rash decision to sell the home I've loved and lived in for more than twenty years because I met a man earlier this week. Come on, get your head out of your—"

"Jocelyn Mae. There's that sass again."

I smirked over my iced tea.

"I do kinda love it on you. Maybe Mr. Cray isn't all bad. He certainly has riled up something." Will had an adoring look meant just for me, and he gave it now.

"Well, not this. I have been thinking of getting out of Westchester for a while. What do I need suburban living for? We fix it, we sell it, we split the profits."

"I'm not taking money for it, Love. I have more money than I know what to do with, and it won't be long before Cookie heads off to the big bakery in the sky, leaving me everything. Such a headache."

Cookie Atwater was the widowed matriarch, and William was her sole heir. Of course, Gabe would carry on the name someday, though I certainly wasn't eager for him to do it with anyone I'd met recently, but it wasn't the time to get into that hornet's nest.

"Speaking of headaches," Will continued like he had read my mind. "What do we think of Miss Frannie?" His eyebrows wiggled while my eyeballs rolled, and I flopped back in my seat. Will howled with laughter. "Tell me what you *really* think, Love."

"She's lovely, and as long as Gabe is happy, I'm happy. And when do I get to hear about Raphe? My lawn needs mowing." I gave Will a sidelong glance when his howl grew to a cackle, and he slapped the table.

"Oh, sweetheart, you little naïve thing." He wrinkled his nose. "My lawn needs mowing—ahhh." He settled himself. "Raphe is fine. Nothing to worry about, I assure you. Sometimes a little break does some good, absence makes the heart—you know, and remember, monogamy is passé. You need to accept that if you are considering getting back out there. But I'm not sure you have the stomach for it, and I assure you Asher Cray or anyone like him is not for you."

"I don't recall asking, and you don't know Asher Cray."

"Oh, I know enough. We worked together; I saw behind the curtain."

"He admitted you worked on *High Art Heist* and helped him invest. He didn't hide it and had nothing but praise even before he knew who you were to me."

"And who am I? Your biggest regret?"

"Never that. I got Gabe. You are my ex-husband, that is all."

"You *wound* me, woman. But I know you don't mean it." He slumped in his chair, and I sighed, suddenly weary of him.

"Fix it, sell it." I rolled up the architect's drawings. "And don't show up here unannounced again. Certainly not in the middle of the night. Do you hear me? I deserve my privacy."

"You deserve the world, and I would do anything to see you get it." He kissed my knuckles. "You know that, don't you? There is nothing I wouldn't do for you if I had the power."

"The power to what?" Gabe and Frannie entered from the front of the house.

"Hey, how was the beach?" I flew to my feet. "A mess after the storm? Why'd you come in the front? Can I get you a snack?" I oh-so-cleverly disguised my Frannie-induced insecurities with litanies of questions and offers of food.

Gabe handed me a package. "Delivery kid out front. Had this for you. Said instructions were inside. Very mysterious."

"He wore a BluWire JFK shirt and said some big shot Venmo-ed him five hundred bucks to drive out here to deliver it." Frannie looked impressed. "Don't suppose we know any big shots flying out of JFK today, do we?"

"A kid?" Will asked. "That's quite the drive."

"My age, all jacked up for making quick cash. You gonna open it, Mom?"

I fingered the package with suspicion. "Maybe later." I looked at three sets of eyes gawking back at me. "What?"

"Open it," the three chorused.

I pried open the brick-sized box to find a note.

FROM THE DESK OF ASHER CRAY

Dear Jocelyn:

In case you want to text, or talk, or video chat even. But I'd avoid the gossip sites for the next few days. A guy's gotta make a living.

See? Normal would have meant flowers, right?

Three-hour difference but try me anytime. I programmed my number in it.

-Asher

"A burner phone, how *practical*," Will jeered.

"It's romantic," Frannie gushed.

"Yeah, he's pretty cool, Mom." Gabe ruffled the curls on my head.

"Okay, gang, what's for dinner?" I asked, trying not to let my desire to text a certain someone on the other side of the country distract me.

"Indian," Frannie blurted.

"Naan Better delivers. Go ahead and order, Gabe. Tikka Masala for me. Your dad's buying. Right, Will?" I winked at Will as I casually walked backward toward the stairs. "Holler when it's here."

"Yes, Love." Will shook his head at my furtive getaway.

Jocelyn: Got your gift. You shouldn't have.

Asher: Selfish, really. I wanted to hear from you.

Jocelyn: Settled in your hotel?

Asher: Yes. Car coming in an hour for early drinks before the dinner meeting.

Jocelyn: High floor, 24-hour room service, pie?

Asher: I'd trade pie for you.

Jocelyn: I don't know how to flirt with my thumbs.

Asher: Lol. You'll get the hang of it, though it has me wondering what you do flirt with.

Jocelyn: My eyes, Mr. Cray. I flirt with my EYES.

Asher: I dreamed of those eyes cross-country today.

Jocelyn: Wow. You're really good at this. Lots of practice?

Asher: Lots of inspiration. See, I met this woman...

Jocelyn: ...

Asher: Hello? Did I lose you?

Jocelyn: I'm here. Maybe we could talk later?

Asher: Sure. Sorry, I didn't mean to make you uncomfortable.

Jocelyn: No. Just a little overwhelmed, maybe.

Asher: I don't know how late I'll be and with the time difference...?

Jocelyn: Right. Of course.

Asher: How late is too late?

Jocelyn: Midnight my time? Maybe between dinner and your leggy blonde?

Asher: Please tell me you're joking about the blonde.

ร

Jocelyn: I am. Promise. Until whenever. No pressure. Really.
Asher: Ok. Until later.

Will knew me too well. I didn't have the stomach for it.

36

Asher

I TOSSED MY PHONE onto the hotel writing desk, lined with brochures, tourism magazines, and a shiny silver ice bucket with short glasses. Hands on my hips, I scowled at my picture glass reflection. *That went well, Ash.*

Colorful ribbons and cellophane took up the entire bistro table set between two armchairs. A fruit and cheese basket with an accompanying bottle of wine overflowed under all the wrapping. A *Welcome to Hollywood* compliments of the movie studio, according to the impersonal card dangling from a curled strip of decoration. This whole process consisted of one big back-and-forth ass-kissing, and I tried to remember why it was so crucial for me to be here. Surely, this is why we have Zoom.

My view of L.A. traffic had me thinking I might miss the screeching tree frogs and other nature sounds of my recent home away from home. But then I noted the blackout draperies and thought at least I'll get to sleep past dawn. No five-thirty sunrise would disturb me here. *Come on, Asher. Snap out of it.* A glance at my watch said I had forty-five minutes until my meet-up in the lobby with Laney and Genevieve. A quick pick-me-up shower, plus fresh clothes, and I'd be ready to play the devilishly charming bachelor-about-town.

I didn't bother to look at the receipts when Laney handed me the multiple crisp, handled bags at the airport. The price didn't matter, but when I saw the tags as I dressed, I couldn't help but chuckle. So much for the *free* trip out west.

One last look in the mirror and I pocketed my wallet, clasped my watch, and grabbed my phone from its charger. A voicemail? *Dammit.* Jocelyn had called. With the phone to my ear, I grabbed my new jacket and headed to the lobby.

"Asher. Jocelyn here. Duh. Oh, jeez. Who says, duh? Sorry, and sorry I missed you. You said you had an hour, so I thought I'd get you before your early drinks got started, but—anyway. So, yeah, I called because I thought— I'd be better talking on the phone than typing on it, but uh, I see now that was a pipedream. Look, sorry about the texting trouble earlier. I'll do better. Try to, anyway. You're great. Okay. Have a great time tonight. Great meeting, I mean. Ha, how many times can I say 'great?' K. Yeah, this was such *a bad idea. I'm gonna stop before you think I'm nuts and decide to stay out west permanently just to avoid this mess. But, well, I'm your mess. Oh my god, no, I'm not. I'm not your mess, I'm not your anything and wow, I just keep talking, don't I? Say goodnight, Jocelyn. Goodnight, Joce— Asher. Goodnight, Asher. Ugh."*

If that wasn't the greatest voicemail of all time, I'm not sure what qualifies. I chuckled as I replayed the message on the elevator ride to meet my agent and attorney. The lobby, all water features and palm trees, thumped with electronic club music beneath the throng of beautiful people sipping cocktails and taking selfies.

"Well, you don't smile like a New Yorker," Genevieve rasped over the noise while she fussed with my collar in motherly fashion, then patted my lapel before pinching my cheek.

"Come on, Gen, New Yorkers don't smile at all." Laney appraised her airport purchases.

"Exactly. What gives, Asher? Didn't realize you were such a big California fan, but you sure look happy to be here, and you don't look half bad."

"You flatter me, Genevieve, but it's not California I'm a fan of."

My grin grew wider. She gave me a gimlet eye, but then I'd swear a glimmer of a smile peeked out as she nudged my chin with her fist.

"Laney Li," Genevieve replied, her eyes still locked on mine. "Let's go make this man some money. He's got better places to be, better people to be with. And how about we call off TMZ? Or whoever you offered up our poor lamb to tonight."

I thought I just got the big sister A-OK, and that notion made it easier to breathe. The three of us stepped through the sliding glass doors to the waiting car and driver sent by the movie studio. The sun shone brighter here than on the other side of the country. Then again, it might have been my new outlook. I pulled my phone from my inside breast pocket.

One last text before my "workday" commenced:

Asher: Best. Voicemail. Ever. Made my night. Talk later.

"So, ladies, what's the play tonight? Charming Asher? Hard-to-get Asher? Aloof and brooding?"

"Not sure you've got the acting chops to pull off that last one in your current state. Hey, Genevieve, is there a play with a *giddy* Asher? *Besotted*, maybe?" Laney walked, talked, and texted at the same time. A multi-tasking necromancer.

"Let up on the guy, Lane. I kinda like it." Genevieve's velvet voice sighed.

Yes. Jocelyn's protector had weighed, measured, and found me worthy.

If ever you are in a situation where "representation" is an option, I cannot say emphatically enough—*take it*. Laney and Genevieve handled the evening with such deftness I knew I had nothing to worry about. Not that I had concerns going in, but the two tag-teamed the Hollywood folks while I enjoyed drinks, a nice meal, and delightful conversation full of praise for my years of published work. And in the end, we shook on a deal, and everyone seemed pleased.

As I have mentioned, I'm a writer, not a movie maker, but I'll happily allow one of the many mentioned *Chris so-and-sos* to steal art on the big screen on my behalf. And though I declined to admit just which Chris was my favorite of all the Chrises, I did recommend the services of the immensely talented art expert who had been so helpful in my research for the novel. And if William needed to relocate out west for some extended period to consult on the film? All the better. Genevieve and I had a good private laugh over that suggestion.

In a blink, the three of us were back at our hotel, in the bar, toasting our success with no Hollywood insiders accompanying us. Laney and Genevieve made excuses and whisked me away before the typical trendy, dark, and noisy night club VIP section with mandatory bottle service and easy access by paparazzi ever came to pass.

"...and how Genevieve jumped in to say, 'Oh, absolutely, we can get a hold of the art expert. I'm sure I have his contact info somewhere.'" Laney squawked while signaling the cocktail server for another round.

"Come on now. Asher mentioned it first. I was just backing our client. But if William needs help moving cross-country, I can have a U-Haul delivered tomorrow." Genevieve played innocent in the scheme while offering me a high-five.

"Oh, I see now. You two are teaming up. A dynamic duo, okay." Laney pointed at her wife and me.

"*Cahoots*, I believe, is the term you're looking for—" I offered.

Genevieve clasped my hand with an endearing look. "Oh, my

lord, it's only been a week, and she's got you—"

"Making it more everyday lexicon?" I parroted her sister.

"Laney, Asher Cray is officially our favorite client." Genevieve may have finished one too many servings of Scotch.

"Well, he is someone's favorite *something*, that is for certain." Laney raised her glass with her wonky version of a smile.

Genevieve leaned in. "Rumor has it, he kisses like a—"

"*Whoa*," I interrupted before any more secrets leaked.

Laney let out her loud honk, and it reverberated through the hotel lobby bar. "Put a sock in it, Cray." Laney leaned across the table with a lascivious leer. "Go on, Gen. I'm listening." We all laughed as we watched the sun set on the day, and I feigned embarrassment. Okay, maybe it wasn't *all* feigned.

"Well, we didn't get too deep into it. I mean, it was early, and I only had the one cup of coffee, plus she's my baby sister—"

Laney honked again, and I'm sure the color had crept up my cheeks, but I tried to play along. "Well, I may not be any Darren Kolchek, but—"

"Oooh, the plot thickens. Darren *who*?" Laney elbowed, but Genevieve blanched chalk-white and set down her glass with a cough. "Gen?"

Air stopped and the noisy bar seemed to hush except for the techno beat pulsing underneath the sudden cloying tension. "Uh, I think I, uh—committed the classic blunder—trying to keep up with Laney and the Scotch. I'm not feeling well. I think I'll— head to our room. Call it a night. I didn't sleep much last night. Jet lag, too." Genevieve's throaty voice wheezed to a whisper as her pallor morphed further to a sickening gray. Pushing back to stand, she looked as though she might be sick. I sprang from my seat to steady her when she stumbled into a potted palm.

"Let me help you, Genevieve." I exchanged alarmed looks with Laney.

"I've got her, Asher. It has been a long day. We should call it early. Come on, hon." Laney had her arm around her wife at the waist, and the two wobbled to the lobby elevators. Laney twisted to me. "Studio visit in the morning. Meet you here."

I simply nodded with a furrowed brow. *What the hell just happened?* Genevieve never met my eye.

37

Jocelyn

THE LAPTOP'S GREEN LIGHT blinked like a Morse code signal calling to me in the night. *You could try. Be brave. Take a chance.* Asher's written words bounced around my brain. He made me want to try, helped me feel brave, willing to take a chance. Those were powerful acts for someone to fuel in another, and let's be honest, that wasn't the half of it.

Best to focus on other things. The next day would be quiet. Will headed back to the city to get things moving on the Westchester house, and the kids would leave early for a day of sailing out of Sag Harbor. I had a list of housekeeping and shopping to do before the holiday traffic picked up, plus a swim my body ached for. My head needed it, too.

My heart skipped a beat when my phone rang, and I thrashed out of my sheets to answer it.

"Is everything all right?" I knew it couldn't be.

"Jojo?" my sister's gritty voice growled.

"Gigi? Are you okay? I didn't think you'd use my new number so soon. Gigi?"

Only her breath rattled through the phone.

"Gigi? What's wrong? Where's Laney?"

"She's in the bathroom. Taking a shower," Gigi whispered, followed by another ragged exhale, too loud compared to her murmured words.

"What's going on, Gi? Have you been drinking? You're scaring me."

"I'm scaring *you*? I'm not the one—" Gigi didn't finish her thought. "You need to get out of that house, Jojo. It's not good for you there."

"What? I love this house. And you were the one who told me I should come here. And I met Asher here."

"Asher. Yeah, he's good, isn't he?"

"I think so. He certainly isn't what I thought he was, but yes, I think he's a good man. Is that what you mean? I think he might be good for me. He has—" I didn't understand where her question came from or why she called so late to ask, but sharing the recent realizations about my romantic life, or the utter *lack* of any real romantic life, wasn't something I cared to delve into with my sister—on the phone—in the middle of the night.

"He has what, Jojo?"

"He has woken something in me. I know it sounds silly, and I don't care to be teased right now, but he has opened my eyes, cleared my focus in a way..."

"Yeah, that's what I'm afraid of." Gigi's words didn't sound meant for me, more like she was thinking aloud. "You should go to sleep, Jo."

"You called me, Gigi. Is there something I should know? Something you aren't telling me? About Asher?"

"About Asher? No. And don't get me wrong. I like the look of him on you." She snorted a sort of sleepy, drunken snicker. The quip sounded similar to Will's comment earlier in the day, and my sister and ex-husband agreeing on anything that involved me caused a hard swallow. "I didn't mean that in an off-color joke kinda way. Not that you would have picked up on it, my sweet little sister," Gigi sighed. "But clarity isn't all it's cracked up to be. Move forward, Jojo. No use looking back, okay? Goodnight. I love you."

The three beeps pulsed in my ear, ending the call, and I had no idea what my sister meant about any of it. And while I had just been told clarity was overrated, I needed some fast and hoped Asher might provide it. I dialed.

"I should have waited for you to call, I know. And believe me when I say clingy is not my thing, never has been, but I just got a weird call from my sister, and I thought you might have some insight, but if you're out or working or tired or got your head in something else, I understand if this isn't a good time. And I realize I probably should have texted instead of calling to see if you were available to speak, but I jumped the gun, and this is new, and I don't know the rules or where to learn them and—Asher?" I gulped a much-needed serving of air.

"I'm not a big stickler for rules, and to be clear, Jocelyn, you can call me anytime, day or night. But phone etiquette suggests you allow the person answering the call to say *hello*, and then you respond with some sort of similar greeting and then allow the conversation to continue from there."

I recognized his joking reprimand, but something felt off.

"I'm—"

"And Jocelyn, don't even think of apologizing," Asher interrupted what was definitely going to be an apology.

"*Uh*, hi," I opted to start over. "How are you? How was your day?"

Asher coughed up a forced chuckle. "Hi, I'm okay. My day was long, but it went well. How about yours?"

I relaxed into the typical phone chit chat. There was something to be said for *normal*, after all. "Okay, I guess. I made some decisions."

Our conversation rallied somewhat. And after a moment's breath, I realized dumping my sisterly drama, as unusual as it was, on the tired lap of a man three thousand miles away probably went against any good advice offered to a person in my situation.

I kept the chit-chat about me and told Asher I wanted to sell the Westchester house. My eager willingness to make the big move impressed him.

He shared some details of his movie meeting and prospects of seeing his story portrayed on a screen, but he admitted his eagerness to get back to writing because it had been so long. We kept the exchange light, and his voice comforted me, the way he told the tale of his day from the rush to the airport and ending at the dinner meeting with powerful movie moguls.

But while I enjoyed the back-and-forth and looked forward to more everyday kinds of discussions like it, an overt distance widened between us. Our puzzle pieces no longer fit just so. Could the actual miles and three time zones be responsible, or had something happened? Did something change throughout the day? And if so, would we find our way back? And what happened with Gigi? All questions I wasn't brave enough to ask as I sat in my dark bedroom with the steady flicker of that darned green light.

38

Asher

MY STOMACH TIGHTENED WHEN Jocelyn's name appeared on the phone screen. I knew I should have called her as soon as I returned to my room, but the writer— the damn researcher—got in my way, and once I clicked one key on my laptop, the rabbit hole opened and down I fell.

I closed the computer on the first ring. *Be cool, Asher. Just talk to her.*

Out of the gate, Jocelyn was jumpy. A sort of panic because of Genevieve's call, a call we didn't mention again after Jocelyn's initial inquiry. I side-stepped it, manipulated the conversation to draw her away from that line of questioning. I'm not proud of my actions, but I needed to get my head around it first. Gather more information before tackling it with her. So, in the meantime, I kept the talk light, almost impersonal. It felt awful. All the promise earlier in the day, and earlier in the week, dissipated even as I wanted nothing more than to grab onto it and make it stay.

Jocelyn yawned, and I realized it was nearly one o'clock in her world, and it felt like it in mine. "Am I keeping you awake?"

"No, I mean, yes, but I don't mind." She tried to find her way into our comfortable spot. Some long-distance version of it anyhow. That's where I wanted her to be, but for whatever reason, we couldn't find it. Whatever reason? No, I knew the reason, but did she?

"I should let you get your rest. Your day starts much sooner than mine." My chest squeezed in the conflict that waged between my head and my—gut.

"I guess you're right." She paused before asking, "Asher?"

I pressed my hand to my forehead in a silent plea that she wouldn't ask a question I couldn't answer or force some sort of lie out of me. I promised her honesty, and now— "Hm?"

"Is everything o—? We're just tired, right? Long day and all?"

I kept to the facts. "It's been a long day, and it's late. Get some rest." I dreaded my voice gave away my worry, and the sound of heartbreak weighed down her not-so-simple questions. I knew sadness flooded those sleepy, whiskey-brown eyes, and I couldn't drag it on any longer. "Goodnight, Jocelyn." I ended the call. *Jesus Christ, Asher. You are such a coward.*

My palms pushed into my eyes, and I struggled for a breath, giving a brisk rub to my scalp. I knew what I had to do. Sometimes, once you jump in the deep end, you have to force your way to the bottom to push back up to get air again. I opened my laptop and stared at the old newspaper clipping headlines scattered in front of me. *Prom Night Peril as Local Teen Goes Missing; Soccer Star Vanished: Runaway or Foul Play?; H.S. Senior Never Came Home, Official Search Ends; Parents Up Reward, What Ever Happened to Darren Kolchek?*

My brain revved. Questions ricocheted through my mind, but the answer I needed would not come from an old news story. The decades-old media didn't have the information I desperately wanted. I would only find satisfaction from one source, but I was too afraid to confront her. What did you do, Jocelyn Durand?

A half-dozen articles I found mostly recycled the one printed before it.

"Last Thursday, June 21, Bayborough High School celebrated their prom. According to friends and family, senior Darren Kolchek, 17 attended the dance with his date, Anne Bismarck, also a senior.

Anne and Darren were known to be a popular couple who dated on and off throughout their years at Bayborough. Friends, family, and faculty all confided the teens often fought. Pictures provided showed them having a good time at the night's festivities."

I had assumed Darren Kolchek was Jocelyn's prom date but thinking back, she never said he was, only that he kissed her. *He wanted to, and he did.*

The article continued.

"Private parties held at other locations are common, but when asked, school officials insisted those gatherings were not sanctioned school events. An attorney for the school district said Bayborough High had neither responsibility for nor obligation to any of the private events that took place after the official end of the prom at eleven p.m.. Unofficial after-parties happened in many locations as far west as Manhattan and east to Montauk.

"Ms. Bismarck and her parents, Edwin and Reba Bismarck, corroborated Darren brought her home by eleven-thirty that night while Darren's parents, Kevin and Charlene Kolchek, believed the teen couple planned to stay with friends overnight at one such get-together. Neither parent knew who hosted the party or where it took place."

A break in the case came a few weeks later, but it never amounted to anything. Still, the newspapers reported.

"In an update from local police, Bayborough classmates confessed to picking up missing teen, Darren Kolchek, on Route 27 on their way to Montauk. The unnamed students claimed the soccer standout acted erratically. One male thought he saw blood, but admitted that in the dark, no one knew for sure. None of the students agreed where or when they dropped off Kolchek, or how much longer it took to get to Montauk once they had."

Who lets out a kid on a scarcely lit island highway in the middle of the night?

The trail, such as it was, ran cold. If this had occurred today, cellphone towers and traffic cams would have pinpointed times and locations in a way police never dreamed of in the last century.

A runaway theory gained credibility when Anne Bismarck eventually admitted she and Darren broke-up that night and he planned to play soccer in some Mexico league. The Kolchek parents disapproved, but Darren was days away from his eighteenth birthday, an adult by law.

The rest of the articles were full of the conjecture and gossip that churned in the small community. I could practically see the eye-rolling as a picture emerged of what life in the Kolchek home must have been. How could his parents be unaware of his whereabouts, so negligent? Ironic, giving the time. Probably unthinkable today, but back then? Ask any Gen-Xer. It's a point of pride. Still, people judge. Anyway, Darren running away seemed the likely scenario, although he never got on the plane to Mexico for soccer training, and there were no indications he ever showed up south of the border either.

What I knew— the *facts* I'd known from an up-until-now trusted first-person account—was that thirty years ago, on a late Thursday night, Darren Kolchek kissed a girl in her family's summer home backyard. *He wanted to, and he did.* And that girl was Jocelyn Durand, a sad, naïve, young woman whose parents had recently died. She had been in the wreck responsible for her parents' deaths. The crash also resulted in a proximal humerus fracture of the girl's left arm, a girl who may have a demon inside her—a demon she somehow figured out how to keep locked down.

I read every article I could find and took copious notes on the subject, trying to connect the dots. Others had the same diagram, I'm sure, minus the intel no one else had. None of *that* information went on paper. No, those details remained with me. No one needed to ask those questions. But how could I find out more? Who could answer my questions? And while everything I knew of her said it couldn't be true, her family insulated her. Kept her practically bubble-wrapped, handling her with kid gloves in a way that had me thinking the impossible.

Come morning, I sat blurry-eyed, pretending to read news off my phone, but truthfully, focusing on the tiny print of the small screen hurt my head. Laney trotted in as a server brought me a second carafe of coffee.

"She'll need a bucket of sugar and a gallon of cream to go with this, thanks," I smiled at the young woman in the apron while gesturing to Laney. The waitress giggled too much in reply, then scurried off red-faced to fetch the necessary fixings for my agent's decadent morning caffeine.

"Genevieve on her way?" I asked.

Laney held up a finger while she emptied the remnants of the sugar bowl into her mug and added coffee, before pouring an unhealthy serving of half and half on top. She sipped and sat back in her chair. "Just you and me today, Ash. The Law Lady has left the building as it were." She took another swig.

"Everything all right?" I knew it wasn't. Last night's sudden illness didn't go unnoticed, and since learning about those long-ago events, I felt sick too.

"Sure," Laney lied. "Another client, another legal emergency. We're a busy firm."

"I understand if that's the way you want to play it, Laney, but I think we both know the truth is something different, and we've never been dishonest with each other in our twenty years, so I don't see the need to start now. Your call, though." Halfway through my cup number three and the dark roast had kicked in.

She grimaced with a head shake. "Yeah. Genevieve hopped a red-eye home. And I don't know why. You talk to Jocelyn last night?" She tried to be casual about the question, but desperation shaded her tone, and I couldn't help.

"I did. She was upset, but we never got around to talking about it." I admitted my own awful truth.

"You didn't talk about it? She was upset, and you ignored it? Wow, Asher, you're not good at this couple thing, you know that? Ya *putz*." Laney mumbled the last bit, but she wasn't wrong. I didn't need to hear about it though, and definitely not from the woman who'd been sidestepping issues in her marriage for who knows how long. Then she dug in again. "Did you hear *anything* I said on the plane?" Her reprimand stung.

"That she's special? To be careful? Yeah, I heard you. But I think you underestimate Jocelyn. She's not fragile. She told me so herself."

"And what would make her say that—to you?"

I returned the question with a stare. "Let's just say, I think there's more to the Durand sisters than it appears. A history. And if you don't feel able to share, I respect that. Gen's your wife, but things won't fly under the radar forever."

"What are you going on about?"

"Spend much time with your ex-brother-in-law?"

"Not if I can help it. What's William got to do with this?"

"He talks when he drinks, and I'd guess he drinks a lot. I don't want to get into that, but you've read Jocelyn's book, haven't you?"

"More than anyone, I'd bet." Laney rolled her eyes.

"That's a bet you might lose, but not important. You and Jocelyn ever talk about her inspiration when you were in revision? Subtext?" Sure, every writer and agent has their own process. Some authors prefer to go it alone. Others enjoy the collaborative route. Laney's insights were invaluable to me. It was worth a shot.

"To be honest, we didn't revise much. That beautiful horror show came to me almost exactly as Watermount published it. Never seen anything like it."

I choked down my last swallow. "Interesting phraseology..."

"What is?"

"Horror show—not the first time I've heard it lately."

"Hey, that literary fiction stuff isn't my thing, but I sold it for my sister-in-law. Watermount Publishing was high off one of my other client's raging success, so they kind of threw me a bone. Their literary imprint hadn't really gotten off the ground. Jocelyn gave it wings. None of us had a clue it would be so big. And when Hollywood types like Craven, and some years later del Toro, came out clamoring for the rights, each time, Genevieve shut it down so fast... What's your point?"

"No point. Let's get this done so we can go home."

"Where'd love-struck Asher go? Where's the goofy grin? What do you know?"

"I know there are more answers there than here. Can we get outta here today?"

"It's pushing it, but I got us a twelve-thirty flight. Lands at 9pm."

"That's why you're my favorite agent, Laney Li. Let's go sign some papers."

While Laney handled the front desk bill, I took care of the breakfast tab and texted:

Asher: 12:30 flight, land at 9pm JFK

Jocelyn: Should I get you from the terminal? I have your car, remember?

Asher: That's a long drive, late at night...

Jocelyn: I'll bring pie ;) ;)

Asher: Look who's a quick study with the flirty thumbs.

Jocelyn: Just trying to keep up.

Asher: With me? I'm not going anywhere.

Jocelyn: Good to know. Last night felt different.

Asher: Let's look forward, not back.

Jocelyn: ...

Asher:: Hello?

Jocelyn: Yes. Let's do that. See you tonight. With pie.

Asher: What kind?

Jocelyn: Of pie? Does it matter?

Asher: Not even a little.

I refused to jump to conclusions about those press clippings. There had to be an explanation. One that clarified Genevieve's reaction to the name Darren Kolchek and found Jocelyn blameless. The woman was bringing me pie, for Christ's sake. Still, hard as I tried to swallow it all, two questions sat like craggy rocks clogging my gullet. What if Jocelyn *did* have a demon inside her? More importantly, what if, thirty years ago, even if only for a moment, that demon got out?

39

Jocelyn

I AM *NOT* A fan of texting. It all seemed fine. Except for the odd suggestion to look forward, not back—nearly verbatim Gigi's cryptic comment from the night before. Everyone close to me mimicked one another, similar vocabulary and phrases on repeat. Will and Gigi. Now Gigi and Asher. Not the first time I've felt on the outside of some inside joke, but none of this felt funny.

Did Asher mention his accommodations? No. And considering it could be midnight before we returned to my peaceful summer home, I assumed he'd sleep here. I had freshened his room, and why shouldn't he stay? Silly for him to go elsewhere, really. Plenty of space and, well— plenty of space.

Gabe and Frannie planned to leave in two days, and they were out at the beach and probably would be until late. In a preemptive move to combat idle hands, I offered to do their laundry so they would take off with clean everything. While that cycled through, I would bake a pie— or two.

"What's for supper, Mom?" Pink-cheeked and sandy, Gabe and Frannie returned home as I planned to leave. "Hey, you look nice. Going somewhere?"

"Yes. Going to JFK to pick up—a friend. There's a pie. Still warm."

"Is it—?"

"Yes." I scurried to wrap up the second pastry to go on the road with me.

"Fran, my mom bakes the best raspberry pie. Prepare yourself. It's life-changing." Gabe kissed my cheek. "A friend, huh? When will you be back? Late?" He stood close, smelling of sunscreen and seawater, but underneath something more manly had replaced his boy scent. When did that happen and how did I miss it? Evening sunlight angling through the kitchen window glinted off his sand sprinkled curls, and his brow furrowed as I looked up at him.

"Who's the parent here? Oh, wait. That's me. Tell you what. If I won't be home before sunup, I'll text you. You kids have fun. Don't burn the house down—it's my last one."

Frannie giggled in the way she often did. "You might just be the coolest mom I know, Jocelyn. I hope I get to see Asher again before we take off for Wilmington."

"Couldn't tell you, Frannie. Don't know his plans." I thought my casual tone sounded plausible as I carried the pie to the side exit. "See you in the morning, unless, you know—I get lucky." I backed out the door.

"In that dress, smelling of raspberry pie? I'll be looking for that text. Have fun, Mom. You deserve it." He winked at me.

"Thanks, Gabe. Goodnight."

I gave myself plenty of time and took a chance on finding a parking spot instead of waiting at the Cellphone Lot. I *did* get lucky. The lingering aroma of raspberry pie taunted me as I waited in the car instead of heading into Terminal Eight. Using the rearview, I reapplied lip gloss and eyed the dessert sitting on the backseat of my Volvo. Who brings pie to the airport? I squinted, then rolled my eyes, scoffing. "What are you doing, Jocelyn?" Before I answered, my phone chirped a text alert. *Thank goodness.*

Asher: Would you believe I've landed? Early? That never happens.

Jocelyn: Guess I'm not the only one getting lucky tonight.

Asher: Huh?

Jocelyn: Oh. I didn't mean... OMG. I meant parking. I got lucky with parking.

Asher: LOL.

Jocelyn: I'm here. Red hot.

Asher: Are you now?

Jocelyn: No! Stupid autocorrect. Red LOT. Top of the deck.

Asher: Oh. Thought you were upping the text game.

Jocelyn: If only...

Asher: God, you make me laugh. Carried on luggage, no baggage claim, headed straight to you.

Jocelyn: Hurry and put me out of my texting misery.

This level of giddiness far exceeded anything appropriate for a woman my age, but I couldn't help it, and since I don't hold myself in check day to day, starting now with Asher didn't feel wise or necessary. No sense hiding it. I liked Asher Cray before I ever knew him, and now that I *do* know him, I only wanted to know more. And after a quarter-century of less than honest living, I never wanted to go back to a life like that.

40

Asher

AFTER THE RUSHED GOODBYE with Laney at the gate, if anyone thought I walked at an unusually fast clip, they were correct. Jocelyn said to hurry, and I had no choice but to abide. I couldn't wait to see her again. Of course, with that enthusiasm came some trepidation. Would my revelations—my *half*-revelations—distort my view of her. Pie or no, would the facts I uncovered foul my perspective, even though Jocelyn would certainly explain it all as soon as I found the nerve to ask. But how? When?

The hot, humid air of Queens hit me as I exited the terminal, and along with it fumes from the long-term parking shuttle idling at the curb. Sweat beaded up immediately, and for a moment, I missed the semi-arid heat of Los Angeles. I removed my jacket I'd worn all day and rolled up the sleeves of my dress shirt. Calm, cool, and collected wasn't happening for me today. I hadn't been all three of those things at once in a week, and only one person to blame. The culprit waited across four lanes of airport commuters atop the parking deck in front of me. It wouldn't be long now.

A good five minutes later, I finally exited the parking deck stairwell and spotted the outline of Jocelyn's head and shoulders. She leaned against her Volvo station wagon, facing away from me and into the night sky. An endless string of red, green, and white trailed across the horizon like Christmas in July, while jet engines roared above, cars honked, and security blew whistles below to keep pedestrians and vehicles flowing safely. Still muggy, the open-air top level offered a sporadic warm breeze, a brief reminder to breathe. *Breathe, Asher.*

She couldn't have heard me in all the noise, but she turned, stopping me in my tracks. Peering over the top of the car, she clutched the raised roof rails, face aglow with a smile and the LED light flooding the parking deck. She was beautiful.

We stared for a moment, still yards apart, neither of us moving as another airplane thundered overhead. When Jocelyn hid her eyes on the backs of her hands, I worried if, in the rush of it all, I hadn't returned the welcoming expression in kind. I took a tentative step toward her as she released her roof rail grip to make her way around the end of the wagon. In three quick steps, I dropped my luggage to cup her face for a kiss, the memory of which I'd been both desperate to remember and trying to ignore over the last thirty-six hours. It also marked the moment I realized I didn't care about the answers to my gnawing questions. They didn't matter. Either way, I wanted this woman, and the events of one night decades ago wouldn't change how I felt.

When our lips parted, we remained wrapped in each other's arms. Heat radiated, but neither of us let go.

"Will was right about that part, anyway." Jocelyn's head rested on my shoulder; her chin raised to speak in my ear.

"Will?" Not the first word I wanted to hear from her.

"Sorry. Poorly timed. Hi." She stayed close but met my eye.

"What did Will get right?" I had to ask.

"He said a break is a good thing. Absence makes the heart— you know."

"Ah. Can't fault that logic. Any other words of wisdom?"

"Nothing important." Those words contradicted the way she fingered the buttons of my shirt and bit her bottom lip.

I knew William had more to say on the matter, but we had time to get to it, and I had a surefire way to get her to stop biting

that lip. My hand slid from her cheek to her neck. Her smooth
skin glistened in the thick night air; her pulse thumped under my
touch. I released her mouth, both of us in need of air. Foreheads
together, my fingers skimmed her collarbone, provoking a lusty
inhale and a tighter grip around my neck. Brakes were failing, and
neither of us seemed to care. Lips met again. My body pressed hers
to the rear of the car, but the gut-swaying sensation of careening
down a hill jolted to a halt when headlights exposed us, and a car
honked as it drove past. Startled, we kept our hold on one another,
our unified gasps from the drive-by scare morphed into snickering,
like busted teenagers.

"Jocelyn?"

"I know." She patted my chest, not meeting my gaze.

"You know what?"

"I know— you're thinking, 'This woman promised me pie.
Where's the pie?'" She returned to playing with the buttons on my
shirt.

I pulled her from the car's rear window with a laugh, the
emergency brake successfully applied for the moment, anyhow.
Another plane rumbled low in the dark sky. Hot air hit my damp
shirt. "God, it's hot out here." Squeezing her shoulders, I fought
to collect myself. "Pie. You mentioned pie."

"I did." She looked at the car. "It's in the backseat. You eat, I'll
drive. It's getting late, and we have a long way to travel."

"Yeah, *uh*." I gave a slight head shake.

"Something wrong?"

"No. Nothing at all, Joss." I took a hard swallow. "Glad to see
you, is all."

"I like that." She gave a shy smile.

"Being seen—?"

"*Ha*. Yes, that too," she breathed a sigh. "But also, you calling me
Joss. No one calls me that, but I like the way you do it."

"I don't want to go to your place tonight." The statement blurted from me faster, harsher-sounding than I meant.

"Oh— okay." Brow furrowed, her smile vanished while she fidgeted with her dress, tucking her humidity ravaged curls behind her ears, eyes to the concrete. The lighting had changed, or her color drained. Spinning on her heel, she darted to open the driver's side door, then swiveled her head back without really looking at me. "Where should I drop you, then?" Her voice sounded strained, high-pitched, tight.

Hands on my hips, I tried not to look amused. "Drop me? I don't want you to *drop* me anywhere." I took slow steps to where she stood. "Jocelyn— Joss."

Her puzzled gaze met mine at my repeating the newly approved nickname.

"I want you to take me home. *My* home. For the night. *Zero* expectations, I promise. It's late, and my home is closer, and I'm beat. But I'd also like you to see where I live, and— I'd like to see *you*— where I live." That realization surprised me. I got a nod and a hesitant kiss in reply before she ducked into the vehicle. I walked around the rear of the car to collect my abandoned bag. The tailgate opened, and without instruction, I tossed the duffel in the back. The sweet smell of pie wafted my way, and for the first time that night, I realized I was hungry for more than just Jocelyn Durand.

41

Jocelyn

LESS THAN AN HOUR later, we pulled into the sloped driveway of a garage in Tribeca. Asher's building dated back to pre-Civil War days and did not have its own parking, but this one was owned by the Tri-State Parking King, a once-notorious bachelor recently married to, of all people, Laney's best friend. It's a small world, after all.

Asher's loft was a quick walk south toward City Hall. Not the busiest part of town at this time of night, but other pedestrians bustled their way around us as we strolled. Our nervous chatter picked up the farther we walked.

"If you can sell the *house* you don't need, surely I can get rid of the *car* I don't want. What I'd save in parking alone could fund my retirement. Gabe need a car?"

"*Ha*. No, not that car. Speaking of, I should let him know I'm not coming home tonight. I mean, that is still the plan? Because if it's not, it is late, and it'll take two hours to get home."

"Jocelyn?" Asher stopped under a dark awning on a narrow side street off Broadway.

"*Hm*?" In my nervy state, I kept walking but made an about-face to rejoin my grinning companion.

"I can't make you stay, but I hope you do. I want you to."

"All right. Got a Duane Reade nearby? I brought forks but no toothbrush." I held up the pie.

"I've got forks *and* a spare toothbrush and anything else you might need. Any other excuses?" His finger lifted my chin in the building's dim sconce light.

"You regularly have unanticipated sleepovers? Regular enough to keep a toothbrush supply? You know what? Don't answer that. Some mystery in life is a good thing, right?"

"Would you believe I was a Boy Scout?"

I yelped a laugh. "No, Mr. Cray, I would not, but I do believe you are always prepared."

Asher shrugged with an impish smirk that quickly turned sincere. "I wasn't prepared for you." He took a beat and then kissed my cheek. "This is me." A single-paned glass door led us into a utilitarian foyer with an elevator and a wide inset of tarnished brass mailboxes for each residence above us. A hung plaque stated the building dated circa 1860.

"1860— with an elevator?" I squinted my skepticism.

"I have indoor plumbing, too, hot and cold running water, electricity, even—it's impressive."

It was too. The apartment stunned me. Old, wide plank floors, huge windows, exposed brick, high ceilings, and all the best in appliances and finishings. The street-level lobby disguised the beauty above it.

"You can pick your chin up off the floor now. I see you were expecting a dump. Let me get the A/C cranked down further. It won't take too long to cool." He wandered down a hall to adjust the thermostat. Stuffy but not overbearing, it felt cooler than outside, where heat still radiated off the hard surfaces that soaked up the sun during the daylight hours. "I need a shower. How about you?"

"Huh?" Dizziness hit with a sharp spike in the temperature.

"Relax, Joss. I'm all for water conservation, but—Hey, give me that pie." He placed it on the kitchen island and opened the refrigerator. "Wine? Beer?"

"Scotch, neat?" My hands fluttered, unexpectedly freed and unsure what to do with themselves. They landed not-so-casually on my hips.

"Uh, sure." He walked toward me to a bar cart set up in the dining area, unbuttoning his dress shirt as he went. "You okay?"

Thank goodness I had relinquished the pie, or there would have been raspberry filling all over the mid-19th-century pine floors. "Me? Yep. You?" I shifted my gaze from his torso to the three large windows several yards away in the living room space. "Great view." I pointed in that direction.

"Yeah, even better when you actually look out the windows." He flattened his grin, barely.

"Is that right?" I asked, well-aware he'd caught me gawking. I made a grabby hand gesture; desperate for the drink Asher took his time to pour.

He silently taunted, using a bar linen to polish the glass before opening the bottle. Once he splashed some liquor into the crystal, he gave me a questioning look. My expression said, "more, please." He tipped the bottle again. Handing me the glass, our fingers touched. Another tease in an escalating game I doubted I could play.

"In all the sightseeing, I forgot to call Gabe." I winked and took a sip of my hearty serving of Scotch, fixing my eyes over the cut-glass on Asher's unbuttoned shirt.

"Oh, you should just text the kid. Believe me, he'd prefer it that way."

"You think?" I scoffed as I dialed and walked away from one beautiful spectacle to the one the windows offered.

"Ten bucks says he lets it go to voicemail." Asher leaned by the fireplace with his own drink.

"Ten dollars against a mother and her son." I *tsked* with another sip. "Hi, honey. Yeah, it looks like I'm staying in the city tonight

... at Asher's. He has a *decent enough* place in Tribeca. I'll be home tomorrow. Crab feast before you leave, right? Okay. You've got my new number if you need me. Right then. Love you. Bye." I ended the call with my third sip of Scotch, eyeing the magnificent view of the Freedom Tower.

Asher walked up behind me. "I should have bet something *way* better than ten bucks. Voicemail, right?"

I couldn't hold my snort. I hung my head in mock-shame. "How did you know?"

"There are some things a son doesn't want to hear his mother say. Sleepover plans rank high." We stood quietly for a moment. "I'm gonna take that shower. I can get you set up in the guest bath, but mine is better. Worth the wait, I mean. If—you wanna—wait." He said all that with his chin just above my shoulder. The heat of his front radiated on my back.

"I can wait," I squeaked.

"Suit yourself." His lips barely brushed my cheek before he walked away. It was the *second* time I gulped Scotch.

42

Asher

I stood under a cold shower and not the first cold shower I'd taken this week. *Careful, Asher.* We'd kicked off a dangerous game of cat and mouse, and I didn't know which of us was which. Suffice it to say, no matter how much catnip got spread around, tonight was not the night—*Jeez, Ash, your metaphors are getting out of hand.* Best to take it down a notch.

"Asher?" Jocelyn called from the other side of the bathroom door.

"Uh, yeah?" *What was happening?*

"Sorry. Your phone is ringing. It says, 'Badass.' Is it important? Should you answer, I mean? And do you mind if I have another splash of Scotch?"

"That's Laney, but I'll check it when I'm done. What's mine is yours here, Jocelyn. Take anything you want. Anything at all." *Whoa, didn't we just go over this, Asher?* I cleared my throat. "I'll be out in a minute."

"Oh, okay," she half-shouted through the door. "Thanks. Oh, and your bedroom is lovely. The exposed brick? So nice. 'kay, sorry to bother you."

Come on, Asher. I knew damn well the importance of that call and encouraging the mouse to drink more Scotch? Or was she the cat?

The air conditioner earned its keep. Company aside, I'd stop sweating soon. The frigid water helped in a couple of ways, and

I dried off and threw on a pair of pajama pants. They came with an oversized button-up top, a gift I'd never worn but imagined it would look fantastic on Jocelyn. So much for the cold shower. I threw on a t-shirt before exiting my room.

"Jocelyn?" I called. "I've got towels out and something comfortable for you to put on once you've showered." I walked toward the living room. "Joss?"

She sat on the sofa, bare feet up on the coffee table, back to me. "It's all yours."

She barely moved, except to raise the glass to her mouth.

"You'll feel so much better."

"Will I?" She didn't look at me.

"Everything all right?"

"Didn't mean to read your text. Really, I didn't, Asher."

I was *this* close to swearing that I had nothing to hide. One stupid syllable from reiterating how she'd asked for honesty, and I promised to give it. Until I remembered the part where I found news articles from thirty years ago that might implicate her in the case of a missing boy. No, I couldn't share that yet, but I'd get to it. Really, I would. Instead, I went with a gutless, non-committal, "Okay."

She took another sip, and I wondered how many sips I hadn't seen.

"What's upset you?"

"I'm just wondering why my sister-in-law is asking about Darren Kolchek. Why is my sister-in-law, who would have no reason to even *know* the name Darren Kolchek, unless you shared it with her? So, why is Laney asking *you* about Darren Kolchek, Asher?" Jocelyn's taut tone was new.

I sat next to her. She only fought my grasp of her glass for an instant when I took it and drained its contents in a single swallow. She'd likely had enough. I registered the burn and pushed on by taking her hand. She didn't fight that much either. I cleared my throat, wishing I had another scalding swig of drink before I jumped from this cliff, but I thought if I let go of Jocelyn's hand now, I'd never get it back.

"Joss? Please look at me."

She did, but the sadness I expected wasn't there. These unfamiliar eyes sent a shiver through me. Or was it the booze?

"Last night, Laney and Genevieve were so amped after the meeting they agreed to give me the night off. No clubbing or paparazzi-inspired hook-ups like usual. We—the three of us—ended up back at our hotel bar, where Laney and Genevieve resumed teasing me the way they had all day. No big deal. But my kissing you—came up. Whatever you want to tell your sisters about me is yours to say, but I didn't want to go there, so, to shut it down. I made an offhand comment. As a joke."

"Which was?"

"I said, well, I might not be any Darren Kolchek, but..." I still held Jocelyn's hand and gripped tighter when I felt her try to pull away. I wasn't letting go.

"Then what?" She pulled at my hands again but then relaxed. "Then what, Asher?"

"Then, Genevieve went pale. Said she didn't feel well because she drank too much, the classic 'trying to keep up with Laney Li' blunder. It happened in an instant. I didn't know—I didn't know what I'd done, how I had upset her. I didn't mean to, or to betray you or any of it. I—I didn't know."

Jocelyn sat quietly for a time. She leaned into me; fingers still entwined with mine. I breathed easier; kissed the top of her head. Letting her speak next felt like the prudent choice, so I waited and watched her examine our hands. Finally, she spoke. "Then what? What happened today?"

"This morning, Laney met me at the agreed-upon time, but

Genevieve had left. Caught a red-eye. Laney didn't say why. I asked Laney to get me back to you as soon as she could. We finished our business, and she got us on the earliest possible flight. Because all I wanted was to get back here. To be here. With you. That's what happened."

"Last night Gigi called me, obviously upset, but didn't say why. Then I spoke to you, and we were—off. Something was off. I told Gi—"

I squeezed closer to Jocelyn, enjoying her heat. The air conditioner hummed in the background, cooling the loft to the point of a chill. "What did you tell Genevieve?"

"I—I told her you were good. You were good for me. That you had—"

I kissed her cheek and held her tighter. "That I what?"

"That you had opened my eyes, cleared my focus, I think I said. And Gigi said—but in a way that made me think she wasn't really speaking to me—she said she was *afraid* of that. Afraid. She said she was afraid, Asher. I have never known my sister to be *afraid* of anything. Ever. And we've seen—" She shook her head then leaned on my shoulder, still exploring our interlocked fingers. I brought them to my lips and kissed the back of her hand.

In turn, she twisted up from her spot to kiss my lips. That sweet kiss escalated, and before I knew it, Jocelyn straddled my lap, her dress pushed nearly to her hips, and her hands pulled at my hair. She tasted like all the best parts of Scotch plus something better, and her intoxicating smell radiated off her warm body, more potent than Scotch. "Jocelyn." My hands met the bare skin of her thighs, and I—

"I'm going to take that shower now." She pulled from me and padded off toward my bedroom while I tried to imagine my third-grade teacher, hairy mole and all.

My head fell back, and I stared at the ceiling, then pushed my palms to my eyes. I heard the shower running and wished I had suggested she take a cold one, a very, *very* cold one. I read the text from Laney:

Badass: Who the hell is Darren Kolchek?!

I replied:

Asher: I'm home. MY home. Going to bed. We'll talk.

I hurried around, cleaning up glasses and putting away the untouched pie. Turning down my bed, I hesitated to climb into it. Best wait. It might be the sofa for me or the guest room for her, but my eyes grew heavier by the minute, the lack of sleep taking its toll.

I sat on the end of my bed when she exited my bathroom wearing my pajama top, and dammit if she didn't look better— or worse— so much better in the thing than I had even thought possible.

43

Jocelyn

I STEPPED OUT OF the bathroom to find Asher waiting on the edge of the king-sized bed, backed by an exposed brick wall. My skin turned to goose flesh in the chilly room despite the warm glow of low hung sconces. The Scotch had gone to my head. An error on my part. Thankfully, the cold shower helped, but with one look at Asher, that heady feeling hit again— hard. God, he was beautiful, but he also looked drawn, exhausted, and I breathed a little sigh of relief. Tonight would be about sleep.

"You were right. I feel better. And thank you for the jammies." I plucked at a button on the giant shirt. The cuffs hung beyond my fingertips and matched the pants he wore.

"You're welcome. I've never worn it—a gift from my *bubbe*—" He shrugged off the rest of the explanation. "Glad it's found a home. You— wear it well."

I curtsied with a grin, feeling silly and took a step toward him. Asher bounded to his feet, making me stop short. We both gave an airy laugh at our awkwardness. "Also, about earlier. I thought maybe you and my sisters were having a laugh at my expense. About Darren. That happens a lot. With them. With Will. Even Gabe. Not about Darren specifically, but—"

"I get it. It wasn't like that, but I shouldn't have mentioned him. I apologize."

"Did you notice how I didn't? Apologize, I mean. Pretty good, huh?"

Asher exhaled all the chuckle he could rally. "Yeah, that's really good."

"So, I can take the sofa or a guest bed, if you prefer. I mean, I don't need to dirty another bed, but if you'd rath—"

"You just showered. How dirty could you be?" Asher interrupted.

I looked at him askance. Evidently, he wanted me to sleep elsewhere. *Ouch.*

"Jesus, Ash." He pinched the bridge of his nose, chastising himself. "That came out wrong, Jocelyn. Totally not what I meant—at all."

"No, that's okay. I get it." I tried to wave off the snub.

"Jocelyn, please. Sleep here. It's the better bed." Asher walked to one side to take a pillow.

"Where are you going?"

"I'll be next door. I have a pullout in my office. Or the sofa, down the hall. Not sure which is more comfortable."

"Why?"

"Why?"

"Why will you sleep elsewhere if this is the better bed? Does my being in it make it less appealing?"

His answer was a quick and definitive, "Nooo. No, not at all."

"So, if I promise to stay to one side, if I swear scout's honor to keep to *my* side, will you feel okay about sharing the *better* bed?"

Asher cocked his head. "That depends, Jocelyn."

"On—?"

"Were *you* a scout of any kind? Ever?"

"Aw, caught me. No Asher, I was not, but the promise is credible."

"How credible?" He squinted with his sidelong look.

"As— credible as you want it to be." I knew I blushed at my reply, but I eyed him straight on as I gave it.

"Can't argue with that. Pick a side." He gestured with his head, wearing a satisfied grin. I scampered to the bed and slid into the smooth, crisp sheets, pulling them up to my chin. Asher pulled on the neck opening of his t-shirt as if to remove it, then stopped. I held my breath. He didn't take off his shirt, but climbed into the bed on the other side, settling in on his back, hands folded across his chest.

Up on one elbow I asked, "This is silly, isn't it?"

"What's that?" His gaze stayed on the ceiling.

"You should be able to sleep without a shirt, if that's how you prefer to sleep."

"It's fine. I'm fine like this."

"But I want you to be comfortable."

"Of all the things happening here—my t-shirt is the least of my concerns."

"You have concerns?"

"Well, not concerns, I guess."

"What then?"

"Real talk, Jocelyn? As your sister-in-law would say."

"Yes, please, Asher." I held my head in my hand, tracing figure eights on the mattress space between us.

"Let's start with your damp hair. I thought it was your shampoo, but you didn't use your shampoo, so it's just the way your hair smells and god, it's the best thing I have ever smelled in my life, and now that it's wet, well, it's *incredibly* sexy, like our first date. But then there are your eyes that give away your mood every time. I could get lost in them, unless—of course, I look at your mouth and Christ when you bite that bottom lip all I can think about is biting it too. And while I have no idea what is under that button-up shirt you have on, I sure would like to unbutton it to find out, and I know it won't disappoint, so it's fine. I can wait. Not a problem. But then those legs. Jocelyn. Those legs I watched walk up the stairs the first night I met you, wrapped in that giant cardigan, those legs under the hem of that nightgown? I haven't stopped thinking about them since, and not a half-hour ago I had my hands on your bare thighs, *my* hands on *your* thighs, and I can still feel the heat of that twelve seconds of my life, so yeah, my damn t-shirt? Not really a big issue for me in the grand scheme of things."

What does one say to something like that? *Is* there an appropriate response? A handbook with options or a blanket comeback? I am rarely at a loss for words. Far more likely, I'm biting my tongue to keep myself from spouting off inappropriately, but even then, I seldom censor myself, and certainly not these days, not since I found myself a divorced forty-something. But here I sat at a loss for words, at a loss for air—at a complete loss.

"Asher?" It wasn't much more than a whisper.

Asher hadn't moved from his stretched out pose on his back, hands still folded across his chest, eyes fixed on the ceiling. I inched closer, watching his chest rise and fall. Slowly. Steady. I repeated his name, reaching toward him, surprised by how much real estate came with a king bed. He still didn't respond, not that I blamed him. What more could he say? I swallowed hard and slid across the remaining acreage until my body rested against his. He smelled of his soap, and his warmth felt good against my skin, still chilled from the shower and the air conditioner continually running to keep up with the New York City summer heat. I kissed his cheek, my lips grazing his late-night stubble. Resting my hand on his hands, clasped on his chest, my chin nudged his shoulder. Asher's rigid stoicism goaded me to have a little fun at his expense. I fought a grin not to give myself away.

"Asher. I have to tell you something. Be honest about something."

He fidgeted in his prone spot. His breathing juddered, but he kept quiet.

"I don't know—it's just—before this goes any further—you and me. Wow, this is harder than I thought it would be." I lifted my chin to kiss his cheek again, deliberately angling closer to the edge of his mouth.

"Jocelyn. What the hell is it? You can tell me." His hand pressed to his forehead. Frustration permeated his whole being as he refused to look at me.

"Kiss me first?"

Asher rolled to his side. We lay face to face, not an inch apart. He gently tucked curls behind my ear and stroked my cheek. I shut my eyes that he read so easily.

"Joss, you can tell me anything, anything at all. You know that, right?"

"I know. I believe that."

"You should. It's the truth."

"I think—I should have brought this up before, mentioned it at least, confessed, you know." I reached to touch his cheek, brushed my thumb across his lips, biting my own to keep up the ruse. Enjoying the torment inflicted on the poor man. "I think—a kiss would make it— easier."

Finally, he moved the last inch, putting his mouth on mine. It was warm and tender, and I could tell he intended to keep it innocent. I had other plans. He had mentioned biting my lip, so I took a nip of his. His closed eyes opened with a jolt of surprise. I pressed against him. Not just my mouth, but my whole body against his. As my soft tongue met his, he released a low groan. Begrudgingly, he withdrew that inch.

Undeterred, I brought the hand he rested on my cheek further into my hair. I kissed his wrist, encouraging him to pull at my curls, the way he had on the beach. He indulged me. Lacing his fingers through the damp locks, he tugged at the root, eliciting a quiet gasp from me.

"Asher." My mouth searched for his again, but he had pulled away and sat up. His back to me, his feet landed on the floor. I stretched to take hold of his t-shirt. He flinched, deciding he'd rather I not touch him. I gave myself a silent reprimand for taking the joke too far.

"Asher?"

"Jocelyn. Talk to me or go. I can't—"

"I'm not going anywhere."

"Then say what you meant to say. What is harder to say than you—what sort of—confession?" Asher stopped talking when I moved.

I sat up too, one leg under me, the other outstretched. My guilt twinged for having a moment of fun at his expense. He took it all too seriously.

"What I was going to say, what I meant to say— what I wanted—should have confessed. It's about what's under this button-up. See, I'm almost forty-seven and gave birth and breastfed for over a year, so I'm just saying— you need to manage your expectations, that's all."

The silence in the loft carried instant weight. Distant street noise thudded on pavement. The sporadic noise of nighttime traffic that doesn't stop in a city that never sleeps. I watched Asher straighten from his slump, his head rising on his stiffened frame as he absorbed my words.

Like some signal, a car honked at a nearby street corner while Asher jumped to his feet, spun to face my sheepish grin. "You *wicked* woman," he whispered with a smile. He grabbed my ankle, dragging me across the bed as I flopped to my back with the firm yank. His ferocious kiss cut short my delighted squeal. "Now, you're gonna get it." He almost growled the playful threat in my ear before taking a nip of my lobe.

"Promise?" I squeaked with more laughter, laughter that morphed to an enthusiastic sigh when Asher's tongue found that spot just above my collarbone. I thought I'd melt into the bedding, a tingling puddle, electricity coursing through me as I clutched at the sheets underneath me.

In a swift roll, Asher gripped my waist, and I found myself sitting astride his hips, him flat on his back. His eyes met mine, a telepathic check-in. I smiled with a nod as his hands squeezed my thighs while we both navigated the next steps. He reached for a button on my shirt, *his* shirt, but I stopped him, placing his hands back on the flesh of my legs. Though he clearly appreciated this arrangement of our limbs, I detected a flicker of disappointment until my fingers moved to undo the first button of the pajama top. I snorted at Asher's new grin and widened eyes. I bent forward, wanting another taste of his mouth. His hands slid from my thighs to hips, and I discovered a startling development underneath me. He chuckled when the "Oh my god" I thought only echoed in my head had actually been uttered aloud.

A few inches from his face, I lifted Asher's chin. My mouth explored until I found a spot in the hollow of his neck. Asher clutched the bedding with his fists as he sighed in a way that made *me* see stars. Squeezing my shoulders, he encouraged me back to the seated position.

"What are you doing?" The lost momentum and his closed eyes worried me.

"Oh, I'm thinking of Ms. Rutledge."

"And who is Ms. Rutledge?"

"She was my teacher for third grade."

"Should I—?" I moved an inch, but Asher quickly gripped my hips to stay put.

He opened his eyes and grinned while returning my hands to the buttons of my nightshirt. Heat crept out from the collar, and

I grew shy.

"Take your time, slow as you want." He took a deep breath, and I rose and fell with it. I released a button from its hole while Asher repeated his steady breath, sending me up and down again, too. The next button rested below my breastbone, and while part of me was eager to move on to the next part, I forced myself to take my time. I let go of my shirt, placing my hands under the hem of Asher's. "Jocelyn?"

"Fair's fair." I tugged his t-shirt, and he obliged me, removing it.

Stroking his firm muscles, my index finger glided along the trail of hair that ran the centerline of his compact abdomen from his sternum to his navel. He interrupted with an *ahem*. I gave him a pout. "Sorry. I'm exploring."

"I see that and appreciate it, but I'd like to do some exploring myself so—" He gave me an encouraging head jiggle with a goofy grin.

My fingers returned to their button task.

"*There* you go." His quietly enthusiastic cheer boosted my confidence. I continued.

The button, second to last on the placket, would reveal most of what I had yet to show. The last button was inconsequential, really. That second to the last one was the true lynchpin, and as the pearly plastic slid through the tight stitching of its corresponding hole, a loud buzzer sounded through a small panel in the wall by Asher's bedroom door. I flinched, then froze, wide-eyed at the harsh noise.

"It's my doorbell." Asher rose to his elbows as we stared at the speaker. When a second longer buzz erupted, I jerked again and rolled off his lap. In seconds, my nimble fingers negated all my button efforts of the last several minutes. Asher slid to the end of the bed and gently yanked on my shirttail. "Joss?"

I looked over my shoulder at his reassuring face.

"It wouldn't be the first time some drunken stranger hit

the wrong number in the middle of the night. The joys of urban living." He took my hand and stroked my fingers with an encouraging squeeze.

"Or a drunken unannounced booty call looking for a sleepover where she knows she'll get a spare toothbrush?"

"What? No, Jocelyn. I promise you. It isn't."

I wasn't so sure. "Will told me monogamy is passé. Particularly for men like you and if I was considering jumping into the dating pool, I needed to get my head around that."

"Wow. That man is such a…" Asher's elbows met his knees, and he pulled at his hair before gripping his hands together under his chin, grinding his knuckles against his jaw. "I don't sleep around, Jocelyn, never have and I don't plan to start. And I sure as *hell* hope you aren't planning to take up the practice. All right?"

I nodded my reply.

"See?" He pointed. "No more buzzing." He kissed the back of my hand, then my palm and beyond my wrist. He'd pulled me between his thighs and rested his ear against my torso. "Your heart is beating fast." His head bent back to meet my eye, his chin to my stomach. As I held his cheeks, I leaned for my lips to meet his as his hands slid up the backs of my thighs.

"Asher," I whispered between mounting kisses.

"Yes?"

"God, I want you—" The buzzer sounded again, long and loud. Whoever wanted inside wasn't letting up this time. I leaped out of Asher's grasp, and he collapsed backward, flat on the bed. I averted my eyes. Evidently, the feeling was mutual.

The buzzer still screamed when Asher limped to press a button on the panel.

"What?!" he barked.

"Finally. Let me in, Asher. We need to talk." Laney Li waited downstairs.

44

Asher

I LEANED MY FOREHEAD against the doorframe, then thumped it with a grunt. Not only for the interruption at the most inopportune moment. That was bad enough. But the reason for Laney's poorly timed drop-in, the topic of conversation, would likely be Darren Kolchek, and I couldn't think of much worse.

The buzzer sounded again.

"Laney Li. Give me a minute, please." My frustration should have been clear, whether in person or through a speaker, but Laney couldn't care less.

"Um, Okay. Is this a bad time, Ash?" Laney's condescending tone didn't match her words. The pissed-off woman grew angrier by the second.

"Gotta say, Laney. It's not awesome." I released the talk button.

"I swear to god, Asher Cray, I have exactly zero f—" Asher quickly pressed the talk button again, cutting off Laney's rant. Jocelyn snickered. She gestured I should let Laney upstairs. I reluctantly pushed the door release, giving Laney access to the foyer and the elevator.

"Here," I tossed Jocelyn a pair of gym shorts I pulled from a drawer. "Cinch those up under the shirt. I'm gonna—" I pointed to the front of the apartment.

"You want this?" Jocelyn held up my recently discarded t-shirt.

"Guess I should." I shrugged and caught the garment she threw at my head with a laugh. "You're killing me, Jocelyn. You are *kill-ing* me." I tripped toward the bedroom door, jolted by the phrase I meant in jest. A chill hit me, and my insides clenched. The elevator dinged its arrival.

I closed the door behind me and tried to clear my mind of two very different notions of Jocelyn Durand battling in my brain.

"He's missing. He's *miss-ing,* Asher. Darren Kolchek was a *kid,* and he went missing decades ago and no one has heard from him since. No one knows what happened to him except—except maybe my wife. My wife. *Genevieve* knows something about some kid who's been missing for thirty years, and it's wrecking her. DE-*stroy-ing* her." Laney exited the elevator, ranting, forgoing the traditional greetings of polite society. "I don't know what to do, who to talk to because my best friend is— uh, what the hell is going on here? Holy crap. Is someone here? You have someone here—you son of a *bitch,* Ash. You stinking son of a—"

"What do you mean, he's missing? Missing how?" Jocelyn scrambled out of my bedroom, stumbling over her own feet as she tried to pull on the gym shorts.

"Jocelyn? Oh, thank god." Laney's tirade subsided. "I thought I was gonna have to kill one of my best clients. Castrate him, anyway. Phew. That's a relief."

Jocelyn engaged in a ridiculous struggle to tighten the drawstring of the large shorts under the long shirttail of my oversized sleep shirt. "Thanks, Laney, but I'd rather you not do that. Not until I've—"

"Whoa. Ladies, I'm standing right here."

Jocelyn ignored my attempt at banter, gaping at Laney. "What do you mean, Darren Kolchek has been missing for thirty years?"

Laney stared.

In an ill-advised effort to wrangle the situation, I stepped in and made the mess worse. Much worse.

"He went to prom, hitched a ride heading to Montauk, got let off *somewhere,* and no one saw him again." I gave my explanation to the floor, but when I raised my gaze, the two women stared at me, eyes wider still.

"You knew?" Laney and Jocelyn asked in unison.

Laney stepped to me with a shove. "You knew, and yet you brought him up the other night? Why the hell—?"

"No, I didn't know then. I didn't know until I went back to my hotel room and Googled him. *That's* when I found out."

"So, the next morning over coffee, when you were all *twitchy* with your cryptic questions, you knew, but didn't tell me. You knew why my wife took off and still you didn't say." Laney fumed too close, looking almost straight up at me.

Jocelyn cleared her throat. Her voice came as a whisper, but she coughed and pushed harder to speak. "But when we spoke on the phone? When we talked, Gigi had called me, and I told you she was upset? You knew then? You knew about Darren then and why my sister was upset, and you didn't say? You didn't tell me?"

"Wait. Genevieve called you?" Laney's focus moved to Jocelyn, but Jocelyn only had eyes for me. Sad eyes.

"Joss," I whispered, reaching for her hand.

"Don't." She recoiled.

"Joss," I repeated.

"Don't call me that. Not now. Don't say my name like that now." She swallowed a gasp. "I think I'm gonna be sick." Jocelyn spun and ran to the hall bathroom. I waited for the imminent door slam. Oddly, it never came.

"Well done, Laney Li." I pressed my palms to my eyes.

"Don't lay this at my feet, Asher. I'm not the one getting caught in lies," Laney scoffed, heading for the Scotch. "I can't believe you didn't tell me my wife called Jocelyn."

"How is that any of my business, or my responsibility, to share? She's *your* wife. And I didn't lie. I would have spoken to her about it—to *Jocelyn* about it—when I knew more. I needed to know more."

"Know more than what? What more is there to know? And what the hell does Genevieve have to do with any of it?" Laney gulped her drink and poured another.

"I don't know."

"Don't lie to me, too. All that— *we've never been dishonest before* crap, in L.A.?"

"I'm not lying."

"You're full of it, Asher."

"Laney, I don't know what Genevieve has to do with it. Haven't got a clue."

"That's *bullshit*, I can tell."

"Jesus, Laney." I chose my words carefully. "I swear I have no information about Genevieve and Darren Kolchek. Not a damn thing."

"Well, you sure as hell know something, you lying SOB and I'm—"

"It's me." Jocelyn reappeared.

My heart sank, and I felt the bile rise in my throat.

"It's me. Asher knows about Darren and me that night. He knows it was me. Darren was with me. And now, I guess Gigi knows, too. But—"

"Jocelyn," I snapped. "Stop talking. Just—stop talking. Let's call it a night. We are all tired. Tomorrow we can hash it out. With clearer heads, okay? We'll take you home, and we'll talk then. Please go get into bed."

To my surprise, Jocelyn trudged back toward my bedroom, her usual bounce deadened by dredging up history.

"Goodnight," she spoke with such sweet sadness, and my stomach lurched again. Jocelyn closed my bedroom door.

"Oh my God, Asher," Laney muttered. "What did she do?"

"For the last time, Laney, I don't know. If I knew—I'd tell you." I couldn't meet her eyes.

Laney paused before she skewered me. "I understand if that's the way you want to *play* it, Asher, but I think we both know the truth is something different." My own words came back at me. "And I believe you don't know. But if you did, you wouldn't tell me. You wouldn't tell *anyone*." Laney gave a humorless snort. "Jesus H. Christ, you couldn't shut her up fast enough in case she was about to—to what? Confess something? Are you afraid of me knowing something? She's my family, and her sister would move heaven and earth to protect her from anyone or anything."

"Careful, Laney." I paced, then stopped near her to keep my voice low. "The way I see it, this goes one of two ways. Genevieve protected her kid sister from someone three decades ago, or—she is protecting Jocelyn from herself to this day. Either way, if anyone finds out, it doesn't end well for the Durand sisters."

Laney took another swig of drink, ingesting the booze and the conjecture.

"Where is Genevieve, Laney?"

"I'm not proud of this, but I tracked her phone. She's in Amagansett. I just needed to know she was somewhere safe."

"Shit. Well, I can't drive there tonight. I'm exhausted, Jocelyn is exhausted, and you've been drinking so—"

"I don't know how to drive, anyway." Laney shrugged with another swig.

"What? How do you not know how to drive?" I looked at the tiny woman like she'd sprung another head.

"Really, Asher. This is the thing? Of all that is raining down in this shitstorm, my lack of a driver's license is the eight-hundred-pound gorilla to knock you flat? Really?"

"Shut up, Laney. You wanna crash here?"

"In The Love Shack, *nah*, I'm good."

I wished I could have laughed at that remark. "Pretty sure we've— missed our window."

"Yeah, biggest cockblock of all time." She pulled her phone from her pocket. "My ride home will be here in—two minutes." She emptied her glass and handed it to me.

"Goodnight, Laney Li." I saw her to the elevator. "Tomorrow we head to—"

"Yeah, I'm going. See you in the morning, not early though. Get some sleep. You look like sh—" The elevator door closed between us.

I set the glass on the kitchen island, and for a moment, I considered the sofa, but the truth was if Jocelyn would let me, all I wanted to do was be there for her.

45

Jocelyn

ASHER OPENED THE DOOR with such care so as not to disturb me. At least I think that's why. Before he returned, I sat upright in bed in an attempt to stay awake, afraid to risk missing him, but the rush of emotions sent me crashing into exhaustion.

It bothered me he'd kept what he knew about my sister to himself. But when I ran the conversations through my mind, I realized he never lied. Moreover, he proved he had no intention of divulging my connection to Darren Kolchek even as Laney berated him. And when I spoke, he begged me to be quiet. Was that to protect me from something? From what? From whom? And what's any of it to do with Gigi?

When the door opened, I sighed a "hi" in relief and pulled my knees to my chest, sitting straighter. "Did she go?"

"You're still awake? Uh, yeah, yes, she left—until tomorrow. We'll go to Amagansett together. Genevieve's there now."

"She is?" I asked. Gigi spending another night at the summer house surprised me. Why would she go there? Alone, no less.

"Aren't you sleepy? You should sleep." Asher suggested, evidently eager to end the talking.

"I am. So tired, but I wanted to see you." I watched Asher's chin hit his chest, and my heart sank. "No? Is that not—"

"No. I mean, yes. I wanted to see you, too."

Fatigue had set in, and we both wore the results of it with weary eyes and slumped shoulders. I mustered a smile to hear he was pleased to find me awake, but Asher's exhausted look included something I couldn't grasp in my own tired state. Nodding, I pulled back the bedding, eager to feel him near me again. Hoping to find the just-right spot and stay in it for hours.

He took a step toward the bed but stopped. "Jocelyn, I wanted to say I'm sorry for not being open about what I knew when I knew it and dodging it when it came to Genevieve."

I nodded. He walked to the windows, closing the heavy drapes on each of them. A remote on his bedside chest dimmed the lights to off. The pitch dark gave me a start, unable to see my hand in front of my face.

"You okay, Joss?" Asher using my shortened name calmed me.

"Yes, it's just so dark." I reached out to find him.

"Too dark? I can get you more light."

"No, it's fine." I waited to feel him lie down so I could nestle into my spot.

"How's that?" Asher's voice came out of the black.

I gave another nod he could only feel on his shoulder. "Goodnight, Asher."

"Goodnight, Jocelyn."

At first, I thought it would be a very long night. No way I could sleep engulfed by the feel and smell of Asher Cray, but I did. I stirred at some point in the night, unsure where I was or how I had gotten there, but then I felt Asher's warmth spooning me, holding me tight and heard his soothing whisper, "Shh. It's okay, Joss. I've got you. Go back to sleep." And I did.

I woke again, but this time, a trace of daylight shone in the narrow edges of the window frames. Asher, still wrapped around me from behind, shared the middle of the bed. Never in my life had I slept entwined with another body, and I couldn't remember a better night's sleep. But now, wide-awake, I needed to get out of the tangle of limbs and sheets for fear of disturbing Asher's rest. Gently prying myself from his strong arms, careful to ease my way without jostling the bed too much, I deduced the man was a heavy sleeper, and was thankful I didn't wake him. Energized and clear-minded, I slipped out of his room in search of coffee-making supplies and raspberry pie.

With a fresh cup of coffee, I enjoyed the daylight version of the living room's view with the smell of raspberry pie warming in the oven. Near the Financial District, street traffic picked up considerably from the nighttime version, and it wasn't hard to see how the quiet of the Hamptons might knock a city-dweller for a loop.

After the drama from the night before, I tried to remember all I could about that June so many years ago. The fact was, I recalled very little and what I did came at me disjointed. Flashes of images that didn't all make sense and assailed me with an ache in my arm and my head. It had been a turbulent time with my parents dying and me having surgery and trying to finish my studies to graduate from high school. On top of that, I departed for France the night of my graduation, to be immersed in a new-to-me country with family who were strangers and spoke little English. My memory included a rush of packing, and Gigi begging me to skip the formality of the ceremony altogether.

After an unusual fight, I'd insisted that we attend. To make amends, she offered to decorate my cast in school colors. We used a combination of silver duct tape and royal blue packing tape she'd bought to box up our Bayborough house to sell. She made overt apologies with the cast decorating suggestion, and we laughed while she wrapped the colorful tape around my arm, covering the grungy white of the weeks-old plaster that ran the length of my arm.

We attended the commencement, but Gigi hurried me out immediately afterward. No time for goodbyes to friends or faculty. Straight to the airport. Of course, in those days, she could accompany me to my gate, and now I recalled we waited a long time for my departure. After dinner in an airport lounge, she bought me gossip magazines and an activity book for the flight with crosswords, word searches, and Mad-Libs, all-in-one. We walked from gate to gate, killing time until I could board. Why had we rushed only to spend hours at the airport?

I never saw the Bayborough house again. It wasn't a place I wanted to revisit, even though I drove near it on every trip to and from Westchester and Amagansett. I never took the slight detour to see it. Then again, why would I?

"Good morning," Asher spoke quietly but startled me from my meandering down memory lane. Worry at startling me etched his face, but I forced a quick smile to put him at ease.

Just as fast, that feigned grin turned genuine as my heart skipped a beat, remembering the best parts of the night before. "Good morning. I hope I didn't wake you." I kept myself from biting my lip.

His anxious look hadn't softened. "Wake me? This morning, you mean?"

"Yes, when I crawled out from under you, practically." I smiled at *that* stretch of memory lane. "When else?"

"So, you got some rest?" It seemed he thought otherwise.

"Can't recall a better night's sleep," I disclosed too eagerly. "I haven't shared a bed in a long time and—never like that." I knew my cheeks betrayed me, but I didn't care. "Careful. I could get used to that arrangement." I hurried by him, self-conscious of my over-share. "Coffee? I brewed a pot."

Asher appeared baffled, but he relaxed as he watched me walk to the kitchen. "Coffee would be great. And do I smell pie?"

"I'm warming it. Nothing better than coffee and pie for breakfast." I brought his coffee to where he stood and kissed his cheek.

"Careful. I could get used to this arrangement."

46

Asher

I WATCHED HER OVER the rim of my coffee mug, smiling as she returned to the kitchen to pull warm, homemade raspberry pie from my never-used oven like the night before hadn't happened. Not the waking hours, the intimacy of the unconsummated foreplay or the disruption from Laney, but the night terrors. The frightened whimpers, the quiet begging with quaking fear—she appeared to have no memory of the night spent scared and shaking.

In the midst of it, I tried to calm her, wake her gently, but what finally succeeded was swathing her in my own body. Wrapping myself, all four limbs, around her and holding firm, a human weighted blanket. She finally wilted limp and lay quietly, but if I released her for long, the twitching started. An agitation that escalated to another round of trembling, mumbling in pleading anguish. By the third time, I knew to tighten my grasp at the first sign, and her body relaxed into mine. I cocooned her from whatever boogeyman she hid from, and while I was relieved to be of comfort to her, the whole incident was shockingly painful to see.

Jocelyn held the pie to her nose and sniffed with an easy grin, absent any angst. From my stool at the kitchen island, she appeared a well-rested, contented beauty, and I couldn't be more confused.

"You're gonna love it." She sang it, but like a warning, and a pang of sadness hit with the inkling that I should be cautious. *Come on,*

Asher. Sometimes pie is just pie.

"I know I will." I forced a grin back at her, but my heart ached, and I couldn't get a deep breath or reconcile this morning's buoyant mood after the *horror show* throughout the night. That phrase alarmed me as pictures flashed of both William and Laney using it.

"You okay? Not feeling well?" Jocelyn set a plate of pie in front of me and touched my cheek. Leaning into her hand, the smell of her skin revived me.

I pulled her to me, setting her on my lap. "I'm fine. Maybe a little jetlagged—Jocelyn-lagged. This has been quite a week."

Her eyes twinkled in the morning sun, and I saw more of her spirit I'd noticed all week at the summer house and the resilience William spoke of days ago. If Jocelyn Durand got knocked down, she got up fast, with a grin-and-bear-it attitude not everyone could pull off with such conviction.

"I'm sorry we have to go back. Not that I don't want to go back—with you. I just wouldn't mind staying here a while—with you." She kissed my lips, then gave a shy smile with a deep breath of resignation. "But Gabe is there, and he leaves tomorrow."

"And—your sister is—" I wasn't sure how to finish that sentence.

"Yes, Gigi and I need to talk. No question." Jocelyn's tone turned curt as she let go, sliding out of my grasp. I tried to hold her, but her abruptness told me she wanted to be freed, and I worried we'd lost connection. A quick glance back at me said she'd felt it too. This was not the morning either of us anticipated, and a part of me wondered if our "missed window" was a permanent situation or merely a momentary setback. The tension weighing at the moment didn't bode well and sitting still made it worse.

"I'll be back in a sec. Gonna grab my phone." I spun on the stool and trotted back to my bedroom. Unplugging my phone from its charger, the home screen showed several missed texts from Laney and a voicemail from a number I didn't recognize.

Badass: Gabe called. Something's wrong. We have to go.

Badass: Where are you?

Badass: Where are you!?! I'm coming there. We HAVE TO GO.

I accessed my voicemail, putting the phone to my ear.

"Asher," Jocelyn called to me from the hall. "If you don't want pie, maybe I can interest you in something else." She stood behind me, and by the time I turned to face her, she had three buttons undone and fingered pivotal number four.

"Jocelyn, stop." My harsh tone surprised her, but rather than apologize, I hit replay on my phone, speaker at full volume.

"Asher. I can't get a hold of my mom. I called Aunt Laney. It's Aunt Genevieve. She's— You gotta get back to the house as soon as possible. Where are you?!"

Jocelyn grabbed the phone from me and hit the call back button. Still on speaker, the call went straight to voicemail. "Gabe. Honey. I'm—we're on our way." She looked at me with pleading eyes. I nodded. "Laney, Asher, and I. It could be—jeez, three hours. Call me when you get this. I'm so sorry." She ended the call and stared at me.

"Your dress is in the bathroom. Laney's on her way. Go. I'm gonna throw some stuff in a bag."

She spun toward the bathroom, then back to me. "Asher, about—" she grabbed at her mostly unbuttoned shirt, wrapping it around her like the cardigan on our first meeting. "This was—silly. I'm so sorry. How embarrassing."

"It wasn't." I couldn't say the words fast enough. My head pounded. "It wasn't, and *please* don't be sorry or embarrassed. Nothing to be embarrassed about. God, you're beautiful—I'm not going anywhere. Focus on your family. We're—the two of us?

We're fine, okay?"

That lip met her teeth, her face doubtful, but she nodded without a word. With a quick jerk, she came at me, clutching my face with a fierce kiss, desperate, like it might be the last one we'd share. A new look in her eyes said she knew something she hadn't known before or she'd made a decision, and for a moment I feared she might be right about that kiss. She took off for the bathroom as the buzzer announced Laney.

47

Jocelyn

Genevieve Durand is the toughest woman I've ever known. My very first memory includes her, and since we are four years apart, few memories of my younger days don't include her. That is, until she left for college, but even then, she wasn't far and did the best she could to keep me... safe. It wasn't unusual for her to whisk me away for weekends in the city. While she initially fought attending Columbia to go to a local university, where she could sleep at home every night, I insisted she get away and, in doing so, provide me a place to escape to... occasionally, anyway.

I don't care to dwell on those days, and to be fair the older I got, the Monsters came less and less, or so it seemed, but I, of course, found more freedom, took more liberty, finding other places to be other than where the Monsters might invade. The Monsters were never public figures. No one even knew of their existence, except, of course, Gigi. Surely if people knew someone would have done something.

The ride to Amagansett could not have been more agonizing. I left Gabe in the awkward spot with Gigi, what Laney referred to as some sort of breakdown. How did I miss it? Then again, how could I have *seen* it? I never imagined the possibility. She was the strong one.

On top of that, I might view the sequence of events with Asher through a comical lens if it weren't so humiliating. The "will they/won't they" trope was on full display, and while Hollywood tells us "they" usually do, real-life felt less accommodating. And the more I thought about it, the more I realized Genevieve's trouble didn't and *shouldn't* involve Asher Cray. It was unfair to him, and it would be best to get him to his things and then get him on his way.

The last moments before I heard my son's plea on Asher's voicemail ran through my mind. Unbuttoning my pajamas as I walked toward his bedroom...*Jeez, Jocelyn Mae. What were you thinking?* I gripped the steering wheel, thankful for the small favor that I could end this before we went down *that* road.

"Are you okay, Joss?" Asher whispered as he placed his hand on my thigh for the briefest moment.

I may have taken an audible inhale at the touch. A glance in the rearview showed Laney typing on her ever-present phone, paying no attention to the two of us in the front seat. "Yes. Why?" I forced a smile. "You?"

"You sort of blanched. Like something came to mind."

"Were you staring at me, Mr. Cray?" I meant to lighten the mood.

"Can't help it. I can't stop—"

I took his hand to stop his talking. "Asher, we need to—"

"I'm going to stop you there, Jocelyn," he quietly interrupted me.

"Ash—"

"No." His head shake was less understated. "We're not doing this now. I get it, I do, but no. We have a long list of things we *need* to do, but none of them are what you were about to suggest. So, no. We'll talk about this later."

"Reading her mind, Asher? That's a habit you're gonna wanna nip, and quick. Trust me." Laney would pinch-hit for Gigi any day, so when Asher's volume climbed, Laney's intervention in some bodyguard role shouldn't have surprised me.

Asher made a slow turn to face the backseat passenger. Laney did not meet his eye. "Not her mind, Laney— her face. She lets it all sit there for anyone to see, anyone who wants to read it. And I'm pretty sure this has nothing to do with—"

"She's my wife's sister and—"

"All right." I stepped in as referee. "Everyone needs to take a breath. We are all running a little hot today, but we are all on the same side here, and I cannot take the bickering. Can we please not do that today—?" My phone rang with Gabe's number on the screen. "Gabe, it's Mom. I'm driving, so you're on speaker with Aunt Laney and Asher in the car. Where have you been?"

"Yeah, sorry. I—mowed the lawn."

"Mowed the lawn? Why? We have the service coming to do that." It occurred to me perhaps I had lost Raphe's services in whatever imploded with him and Will.

"Um, maybe we can talk about that when you get here." Gabe sounded strange. Muffled. Had he been crying?

"Is Genevieve okay? She won't answer me." Laney's angsty worry was new to me and probably her reason for lashing out at Asher.

"Yeah, uh, she's sleeping now."

"Sleeping?" Laney and I asked in unison.

"I'll explain things when you get here, okay, and just so you know, I'm not leaving for North Carolina tomorrow. Frannie left without me. I'm staying here."

"Left? Gabe?" It was all I could do not to pull over so we could speak privately.

"It's okay, Mom." He paused, the sound of blowing his nose filled the car.

"Gabe, I don't care if *it's* okay. I care if you're okay."

"*I'm* okay, Mom. I'm *o-kay*."

"We'll be home as soon as we can." I white-knuckled the wheel again.

"Take it easy in that holiday traffic. Love you." Gabe ended the call.

Asher touched my forearm, a gesture meant to calm me, and much to my surprise, it did. I let go with one hand to hold his and relaxed.

"I might have said this already, but you are the greatest mom—" Asher spoke softly, but Laney jumped in also.

"My nephew's pretty awesome too."

"Well, thanks, and I agree on the second part, but I can't take all the credit—"

Laney interrupted with her loud honk of her version of laughter, with Asher joining in right along with her. I appreciated their shared moment as I refocused on the road. When I released Asher's hand, he tenderly kept hold of mine, and foolishly, I let him.

48

Asher

THE EXCRUCIATING DRIVE WITH mounting holiday traffic was
nearly three-hours of wasted time. If Laney hadn't been there, we
could have talked. I would have figured out a way to ask about
that long-ago June, gained insight, but none of that mattered. We
weren't alone, we couldn't talk about it, or anything of substance.
And I sure as hell wouldn't let Jocelyn go down some "bad timing"
road, a "let's cut bait" kind of conversation, like she attempted on
our first date. No, that wasn't happening and certainly not in front
of Laney. All I could do was endure her worry-induced pallor while
squeezing her hand for reassurance. Add Gabe's odd vagueness,
and I'd never felt more powerless.

When we pulled into the pebbled driveway, everything appeared
quiet, routine, undisturbed. The mowed lawn and charming old
house made an idyllic setting. But I couldn't help but wonder what
this picturesque scene hid, and I'd been curious since that second
morning.

"Let me out here," Laney snapped as we inched down the drive
toward the garage. Jocelyn hit the brakes, and Laney jumped from
the station wagon. The slammed car door jolted Jocelyn. Shards of
a broken mug lying in splattered coffee flashed in my mind.

"Joss?" I whispered, but she only had eyes for the car door, the
offending disturbance. Her brief catatonia passed as she forced
a hard swallow, followed by a slow-motion blink. Her eyelids
squeezed tight and opened again when another shudder brought

her back from wherever she went to in those brief moments. "Joss?" I repeated.

An instant smile appeared, an ersatz grin, just like first thing that morning. It, too, only lasted a second. "Sorry. Spaced for a moment." She let off the brake and crept down the drive to park in the garage next to my own silly car. When she turned the engine off, she kept her gaze straight ahead. "I appreciate you being here. Coming here."

"Well, you had my car—" I jested with a head tilt to the vehicle beside us.

"Oh. Right. Good." She twisted over the backseat, looking for her bag, careful not to look at me.

"Joss, I'm kidding. I came to be with you." I knew she wasn't buying it.

"Okay." She reached for the door handle.

"Jocelyn," I hadn't meant to raise my voice, but her shoulders rose with the slight uptick. "Sorry." I lowered my voice.

"No, I'm sorry, Asher."

"Why are you sorry?"

"This won't work. I'm not—You don't really—We're not gonna work. You should go. Take your car and your computer and go." She opened the door while I scrambled out my side of the car. I reached her before she cleared the garage, not letting her pass. She still wouldn't meet my eyes.

Careful to keep my calm, I tried to touch her, but she deftly moved out of my reach. I understood, respecting her unspoken request. "Jocelyn? Are you letting me go, or—are you telling me to leave?"

She nodded, her gaze still to the concrete.

"That isn't a yes or no question. Are you letting me go, or are you telling me to leave? Do you not want me—?"

She sighed an out-of-the-blue chuckle I couldn't reconcile.

"Well, if you don't know—" she shook her head, "I'm definitely doing it wrong. I guess I shouldn't be surprised—"

"Not like that. This isn't about that? This has never been about that."

"Never. It was never about—"

"Okay, yes, there have been moments, some really great moments that have been about that, but it's more than that, more than—Is this what you think this is? You're some conquest, some potential notch in my—Wow." I grimaced, letting this new information sink in as we stood in the heat of the garage.

"Don't get all hurt, Asher. I'm flattered, really. But you were pretty clear with Will the other night, and while I *was* curious about being properly f—"

"Jocelyn, stop."

"You said that this morning, too. *Jocelyn, stop.*" She took a deep breath and her smile resumed. "No harm, no foul, Asher. My family needs me right now. My son, my sister. And while a romp with you sounded fun—the attention was nice—bad timing aside, it's not for me, plus the whole mixing business with pleasure no-no, so I'm afraid you're going to have to look elsewhere for your Hamptons summertime fling. But thanks for considering me. Like I said, flattered." She reached up to pat my cheek. That was her mistake because her dismissive gesture included eye contact and I had been a quick study.

I chuckled now. "Oh, Jocelyn." I shook my head in mock-disappointment. "Now, I'm in a quandary."

"Why is that?" She stood firm in her confident air.

"I don't know if I should break the news to Gabe or let him go on believing his mother has no notion of guile. He seems to believe you are incapable of deception. Now I know differently. Or maybe it's just, like me, he's broken the code, knows the signs. I'll ask again. Are you telling me to leave? Because I will not stay if you don't want me here. But if this is about you giving me an out, thanks, but no thanks." I walked to the tailgate for Laney's and my bags. "You almost had me there, but your eyes don't lie. Nice of you to offer the opportunity to bolt, but I'm cutting back on cowardice these days. You're gonna have to look me in the eye and say the words—oh, and *mean* it."

49

Jocelyn

GAMBLING HAS NEVER BEEN my thing. Going the safe route is the right route and always has been. And while my attempt to give Asher a free pass to walk away was altruistic, it was a heck of a risk. I leaned against the station wagon for a moment. Dishonesty didn't come naturally to me, and I don't tolerate it in any direction. Ironic, considering my marriage, but that past has made the truth even more important. I should avoid taking part in deception, if only because I'm just no good at it.

Decision made and balance found, I jogged toward the house. "Asher," I called. "That wasn't a test."

He turned, wearing a satisfied grin. "But if it was, I passed, right?"

"It wasn't."

"Okay." The grin vanished, but he stared.

"It *wasn't*." The third time nearly convinced me.

Asher set the bags on the ground and walked to face me. "Do you trust me?"

I lifted my gaze to the clear sky, unsure how to answer. The sun beat down, but I appreciated being out of the city. My own turf. "I don't *not* trust you."

Asher's brow rose.

"What I mean to say is you're not the one who hasn't been trustworthy."

We stood in the heat, surrounded by birdsong and the rumble

of a postal truck between the metal-scraping open-and-shut of mailboxes on the delivery route. He finally spoke, "Well, hell, Jocelyn, that sounds like something we probably ought to discuss because without that, we're just spinning our wheels, aren't we? But you've got a kid to see to, and I won't get in the way of that. Find me when—"

"Hello, Ms. Durand."

I shielded my eyes as I waved to Felix, the mailman, with another phony smile. At the same time, Asher returned to the overnight bags near the side door. He didn't finish the sentence but took up the bags and went inside. Sometimes the truth hurts, and it looked like this was one of those times. I went in search of Gabe.

There isn't much in this world that will get you more tuned-in to what's important in life than coming face to face with your own hurt child, even if he stands a head taller, fifty pounds heavier, with a week-old beard. When your kid hurts, you hurt, but your hurt comes with a strong desire to fix it all with a side order of retribution. And while full-Martha was my default setting, I switched gears to full-Mama-bear when I heard Gabe sniffing and saw his bloodshot eyes. How dare that no-good Frannie—that neuro-comparative-literature-whatever succubus...

"Hey, Mom." Gabe placed his clean, folded clothes in drawers in the downstairs bedroom.

"Hey, kiddo. You all right?"

"Yeah. It'll pass."

"That's good to hear. I'm impressed by how mature you are."

"Mature? Okay."

"Can I do anything? Get you anything?"

"Well, I might break down and take an antihistamine if we have something."

"Oh. Wait, what?"

"Yeah, mowing the lawn sent my allergies into overdrive. I'd forgotten how the eyes itch and the snot just keeps—"

"Allergies? This is allergies?"

"Yeah. What'd you—did you think I was— crying? Come on, Mom. I'm a dude. A college dude. Sure. Seeing Aunt Genevieve drunk and digging holes in the yard was weird. Don't get me wrong. Freaked me out a bit, but—"

"This isn't about Frannie?"

"Frannie? No. I'll see Frannie in Wilmington." He stopped his chore and cocked his head. "She went ahead. There's weather headed up the coast, so my boat captain is staying in Savannah a couple of days to wait it out. I don't need to report until Wednesday. She hitched a ride with some beach bum friends of ours making their way to Miami. Stopping off to see her boyfriend in Ocean City, then down to Wilmington."

"Come again? Frannie has a boyfriend?"

"Yeah. I told you it wasn't a big deal."

Monogamy is passé. I exhaled and rubbed my temples, wondering how many minutes of my life I had relinquished to the stress of thinking my poor baby— "Did you say Gigi dug holes in the yard?" A whole new world of stress opened up.

"Yeah, well, one hole, a big one, though. In the new garden spot Raphe put in this spring. I tried to put it back together, but she tore it up pretty—Mom?"

I took off to find my sister.

Barreling up the stairs, I ran into Asher at the landing turn. Literally.

"Whoa," Asher murmured.

"Sorry." My attempt to hurry by him morphed into a back-and-forth dance where Asher and I tried not to touch one another, and I avoided eye contact. Asher's ability to read my face proved to be a significant disadvantage, and at the moment, I felt vulnerable enough.

"You okay, Joss?"

"Yep. Uh, nope. Uh, not sure, really." I kept my eyes down but pointed in the direction I needed to go. He stepped out of my way, and I bolted up two stories to Gigi's old room on the top floor. Laney opened it when I gave a timid knock and stepped out to join me in the hall.

"She's—asleep. Well, from the smell of her, passed out. Probably best to let her rest. She doesn't sleep so great here."

"I talked to Gabe."

"Me too. Her middle-of-the-night gardening exploits?"

"Yeah."

"Yeah?" Laney looked up at me for some explanation.

"Yeah, what? I don't know anything about it. She didn't say *anything* to you?"

"She did. One thing." Laney gave an incredulous look. Then eyed whoever climbed the stairs behind me. "She said, 'call William.'"

Asher stood at the top of the stairs, shaking his head. "That sounds like my cue."

50

Asher

"Cue to what, Asher? Leave? You and me both," Laney grumbled. "Oh. You're not kidding." She shooed us away from her door. I headed toward the first floor, but Jocelyn grabbed me by the arm, dragging me to her bedroom. No, I didn't imagine this was some fantasy come true. *There's the old Asher we know and bear.*

Jocelyn released my arm, returning to shut the door while I cautioned myself of the dangers of breathing through my nose in this space. The narcotic-strength of Jocelyn's scent would have me under its spell if I let it. *Lean into the mouth-breather reputation, Ash.*

"This feels like déjà vu. Are you leaving?" She asked from behind me.

I appreciated not seeing her face. It made it easier to lie. "I think it's best." A hum took over as soon as I said it. I don't know where it came from, but it grew louder, filling the silence; eventually earsplitting. *Don't turn around, Asher.*

Jocelyn finally spoke, but I wasn't sure she spoke to me. Whatever she said, I couldn't make it out over the tinny whir assaulting my ears. I recognize the unlatching click of the door to the hall. Jocelyn walked by me, beelining to her bathroom. She closed that door without ever looking at me. I eyed my computer on her writing desk but left it to collect my duffle before I changed my mind.

Gabe blew his nose when I lumbered into the kitchen on my escape to the garage. "Wow, this is like déjà vu. Me in the kitchen. You with your bag like you're leaving."

"Yeah." I looked to the stairs and back to the kid, who was so much like his mother. Other than his height, I didn't see an ounce of William in him. The rest was all Jocelyn. "It was a real pleasure to meet you, Gabe." I offered my hand to shake his.

"*Oh*," he stumbled off of his barstool, "You're going? Like for real this time." He dropped his used tissue and wiped his hand on his shorts, but we both reconsidered the handshake. "Sorry, allergies."

I shook off the apology. "Yeah. Think I'll head out to find a quiet spot, dig in, and write. That's why I came in the first place."

Gabriel sat. "Somewhere local? Cuz it's fourth of July weekend. Not a hotel, motel, or Airbnb to be found on Long Island, so probably best to wait until after the holiday—if you can."

Another glance toward the stairs. "Not sure that's a good idea."

"No?" The genial kid I liked so much turned gruffer. "Trouble in paradise? Or did you get what you wanted in Tribeca and now you're done?"

The bluntness from Durand-Atwater offspring shouldn't have surprised me, but I was tired of being second-guessed. Then again, I had a reputation, might as well roll with it. I'd taken a punch before and could handle one now. I'd be ready for it. Plus, I'd deserve it.

"Hey, Gabe. You know how it is. But I didn't take anything that wasn't— offered." I lifted my chin more than I'd anticipated to keep eye contact when Gabe got to his feet again. Had he grown an inch or two since earlier in the week?

"Hey, you two. What's up?" Jocelyn floated in, snagging an apron off a hook, tying it at her waist. "I'm a little late getting started and I know we have some extra time now that you don't set sail tomorrow, which I'm not even a little sad about, Gabe, but we did plan to have crabs tonight." Jocelyn busied herself, pulling out bowls and produce, as well as staples from the pantry. She preheated the oven. "And the weekend is only going to get busier with the tourists, so tonight's the night. Which means I'm going to need you two to head for the fishmonger. With five of us, a couple dozen should do and then some, don't you think?"

"Thought Ash had to go." Gabe stepped back, either to give me room, or himself a better angle to land his clenched fist.

"Leaving?" Jocelyn scoffed. "Not on a holiday weekend. I know he needs some quiet, so maybe we give him the downstairs? What do you say, Gabe? Give the writer room to—you know—write."

"I'm not sure that's a great idea, Mom. I mean, if the man really needs to go, he can make it to the city easy. All the traffic is coming this way and he'll never find a room here for the weekend."

"He has a room. Right down the stairs and he is welcome to it as long as he wishes to stay."

"Mom, I think he should go."

"That's not up to you, Gabriel." It was the first time Jocelyn looked at her son with patent authority. "Why don't you clear out down there and move into my childhood room. We'll move your aunts where Asher was last weekend. A little rearrangement. Easy to do. I prepped all the other rooms before I left, and I will do a quick change of sheets and towels downstairs while you two fetch me my crabs." Breezy Jocelyn returned in all her hospitable glory. I wanted to hurl.

"Jocelyn?"

She paused before answering, "Yes, Asher?"

"You can just give me the sheets and towels. I can make a bed." Gabe and I hadn't broken our eye-lock.

"Oh, I don't think so, Ash. My hospital corners are legendary."

"I have no doubt, but really—"

"What has gotten into you two today? Acting like you're in charge or something. Please do as I've asked." Her voice pitched higher than typical, and she feigned any sweetness, but her words were unequivocal.

My fingers had gone numb holding my duffle over my shoulder this entire episode, so I happily set my bag on a neighboring stool. Gabe gave me a sizable shoulder shove as he headed to collect his belongings, leaving Jocelyn and me alone in the kitchen. She hadn't stopped moving since her happy homemaker routine began.

"Joss?" My saying her name brought her frenzy to a halt, but her gaze kept out the kitchen sink window.

"You shouldn't call me that anymore."

"What?"

"You heard me."

"Why?"

"It— hurts me, so will you please stop?"

"Jesus, Joss."

She bowed her head. In prayer? Deflecting a blow? "Please?"

"Sorry, yes. I'll stop."

"Thank you. What did you say to Gabe to upset him?"

"I, uh, I— nothing really. He made an assumption, an assumption about you and me, based on my—reputation. I let him believe it was true. I didn't lie. I just didn't correct him."

"Why?"

"Why?" I didn't understand her question.

"Why would you let him think that? Why would you let him think that— about his mother? Why are you—? What did *he* do to deserve that?"

"It's all yours, Mr. Cray." Gabriel came through the basement door with his clothes shoved in his giant backpack. "Everything all right?"

My face must have shown how much sicker I felt.

Jocelyn's smile returned. "Asher was telling me he had a little fun at your expense. I take it his *joke* didn't land well. That's happening a lot lately."

I'd rather take Gabe's punch over that barb any day.

"And not that it is any of your business, young man, but nothing happened in the city. Asher was a complete gentleman, much to my chagrin. So tired, really. Could hardly stay upright, if you know what I mean."

"*Mom*," Gabe gasped at his mother's out of character quip. It almost made me laugh, too, except I knew, behind all her newfound humor, I had hurt her... again.

"I know. Your Aunt Laney is rubbing off on me. Now go move your things upstairs and then take this *perfect* gentleman and show him how to pick crabs. *Ha*, but knowing his reputation, he's probably had them before." Jocelyn tossed a dishtowel in my face.

Gabe roared with laughter. "Oh my God, Mom. Too funny. Laney and Gen will never believe you made those jokes. You'll have to back me, Ash." Jocelyn's son headed upstairs, still chuckling at his mother's raunchy humor at my expense. Letting her have the moment seemed the least I could do.

Her laughter died out, and she turned to me. All the sadness came back. So much for what you see is what you get. My saving grace? She didn't cry. Thank God for that.

"I didn't do it to *hurt* him—or you. I did it so he would just hate me, be glad I was gone. I didn't think of what else it said—about you. I wasn't thinking. I'm an ass. I'm sorry." Everything spiraled. "Can we stop—rewind an hour—forget I said it was best for me to go. It wasn't. It isn't. I didn't mean it, Joss—Jocelyn. I didn't—"

"I know, Asher. I know it isn't best. I know you didn't mean it. I didn't mean it either, but here you are, halfway to the door with a packed bag."

"Tell me where to put my bag, Jocelyn. I'll put it wherever you want. The car, the basement, the barn—"

"My room?" That option startled me and I'm sure my face said as much. The suggestion surprised her, too, apparently. "Oh my God, I'm my monst— my mother." Jocelyn gripped the counter as her knees buckled. Blood drained from her cheeks. I didn't understand the comment but let my bag fall to the floor to grab Jocelyn before she did the same.

"Hey, Ash. Sorry about before. Late night, plus Benadryl. Let's hit it. Crabs are calling," Gabe called out, bounding down the stairs.

Jocelyn's arms wrapped around my neck and her mouth found mine.

"Whoops, you crazy kids." Gabe spun one-eighty. "Holler when you're ready to go. I'll unpack. *Again*." He tromped back upstairs while Jocelyn clung tighter to me as the kiss intensified. I lifted her onto the counter and her legs encircled my hips, pulling me close. She released my mouth, ducked her chin, finding her way to my neck. I forgot myself and allowed her access to my weak spot. The woman paid attention. I had to give her credit.

"Jocelyn," I whispered the plea.

Firmly holding me with her legs, those strong swimmer's legs, she leaned back on her palms while we both steadied our breaths. She assailed my mouth again, then murmured in my ear as she yanked my shirt. "Take me upstairs," she breathed in my ear before her teeth found my lobe.

"I can't." Where I found the fortitude, I couldn't say.

"Yes, you can."

"I can't. Everyone is upstairs. God, why are you—" I don't know if she meant to shut me up, but her tongue was in my mouth again. I pulled back as Jocelyn's fingers found my belt buckle. "*Whoa*, Jocelyn."

"Take me downstairs, then." She kissed me again. "Asher, please."

The whole scene played out like a movie in my head. I could throw her over my shoulder, carry her downstairs like some caveman, ravage her the way I'd thought about more than once, and she probably never knew was possible, and we would both be happier for it. And yet my brain screamed *no*. I took her firmly by the shoulders. "No, Jocelyn. Not like this. We were just—"

"Fighting? Yeah, I'm seeing the appeal." She almost smiled as she slid off the counter. "You know what *would* be better? Less talking, more doing." Her mouth found the hollow of my throat again, and I tossed her back onto the kitchen island, lustier than the first time.

My hands were in her hair and tugged. "I kinda like the talking."

Jocelyn gasped my name as she flailed her arm, knocking over a glass tumbler. It shattered on the hardwood floor.

"Mom?"

She shoved me with another yelp.

"Jojo?" Both calls came from upstairs.

"Yes, everything's— fine." She forced a cheerful tone, flustered in the mayhem. "I dropped a glass. Slippery fingers. We've—I've got it." She slid off the counter again, but I couldn't help pulling her face to mine. "Go. Downstairs." She kissed me. "Take your bag. Unpack. *Go.*"

I wasn't exactly sure who I walked away from in that kitchen. She looked like Jocelyn and smelled like Jocelyn, tasted like her too, but something new emerged, and if I'm honest—and I try to be—I looked forward to exploring that new side further—and soon.

51

Jocelyn

THE BLOOD SHOULDN'T HAVE been a surprise. I had cleaned the floor but, distracted, missed the stray shard of the glass hiding in plain sight on the edge of the kitchen island, the one piece left behind when the rest of it shattered on the floor.

"Darn it," I hissed and raised my palm to eye level, studying the protruding sliver in the meat of my hand. Blood trickled down my wrist, the thin red line growing longer as I slid to the floor, lost in thoughts of the woman who bore me. How she stayed with a man who hurt her. Did the fighting make her feel alive? Seen in a world that seemed to pass her by?

"Good lord, Jojo. What are you doing? Where's Asher?" Gigi, showered and rested, lunged for paper towels before kneeling at my side.

"Asher? Downstairs. We're playing some musical beds." I only had eyes for my wound as Gigi gently plucked the glass from it. More blood flowed.

"Sounds fun. Raise your arm over your head." She pulled my hand, and I flinched when she extended my old injury in a way it refused to move.

"Fun? Oh, not him and me. You all. He's moving downstairs, Gabe is moving to my old room, and you and Laney can move to Will's usual spot." I climbed to my feet with a momentary head rush.

"That's not necessary, Jojo." She applied more pressure when the bleeding didn't slow.

"It's been decided." I yanked from her grasp and bloody paper towel dropped to the countertop.

"That's a lot of blood, Jo. Do you need stitches?" Gigi hurried to hide the evidence and shoved more clean paper towels in my direction.

"It's not, really. I'm fine." I eyed my sister for a moment. "What about you? Think we need to— talk."

"Yeah, I hear Asher might head out. Can't be poor hospitality, so what gives?" Gigi walked to the pantry while she tried to control the conversation.

I wouldn't have it. "He's not. Crisis averted. And I'm talking about you, and you know it."

"It was nothing. Drank too much. It happens. Rarely, but it does. Forget it."

"You dug up my yard, Gi. Kinda weird." I watched my big sister pull a first aid kit from the top shelf she could reach from her tiptoes. I needed a step stool.

"Yeah, I know better than to mix my booze. I don't remember that flowerbed even being there." She returned to where I stood and beckoned for my hand so she could care for my injury. Gently pulling back the paper towel, Gigi breathed relief to see the bleeding had tapered.

I opened the red and white metal box at the sink. "Newly planted this spring. Used to be overgrown, natural. I wanted more peonies, so Raphe came in and cleared it, added some hardscape. I considered some in-ground lighting. Good thing I didn't—"

"Raphe did it?" Gigi cleaned the cut, dried it and applied an ointment before opening a large band-aid to cover the inch-long wound. Her interruption, though casual, indicated she stopped listening after hearing the landscaper's name.

"Who else?"

"I mean, Raphe himself, or his crew?"

"I don't know." I shrugged and threw away the rest of the bloody mess on the counter.

"What do you mean you don't know?" Gigi snapped but quickly lightened her tone. "*I* need to know who to apologize to. Did *he* do the work or his—"

"I wasn't here, Gi, but I assume he did it. He refuses to charge me, so I think he does the work on his own time. What's it matter?" I began with dinner prep despite the lack of our main course. And where was Asher? "Raphe says he likes to do it and doesn't get to 'play in the dirt' as much as he did before all his success. A break from pushing paper, he says. Though it is strange—"

"What's strange?" Gigi didn't hide agitation well.

"I haven't seen him in a while. His lawn crew in Westchester, yes, but here, nothing. And him? It's been weeks, *months*, actually. I haven't even thanked him for the new peony bed, which, I gotta say, looks pretty puny, even before you took your shovel to it. But since he and Will—"

"Speak of the devil." Laney walked in undetected. She's the only one small enough to get down the old stairs in silence. She held up a phone. I gingerly dried my hands on my apron before reaching for it. "Uh, nope. Not for you. It's Genevieve's phone. He's asked for her."

Gigi snatched the phone, dashed through the living room, and out the French doors. Laney and I shared a confused look, but per usual, Laney didn't dwell on it.

"What's for supper?"

"We're picking crabs tonight. Jícama slaw, baked sweet potato fries, and cornbread," I declared with pride.

"God, I love coming here, Jocelyn."

"Well, I'm behind so feel free to roll up your sleeves."

"To cook? Uh, no. No one wants my help in the kitchen. Trust me." Laney pulled her phone from her pocket. I wasn't the least bit surprised.

"I'll help." Asher hurried from the basement. "Put me in, coach. Tell me what to do. Hey, what happened?" He took my bandaged hand.

"Broken glass, one. Jocelyn, zero."

He cradled my hand, then brought it to his lips, kissing it.

"You okay?" He asked the loaded question with an overly concerned expression for a band-aid, even a large one. It was a question no one ever asked my—

"Better now," I said, pulling from his gentle hold. No, this man was no monster.

"Aww. *Gag*. Kidding." Laney chirped behind me.

Her immature mocking coaxed my first real smile in a while and tensions eased. I lifted my chin, placing a tender kiss on Asher's lips, then dragged him to the sink to introduce him to jícama.

52

Asher

THE CLINK OF BROKEN glass being swept sounded overhead as I trotted down the stairs to my new lodgings in the basement. I pushed through the door of the spare bedroom and tossed my duffle on the stripped king-sized bed. A neatly folded set of fresh bedding rested on one edge, but I flopped on the mattress, my heart and head still racing from all the commotion upstairs.

Flashes of the frenzied encounter with Jocelyn tightened my stomach. The corners of my mouth curved upward, and the recent memory ushered in a lightheadedness that kept me on my back. I pressed my palms to my eyes, torn between snapping out of it and allowing myself to relive it a while longer. For a woman who lacked experience... maybe that was the thing... decades of pent up... I grunted to sitting, deciding to sober up.

Focus, Asher. Her mother. What was the talk of her mother about? Some realization nearly brought Jocelyn to her knees and my poorly thought-out strategy to sway Gabe and make a speedy exit brought me to standing. "Jesus, Ash. What the hell?" God, I needed a run. I dragged my bag to me to unload its contents. Half my button-down pulled from my jeans and recalling Jocelyn's hands on my belt buckle stirred more distraction. I tucked in my shirt and closed the drawers. *Information, Asher. You need more information.*

I exited the guestroom in search of the photo albums with Juliette Durand on my mind. The *Mrs.* Durand shared similar features with Genevieve, taller with a broader nose. I wondered if she also had the lighter colored eyes. The photos I remembered included Juliette in sunglasses. Not unusual, but being light-eyed myself, I know we tend to be more sensitive to sunlight. Genevieve's eyes were hazel. A mix of green and brown, much lighter than Jocelyn's brown version, though hers held flecks of gold that sparkled like there might be magic... *grrr, focus.*

I speculated Juliette possessed lighter eyes like Genevieve's because every photograph had the woman wearing sunglasses. Typical for sunny summer days. It hadn't struck me when I looked at the photos last week, but now I focused on the matriarch. The consistency was unmistakable. Every single picture. And the more I studied the images, the more I saw of Genevieve in Juliette. The shape of her face, the curve of her mouth, the jut of her chin. The next regularity knocked the wind out of me, and I flipped through every page in search of some discrepancy, something to contradict the narrative forming in my head. I found none. Sleeves. Long sleeves and a variety of scarves around her neck. In the heat of summer. Every single photo. A bigger picture came into focus. An ugly, terrifying picture. Monstrous, even.

I removed the last two photos of Jocelyn dated June the year she graduated high school and slipped them into my back pocket, trying to quell my burbling rage.

"I'll help," I offered before clearing the top step. "Put me in coach..."

I peeled something called jícama for a salad and learned what it meant to *julienne* something. Gabe joined us and tuned in music to hum in the background. The young man and I shared a nod, indicating I was back on track, if not completely forgiven. His mother's mood was calm and genuine, and I noticed his relief at the change. Like me, Gabriel Atwater was an observer. I don't think much got by him, at least concerning his mother, and I took solace knowing the two of us were on watch now. If only I knew what we were on the lookout for. Why did everyone handle Jocelyn with such subtle but deliberate care?

Laney sat quietly on the sidelines working on her phone with regular glances to the patio beyond the French doors, where Genevieve paced with a phone to her ear.

Jocelyn was a whirlwind, a controlled force, and despite an injured hand, buzzed around the kitchen like she had *four* capable ones, cutting, mixing, pouring, whisking all to the digital beat of the 1980s.

"Should Gabe and I head out?" I placed my hand on the small of Jocelyn's back, having finished peeling sweet potatoes. Her immediate reaction to the gesture appeared like surprise, but a warm smile encouraged me to keep close.

"Yeah, I think you two should go make nice. He's in the backyard, cutting some arugula for the slaw." Jocelyn's observation that her son and I needed to "make nice" called back my idiocy and her unintended embarrassment.

"Jocelyn, I'm so sorry about—" I spoke quietly with an ardent head shake, still wrecked by my stupidity.

"Shh, we're past that now." She tugged on my shirt, drawing my eyes to hers.

"I need you to know—"

She stopped my apology with her lips, and I was glad to have the counter to lean against. "I do like how you shut me up, Ms. Durand." I smiled.

"Oh, I like the way you make me make noise, Mr. Cray." Her

tease whispered in my ear surely brought color to my cheeks and I thanked the images of Ms. Rutledge I kept on standby. Who knew forty years later, the old woman would become a near-constant in my life again?

"Good news or bad news?" Gabe entered with a colander full of leafy greens and a pair of kitchen shears.

"Bad news first, Gabe, always bad news first," Laney piped up from her spot in the corner.

"Dad's on his way."

Well, where Ms. Rutledge failed me, William Atwater came to the rescue. No doubt my grumble was audible, at least to Jocelyn. She stepped on my foot and gave me a commendable elbow jab.

"Didn't realize we invited him. What's the *good* news?" Jocelyn frowned in resigned disappointment.

"Aunt Gen asked him apparently, but he insisted he bring us crabs."

Jocelyn turned from the sink and let go of her large chef's knife on the kitchen island with a noisy *clang* that startled everyone. "Jeez Louise. *Again?*"

Laney and Gabe nearly fell over in honks and laughter. Gabe's allergies ramped up again from his arugula haul and tears streamed down his face. Laney squawked, "Jocelyn made an STD joke. The 'jeez Louise' tracks, but my *God*. The world is upside down. Ash, you gotta put that in a book. You can't make this stuff up."

I chuckled along too, awed by Jocelyn for making light of the new situation. Still, underneath it, I saw one more example of this woman getting knocked down and clawing her way to standing again, a smile affixed. But like me, Jocelyn had to wonder why Genevieve summoned William and why he was so eager to come.

53

Jocelyn

MY KITCHEN HUMMED WITH a house full of people, making me smile as I sipped wine. A smidgeon of guilt sprang in my chest when an across-the-room grin from Asher made me wish everyone else would disappear. A quick replay of earlier activities on that kitchen island sent an inner heat in all directions. My wine went down fast. Too fast.

Will's arrival was more subdued than I had feared. He and my sister made a quick exit to the patio. Neither Laney nor I received an invitation to the flagstone summit, and our shared glance was the only "mention" of the snub.

Supper was a feast with a healthy dose of angst simmering underneath, but the evening also signaled the beginning of a Hamptons holiday. Laney and Gigi buried themselves away in fresh new quarters with tight lips and stern moods, while Will and Gabe claimed to have impromptu father and son plans. None of that guaranteed the sort of privacy I wanted with Asher, but it would provide some alone time. Still, I couldn't escape the familiar feeling of tiptoeing around secrets.

"Want that patio date drink? It's about that time?" We had finished cleaning the kitchen and nerves rippled through me as Asher gently redressed my hand. First aid never felt so sensual.

Asher's concentration was laser-focused, aligning the wide bandage across my palm. "What time?"

"The magic hour," I reminded him.

"Ah, yes, the magic hour."

I grabbed two fresh glasses and a bottle from the wine fridge, holding them up for approval. Asher nodded.

The show had already started, and fireflies flickered everywhere. The pool beyond the yard looked appealing. "Do you swim, Asher?"

"Not like you swim, but yes, I can swim. I even thought to throw in swim trunks this time."

"That's too bad," I flirted.

"What? *Oh*, I see. Once the suggestive jokes start, there's a never-ending supply, huh?" He held the fingers of my injured hand across the armrests of wrought-iron patio chairs.

"Sorry about earlier with Gabe—" I caught myself in another apology.

"No, you said we were done with that, and I deserved what I got and worse."

I sat up in my seat. "No one deserves to be embarrassed or hurt."

"No, of course not." Asher's thoughtful reply reflected mine.

The tree frogs accompanied the fireflies with the addition of crickets. I'd forgotten how loud nature could be. Memories of childhood summers came to mind, urging me to look up at my old bedroom.

"When Gigi and I were little, nights like this were—uncomfortable." I kept my eye on the mullioned windows.

Asher's grip squeezed. "How so?"

"We didn't have air conditioning and on the second floor, the heat hung in the eaves with no crosswind. Sometimes Gigi would sneak into my room. They connect with the bath. She'd take out the screen, and we'd sit on the windowsill, trying to catch a breeze, but it did little good."

"You should have gone to the sunroom. Could have found cross-ventilation there," Asher made the benign suggestion, but I bristled and took back my hand.

"No. Not really an option." I pushed aside a sad but silly memory of ignoring rules and broken charms. "Anyway, installing A/C was the first renovation I had done here."

"What happened?" His direct question surprised me and wasn't one I wanted to answer, but the last thing I wanted was more distance between us.

"That night? Nothing. It was nothing," I blurted, realizing too late I'd misunderstood the question.

He cocked his head. "I meant now. What happened just now to make you let go of my hand? What night are you talking about?"

54

Asher

YOU WANTED ANSWERS, ASHER? Time to ask the hard questions and Jocelyn just opened the door—or window, as it were.

Jocelyn sipped her wine instead of talking. Nearly dark, ambient light from the distant kitchen lit the patio enough to see her set jaw. I hesitated to push, but the time was now, and the sooner I knew things, the sooner I could do what needed to be done. And no, I didn't know what that might mean, but I knew it didn't matter. Nothing would stop me from protecting the reticent woman sitting to my right.

Jocelyn put her hand within reach, and I took it as a sign. With a gentle hold again, I bided my time, hoping she would speak. No such luck. I offered a verbal nudge.

"You told me once—" I didn't get far before Jocelyn interrupted with a laugh.

"'I told you once?' That sounds like, 'Remember that time years and years ago?' We've known one another a week, Asher. *You told me once...*" she repeated with a snicker.

"Doesn't it feel longer? Like we've known each other longer?" I asked in all seriousness because, to me, it felt like a life—

"Like a lifetime," she said precisely what I thought. "In some ways," she added the unfortunate caveat and finished her glass of wine. Foolishly or not, I refilled it, topping off mine too. She took another sip. "I mentioned once—" she pretended to look at a watch she didn't wear and smirked. "I mentioned how beginnings get short shrift, and you suggested that while they were in the rearview—endings come barreling at you." Jocelyn got thirsty again.

"Not sure I like this conversation's trajectory, Joss. Jocelyn." I quickly corrected myself.

"No, I like you calling me that. I won't—I won't take that from you again. Promise."

I kissed her fingers. "You were talking about endings?" I needed to keep the momentum.

"I said endings sometimes come out of the blue, catch you unawares—"

"No, they don't. Not in hindsight, anyway. Not if you're paying attention."

She stood with unexpected speed, but I followed. Reaching for her arm, I caught her elbow.

"Jocelyn, that wasn't meant for you. I mean, I wasn't saying *you*—" A couple glasses of wine and— *what the hell, Ash?*

"You should let go of my arm, Asher."

"Don't push me away, Joss. Why are you pushing me away?" I appreciated the darkness. I'm not sure I would have asked in a lit room.

"Pushing *you*? You're the one who jumped from watching fireflies to accusing me of willful ignorance in my marriage."

"Your marriage? Is that the sore spot? Your *marriage*? I don't blame you for your marriage choice, Jocelyn. Who would? You married the safe pick or thought so. For all his faults, he was a smart guy who *liked* you—*cared* about you, and thank goodness because, statistically, it doesn't usually go down that way."

"Statistically? I'm a statistic? You are a charmer, Mr. Cray."

"Yes, the *good* kind of statistic, the kind where you got out alive. Lived to tell the tale. *Literally*. But I didn't understand until today. The hours I've spent combing through your words. For years, I pored over every gorgeous sentence, inspired to take a chance on something not even close to what you created. Only to have it all explained with one —"

"You don't know—"

"Then tell me." I didn't want to know, didn't want to hear it, but how else could I help?

"Weren't you the one who said we shouldn't look back, only forward?" Jocelyn had me there.

I walked away, crisscrossing the grass toward the pool. God, it was hot. The air hung heavy and wet, so I kept moving, if only not to be smothered in the dark. My mind dove into passages of the decades-old book. *"The frightening house with a will of its own."* A will of its own. A *Will* of its own? I jerked at Jocelyn's hand on my back. She had snuck across the yard in nature's nighttime racket.

"I'd apologize, but I know you don't like it when I do that." Pale moonlight emerged from thick clouds I hadn't noticed. It lit the yard in an eerie bluish-white. Jocelyn's tanned skin looked even darker. She gazed up at me and smiled, her mouth highlighted by the ghostly light.

"I want to show you something." She faced the back of the house, and I followed suit at her side. "What do you see?"

Beyond the patio, the floor to ceiling windows and French doors of the first floor shared a dim glow barely backlit by light further inside the house. The second floor had a set of symmetrical windows, one for Jocelyn's childhood room, the other for Genevieve's. Gabe left on the overhead lights in his mother's old room. Genevieve's room stood dark. When the image hit me, I sucked in a gulp of air.

"Say it. I want to hear you say it. No one repeats my favorite lines."

My chest tightened and my eyes found my shoes in the freshly mown grass. *"With a subtle smile and a wicked wink, the house hid all the secrets inside its outwardly ordinary walls."* I looked to the author when I finished reciting that line. Her upturned face, serene with closed eyes, glistened in the humidity.

None of that changed, and she barely moved when she spoke again. "And the next line? Do you know the next line?"

I cleared my throat, almost wishing I didn't know it. *"It was a very crowded house."*

She leaned into me with a playful nudge. "You're officially a superfan, Mr. Cray."

"I could have told you that long before today. Thought I did, actually." I returned the shoulder bump.

"Durand women don't cry."

It was an odd statement, out-of-the-blue, but I could attest to it. And since I didn't know where that line of dialogue might lead, I kept my mouth shut.

"A shame, really. I imagine a lot gets *freed* with a good cry." She started an airy laugh she didn't indulge. "I suppose the trouble with that is— a *lot* gets freed with a good cry." Her eyes opened, remaining skyward as she continued. "We brush our hair, change our sometimes— soiled clothes, take a mini timeout."

"I have seen your version of that too many times this last week."

"*Ah.* Learned behavior. The number of times I watched that woman get up off the floor would—"

My protection instinct reared its mighty head. I wanted to save Jocelyn from her own words, but letting those words out into the world might be her saving grace, and how could I think of stopping her salvation? Enduring that pain would be worth it. Or is that a lie told over and over until it becomes a kind of truth?

"Well, it was enough that I made choices to ensure it never happened to me. Of course, we know the irony is— it did, anyway. Sort of. In a kinder, gentler way but, nonetheless. Playing it safe, the prudent choice bit me in the—ass." She checked up on the unusual-for-her vocabulary but only for a moment. "I ended up living a different lie, took a different beating. No, Will *never* hit me, not ever. But the abuse he inflicted came in the form of deceit, neglect, gaslighting. And every time I picked myself up, I prayed my son didn't notice. Hoped he didn't see."

Maybe I made a noise, or Jocelyn actually could read my mind.

"I know, Asher. Gabe saw. Gabe saw everything, and that will haunt me for the rest of my days."

"Why do you—why is Will—William still in your life?" I shook my head, raised my hands to backpedal. "I'm sorry. That's not my business."

"It's not? The people in my life are not your business?" Jocelyn moved to stand in front of me and gave a tug of one of my belt loops, forcing a minor impact of our sweaty bodies. Her arms wrapped around my waist. "With whom I may or may not be in *cahoots*— makes no nevermind to you, Asher?" Her face was in my shadow now, but those eyes still sparkled.

I pulled her tight and kissed her. "It matters." We kissed again. "But I would never presume to know better than you."

Jocelyn grabbed my face. "*That* might be the sexiest thing a man has ever said to a woman."

I tilted back my head to laugh, baring my weak spot. Jocelyn pounced. "Jocelyn, you can't do that," I grunted, making no effort to stop her. "Jocelyn."

"Why? If it makes you feel good, it's what I want to do." She continued, and for me, staying upright was—well, let's say, a mixed bag.

I wobbled. "That may be the sexiest thing a woman ever said to—no, you should stop." With a firm hold of her shoulders, I nudged her away, kissing her mouth in the separation. "We haven't finished talking."

"Okay," she pressed in to stay close, and I encouraged it despite the shirt sticking to my skin, "Why is Will still in my life? Because Will is the father of my son and Gabe is the best thing I ever did. And Will loves me, in his way. He wants me happy and safe, and sometimes I'd swear he'd break the law to ensure it."

"Yeah, I think he might if he hasn't done it already." Genevieve's sultry voice startled Jocelyn and me when she stepped out of the dark. "And he's not the only one."

55

Jocelyn

DESPITE THE STIFLING MUGGINESS and clinging to Asher's radiating body, a chill ran through me. Instinct tried to pull me from his embrace, but Asher held tighter, muttering a curse. I craned my neck to meet his eye. "What?" I mouthed.

He only gave the slightest head shake in reply.

"Asher. Why don't you head inside." Gigi often made demands that on the surface sounded like suggestions. They rarely were, but Asher only had eyes for me, and clearly he planned to go if and when *I* told him to go.

"Anything you have to say to me, Gigi, you can say in front of Asher."

"Not this." Gigi's curtness cut sharply, even for her.

I don't know why I chose that moment to push back. "I said *anything*, Gi, and I meant it." I hadn't let go of Asher's waist. He clenched his jaw with a subtle nod of support.

"I was speaking to Asher, and Asher has written enough, done enough research, to know that as his legal counsel, if I advise him to go inside, he damn well better *go inside*."

"As his legal counsel? Don't think there are any contracts on the table, Law Lady, and Asher has done nothing wrong." I let go of him and faced my sister, who stood between us and the house, *almost* sure I spoke the truth.

"You're right. He hasn't done anything wrong—yet, and as his attorney, I would like to keep him free from peril moving forward.

The less he knows, the better."

I held my sister's eye for a beat, then looked to him. His eyes focused on the ground, but he shook his head no.

"Gigi, you're scaring me a bit. This feels a little dramatic, even for you." My mouth dried up, desert-like, and my heartbeat pounded in my ears.

"If you care anything for the man and I think it's clear you do, you tell him to go inside." Gigi's rasp insisted I obey.

I moved back to stand in front of Asher and took hold of his hands with a tight squeeze. His were warm while mine had turned cold and clammy. "Asher, you should—"

"Don't," he whispered.

"I don't know what—"

"Joss, please don't send me inside. I can help. Whatever you did, whatever it is, I can help. It doesn't matter. I don't care." His light blue eyes looked wild in the moon's glow, and I didn't understand what he said. I heard him but couldn't comprehend his meaning. Nothing made sense. The pulsing in my head rolled down my body, throbbing in all my limbs. I released Asher's hands and looked at mine. My tight grip had reopened the wound in my palm. Blood seeped through the band-aid, black in the nighttime shadows.

"What I did?"

He held my face in his hands and gave me a tender kiss. "I don't care," he murmured.

"What does that mean? You don't care."

"It means it doesn't matter. I care about you. More than anything, I think. I—I care about you more than anything." His words sounded as though he came to the revelation just as the syllables fell from his lips.

I gave a small smile, breathed a slight sigh, and rose on my toes to kiss him. "I care about you, too."

He relaxed some, offered a shy grin too, with another sweet kiss. "Asher, I'm gonna need you to do something for me."

"Anything. Anything you need, Joss." He waited, eager to help.

"I'm gonna need—" I leaned around to look at Gigi before refocusing on Asher. "I'm gonna need you to go inside now." I nodded with wide, reassuring eyes, reaching up to touch his cheek. He rested his head into my hand. "Go on now. I'll see you soon." I looked around him again to nod to my sister, waiting patiently in the dark.

Asher gave me a moment to change my mind, but both of us knew that wouldn't happen. With a slow turn and heavy feet, he trudged toward the house, still displaying its wicked wink. He stopped beside my sister, but if he spoke to her, the incessant nocturnal din made it impossible to hear him. She took a brief hold of his forearm before he continued on to his exile.

I held my breath, still confused by the histrionics of the scene and thought if Asher glanced back, gave me one more glimpse of his caring face, everything would be all right. That would be the thing to cast the spell to save us all. The longer his slog across the yard, the higher my anxiety rose, but when he opened the French door, he gave me what I needed. One more look.

"I don't enjoy playing the heavy, Jojo, but I need to protect your boyfriend. He's one of my wife's biggest clients."

"One of *your* biggest clients and calling Asher my boyfriend feels a little—weird, Gigi."

"I don't have clients if I'm not a lawyer anymore. And do you prefer 'lover,' Jo?"

I tried to cover my immature giggle with a cough. "Would that he was, Gigi." I rolled my eyes. "And what do you mean you're not a lawyer anymore?"

"I mean, I'm pretty sure we don't get through this without me getting disbarred, and that's if we're lucky. That's the best-case scenario. Wanna take a seat?"

My confusion compounded, but my sister's calm provided some comfort, and I knew whatever issues we faced, she could find a solution to any problem. She always did. Gigi took care of everything. "How about at the pool? Stick our feet in? It's hot out here."

Gigi shook her head and shrugged. "Sure, Jojo. Seems appropriate." She walked by me, headed straight to the pool's edge. I watched her hesitate, then kick off her shoes, roll up her pants, and squat to the concrete to dip her feet into the saltwater. I couldn't remember the last time she'd been near it, much less in it, and joined her, wishing I had more wine.

Once settled, I tried to enjoy the water that wasn't cool enough. I leaned back on my palms then hissed at the sting of the cut on my hand.

Gigi gave no preamble. "I need you to think back to that night, Jojo. And tell me everything you remember. *Everything.*"

"Oh, not you too," I scoffed.

"What does that mean? Who else have you told? Good lord, Jojo. Who else knows?"

"Whoa. I don't even know what night you all are talking about. There have been a few."

"Who is 'you all?'"

"You and Asher. He just asked me about some night, though I guess I kinda brought it up first, but I was talking about—well, nothing he would know about. What are you talking about?"

"Prom night, Jojo. What happened on prom night?"

"Nothing. I barely remember prom night. Wait. Is this about Darren Kolchek?"

"Yes, Jocelyn. It's about Darren Kolchek." Gigi's patience waned.

I didn't like it when Gigi called me Jocelyn. It didn't happen often, but when it did, it never meant anything good. "I don't know anything about that. Yes. He was here, but then he wasn't. As a matter of fact, the last time I saw him, he sat exactly where you do now. Tuxedo pants rolled up to his knees, feet in the water."

"Then what? It's okay, Jojo. You can tell me. I don't care and it doesn't matter. I can help."

"Okay, the double team is feeling a bit contrived, Gi. You two parroting each other like you rehearsed this." I splashed my toe out of the water.

"Huh?"

"Asher said the same thing. *I don't care; it doesn't matter, I can help.* I don't know what you two think I—wait. Do you think I—you think—Asher thinks I—?" Another chill ran through me, and my throat tightened. My brain screamed at my limbs, begging me to get up, but I couldn't move.

"Jojo. Just tell me what happened."

"I don't know. I don't remember—"

"It's important. I know you don't want to but—"

"Shut up, Gigi." I rolled to my hip, forcing my legs under me and scrambled to my feet. Dizziness hit and I stumbled before righting myself to hurry to the safety of the house, the protection of my bedroom.

The frigid A/C delivered another blow to my system. Asher jumped from his stool the moment I crossed the living room threshold. Laney waited with him but stayed in her seat. Gigi followed fast at my heels. All three said my name—three different versions of it, at once.

"Stop. All of you. I need a minute and some space. I need air. I need—" No one spoke. "No. I have questions." My eyes darted to my sister. "Is Will involved in this? Is he a part of this?" I pointed and flung my hands around at the threesome. "And what about Gabe? What have you said to my son?" Blank faces stared.

"Someone answer me."

"Gabe isn't involved. I wouldn't do that." Gigi took the role of spokesperson. "And William is—William is looking for some answers. He says we've—*I've*— got it wrong."

"We? You three? You three think what? That I'm like them? Really, Gigi? Those Monsters? I mean, logistics aside—forget the chiffon, and the heels, the cast from shoulder to hand, or the size difference between us, between Darren and me. Darren the six-foot-tall athlete. I mean, it's me. How?"

My questions were for Gigi, but I looked at each of them for answers. Laney dropped her gaze first, the one with the least to lose. As seconds ticked by, I wanted to escape. To find my way to my bedroom so I could piece together any memories of that long-ago night. The only path meant walking past Asher. I stopped in front of him, setting my hand on his chest. "Asher?"

He looked me straight in the eye, but he only said, "Jocelyn." His head gave the slightest shake when he placed his hand on mine.

"I can't—I can't believe *you* think I'm—a monster." I ripped my hand away and hurried to the stairs.

Buried in the noise of my stomping feet, I thought Asher said my name again, and Gigi said, "Let her go, Ash. Let her go."

56

Asher

I DON'T KNOW WHY I listened to Genevieve instead of hauling ass upstairs to be with Jocelyn, but a part of me thought Jocelyn's sister knew best. Then again, Genevieve was the one who seemed confident her sister was involved in this mess in the first place. What did Genevieve know? Why was she sure her sister needed protection? Why did I believe it too?

"I don't think she knows anything." Genevieve's tone reeked of utter disbelief.

"Jesus Christ, Genevieve. What the hell are you doing then? Why would you put her through this? What's the fucking point—"

"Back up, Ash." Laney jumped between Genevieve and me. "Don't speak to my wife like that. Ever."

"It's okay, Laney. I thought if I pushed, she'd come around— I did it wrong."

"You sure as hell did. Come around? I don't care if you're her big sister. You just destroyed her. She thinks we all believe she's a—a monster. And of all things to compare herself to—her— *your* parents? Christ." I struggled to keep my anger in check, my voice low volume.

"What do you know about—did she talk to you about—?" Genevieve reached for her throat and went ashen like she had in the L.A. hotel bar. I didn't admit to any of it, but my silence said enough. Genevieve's attitude changed. She sneered. "Good lord,

Asher. Why couldn't you just *screw* her like a real man?"

"Whoa, Gen. Come on, now." Laney switched to my defense. "What the hell, Hon? He's my friend and a good one.

"He's your *client*, Laney. And you get too goddamn close to your clients."

"Not *all* my clients, and I think you know your sister's lucky to have Asher Cray in her life. Damn lucky."

"Lucky? Even the closeted queen figured out how to get the job done. This one can't close the deal. Tab A into slot B, Ash. It's not rocket science. Maybe he's blocked in more than just the writer variety. Sad, really." Genevieve's fake frown dripped with sour sarcasm.

"Genevieve," Laney almost shouted and Laney *never* shouted.

"It's okay, Laney." I stepped in with a forced chuckle. Truthfully, the words hit hard, but I'd seen a version of this earlier today. That play actor was the *other* Durand sister, but with a similar tactic. "You can insult me, Genevieve. Embarrass me. Try to shame me into bowing out. It's not happening. You are— better at it than your sister. I'll give you that. Probably because you have less apprehension about actually hurting me, which is—good to know, I guess. But I'm not going anywhere. I don't believe she could ever hurt anyone, and I can't for the life of me figure out why you would want her believing we all think she is capable of—violence." Saying the word aloud hurt even as Jocelyn's raging lap swim came to mind. Her furious strokes. The animalistic cry as she roared out of the pool. The blood that trickled down her legs in the aftermath.

"Well, not all of us," Laney interjected. "Not William, apparently. He got a pass. Where is he, anyway?"

The notion of William winning the role of *Good Guy* made me queasy. The drunkard who believed his ex-wife had a demon inside her continues to get off blameless—*bloodless*.

"Trying to get a hold of Raphe."

"Why? What the hell does Raphe have to do—?"

Laney caught my eye and shook her head no.

I obeyed, swallowing a growl. "I'm going to talk to her." I made it to the foyer before Genevieve called out to me. I stopped.

"Asher. I'm sorry. I didn't mean—I didn't mean *any* of—"

I walked upstairs without letting Genevieve finish.

The house got very small. That was to say, I found myself outside Jocelyn's door in no time and I wasn't sure of my next move. *Knock on the door, Asher. Go from there.* I knocked.

"Unless you're Gabe, go away." Jocelyn's voice sounded quiet and sad, but resolute.

I leaned my forehead on the door and let out a long, slow exhale. "Jocelyn, I know you're mad or sad, or worse— disappointed, and I may have jumped to some conclusions, made snap judgments, and I'm sorry for that. But I never could connect the dots. I never believed you were capable of—of doing anyone harm. And I knew explanations could be, *would* be made, no matter what happened. I'm here to help you. And I'm not going anywhere. You can push, your sister can push, but I'm staying put. I will sit outside this door until you open it."

The wooden four poster squeaked, and the hushed shuffle of feet moved across a rug and the hardwood floors. The click of the antique bolt lock echoed in the hall, and I held my breath to see if the door opened. When it didn't, my stomach sank. I chanced turning the knob, relieved when I gained access, but only a crack.

"Joss."

Her face peered through the inches-wide opening. "Asher, I—I think I'm in trouble."

"You're not. We're gonna figure it out. There's an explanation and we'll find it, I promise."

"You can't promise. You don't know—"

"I *do* know. I know you wouldn't hurt anyone intentionally, not without good cause."

"No, Asher. You don't."

I let another breath go. *Another tactic, Asher? Plan B?* "Okay, Jocelyn. Why don't you let me in, and we will go over every detail you can recall about that night. You can close your eyes and walk me through it. Maybe I'll see something you don't. I might ask a question you hadn't considered. Let me help."

Her expression was new. Not one I'd seen until tonight, but my gut said it was the look of unadulterated fear. That's when I leapt to another conclusion—a sickening one. "Joss? Are you—are you afraid of *me?*"

"No. God no, Asher. I'm afraid—of me."

My head bowed with relief. "Jocelyn Durand. Let me in."

She did and proceeded to tell me everything she could recall from her prom night and the reasons she got foggy about the events became apparent, and while it didn't exonerate her, it chalked up more points in the innocent column as far as I was concerned. Of course, I'm not law enforcement, but I knew enough, enough to be dangerous. Jocelyn's rehashing of that long-ago night also made one thing crystal clear, and it burned inside me. Genevieve Durand knew something I didn't, and she wasn't sharing.

"That's how I remember it. *What* I remember." Her thumb stroked the wound on her palm, her focus on the bloodied bandage.

I leaned back on the bed's headboard and spoke barely above a whisper. "May I ask some questions now?"

She shrugged her permission.

"Was Darren dirty? Did you notice mud or dirt on his clothes or his face?"

"*Hm.* It was dark. Darker than tonight, cloudy, moonless, and I didn't turn on any lights."

"It's important, Jocelyn. It can help with the timeli— it's important." I pushed, but gently. She'd been steamrolled enough already.

"I don't know, Asher. If I knew, I'd say." Her frustration grew.

"Okay. And you said he acted kind of weird?"

"Sort of. But Darren didn't smell like alcohol, and I would have known that smell."

"Anything else? Other smells? Weed?"

"No, I wouldn't have known that scent, but I remember chlorine. Pungent. The pool company must have just opened the pool. It was a service, the same service we have now except it was chlorine then, now it's saltwater. Scheduled in advance, I guess, because my parents were—"

"Yeah." I didn't need her going down that road right now and drew her back to the details she had shared. "So how long do you think it was from the time you took the pain pill until—?"

"I don't know. My arm ached. That's why I called it a night. My girlfriends went off to party, but that was never my thing, anyway. The strap from my sling was rubbing my neck, so I took it off." Jocelyn gripped the back of her neck like she felt the irritation of the sling all over again. "We were sitting on the edge of the pool." She stopped, but I could tell she was trying to see it in her mind's eye.

I clenched my jaw, unsure about the next question. As sick as I felt, I knew it had to be asked, but the idea of it, the thought of— "Jocelyn? Did—did Darren hurt you?"

"Hurt me? How?"

"Did he touch you when you didn't want him to? Go too far? Did he—?"

"*No.*" Her answer was adamant. Too adamant?

"If he did, if you didn't want whatever he was— if you fought back?"

"No, Asher. It wasn't like that. It was sweet. He even—" She paused mid-sentence and took hold of her once-injured arm but wore a small smile. "He *did* hurt me." She breathed a hollow laugh. I stiffened, tightening both fists. "He kissed me. He asked first, and I said no because he had a girlfriend. Annie, Anne Bismarck. God, she was pretty, and they were a couple. Off and on, I think, but all year. Maybe longer."

Everything Jocelyn said corroborated what I had read in the news articles. She was quiet again, the grinding of her brain gears almost audible. The rhythms of the night creatures played in the background too. She needed to continue, but I didn't want to hear the next part. Still, I asked, "But he did anyway? He kissed you anyway? Even when you said no?" I tried to relax my balled hands, keeping my tone calm.

"No. He explained he and Annie had broken up that night." Jocelyn sighed. "I don't know if that was true. But it was Darren Kolchek, and he asked, and I was seventeen and never been kissed." She shook her head and took a brusque, deep inhale. "So, I let him." She shrugged. "That's when he hurt me. He didn't mean to. He was joking around, I think. Pretended like it was such a good kiss, he fainted. Fell right over, slid down my arm, the cast, and his head landed in my lap. *Ugh,* it hurt. But he still played like he was unconscious. I pushed him off me. He was heavy—like he could have been asleep, but he wasn't. He apologized, and that's when he asked for some water. Real groggy. I was sleepy by then too, and my arm throbbed after he landed on it." She clutched at her arm, reliving the pain. "So, I went inside to get water, but before I came back out, I—" She put her head in her hands, hiding her face.

I sat up to touch her, ran my hand down her back, encouraging her to continue.

"I took a second pill. Yes, I probably knew better, but I hurt all over, and I wanted to sleep, so I took one, *another* one. When I went outside to take him his water, he was gone. It was dark, but I called out for him. Quietly though, because I didn't want to wake Gigi."

"Wait, Genevieve?"

"Yes. That's why I never turned on the lights. Our rooms are on the backside. Why?"

"I didn't realize Genevieve was there. Here, I mean. You hadn't mentioned that."

"We—well, *she* was getting the Bayborough house ready to sell and keeping her big sister eye on me, though she sorta gave me carte blanche that night, and this might surprise you, but I was a bit of a goody-two-shoes, so—"

I huffed a laugh at the vision of her in pink chiffon, then forced myself to concentrate on the story details. "Weird, though, right? That she *chose* to sleep here?"

"The other place was in boxes and, well, not our favorite place, really."

"I thought *here* was not her favorite place." I teetered on the cusp of betraying Laney's confidence, but it seemed necessary.

Jocelyn rotated to see me.

"Laney mentioned something."

"That's true, but that didn't happen until later—until—" The color drained from her face.

"Jocelyn? Do you remember something? Something from that night? Maybe the next morning?"

She shook her head. "I'm tired now, Asher. I think I need to sleep." Her abrupt end to our conversation said volumes but not enough.

"You're doing so well. Let's keep going." I slid toward her, put my arm around her shoulders, but she pulled away with a jerk.

"Sorry. So tired all of a sudden." She rolled over and inched up, laying her head on a pillow on the other side of the bed.

I hesitated to prod further, but I'd struck a nerve. Something new came to her and Jocelyn shut down, shutting me out. Leaving her was the last thing I wanted to do. I moved to lie close to her, cocoon her again like I had the night before, my hand on the outside of her thigh. Her smell filled my head as I settled it on the same pillow.

"You should go, Asher." Jocelyn didn't move.

I could barely track her breathing. My hand traveled from her thigh to hold her at her waist—

"I'll see you in the morning." Her dismissal left no room for doubt.

I opened my mouth to argue but knew better. Kissing the back of her head, I drank in another gulp of her scent, then paused on the opposite edge of the mattress in hopes she would change her mind. But whatever occurred to Jocelyn superseded any other notions she had about me staying in her bed. Not how I imagined the night would end. Don't get me wrong, I can read a room, and I know there's a time and a place, but I hadn't seen myself sleeping alone tonight.

I crept to the door, the whine of its hinges loud in the silence of the big old house.

"Asher?"

I sighed in something like relief. "Yes, Jocelyn." It was premature.

"Goodnight." That word hammered the final nail in the evening's coffin. I shuddered at the clichéd metaphor.

When I found my way to the living room bar, Laney had beaten me to it and scared the crap out of me when I flipped the light switch.

"Got the boot, huh?" She raised her glass.

I nodded. "You?"

"Yep. Sorry about Genevieve earlier. It's not you. No one will ever win over her sister." Laney took another sip. "No one. Ever."

"Yeah, the feeling's mutual. I mean for Jocelyn. She's gonna go down trying to keep Genevieve up, and I don't know how to stop it."

"What the hell does that mean?"

My opinion of Genevieve had taken a hit tonight and continued to plummet. "It means your wife is into this up to her eyeballs, and she's not doing Jocelyn any favors."

"Says the guy with no siblings, no family, zero attachments in quite some time."

"You're right. Family has never been my thing. I don't relate. But I guess going through what the two of them faced growing up, what they survived, they lean on each other. No matter what. I mean, who else can they trust, right?" I eyed Laney over the rim of my glass. An ignorant look came back. "What the hell, Laney Li?" I poured too much Scotch on top of my initial dose. "Do you even know who you're married to?" I recorked the crystal decanter and flipped the switch again, leaving my agent in the dark. The symbolism was overstated, even for me.

57

Jocelyn

How many times can you push away a man and expect him to come back? Is it covered in that elusive manual I never got around to reading? Truthfully, Asher would be better off if he ran; ran far away from whatever trouble had found its way to this house. It's not what I want, but it's best. Isn't it?

While I struggled to piece together the events of prom night, the morning after played back with more clarity. I say morning, but it was well after noontime. The clock said *late* when I went to bed, though *passed out and still dressed in formalwear*, paints a more accurate picture. The narcotics were potent, and I'd taken too much. They left the previous night in a thick haze, and I slept away the morning.

A more recent memory flashed of the morning in Asher's loft when I had first replayed those long-ago June days. I recalled my argument with Gigi about skipping graduation and her apologies made with my cast decorating project, but in reality, the fighting had started *before* graduation morning. The day before, the day after the prom, Gigi ruled like a tyrant. Nothing I did pleased her, and we couldn't get out of Amagansett fast enough. We'd hurried home to the Bayborough house full of horrible memories and half-packed boxes.

The whole day she'd snapped at me from the moment I came out of my room, still dressed in my prom get-up. Somehow I had dirtied my gown, a big brownish smudge soiling the lap of the skirt and my cast too. Asher's mention of dirt on Darren pinged something. Gigi had berated me for ruining the dress and then, in silent fury, pulled it from the heap in the backseat of her car and threw it into a dumpster at a gas station when we stopped to fuel up on the way home. She acted so unlike herself, and when we got back to Bayborough, she sent me to pack for my trip to Èze. Later that evening, I emerged to find her asleep on the family room sofa. Crashed out early, like she hadn't slept the night before. She even admitted it and thus began the days of Gigi *not* sleeping at the summer house. *That* was the start of her resistance to visiting Amagansett.

I lay still on my bed, but the sensation of movement sloshed in my stomach and my brain. Staring at my hands, the faint sting of my cut under the blood-stained bandage sparked another detail. Gigi wore a bandage on her hand that day, her right hand.

Graduation day. Gigi eventually acted more herself and we had fun wrapping my dingy cast in bright silver and blue before going to the high school for commencement. The ceremony had hardly ended when Gigi, who stood on the sidelines having never taken her seat, grabbed my good arm, saying we had to leave immediately for the airport. I didn't get to say goodbye to friends or teachers, no pictures or hugs.

But then I remembered my sister taking me the long way around the school's auditorium. "It'll be faster this way, avoiding the crowd. International flights can be hectic, and I don't want to take chances," she insisted. I knew nothing about air travel, but I think I rolled my eyes (as seventeen-year-olds do) at my big sister taking her "parental" routine too far. Salmon swimming upstream, she pulled me through the onslaught of attendees all walking the opposite direction. Backstage, we exited a door to a loading dock. But why?

The scene played out in front of me vividly, like on a movie screen, and two things struck me. Four, actually. The two uniformed police officers we avoided standing at the front entrance of the auditorium, and passing two police patrol cars with lights flashing after exiting the school's parking lot as we sped to JFK airport.

Two months later, my sister picked me up at JFK and drove me straight to Greenwich Village. The car overflowed with trendy bedding and school supplies, new clothes, and colorful coordinating storage containers. All a girl needed to set up her new living quarters in a ten by fifteen cinderblock room. No, not a prison cell. Urban college living. We'd eaten pizza and ice cream while walking around campus and when I met a boy named Will with a meticulous five o'clock shadow and the subtle frosted-tips of George Michael (*ahem, hello, red flag number one*), Gigi left me to begin my new life while she headed to New Haven, Connecticut to start hers.

I hadn't slept. Earlier movement in the hall, long after I banished Asher, stirred me, but I didn't hear anything now. I washed my face and brushed my teeth, and after applying a new bandage, I changed into a nightgown and a bathrobe. On tiptoe to Gabe's room, I dared a peek. All arms and legs, he lay asleep and alone. I closed his door. My eyes adjusted to the dark with the help of a streetlight beyond the sunporch. I decided not to open Gigi's and Laney's door.

My butterflies got rambunctious when I hit the first landing headed downstairs. The basement door stood open, but Asher had closed his. *If I were to wake in the night and find my way to your door, would it be locked?* My knuckle tapped gently on the solid door. Nothing. The sound sleeper likely wouldn't wake, but I rapped louder and heard the creak of the bed frame. With a silent prayer, I held my breath, hoping to hear Asher's voice. Instead, he opened the door.

The basement bedroom had two narrow glass-block windows high on the mostly subterranean walls. It was dark, but I made out Asher's broad shoulders and sculpted torso, finding myself tongue-tied with unusual concern for the state of my wild nighttime curls.

"You okay, Joss?" One of us had to speak, eventually.

"Yeah, yes. I was—I wondered if—?"

Asher stepped back and opened the door wider. "Pick a side."

Relieved, I scampered to one side of the bed, removed my bathrobe, and climbed into the already warm bed, scented with Asher's now-familiar sleep smell, taking my spot right in the middle. In a moment, the weight and warmth of Asher Cray surrounded me, and I fell asleep in no time.

58

Asher

IT WASN'T RIGHT TO feel this good, when outside these sheets a world of trouble lurked. But even as the sun rose and the small block windows filtered light into the room, some spell had yet to be broken, and I swore I wouldn't move, breathe even, to keep the magic alive in this dim hideaway.

I don't know what time Jocelyn joined me in the night, but I was relieved she had. It must have been late, as daybreak found us quickly while she continued to sleep unbothered. She'd flinched twice, and I feared a repeat of the overnight in my loft, but I held tight, and she relaxed into me without so much as a whimper.

Questions remained, of course. What had occurred to Jocelyn last night to force my abrupt dismissal? Why did she change her mind and search me out? And was it fair of her to expect me to be at her beck and call? *Fair? Come on, Ash, life isn't fair.* I caught myself before chuckling at the notion I would ever turn this woman away from my bed. Sad? Maybe. The truth? No question.

Focus on other things. I worried about my agent friend. The wide berth she'd given her wife concerning her past was problematic, and while I couldn't do anything about it, a reckoning would come, and the effects would bleed over, impacting the woman snug in my arms. Little to do with Genevieve Durand wouldn't influence Jocelyn, and I wanted to mitigate any negatives. But I also guessed whatever prompted my expulsion from Jocelyn's bedroom had Genevieve's name all over it. Somehow I needed to keep from being excluded, allowed to help. *Lean in, Jocelyn.*

As if she heard my thoughts, Jocelyn released her hold on my arms wrapped around her, stretching hers long, her shoulder blades pressed to my chest. A sweet grunt accompanied it all. I held my breath, hoping it wasn't the end of our entangled state. A mini jolt told me she registered her current situation, realized where she was and who she was with, and I smiled when I felt her ease back into me with the quietest contented sigh.

Her comfort stirred my own deep breath. That lungful betrayed me.

"You're awake," she whispered the playful accusation.

"Shh, no, I'm not," I replied with a gentle squeeze.

She twitched with a snicker, then allowed us another moment in our human knot.

"Sorry about last night."

I held tighter. "I'm not."

"Not this. The earlier part. Pushing you out."

"Yeah, I'm gonna need you to stop doing that." I am rarely accused of being indirect.

After a few seconds, she simply replied with a slow nod.

"You said my sister *pushed* too?"

"*Ha.* You could say that."

"You're still here. Couldn't have been but so bad."

"You don't want to know, but yeah, I'm still here."

"But I *do* want to know." Jocelyn twisted, trying to see me.

"Sure. Why not? She insulted my manhood, my inability to *close the deal*, I believe was one of the ways she referenced it—"

"*One* of the ways?"

"*Uh-huh.*"

"Must have stung."

"Only because it's true. And the ease with which you two discuss such things will take some getting used to, but I am up for a challenge."

"Yes, *ahem*, I noticed," she coughed, evidently noticing my body appreciating hers.

"*Jocelyn,*" I tried to sound aghast.

"Just kidding. I know it's a morning thing. Nothing to do with me."

"Well, whoever fed you that line was—oh. Crap." I scolded myself for speaking without thinking. William Atwater had become quite the regular third wheel. Jocelyn's new grip slackened.

I let go of her and rose on one elbow. She didn't move. I tucked curls behind her ear, revealing her cheek and bent to kiss it. Her eyes closed. My head rested on my fist as I surveyed her back. Jocelyn had tan lines that highlighted her sculpted muscles, a strong, lean figure made possible by the swim regimen.

She lay, legs bent, one atop the other. When I placed my hand on her nightgown covered knee, she straightened it, giving way for my hand to glide up her side a fraction. Inch by inch, I gathered the thin, soft fabric until my fingers met Jocelyn's firm, bare thigh. Her muscles tensed as her hips inched into me in an alluring act of encouragement that made me doubt she was as nervous as I was as we waded into uncharted waters.

"Jocelyn?" I murmured in her ear, brushing my lips across it. She placed her hand on mine and gradually drew it, along with her nightgown hem, clear to her waist, introducing me to the lacy band of her panties. No sooner had my thumb slipped between the lace and smooth skin of her hip than a knock rapped on the bedroom door. I released Jocelyn's undergarment with an exaggerated snap of elastic, flopping to my back with a mumbled, "*Seriously?*"

My bedmate curled into a ball with a snort, followed by an uncontrollable laugh she muffled with her pillow.

"Asher, are you awake?" Laney spoke in a loud whisper through the door.

"No, Laney. I'm asleep. In the depths of a nightmare. A recurring nightmare, featuring *you*," I replied while putting on a t-shirt. Jocelyn buried her face in her pillow again.

"Not sure my wife will appreciate hearing you're dreaming about me—repeatedly, no less. Chances are it won't please her sister either. I suggest we keep that on the DL." By the time she got to the *down-low*, I had opened the door a few inches. Despite her jokes, concerned eyes looked up at me. "Speaking of—they're gone. Both of them."

Without a word, I opened my door fully, providing a view to my bed—and its occupant.

Jocelyn rose on her elbow and gave a meek wave. "Gigi's probably at the pier. She does that."

Laney looked away and practically whispered, "Sorry, man. I'd high-five you, but my wife is kinda missing and things have been a bit of shitshow lately. Plus, it's my sister-in-law, so..."

"Well, I haven't earned that accolade yet, *so*..." I mimicked. "We'll be upstairs in a minute, okay?"

"Thanks, Ash. And again, apologies for—you know." Laney turned on her heel toward the stairs.

I closed the door, sorry the world of trouble had once again found its way into our refuge. Matters only got worse when Jocelyn's tan leg peeked out from under the top sheet, tempting me back into bed. That peek included a glimpse of lace I had only fingered, not seen. Pink, of course. My palms pressed my eyes. "You've gotta get out of my bed."

It was Jocelyn's turn to collapse back, disgruntled. "I know," she sighed. "Nice of you to own up to not closing the deal. Unnecessary, but nice."

"I'm nothing if not a gentleman. Besides, some credit I don't want until it's due. Now, get out of my bed," I groused.

Jocelyn rose on her elbows, cheeks darkened, and eyes wide while her teeth found that bottom lip. She *really* needed to stop that.

I watched as she rolled off the mattress but spun with a jerk when the sun shone through, catching her nightgown with cruel precision and spectacular results. "Your robe is—" I flailed, pointing over my shoulder to the opposite bedside, careful to focus on the door.

Evidently enjoying my discomfort, she took a circuitous route to fetch her garment. A path that crossed between me and my point of forced concentration and included her hand skimming across my t-shirted torso with a doe-eyed look from under long lashes. Jocelyn Durand had a definite playful side that, on occasion, tended toward mischievous. Needless to say, my eagerness to explore those avenues thoroughly, and *god help me* soon, ran high.

59

Jocelyn

THE ADAGE ABOUT NOT playing with fire, lest you get burned, weighed heavy on me but not in the way any sage advisor would welcome. I looked forward to taking any heat Asher Cray cared to rain down on me. Considering all the trouble surrounding us, my distraction was wildly inappropriate, but I couldn't help myself. Hurrying upstairs with Asher right behind, I needed to clear my head and focus on the Darren mystery, how it appeared my sister knew more than she was letting on, and why she believed I had anything to do with it.

"I need something from both of you," Laney said before Asher and I had cleared the door from the basement.

"Well, considering you haven't been the least bit of an imposition on me *yet* this morning," I cleared my throat with an exaggerated cough, "what can I do for you, my favorite sister-in-law?" My sass on full display garnered a chuckle from Asher and Laney's scary version of a smile.

"I'm your *only* sister-in-law."

"Exactly." I sashayed to the coffeemaker, glad to see someone had brewed a pot. "What do you need?" I poured a cup for Asher and myself, noticing Laney had her own.

"Yours is easy. I emptied the sugar bowl. Got more?"

"Of course. If that's all you want, now I feel bad for the snark." I feigned a frown.

"Well, Asher's favor is more—well, *more*." Laney stared at her dashing client and sudden tension filled the typically light and airy room, that seemed so much less so lately. Asher stood still with a steaming mug of coffee halfway to his mouth and waited for Laney to continue. "I'm gonna need you to call Harry."

My gaze went from Laney to Asher and back again. His coffee never made it to his lips. In a slow-motion sequence, Asher lowered the cup to the counter, leaned with both hands widespread, and lowered his head. Whatever the backstory with Asher and this Harry, the mention appeared to knock the wind out of the man holding himself up on the sprawling slab of quartz in my kitchen. My flight response kicked in and I couldn't move fast enough.

"*IIII'll* take my coffee—elsewhere."

Asher lifted his head with a subtle shake at Laney.

The two spoke to me at once:

Asher: "That's not necessary."

Laney: "Good idea."

I grimaced, stuck to my spot.

"Why?" Asher asked.

Laney gave a raised brow side-eye. "*Uh*, because Jocelyn doesn't know—"

"Not that," Asher interrupted. "Why do you need me to call Harry?"

"Because we got *bupkis* and Harry's the best. Because Harry will find out what we need and fast. Because Harry will drop everything if you call."

"Well, sounds like Harry's our *guy*," I chirped with a sip of coffee.

"Not exactly." Asher kept his glare on Laney.

"So, who's Harry again?" I didn't understand the issue, so I tried to keep things on the light side.

"Harry is a P.I. A private investigator Asher has—used—from time to time."

"Consulted with," Asher added. "Like I did with William."

"Sort of," Laney scoffed. "Pay structure varied a bit, I'd guess—"

"Come on, Laney," Asher mumbled.

"Just sayin', you two *consulted* a *lot*." Laney shrugged.

"I say call this Harry fellow. I've got questions." It seemed an easy decision.

"It's not that simple, Joss."

"I'm not asking for favors. I'll pay. The going rate plus some—for speed. The sooner we track down Darren, the better—What's wrong? Is this Harry *not* the best? Something untoward I should know? Because if he has a tendency to— I don't know—push boundaries, color outside the lines—well, that could come in handy. I mean, I'm not saying I'd condone busted kneecaps, but a couple of broken fingers...?" I might have been joking, then again... desperate times.

"More like broken hearts." Laney shoveled several teaspoons of sugar into her fresh cup of cream with a splash of coffee.

"All right, Laney Li. Time for you to go." Asher's strained tone sounded like it came from under a hefty weight.

"Make the call. You owe me, but this is the last time I'll come to collect. You have my word." Laney patted his shoulder and headed upstairs with her mug.

Having exhausted all efforts to stay upbeat, I didn't understand the duo's back-and-forth, but I didn't like the feel of it, any of it. Asher's brain obviously ran the calculations, weighing some list of pros and cons, and none of it brought me any solace.

"I'm going to go put on a swimsuit. I need to—burn some—swim. And I can see you're struggling with something. If I can help, I'm here for you. But if this is something you need to deal with on your own, I'll respect that. Then again, you promised me honesty and there has been an emphasis put on trust, so before things go much further in this game of two steps forward, one step back we've been playing, you may need to lay your cards on the table."

Asher huffed. "This from the woman who kicked me out of her bedroom last night with some sudden realization you apparently have no intention of sharing?"

Well, you walked into that propeller, Jocelyn Mae. I set aside my coffee, no longer interested in it. "I'm sorry, Ash."

"No, I'm sorry. You didn't deserve that. I shouldn't have—I don't want to go backward, Joss."

"That was when Gigi stopped sleeping here," I blurted my revelation from the night before.

"What?" Asher cocked his head.

I took his hand, leading him to the comfort of the sofa in the living room. I sat close but kept my eyes on the French doors and the green space beyond them. "Something happened that night. I don't know what. But the next day Gigi was so unlike herself; she threw away my dress, then we fought about going to graduation..." I let it all tumble out of me, the cast decorating, the hurried departure from the graduation ceremony, the unexplained police presence, the hours at the airport, and how, when the summer was over, it was like none of it ever happened. "I never thought of it again. Never went back to Bayborough. Never even thought of Darren Kolchek until I met you."

The more I talked, I couldn't understand why I ever considered hiding it in the first place. Asher stood on my side wanting to help, and would never do anything to hurt my sister, or Laney, or me. He listened without interruption. Held my hand with encouraging squeezes and kind eyes, and when I finished, relief washed over me, and I leaned against him, head resting on his shoulder. A minute went by with nothing but the muffled sounds of a neighboring lawn trimmer and the overhead fan chain clicking on the fixture glass. The next minute added a buzzing in my ears because the relief had subsided, and new angst bubbled up between us. With a hard swallow, I sat up to face the stoic man sharing the sofa, afraid I'd made an error.

"What? What is it?" My brows could go no higher.

Asher bent forward, elbows to knees, and cleared his throat. "I don't—okay, so—It's not a big deal—"

"Jeez, Asher. Out with it." I rushed to stand, my skin prickling with anxiety.

"So, Harry— is short for Harriet."

60

Asher

JOCELYN SPUN ONE-EIGHTY, HER focus moving from the view of the sunny morning to me. I didn't see anger or hurt, merely a questioning gaze, an innocent request for more information. That's when I remembered who was asking—the brilliant yet naive woman with only a wee notion of guile. "*Uh*, she and I—Harry and I used to—"

"Work together. Yes, I heard."

My head wobbled from side to side. "Yeah."

"Research. You said."

"And—sometimes more than that. Surveillance vans, junk food, late nights." I winced, waiting for Jocelyn to *carry the one*.

"Oh. Okay—*Oh*. I see. O-kay." The color rose out of her robe, and she fidgeted with the tied belt. "I see. All right. And was this—*um*, am I allowed to ask questions?"

"Yes, of course. Anything you want to know. Shoot." I leaned into the cushions, bracing for whatever came next.

"When?"

"It's been more than a year since I've seen Harry."

"More than a year? That would make her the last—kiss?"

"No, *you* were the last kiss. And the *next* kiss, if I have my way." My attempt to charm her missed its mark, and I sat up straighter in the failure. "*Uh*, yes. She was the last—"

"The kiss-kiss that wasn't romantic?"

"Wow, Joss. Your semantic recall is impressive, if not—

unfortunate." Frankly, Harry and I had never been *romantic*. We'd been a fun and easy means to a "happy ending" and great night's sleep. At least in my head. Harry's too, right? *Hmm.*

"So, you kiss-kissed this woman over a year ago but in a decidedly *un*-romantic way and yet Laney feels this woman will not only take your call but drop everything when you do—because—why exactly?"

Busy avoiding the Indiana Jones-like boulder barreling at me, I missed the footfalls on the stairs at the front of the house.

"Mom," Gabe bellowed. "I woke up from a dream about rainbow pancakes and I think I'm gonna have to call in a favor." He entered with a groggy stretch and bedhead curls, opening the refrigerator before looking at us. A carton of juice to his mouth, he took a long swig before lowering the container with a grin. "What'd I miss?"

"Asher here is telling me about the last woman he kiss-kissed—"

"Joss, you need to stop saying it like that," Asher interjected.

"Sorry. Asher was telling me about the last woman he *un*romantically kiss-kissed. But he was getting to the good part where we find out why, after more than a year, she will undoubtedly take his call and drop everything when his name shows up on the caller ID."

"Joss—"

"No, Ash. Don't worry, Gabe's cool. Ask Frannie's boyfriend. Or Will. Because monogamy is passé."

"On second thought, forget the pancakes. I'm good. It's practically lunchtime. Maybe I'll call Dad. Meet him at The Funky Brunch. Asher." Gabe gave me a nod and backed out of the kitchen in a hasty exit, taking the juice with him.

Jocelyn waited until Gabe was gone. "This is silly."

"I agree. Obviously, I won't call her."

"Yes, you will."

"No. It's—it's not worth it, Jocelyn."

"It's not worth Gigi and Laney?"

"It's not worth you—losing you."

"*Aww.* Losing me? Asher, you haven't *had* me. Remember? Can't lose what you— never mind, nothing is more important than Gi—"

I raised my hand to stop Jocelyn from telling me what I already knew. Genevieve was priority one. Next, came a rash move. I didn't think it through. Didn't have a plan but pulled my phone from my shorts and dialed. Jocelyn cinched up the belt on her robe like her work here was done, but I took a gentle hold of her arm before she left the room. Let's not forget she insisted I call. I did it for her.

"Harry...it is... Wasn't sure you'd answer this early in the day—or at all. I know how you like to keep late nights...Yes, I remember... *Ha.*" My stomach lurched as Jocelyn pulled away, but I held tighter. "Nice to know I'm still in good standing... yeah, it has been a minute... what's new? Well, I could use a good P.I.... Sorry, I could use the *best* P.I....Oh, I figured business first...Well, if you're really asking—?... I know, I know, you never were one for the small talk... that's why I—...Okay, truth is, I met this woman and, well, she's amazing." I released my grip on Jocelyn. "Makes me a little squirrely, but—in a good way, you know?..." My pulse sped up. "Serious? As a heart attack, Harry... No, I'm the lucky one, but nice of you to say."

Jocelyn's head rolled back, brown eyes to the ceiling fan, but I kept my eyes on her. She shook her head, then met my gaze, mouthing the words, "I'm sorry," and stepped in to rest her head on my chest.

"Hey, Harry, can you hold on for a sec?... You know me, can't walk and chew gum... Just a sec." I hit the mute and lifted Jocelyn's chin. "We good?"

She nodded.

"Why don't you go take that swim?"

She hung her head again. "Why are you putting up with me?" She held my hand but only had eyes for the floor.

"Wow, Jocelyn Durand, for such a bright woman, you sure can be obtuse. Use that wildly creative mind of yours."

"While I appreciate the critique sandwich, that's not exactly an answer, Asher Cray."

"Let's just say I've got this feeling you're worth it." I winked. "Now go get changed to swim. I'm setting up a meeting with the best P.I. I know, and you should be there."

Jocelyn swallowed a mini-gasp and looked at me askance.

"You should be there," I repeated with a confident smile. She nodded, kissed my cheek, and headed upstairs to change for her workout.

"Harry, sorry. When can you squeeze me, uh, *us*, in?"

As one might expect, much of Harriet Smith's work took place *after-hours*. Yes, her birth name was Harriet Smith. Growing up, she went by the perhaps more feminine nickname of Hattie, but in the P.I. game, a name like Harry Smith got far more calls than Hattie Smith, and when a woman answered the phone, most potential clients made the assumption she was the front office person. When faced with stellar results, few clients cared about the investigator's gender. Results speak volumes and Harry delivered.

Harry kept a pretty full calendar in the nighttime and reserved daylight for sleep and the criminology classes she taught at a local university. But considering our case dated back thirty years, the hour was inconsequential. I promised Harry a good payday, so she was eager to get to work. Despite Laney's perverse supposition, my compensation structure for Harry Smith *was* like that of William Atwater, better even. And no, I'm not blowing my own horn. Business is business and thought we hadn't seen each other in a long time— well, Harry and I would be *strictly* business forevermore as far as I was concerned.

"Where'd she go?" Gabe returned from his self-imposed ousting.

I was rereading the old news articles about Darren Kolchek after sending them to Harry with a list of thoughts, questions, and details I thought might be pertinent, but closed my laptop when Gabe approached. "She's in the pool."

"Probably best. She can take it out on the water, not the innocent bystander—or you."

"Your mom and I are fine, Gabe." I don't think Gabe needed or wanted reassurances from me, but I felt the need to give them. More was going on than he knew, and his exclusion— whether I agreed— didn't fall under my purview.

"That's cool, Ash. I'm just happy to see her care. It's been a while and never like this. This is different, so—I'm probably telling you more than you should know. Then again, I'm not a big fan of leaving people out of the loop in important matters." Evidently, Gabriel Atwater had the familial talent of saying one thing while making me hear something else. But as I said, his being shut out wasn't my call.

I gave the kid a steady stare for a beat, hoping he would pick up on my sympathetic agreement. "You catch up with your dad?"

"Yeah. Dad's more flighty than usual, if that's possible. We planned this great overnight out on the water. I rented a boat for us, but then he took off on it *without* me. Left before I even got there. Something about needing time alone out on the open sea in total darkness. One with the universe or some such. I'm guessing you're to blame." He smirked. Gabe's willingness to share had its pros and cons, but I opted to appreciate his candor like I did his mother's.

"Not sure I really care, Gabe. About your dad, I mean. Your mom, on the other hand—"

"Good for you, Asher," Gabe jumped in. "I wouldn't want it any other way."

"Glad to hear it, because I *do* care what you think."

"Ash, you had me at *discombobulating*," he chuckled with a heartening nod but then turned solemn. "And I hope whatever is going on here, whatever this weirdness hanging—whatever it is, I hope you've got a handle on it. I'm not an idiot, but I am in the dark. Plus, I've got a research team to meet in North Carolina. I'm only going because I trust you're—"

"I've got it, Gabe, and your mom. Promise." I stood, positioned myself face to face with the young man, and extended my hand, hoping he detected more confidence than I really possessed.

He took it with a firm grasp and a set jaw, but his eyes betrayed some fear. With a brief squeeze and a lifted chin, I telegraphed my guarantee, and I watched the kid breathe relief and give his thanks without uttering another word.

He pointed to the backyard. "I'm gonna say a quick goodbye to my mother the mermaid before I meet Dad. Maybe we'll get a night out on the water after all. I'll give him your regards." His chuckle returned.

"Be sure you do." With an encouraging thump on Gabe's shoulder, I watched him trot to the French doors and out to see Jocelyn. My phone pinged a text from Harry. She works fast.

Harry: A quick search brought up a discrepancy from the few details of your version of events. See the attached police report. Note the driver. Significant? Interview stuff will take longer, but I'm on it the rest of the day. Macallan

12 still works but bring the 15 if you're joining me. Screw it. Make it the 18.

61

Jocelyn

I STAYED IN THE pool for longer than usual. Typically, the minutes fly by during a swim. There is no mandatory distance or time. It's me and the stroke, all I need to allow my brain to work through an issue, but it's my body that tells me when the session ends. I took slow laps; afraid my limbs would wear out before I could solve all the world's problems. Avoiding anyone and everyone was an added perk. Of course, I spoke to Gabe when he came to say goodbye, assuring him I was all right, and wished him a pleasant late lunch with Will.

"And maybe lighten up on Asher. Everyone's got a past, Mom. And his past brought him to you. So, in a way, you kinda owe that woman your thanks, right?"

Forearms on the pool's edge, I squinted into the sun, peering up at the astute young man standing above me. Where the kid's wisdom came from, I couldn't guess, but I beamed pride to know he was mine. "Thank you, Gabe."

When Gabe left to meet his dad, I continued with my leisurely back-and-forth in an effort to organize my thoughts, what I knew, what I *thought* I knew. The worst was the realization that yet another person I loved and trusted with my life had thrust another decades-long lie upon me. How could I believe or love another? And what did that mean for my future?

"You had no right, no place, no *business* getting involved in this, Laney. Why? At the very least, you should have asked me first, *talked* to me. I'm your wife." Gigi had reemerged after her dawn disappearing act, her rasp further strained with sorrow.

Wrapped in a swim towel, I intruded on Gigi and Laney mid-quarrel. Asher found himself stuck between the two women, part referee, part interloper, one hundred percent ill-at-ease. Tensions in the room seethed, fists clenched, arms crossed tightly, and no one looked at each other until I entered. Asher's face begged me for escape.

"Talk to you? Because this is something you've been *dying* to open up about since—forever? Jesus H. Christ, Genevieve. If you only knew what the mere *mention* of this place does to your face. I'd burn it to the ground to never have you feel that—that pain or fear or sadness, whatever tortures you from the inside. Do you have any idea how it feels to *not* be able to fix it, relieve you of whatever that thing is? To ease your suffering?"

The desperation in Laney's voice and the grief on the faces of both women tore at my heart, but Laney continued like no one else could hear.

"I have never failed at anything except this. The one person I would give everything to be content, free from burden, and I can't do the job. And it's a failure I stare in the face every single day, because, at the same time, it is the *only* face I want to see every single day."

My sister's reticence to share could only be to protect someone else from what she deemed a more dangerous secret—a threat so devastating it was worth sacrificing her own well-being and her marriage. Only one person fit that description. One person she would protect with such vehemence and for so long.

I shivered in my dripping state. The central air bombarded me and my damp towel did more harm than good. "Gigi?"

Like an injured animal, Gigi's eyes pleaded to be freed from her agony.

"It's okay, Gigi. You can tell her. I know you've kept the secret to protect me, and I love you so much for that, but it's time now. You've carried the burden long enough. We can't keep going like this. I should have made you stop a long time ago."

A mix of fear and confusion pulled from my sister's face, contorting it in a way I had never seen. The tall, strong woman who had been my constant from my earliest memory crumbled in front of me. Asher caught her, easing her onto a stool at the kitchen island. She wrapped her arms around one of his, but then quickly released him with a non-verbal apology. Laney took his place as Gigi's support while Asher walked to me, dread in his stare.

"Maybe we should give them some privacy, Asher." I gestured to the front hall.

His earlier look for a way out disappeared. Clearly, he was eager for some clarity, too. "I'll go get dressed and we can go meet your—friend and see what— Harry knows."

"What?" All three of them looked bewildered.

"Jojo? What *Harry* knows? How would Harry—? You still don't— Good lord, Jo." Gigi stood. A new emotion billowed out of her, like anger, but it included a wholly unfamiliar addition. Tears. The sight of it wrecked me. She took off upstairs, followed by a shocked Laney, whose pleading eyes wanted an explanation from me I couldn't give her. Laney disappeared to the front hall and up the stairs.

Another shiver hit me as I examined my pruned toes. Evidently, my scheme to get Gigi to tell all failed. Lying simply wasn't my strong suit.

"Jocelyn, what are you doing?" Asher whispered.

"I'm going to shower and dress. I'm freezing. Excuse me."

62

Asher

STILL IN THE PROVERBIAL dark, I didn't know how to protect Jocelyn, especially when she acted as her own worst enemy. I paced, waiting for her return from getting dressed but wasn't sure she wouldn't avoid further confrontation. Obviously, we were all in the dark except for Genevieve, the one desperate not to enlighten any of us.

Footfalls on the stairs finally signaled someone's approach.

"I'm trying to relieve my sister of whatever burden she's bearing. It's what a good sister does." Jocelyn entered the kitchen, speaking like our conversation, more than an hour ago, never ended.

"Joss, you don't even know what that burden is. You don't even know what—"

"I know whatever it is has to do with me. I know she wouldn't put herself through this, even her wife through this, for anyone *but* me, and if giving her permission to clear her conscience saves her from whatever prison she has locked herself in, then so be it."

"Even if it puts you in a *real* prison? Why are you so damn desperate to take the fall?" My powerlessness triggered anger that spat out like venom. "I'm sorry. I didn't mean to shout."

She shook her head with her focus on her fingers, then inched to where I stood. With an inquiring squint she asked, "Why are you so desperate to believe I did something wrong?"

"*No*, I'm not, I'm—"

"You're afraid I did. Somewhere in there, you're afraid I hurt that boy." She placed her palm on the side of my head. "You think I'm capable of something horrible—"

"We're all capable of doing horrible things." My volume climbed again with fear and frustration at Jocelyn's inability to see the danger of the situation. "All of us and in a perfect storm—even you. And it was a perfect storm, Jocelyn. A *goddamn* perfect storm."

"What does that mean?"

"Jesus, Jocelyn, you were hurting. You were tired, and you had taken a narcotic. Too much of it. He caused you more physical pain, and let's not forget your grief. You were mourning the loss—"

"I wasn't," she interrupted with a forceful bark.

Jocelyn's broadcasting eyes aired her inner conflict, and her lip found its way between her teeth. Sadness showed but something more too. Embarrassment or maybe shame filtered through the strained guise.

"You weren't feeling those things? You made it up? You lied to me about what happened?"

"No, Asher. I told you everything I remember, exactly as I recalled it. I promise." She took my hand.

"Then what—"

"I wasn't— grieving. I had never felt so—good, aside from the physical pain. I was relieved. Free. My parents were dead, and I was *relieved*. God, I *am*— a monster."

"No, you were—" I pulled her to me, but she stood rigid. I couldn't coax her into her just-right spot. "You were a kid who witnessed awful things, and those awful things weren't going to happen anymore. It was completely natural for you to feel—relief."

Her stiff stance eased some, her body softened into mine.

"Asher, I didn't hurt Darren. I'm certain I remember it correctly and it was just as I said."

"How are you so sure? I believe you, but..."

"Because I don't remember the car accident and it feels different."

"I imagine forgetting a car wreck is normal, right?"

"It can be. If there's brain damage. But then there's dissociative amnesia. Forgetting due to trauma." Jocelyn explained it like it had nothing to do with her. Clinical, as if she'd done the research, but somehow didn't believe it pertained to her situation. "They said—the doctors—that mine would probably be temporary. A car accident, one *without* brain injury, shouldn't mean permanent memory loss. I've studied it. It's possible, if something horrific happened, it might take longer, or even never reverse, but that doesn't fit my case. Still, I don't remember anything. Why we were in the car, where we were going. Where we were traveling from or anything leading up to that car ride. Nothing. It's blank, not a flicker. Only waking up in the hospital, days later with Gigi at my side. And even that part is hazy."

"Four days," Genevieve's low hoarseness growled out in a whisper. She cleared her throat. Jocelyn let go of me to see her sister, red-faced from crying.

Jocelyn gasped at the sight.

"We need to talk, Jojo."

"No holding back, Gigi. No more protecting me. I want to know everything, and I want Asher to know it too, and Laney."

Genevieve looked back at the stairs. "Laney knows now."

Jocelyn looked to me before taking my hand to move to a sofa in the living room. I couldn't help but remember Jocelyn confiding that Durand women don't cry. *A shame, really. I imagine a lot gets* freed *with a good cry... I suppose the trouble with that is— a* lot *gets* freed *with a good cry.*

I couldn't keep my mouth shut. "Why four days? Why did they keep her sedated for four days?" I asked the questions, but Genevieve rightfully directed the answers at Jocelyn.

"They tried to bring you around— a few times, but you were terribly agitated, and they couldn't keep your arm stable. It was to save your limb, really."

"And the memory?"

"We assumed it was from sedation. Days kept intubated can do that, but it would come back, eventually. But it never did. The slate wiped clean. An amnesia of sorts." Genevieve retold the tale with a distance, a faraway look, and a gruff narrator's tone with a fairy tale cadence that made me think of Frannie. The story was only going to get darker.

"Yes. Dissociative, but that's normally due to extreme trauma. It doesn't fit."

"It doesn't?" Genevieve asked like she thought otherwise, but Jocelyn wasn't listening.

"And how do you know my memory never came back?" Jocelyn asked slowly, like she hoped to discover the answer on her own before she finished asking it.

Genevieve huffed out an airy laugh. "*Ha*. Because we would have talked about it."

"Why? I don't remember you ever asking me about it. Not that I could have told you. But since you weren't there until afterward, I assumed you didn't want to know."

"I wished I could forget. For a time, I stewed in jealousy of your ignorance."

"But you weren't—How would you—oh my God, Gigi? Were you—? Gi—gi." The color drained from Jocelyn's face. She held my hand but released it to take Genevieve's. It wasn't until she let go that I realized how cold she'd gone. But all I could do was sit and watch her world collapse under the weight of decades-old nightmares creeping back to plague the present. Another round of pain on the road to her salvation? Or were we perpetuating the lie that all this would be worth it?

Jocelyn bolted from her seat. Genevieve gasped and clenched her fists, burying her eyes. More tears streaked down her mottled face. She didn't want this any more than I did, and yet here we were goading it to happen.

"You came home. A surprise. You'd traveled some because you had already gotten your acceptance to Yale Law, but you came back. It was supper time, *his* supper time. But she was so excited to see you. Where had I been?"

At that moment, I thought Jocelyn was merely thinking aloud, but Genevieve answered. "At the library, working on your final English paper."

Jocelyn gasped again. I didn't want Genevieve filling in the holes. Too fast and Jocelyn couldn't prepare herself. My silent plea to Genevieve begged her to let her sister go slowly. Jocelyn always wanted to go slowly.

"Yes. By then, we knew to get home to help for mealtime. We never knew what kind of day it might have been, so getting home to help get dinner on the table mitigated the— unpleasantness any kind of delay caused." Jocelyn's vacant eyes stared at nothing in particular while sharing the matter-of-fact detail of daily life in the Durand home while my stomach churned at her use of the word *unpleasantness*. An understatement if ever there was one. "It was wonderful to see you, but I also wanted to get my paper done, not that it was due, but I wanted to finish, and you said—"

"I told you to go write. I would take supper duty." Genevieve filled another blank, and I swallowed back my desire to call a timeout.

"Oh, Gigi. I shouldn't have—If I had just—"

"No, Jojo," Genevieve growled out the emphatic dismissal.

"Not your fault. It was never our fault. Not when you were four, or six, or seventeen, or any time in between. The Monsters did what monsters do and none of it had to do with us."

"Except you—" Jocelyn's fingers smoothed the hair around her sister's face and sweetly caressed her cheek.

"Not my fault either," Genevieve interrupted Jocelyn again. "We can't help who we look like, and I looked too much like her, I guess. But he came home slamming the door. Before he even saw me, the Monster was prowling. It was one of those days."

"The door slammed," Jocelyn whispered the memory and grew paler still, corpse-like.

I stood to end the rehashing of this episode of the Durand Family Horror Show. I'd had enough and Jocelyn didn't look as though she could take much more.

"Why, Gigi?"

"Who knows, Jo? It didn't matter. But I was out of practice, missed a signal, or something— because it happened so fast, she hit the floor— so fast. And then—"

"Stop, Genevieve," I insisted. "Let's just take a minute."

"No," Jocelyn interrupted. "We didn't have a minute. That was my mistake. I hesitated, so by the time I got downstairs, you were— Gigi—you were on the floor, too." Jocelyn pressed her fingers into her brow with a quiet groan that morphed into a strangled cry. "*You* said it. They were *your* words. Your *voice*."

"What words?" The question flew from my mouth. I hadn't meant to ask.

"I'm not—fragile. You can't— break me," Jocelyn stammered out her sister's words. Words she'd apparently said thirty years ago.

"Oh my God," I muttered.

"And he laughed—he laughed, Gigi. He laughed as he grabbed you. He grabbed you by the—he had you by the throat—against the wall. You turned purple, and he squeezed." Jocelyn's next guttural sob began low but grew out of her as she pushed on her eyes, trying to make the image cease. Or maybe she wanted to see it more clearly. But her awful wail came to an abrupt stop. She relaxed her hands, fingers trembled in her lap. "Then you were on the floor— and she was on the floor— and *he* was on the floor."

"You saved my life, Jojo." Genevieve touched her own throat. "You saved me, and I was lucky. Any longer, and I never would have spoken again. Even if I'd lived, I'd have never been able to talk again."

"Your voice is because of—?" The new information gored my gut. I cringed. Genevieve Durand and I had worked together for more than twenty years and I didn't know her husky rasp had been caused by injury. I'm not sure anyone did. "Jocelyn? How did you get him to let go?"

"She—" Genevieve started, but Jocelyn took over.

"I hit him. Took his legs right out from under him. The wrought-iron fireplace poker." That vacant look returned, her hands blotched in red and white still quivered.

"She snapped his tibia in half with the force of the blow. Never said a word. She helped me to my feet, smiled even, and placed the poker back on its stand. She sat on the sofa. A zombie, not really there. Do you remember—"

"We were in the car. Just me and the Monsters," Jocelyn recounted this part of the event with a remote tone. More memory clawed its way from Jocelyn's decades of fog.

"Yes. We got him in the front seat and you in the back behind Mom. She said I should go like I had never been there, and you and she would take him to the hospital. We didn't even know she could drive. She never had. Well, I guess she couldn't really because..."

"We didn't make it. They didn't make it." Jocelyn caught my eye, sending me a message I couldn't read. The sadness seeped but also a recognition of something. A new memory? She had more to say but couldn't or wouldn't, at least not yet, and she wordlessly asked for my help.

63

Jocelyn

DETAILS OF THE WRECK returned to me. Not the immediate aftermath. I still had no memory of that, but the run-up to it played back for me as clearly as the incident with Gigi and the fireplace poker. Specifics only I knew, because no one else lived to tell the tale. Some stories shouldn't ever be told. Frannie was right and I'd learned that lesson the hard way, some twenty years ago with my book, on a very public stage. I had no plans to make that mistake again, but I still wasn't any closer to knowing about Darren Kolchek, and I *needed* to know.

"I'm tired, Gigi, and I know you are too, but I need to know what happened on prom night. I mean—" I looked to Asher, "what you think happened. Because I—"

Asher stepped in to relieve me. "She went over every detail with me. She has a very clear recollection of that night, and it's why she's so sure she had nothing to do with it. Am I saying that right, Joss?"

I nodded.

"That was the difference. Jocelyn eventually remembered prom night, but not the circumstances of the car wreck, but the *not* remembering felt different to her."

Distracted by the revelations of the first incident, I was thankful to have Asher take the helm for the next part. He walked Gigi through the series of events up to and including my going inside to get water for Darren, taking the second pain pill, and returning to the patio to find Darren gone. He left out the kiss.

"You looked everywhere for him? Called for him?" Gigi asked the questions, drawing me back from the horrifying loop running through my brain.

"It was so dark, Gigi. And I didn't want to wake you, but I walked out to the patio and—"

"The patio? That's it? You didn't cross the yard?"

"No. I'd have seen him from the patio. He was gone. And I was aching and exhausted and—loopy. I didn't stay awake for much longer. Remember, I never even got out of my dress?"

Gigi shook her head with a new burst of energy. She got to her feet at an agitated pace. "Yes, the dress with *blood* on it, Jojo. And down your cast. A streak of—"

"Mud, wasn't it mud?"

"No, it was dried blood, Jo. How did he bleed on you if you didn't—"

Asher jogged to his computer. The screen came to life with pictures of news clippings. He scrolled and flipped from window to window. "Here." Asher quoted an article. "*One male thought he saw blood, but admitted that in the dark, no one knew for sure.*"

"What are these?" I watched the words and pictures of decades-old newspapers blip by back-and-forth as he looked for more information.

"News reports from the days and weeks that followed."

"And you didn't think I should see them?" I tried to navigate how in-the-dark I had been all these years.

"I—I didn't—" Asher tried to reply, but Gigi bulldozed over him.

"So, he was bleeding *before* you saw him?"

"I don't know."

"But the blood was on you, Jojo. How?"

I sighed and retold the kiss and Darren's silliness and how he'd aggravated my already throbbing arm. "And I pushed him off my lap and he slurred an apology sort of and asked for water. He seemed sleepy too. So, when I came out with the water and he was gone, I assumed he had left. And I fell asleep."

Gigi's pacing grew more animated. "So, say he was bleeding from some other incident. He could have been seriously injured. A bleeding head wound? And he was acting weird but not drunk? And he passed out on you, and his head ran down your arm and landed in your lap? Good lord." The cross-examination lacked any opportunity for answers. Classic *Law and Order* Genevieve.

"That all fits the newspaper narrative. If Darren got into a fight somewhere. Breaking it off with Anne Bismarck? An accident where he fell? Or got pushed?" Asher eagerly followed this theory and Gigi's movements around the room from his seat next to me. "So, she didn't do anything, see?" He grabbed my hand for an encouraging squeeze. "Jocelyn didn't do anything."

Gigi hadn't settled down. In fact, she escalated more flustered and red-faced.

"What's wrong, Gi? Why are you acting like this is bad news?"

"I—You have to know I—It had only been a couple of weeks since the other—incident. And you weren't talking about it. You didn't ask questions. Played along when we told people I had laryngitis and wore constant silk scarves of Mom's like some sort of creepy tribute to her, until my bruises healed."

"I don't understand, Gigi."

"I didn't either, but it was like you were there but *not* there. When you saved Mom and me, in that moment, you didn't speak or yell or blink even. You lashed out with such fury and with the strength of a man twice Asher's size. It was not— human, but at the same time, calculated, precise without hesitation. Your expression lacked any emotion. It was the most terrifying thing I'd ever seen, and it was my baby sister, except it wasn't. And I thought—I thought it had happened again, that it—"

"That it got out. Again," Asher whispered.

The two women asked, "Huh?" in stereo.

I looked at them and their wide eyes.

"Nothing. It's nothing." Asher brushed off my question to focus on Gigi. "But it didn't, Genevieve. It didn't. It was a one-time thing to save you. The one person who had always looked out for her. It—*she* saved you and it never—got out—it never happened again. So, we're in the clear, it's all right."

"No. No, it's not all right because, I thought it had so I—" Gigi pulled at her hair, frantic. "I had to protect her—like she protected me. I had to. You understand, don't you?"

"I do, Gigi. I understand you have always protected me. But this time, you had nothing to defend."

"I didn't know. I thought something happened and you—it—happened again and—"

"But it didn't. I promise. I didn't."

"I know. I know it *now* but—"

"But what, Genevieve?" Asher's harsh exasperation pushed Gigi to erupt.

"He was in the pool. Darren was at the bottom of the goddamn pool," Gigi belched out another long-held secret in an airy, hoarse scream.

64

Asher

AFTER ALL MY MISGIVINGS about Genevieve, now I stood in awe of her. She did what only an extraordinary sister would do—pull Darren from the water, strip him of his things, grab a shovel from the barn, and start digging. All night. She dug so deep no one would find him.

With Genevieve and Laney tucked away upstairs again, Jocelyn and I sat in the living room. The truth hung heavy in the quiet, accompanied by the hiss of the sprinkler sputtering to a start as the metal heads popped out of the ground, ready to get to work. It signaled early evening, the precursor to the magic hour, but I wasn't sure the magic hour would ever be the same. Looking out over the lush yard with the knowledge it also held a body, the final resting place of a boy Jocelyn Durand was the last to see alive, changed the magic. No wonder Genevieve abhorred this place.

Knowing what happened, how and why, didn't help much. At least the worst-case didn't apply. Jocelyn did nothing wrong. A rabbit hole of research for a novel I wrote years ago also taught me if Darren was at the bottom of the pool, as Genevieve said, he was dead before he hit the water. Dead bodies sink, initially. Drowning victims stay afloat longer. There was nothing anyone could have done to save the boy, certainly not a one-armed teenaged girl in the middle of the night. If anyone raised that question, I could share some insight. Still, I had other questions itching my brain and while I could avoid it in the short-term, eventually I would need to scratch.

Genevieve's hill might be a steeper climb, and while all of that weighed us down, something else had occurred to Jocelyn. I read those expressive eyes, and she knew something more, something she hadn't remembered until this evening, and it pained her.

"Can I get you anything? A drink? Food? A place to lay your head?" Physically and mentally exhausted, I couldn't imagine Jocelyn's state.

She curled up next to me, nestled into her spot, and in an instant, I relaxed. The empty spots were full again. Her freshly washed hair intoxicated me, and I could have fallen asleep where we sat until her breathing changed. The night of revelations hadn't ended.

"You can tell me. You don't have to, but you can, you can tell me anything," I whispered the reminder into the top of her head.

It didn't feel like laughter would be on the night's agenda, but she snorted the start of something close. "How'd you know?" She tilted her head, but I held tighter. "Maybe I'll take that drink."

"What'll you have?" I twisted out from under her, but she grabbed my shirt and kissed my mouth in a heated way that said the answer was *me*. And just like the troublemaker he has always been, my inquisitive brow asked questions when he should have kept still and played along.

"Sorry." She let me go, smoothing the rumpled shirt she caused. "Scotch, neat."

"No need to apologize. One Scotch, neat, coming up."

"Just one? You won't join me? Don't make a girl drink alone."

I returned with two short pours, and as I suspected, hers was gone before I sat. I offered her mine, and she took it. It was shaping up to be a difficult evening, and I didn't know the half of it.

"Maybe you should tell me. You know—save your mouth from anymore Scotch."

"There is plenty I could do with my mouth that doesn't

involve—" Jocelyn kissed me again and the Scotch and her smell blended in the heady way they did.

I nudged her away. "Talk to me. What did you remember?"

She wiggled her head and handed me her—my— empty glass with a look that said, "more." I rose and poured her another, waiting for her to continue.

"She drove. I don't know if I told anyone different. I don't remember being asked, but if someone did, I would have said *he* drove. Not to lie, but because he *always* drove, it never would have occurred to me it would be anyone but him at the wheel. But it wasn't. I know that now." Thankfully, she nursed her third drink.

"I know. I've seen the police report. They knew Juliette drove. I'd made the assumption he drove, too, but not because you said so. You never said—to me, anyway. But the police report made it clear. And I saw no notation that anyone had questioned you about it, that you told them wrong. Nothing in the paperwork. I don't think you need to worry about that part anymore." I thought I would feel some relief with her disclosure. Her realization was of no consequence unless she had more to share. I braced myself.

She took a ragged breath in and blew it out, trying to keep a steady stream. She had to be feeling the heat of the booze as she drank too much, too fast. "I remember it now. We headed to the hospital."

"You weren't, though." I caught myself. I shouldn't have interrupted, corrected her version of events.

"*Hm?*"

"Sorry. Go on." I took the lowball glass she handed me and hesitated when she elbowed me for another round. "I don't think you should—"

"Asher. Please." Against my better judgment, I obeyed while she kept talking. "He came to."

"What?"

"He woke up." She paused, waiting for her glass. "The pain must have been—excruciating. He bled, but not a lot. More from his head than his leg. Maybe he hit the mantel on his way down. The bone tore right through his shin flesh, though." She described gruesome injury with an odd fascination and a faraway look, then sipped again. "He lunged for me in the backseat, but he couldn't reach. *God,* the rage. He shrieked, *'I'll kill you.'*" She almost laughed again, but instead took another swallow. Too far gone now, it didn't matter how much she drank. Not really. She wouldn't be awake long and how could I deny her anesthesia. "That's when she turned to the industrial park."

"You remembered that, huh?"

Again, her account matched the official report.

She churned the amber liquor in her glass. "Did you know swirling the Scotch makes it harsher, burn more?"

"I did. Laney is quite the mentor."

"Isn't she?" Jocelyn finally relaxed back into me, quiet but watching the liquid eddy.

"I wonder if someone found swirling her drink is trying to punish herself. Make it hurt more going down." She stopped when I put my hand on hers to hold the glass still.

"I'm careful only to do it when on the rocks, to weaken it. Water it down." I admitted, wanting to keep the conversation going.

"Takes a real man to admit he prefers a weak drink, Asher Cray."

I chuckled, "It takes a real man to do many things, Jocelyn Durand." I kissed her cheek, not intending to rile the intoxicated woman in my lap. Bad call. She squirmed around and pounced. A difficult evening, indeed.

"God, you're a good kisser," she gasped the words when she came up for air then emptied the glass with a blistering swallow.

"Well, like I said on our first date, it's really a team sport. And you more than hold up your end, but we have to stop now."

She looked around the room and nodded as if she understood. Rolling off my lap, she flailed a moment, then found her spot nestled next to me. I took her empty glass before it found the floor. Nothing but the passing out to do now. Or not...

"He didn't wear a seatbelt." Jocelyn didn't slur her words, but I had little doubt she was drunk. The delivery, not the content, gave her away. A giddiness rippled through it at the same time her speech slowed. "Neither did she," she added. "Well, not in the end."

These details appeared in the report as well. Juliette hit the windshield, and the impact ejected Hugo because neither wore seatbelts. They crashed into the center pier of an overpass in a front-end collision after rounding a curve.

I held Jocelyn, gently rocking, keeping my voice low in the hopes I could lull her to sleep. "You were lucky. You wore a seatbelt, and the vehicle struck head-on. The arm fracture resulted from what the report called *human collision*. Your left side hit the door, your upper arm meeting the steel frame under the window. Under the circumstances, you sat in the best position possible."

I misconstrued the noise at first. She covered it with a cough but relented and let the laugh go before blurting, "Never knew the woman to be such a planner." She snorted another drunken guffaw.

My stomach lurched. "What are you saying, Jocelyn?"

"I'm *say-ing*— I *never* sat on that side of the car. It was Genevieve's side. I'm *saying* she told me where to sit and to be sure to latch my seatbelt. I'm saying she *unbuckled her* seatbelt," Jocelyn over-enunciated each word. "And while the car sped up, as she pressed the accelerator to the floor and the engine revved louder, she said she loved Gigi and me and then yelled, *'brace yourself, Jocelyn!'* The last thing I saw was concrete... *Ta-daah*."

"Jesus Christ." I hadn't imagined any of the grenades that went

318   KELLY ELIZABETH HUSTON

off that afternoon, but this third one hit hardest.

"Of course, now I'm left with this truth bomb, this fresh reminder of the horrific reality of how desperate the woman must have been. The woman I have spent my life hating for staying. I hated her for making us stay. And her solution? Her solution was—*that*? *Too much* and too late. And yet—"

Crashing the car was quite the calculated risk for a mother to take with her daughter's life at stake. Then again, she would have known her daughter's life was in jeopardy, no matter the circumstances in the car. And the trauma caused by the accident covered the injury Jocelyn had inflicted on her father. The remote section of roadway in a recently shuttered industrial park saw little traffic, so some time passed before emergency responders arrived, though no indication in the report how long. And with a single-car accident, little investigation took place. Harry had gotten her hands on pictures if I wanted to see, but Juliette Durand had concocted a brilliant plan.

Jocelyn drew me from my mental reading of the police report with a head jerk. She pressed into me. Her breath warmed my neck before I understood her intention. Ducking her cunning assault on my weak spot with a bit of an inappropriate laugh of my own, I allowed her lips to land on mine rather than the hollow of my throat.

"Jocelyn," I spoke through her continued blitz. "You should go to bed."

"Yes, we should," she agreed and amped up her charge. "Please."

"No, Joss. You're drunk."

"I know I'm drunk. I want to forget again. And I thought alcohol would do the job, but it hasn't, so now I'm asking you. Please. Please take me upstairs and make me forget." She stared me down with the plea and placed the most tender kiss on my lips before I grabbed her by the hair the way she liked. Sighing a *yes*, her mouth landed on mine, and I picked her up to carry her to her bedroom. I navigated the stairs in the dark with remarkable skill and carefully closed her door before placing her on the bed.

She scrambled to her knees, weaving with her eagerness to undo my dress shirt. "There's no rush, right?"

I shook my head and gave her access to my vulnerable spot while she made slow work of my buttons. Almost out of the oxford, a thought hit me. "Wait." I pulled from her, dizzy with lust and the booze that had us spiraling out of control.

"What's wrong?" She pulled my shirttail.

"Do we—do we need, uh—protect—"

"No." But she bit her lip.

"Jocelyn?"

"Don't overthink," she sighed the words like they were for *her*, not me. She hesitated.

Momentum slowed, doubt crept in and I wavered.

The streetlamp light slipped through the plantation shutters, striping lines on the bed linens and across her body. She wore a sleeveless cotton dress with a rounded collar, and buttons that ran the front of the knee-length shift. Innocence personified. With the first two buttons undone, she reached for number three to begin the reveal. By button number six, I realized the small size and large number of round plastic stitched disks staring back at me and I may have cursed some unsuspecting clothing designer. The karma was quick and came by way of—you guessed it—a knock at the door.

"No," Jocelyn whispered and pulled at my neck to kiss me. "Ignore it," she hissed and pulled my undone shirt from my arms.

I grabbed her by the waist, willing to comply when another knock sounded, and Genevieve's low tone came through the crack of the door, desperate for her sister.

"Wait, Asher," Jocelyn gasped.

I released her, already able to see the scene's end. I knew the score.

"What, Gigi?" She called to her sister.

"Can I—can I sleep with you?"

"*Uh*—"

"Please, Jojo. Just for tonight?"

"Hold on. I mean, yes, of course, Gi. Just— hold on."

I bent to pick up my discarded button-down, hurrying to re-button it while Jocelyn did the same with her dress.

"Asher, I'm—"

"Yep." I avoided her reach this time.

"She's my sister."

"Yep."

"It's been a rough day."

"Yep." I let my shirttail hang. "Will you tell her? About the wreck?"

"I don't know."

"You should tell her. Enough secrets. Tell her the truth."

"I'm not sure. I don't think she needs to know. What good—"

I moved on to other matters, distracted by my impending next steps, wondering if I could manage the fallout. "I assume I can use the door. I don't need to haul ass out the window, do I?"

"The door's fine."

If I'd been paying attention, I'd have heard the miserable hurt in her reply.

"Right, night then."

"That's it? '*Night then?*'"

I swiveled back for a rushed kiss to her cheek. "See you tomorrow." Shoes in hand, I opened the door to a wide-eyed Genevieve clutching her bathrobe at her chest.

"Asher."

"Counselor." I nodded.

"Sorry, I didn't—"

"Nope. I've been *dismissed*. She's all yours." I landed on the first floor before I knew it. Tossing my phone on the island, I slipped into my shoes and tucked in my shirt before typing my text.

Asher: Same spot? I'll bring the bottle.

Harry: Yes. And Yes!

I chuckled. Harry always was enthusiastic.

"Going somewhere?" Laney lurked in the dark again.

"Yep." I played off my minor heart attack.

"Should I ask?"

"Not gonna start lying now. I've got an expensive bottle of Scotch to buy and a P.I. to meet. Don't wait up."

"I tried to warn you. Nothing is getting between those sisters, Ash. There's nothing to be done about it."

"Oh, I know one thing I can do."

"Asher. Don't do this. You don't want to do this."

"You were the one who made me call her in the first place. Remember that, Laney Li. This can of worms belongs to you."

I grabbed the keys to the stupid car I thanked heaven I had and exited the side door. At this time of night, I'd be in an apartment in Queens with good company in less than two hours, drunk in two and a half.

65

Jocelyn

GIGI DIDN'T MOVE IN the night. She latched onto me and never let go. It seemed unnatural how fast I sobered up, but when I heard the popping of pea gravel made by a car leaving the property, I knew Asher had left, and it defogged my drunken brain and fast. I didn't hear him return, and my gut told me he hadn't. Still, my heart hoped I had missed it during one of my short dozes in the wee hours.

I took solace in Gigi's peaceful night. It helped to know she finally slept in this place again, and if I had any hand in that, I had no regrets. That reeked of a lie, but what was done was done.

Rain only seemed appropriate. With the dismal activity of the day before, and Gabe's imminent departure, clouds and showers seemed like the right call by Mother Nature.

"Where's Laney?" Gigi jolted awake, letting go of me, and scrambling from her spot.

"I don't know. You've been holding me captive. Glad you slept, though."

My big sister thrust her arms through the sleeves of her bathrobe in a rush to find her wife.

"How'd you do it, Gi? How'd you forgive her?"

"Who?"

I just stared.

She cinched the silky tie at her waist. "There wasn't anything to forgive. She did the best she could, and you can't ask for more than that. Demanding more than another is capable of makes *you* the monster. And you aren't, Jojo. And I'm sorry I ever thought otherwise. She gave all she could, so there's nothing to forgive."

Gigi didn't know how right she was, but I didn't think her learning the truth, despite Asher's opinion, would help bring her any more peace than she had already found. She didn't need another secret to carry after finally ridding her conscience of one she'd carried for thirty years. Genevieve Durand had done her time.

I reached for her, and she bent to kiss my cheek. I flinched, offering her the one cheek Asher *hadn't* kissed before his hasty exit. In case it was the last, I didn't want it replaced. Gigi noticed the abrupt move but didn't comment, intent on finding Laney.

Taken aback by the hour, I supposed the weather was to blame for our late sleep. The soothing sound of gentle rainfall and the darkened skies combined to make the perfect atmosphere for lazing in bed. The idea of doing that with Asher riled butterflies, but his absence now forced a groan into a tightly held pillow. But what if I had missed his return? Clambering from my high bed, I realized I could join him in his room in the basement.

Still wearing my dress from the day before, I hurried from my room and down the stairs. Gigi and Laney sat holding hands at the kitchen island. The smell of coffee filled the air. Laney caught my eye mid-sip, giving a slow head shake that told me my plan to idle the morning away wrapped in Asher Cray wouldn't happen. My eyes begged for more intel and her reply made the sinking feeling fall further.

"Did he—?"

"Pack? No, his things are still here." Laney had done her own reconnaissance. "Of course, the *schmuck* might ask me to collect them for him."

"Laney," Gigi shushed her. "He'll be back, Jojo. And if not, we'll burn his stuff. Promise." She winked.

My ill-conceived antics continued with a phone call to Asher's cellphone when I trudged back to my bedroom. It went to voicemail, but immediately, like he had dismissed the call on the first ring. My chest ached. Then my phone pinged.

Asher: Can't talk now.

Bile burned my throat with remnants of last night's Scotch. I lay down when the room spun, and held on, experiencing a sort of delayed drunkenness. A moment later, I staggered to my feet to purge the sickness inside me. When I finished retching, I peeled out of my dress and stood in the shower, hoping the hot water would wash away my dread.

In true Durand woman fashion, I exited my room, refreshed, a smile adhered to my face. Gabe had returned, and I made rainbow pancakes before his watery departure for North Carolina.

"So, you had a good visit with your dad?" I sifted flour while Gabe drank coffee light and sweet, a la his aunt Laney.

"Yeah. He acted incredibly cool, actually. Adjusting to the new dynamic we have. It's about time." Gabe's matter-of-fact delivery often surprised me. To be so self-aware at such a young age was a marvel. "We're gonna be all right. Though he did clam up when he got a call from some guy. A couple calls, actually. He took them privately, so I don't know the details."

"Maybe it was Raphe," I suggested while I whisked.

"Nope. Some guy he called Harry." Gabe shrugged while I sent the batter-dipped wire whisk flying across the kitchen island. "Whoa, Mom."

"Whoops." I reached for a towel to mop up the mess. "Three minutes until pancakes," I called out, eager to move past the mention of Harriet Smith.

"Hey, I know Asher will be bummed, having missed saying goodbye. Uh, he—"

"Stop, Mom. He called and told me you might try to make up some excuse for him taking off and fail spectacularly. *Nailed* it. He sure has your number." Gabe loaded the last of his cleaned clothes into his backpack. "He explained he had to pick up some research from a consultant he hired for research on a new book. That it was time-sensitive. Sounded plausible, and I'm a pretty good judge of character, so whatever he's up to, I'm sure it's a noble pursuit."

Gabe's aunts both snorted at his comment, but I took his use of the phrase *noble pursuit* as a good sign.

"I'm glad he spoke to you."

"He's a good guy, Mom."

I had an unusual lump in my throat and found it a challenge to make eye contact with my son.

"And you're a great catch, if not a bit discombobulating. Trust him. But trust yourself even more, 'kay?"

I wished away my sick gut and tight chest, finding hope in my son's canny advice. "Discombobulating? Great word, but who's the parent here again?" I reached up to nudge his chin.

"We have never been particularly traditional, have we? No reason to start now. I'll text when I arrive. Then I'm only ashore once a week for the next five weeks. I'll be sure to check-in."

"Give my best to Frannie."

"If I see her, I will, but plenty of other fish in the sea, as we marine biologists like to say."

"There certainly are. Cast a wide net, Gabriel James Atwater."

"Hook the one you got, Jocelyn Mae Durand. He's a keeper."
Gabe kissed my cheek, and again I offered the one Asher had not
kissed. Apparently, I still had doubts.

66

Asher

I DISMISSED THE CALL at the first ring for a few reasons. One, it hurt. The shrill pitch of the pulsing noise sent a searing pain in my soused brain. Two, I knew talking to her, unprepared and hardly awake, wouldn't do anyone any good. And three, I didn't want to wake the other person in the room. I wasn't ready for that "good morning" scene either. I sent an auto-response to the call. Three short words, nothing to read into there. I peered under the luxurious sheet and then covered my eyes to focus on the details of the night before, but the dueling jackhammers pounding my temples from the inside out slowed progress.

"Coffee might help." Harry leaned into the wide cased opening delineating the sitting area from the sleeping space in the apartment's one bedroom, a quick jaunt from St. John's University where she taught. "A quarter pounder with cheese and a Coke used to be my go-to. Don't get me wrong, it's still a cure-all, but I've noticed, now I've turned thirty, I need to watch what I shove in my pie-hole."

What? Did I forget to mention Harry was young?

"Never saw you going the way of the health-nut, Harry. What a difference a year makes." I kept my eyes to the ceiling, furtively feeling around for my shirt.

"You have no idea, Ash. And uh— I hung them up."

"What's that?"

"Your clothes. I hung them up. Figured you wouldn't want to

wear wrinkled stuff today, so I hung them. Seeing as you didn't bring a change with you."

"*Ah*. Thank you." All I wanted was to get out of there, but not before rinsing out the remnants of whatever animal died in my mouth overnight.

"Fresh towels and a toothbrush in the bath for you." Harry seemed to read my mind. "Probably not as fancy as your flat if I had to guess, and I do because even after a year I never merited an invitation, but I followed your suggestion to keep a toothbrush stash. Makes those unexpected sleepover guests feel— special. It really is the little things."

I forced myself to sit, then braced for the throbbing that followed. It vibrated down my body as I swung my legs to set my feet on the floor. Jesus Christ, I was never drinking again. Pretty confident standing wasn't yet in the cards, I got on with the next uncomfortable part of this morning-after.

"So, I should apologize for last night."

"Ya *think*?" came Harry's speedy reply.

My elbows found my knees and my fingers clutched at my hair. Somehow the tugging alleviated some pain until I remembered pulling at someone else's hair, blonde curls. A new pain erupted. This one in my chest. "Wait, what's that mean?"

"Oh, God, Ash." Harry had a great laugh when it wasn't crowing at your expense. "*Hoo-boy*. I toyed with dragging you along. But it's so terribly cruel to mess with the elderly."

"Excuse me?"

"Relax, Grandpa. Nothing happened last night."

"What?"

"Well, aside from the drinking and the bitching and the moaning— and *not* the good kind."

Still bent over, I twisted to look through split fingers at the mouthy redhead. She rolled her eyes and spun toward the stairs;

her flowery silk kimono whipping around her.

"Really?"

"Yes, really. I slept on the sofa. Now go wash off your stench and that new shit-eating grin and take me to breakfast. While this little reunion has been a real treat, it's time to get to business." Harry shooed me off to the shower.

"Bitching and moaning?" I stuck my head out of the bathroom.

"And whining. Oh, God, the whining." She shook her head and sipped her coffee. "Asher."

"Yeah?"

"It was kinda sweet, and *you* should have more faith in yourself, you old geezer. Now hurry. I'm starving."

It might have been the best shower of my life.

Rico's Diner was a quarter-mile walk from Harry's warehouse duplex, give or take, and a bit of fresh air would have done me good if a July day in Queens had any of that. Still, with chrome stools at a stainless-steel counter and booths lining the windowed walls, the aroma of sautéed onions and maple syrup wafted to me, and I thought there might be hope for my survival yet. I felt well enough that a phone call to a certain traveling marine biologist-in-the-making felt in order. Plus, I knew neither of us would care to have the chat drag on long, so I took the chance. I'm glad I did.

Harry carried a well-worn leather messenger bag across her body, and I guessed it held some information I'd find pertinent. But the truth was, until I had some bacon, I didn't want to hear a word about it.

"Holiday, so I'll have to charge you time and a half." Harry scrounged through her satchel, pulling out a pad and pen.

I nodded as I pulled off my sunglasses. With overcast skies, chances were the Ray-bans gave little help to the eyes bulging from my skull. I tucked them in my breast pocket. "Not a problem, Harry."

"Did I say time and half? I meant double time and a half." She grinned over another cup of coffee.

"Just send me the bill, but since when do we haggle over payment?"

"Since my Asher Cray *benefits* package got cut off."

"Ouch." I kept my gaze on the laminated menu. It was late for breakfast, but you could order it at Rico's day or night, and the short-order cooks could grill, fry, sauté, or broil pretty much anything for you. I've eaten many meals in these booths, and it never disappoints, but the racket never bothered me like it did this time. And looking across the table at the black leather jacket—despite the heat—tight t-shirt and ponytail wearing ginger, I chastised myself for my behavior the night before.

"What's up, Ash?"

"*Huh*? Just feeling lousy. *Uh*, thanks for—keeping me out of trouble last night."

"I obviously didn't keep you one hundred percent trouble-free."

"The worst kind of trouble, though. We could have—"

"*Uh*, nope. Can't take credit for that. You weren't buying what this gal had to sell, much less tried to give away for free. Not even a little. Not my finest moment, so I'd like to—do like Elsa."

I squinted my ignorance at her with a painful head jiggle.

"*Let it go*—oh, never mind. Besides, it's good you've found someone your own age."

"I mentioned her age? Weird."

"No. I learned her name, heard about her blonde curls and her

Macallan-colored eyes— and her legs."

"Oh God." I signaled for more coffee.

"There's not much I don't know now about Jocelyn Mae Durand. But you failed to mention she was once Jocelyn Atwater, as in that award-winning writer of the book you harassed me about until I read it. The one that scared the shit out of me. I made you sleep at my place for like a week."

"Sleep?"

"Shut up, Grandpa. So, the ex-husband—"

"Let me stop you right there, Harriet. I'm going to need to ingest some serious grease before I hear about William Atwater."

"Ah, so you know him, huh? He's a peach."

"You've met?"

"Phone— but I've got good visuals of him, too."

"I'm more interested in the Bayborough folks of thirty years ago."

"Well, shit, Asher. I was warming up to that. Easing in, a little slap and tickle before the big—"

"Did you always talk like this, Harry?" I massaged my brows.

"Like what?"

"Never mind. Tell me about Anne Bismarck."

Our food arrived, and she told me what she'd found.

Sometimes it's interesting to look back. The pretty girl from high school who ends up aging poorly, embittered, never leaving her childhood home, much less the town. The decidedly middle-class neighborhood. The tidy yards and small brick ranches with neatly painted matching trim and shutters that experienced a turn with blight and never recovered. Those same houses suffered peeling paint and weedy lawns now. Rusted railings on steep concrete steps lead from crumbling sidewalks to cracked front walkways with squeaking wrought iron security doors that didn't welcome anyone. When you live in a world that has seen such renewal and skyrocketing property values, it's surprising to discover places that, instead, deteriorated, falling victim to a changing economy. If you wanted an illustration of a segment of society that got left behind, you needn't look any further than Bayborough.

Families like the Kolcheks and the Bismarcks were two such examples of blue-collar households who didn't thrive in the new century but rather withered on an unnurtured vine until the earth swallowed the shriveled remains.

Anne resided in the same house she'd lived in on the night of her senior prom, and grumpily chained-smoked generic menthol cigarettes on the front walkway, telling Harry Smith the tale of her break-up with Darren Kolchek. Ms. Bismarck demanded fifty dollars for the trouble. Harry surmised, despite Anne's crankiness, she was happy to have someone to talk to about anything. Including how, thirty years ago, her drunkard of a father, who had "downed a few" that night—like *every* night—got in the face of the teenaged boy who broke his daughter's heart. Eddie Bismarck shoved "that boy" down those concrete steps, and Anne was reasonably sure Darren lost consciousness for a moment when his head struck the sidewalk with a harrowing *crack*. She never heard from Darren after that and blamed her rotten father.

Harry thought Anne spoke a bit too merrily with the recap of her dad's agonizing year of liver failure. It culminated in him eating his gun, leaving her and her mother with nothing but a pile of medical bills and a horrendous, bloody mess in the garage. Anne uttered the phrase, "good riddance" many, many times.

The Kolcheks didn't find their happily-ever-after either. The couple divorced, and while broken marriages are not atypical when parents lose a child under any circumstance, family, and neighbors both said the pair should have split long before, better yet never married at all. They were also both deceased now, but people who knew them thought they had heard Darren *did* take off to Mexico to play soccer, and wasn't it nice the sweet young man escaped the drudgery of Bayborough to go off and do the thing he loved most. Of course, I knew it was just another example of the lies we tell often enough they become a kind of truth.

"Now, I can't find any sign the kid left the country, much less arrived in another one. I suppose if he hitched his way, it's possible. Kids are scrambling to cross over here to get away from their awful home life. Stands to reason he could have done the same going the other way. It sure would have been easier to do thirty years ago. Then again, it could have been a lethal head wound, just no one found the body. I'll keep digging if you want." Harry awaited further instruction.

"No. No more digging. There's been enough digging." My stomach churned, and I didn't think I could blame it all on the Macallan.

"Suit yourself. That should cover it then. I'll send you a digital file with all my notes and photos, along with a very, *very* expensive bill."

"Sounds good, wait. You mentioned William Atwater." Damn my curiosity.

"Oh, yeah. It's probably nothing, due diligence is all. I spoke to him twice."

"Once wasn't enough?" I grimaced into my now cold coffee.

"Would have been. But when I catch someone in a lie, I like to circle back. Revisit. Allow them to make things right, you know. And he did, well enough, I suppose."

"Tell me about it." The hairs on the back of my neck prickled.

"Tracking people's movements is so much easier nowadays. I found out he took a late night pleasure cruise day before last."

I breathed some relief. "Yeah, I know about that."

"Oh. Good then."

"Just curious. What was the mix-up?"

"Well, I tracked him because of his son," she checked her notes, "Gabriel James Atwater."

Another wave of nausea roiled with the mention of Gabe and my respite ended with a thud.

"Seems Gabriel rented the boat. Father and son are both licensed for small watercraft. I checked. Not unusual for Southampton locals. But then Daddy Venmo-ed the near exact amount back to the kid. Well, the exact amount plus one thousand dollars. I thought it must be a reimbursement. Correctly, I might add."

"Why'd you think one had to do with the other?"

"Because only Daddy shows up on security video accessing the boat. Daddy wheeling an oversized duffle bag. An oversized duffle bag he did not disembark with come the break of dawn."

"So, what was the lie—or misunderstanding?" I doubted my casual tone played well.

"When I first spoke to William, I hadn't seen the security footage. So, when he told me in passing, he went out for an overnight with his pal Raphe, I didn't question it. But then I saw the video. Guess what?"

Afraid if I opened my mouth, I might vomit, I simply shrugged with a grimace.

"No Raphe. The senior Mr. Atwater traveled alone, at night, on a boat—he didn't rent."

Moments like these, I cursed my vocation. It's a rare occurrence, really. Having a brain full of factoids and other trivial pursuits made me a hoot at parties... when I went to parties. Being able to whip out the meaning behind the back-and-forth of mourning doves or how butterflies taste flower nectar can boost a guy's quixotic point tally. But knowing it's unlikely to find any discernible remains of an unprocessed body buried more than three feet deep and three decades ago in Long Island's notably acidic soil isn't information I wanted to possess. But there I was, desperate to stretch my legs, and regrettably well-informed, thanks to another of my blockbuster books. "His response?" I asked.

"Oh, you know, Raphe was *supposed* to go. That had been the plan, but then Raphe canceled at the last minute. And while I found no sign the two had communicated for weeks, I found a logged call from Raphe's phone that pinged in Manhattan to William's phone in Sag Harbor that night. The cancellation call, I presume. Anyway, I didn't see how any of that connected to you so...Plus, he and Ms. Durand divorced a few years back. If he planned to *off* anybody, I mean, if *anyone* was gonna find their way into William Atwater's giant duffle, it would be his ex-wife. The size of the alimony check he cuts her every month? Shit. He must *hate* her, or— he *loves* her, but I think we both know that's not likely the case... Asher?"

Cold ran through me. "What? Oh, yeah, divorce, it's an ugly business. Thanks for all this. I'll be looking for that bill." Tossing a twenty on the table, I took the check to the register, eager to escape the diner racket. Harry followed.

"Does William know *why* you were looking at him?" We walked to my car.

"Come on, Ash. You know me better than that. It's never coming back around to you."

"Okay. So why did you look into William?"

"Uh, cuz whenever I investigate someone, I always open a file on those connected to them, too."

"But I only asked to see the police report of the car wreck. Not for you to investigate anyone. Not for you to pry into Jocelyn

Durand or her family." I kept my cadence matter-of-fact, but it unnerved me that Harry had snooped so far and as the day went on, my concern for Jocelyn's safety grew.

Harry stopped with her gaze to the sidewalk. "I guess I needed to know more about the woman with the magic touch. The one who seems to have conjured the spell to domesticate the wild Asher Cray." She rattled her head, taking in a ragged breath, and moved on. "Anyway, I hope the police report helped."

"Oh, sure. Jocelyn had little memory of it. Typical. I thought a glance at the report might clear up some stuff. Ancient history, of course, but if I could help, I wanted to be that guy."

Harry shook her head with an off-set jaw. "Who even are you?"

Apparently, I was a changed man, but I didn't know how to explain that to the young woman standing in the drizzle that picked up strength.

"And the cold case? When will I read the fictionalized account? The next Cray bestseller?"

I had no qualms about misleading Harry about my interest in the missing Darren Kolchek and stretched in preparation for squeezing into my MG. "I don't know. Not sure it's a story I want to pursue anymore. Not really feeling it now." I shrugged.

Harry looked at me askance.

"I've got this idea about a beautiful divorcee who lures an unsuspecting novelist to her coastal home, holding him hostage."

"Victimless crime, huh?"

I laughed through my hangover. "Funny. That happens to be the working title, Harry." I ducked into the driver's seat.

67

Jocelyn

"So, I GET YOU might be angry, Jocelyn, and you have every right. I was a jerk— but I thought if I could get some answers, it might help. Help you and help Genevieve. Help us. So, I went to where I knew I could get some answers." Asher barreled forward when I answered on the first ring. "But being a self-centered prick who has never had to check in or ask permission, I took off with little regard for how that might look or feel, and I apologize. I have some learning to do when it comes to—"

"*Hello*, Asher." I interjected. "See, that's how this works. One person calls and lets the other person answer that call with a *hello* or some other greeting. They respond in kind, and then the conversation goes from there. At least that's how someone explained the process to me not so long ago."

"Hi, Joss."

We both paused and momentary relief flickered hearing him speak my name.

"Did you— get what you needed— from Harry?" The fully-loaded question hurt as it came from my mouth.

"Jocelyn—"

"I meant information, of course. I heard you were picking up some time-sensitive material from a consultant you hire from time to time." I wanted him to know Gabe informed me of their chat. "Did you get what you wanted?"

"I did." Asher's brevity stung.

"Good to hear. Not too costly, I hope."

"I guess that remains to be seen. The invoice is still outstanding."

"Sure, I guess sometimes it takes a while for these things to shake out. Investment versus gain, and whether short-term reward was worth sacrificing some long-term possibility." I bit my bottom lip, hearing a quiver in my voice.

"As long as you make the final judgment with the facts. Not swayed by some media bias or hype, sometimes some good old-fashioned gut instinct is involved."

"Yes, of course." That was my attempt at being concise, but it didn't hold long. "Do you—know when we might be able to—go over that information? Face to face might be best, under the circumstances. Unless the logistics of that are inconvenient." I stared out the kitchen sink window as a gentle rain continued, as it had all day. Speaking in metaphor aggravated my hangover.

"Well, some of the reporting might interest more than just you. And since I see Laney Li and Genevieve are still in Amagansett, sooner would be better than later, I think."

"Oh, yes. Good thinking—wait, how'd you know they're still here?"

"I just stepped onto your front porch and saw Genevieve's car through—"

I tossed my phone and ran. Wrenching open the front door, I pushed the screen wide and landed in Asher's arms, clinging to my just-right spot. His fast hand caught the screen door to keep it from slamming.

"Jojo?" Gigi called from inside, but I didn't reply. "Asher," she acknowledged him before she carefully closed the heavy door to keep the A/C air in, and giving us some privacy on the portico.

"You okay?" He finally spoke, still wrapped in each other's arms. I nodded. "I'll be better once we burn these clothes."

"What?" He wheezed a short laugh into my hair.

"They reek of a distillery and bacon grease and—" I sniffed again.

"We'll burn them." His grasp lessened, but I held tighter.

"I'm not ready to let go."

"Good." His hold grew stronger.

"I mean, I will eventually because, um, bacon grease—but I'll endure for now." With a head tilt, I eyed Asher's neck. His Adam's apple moved with his quiet chuckle, but when my fingers brushed the hollow of his throat, he fell silent with a hard swallow. "Asher?"

"Hm?"

"I—I can't apologize for last night. I mean, I'm not going to."

"Okay."

"I was upset."

"I know."

"And Gigi needed me."

"I know."

"And I drank too much."

"Oh, I know."

"And that's not how I want for us to—"

"I know. Me either."

"Thank you for understanding, Asher Cray." I patted his chest.

"Thank you for not apologizing, Jocelyn Durand."

"I guess we're both learning, huh?"

"I imagine there will be a few more lessons along the way, yes. But I'm looking forward to the education."

I sighed.

"What's that?" He whispered into my hair.

"The depth and breadth of what I don't know—well, I haven't even got a clue."

"Okay," Asher coughed. "Before I start formulating a lesson plan, we should make another plan—with Laney and Genevieve, I mean. And—I can't believe I'm saying this— maybe William too."

Asher's suggestion that Will join us surprised me, but I took comfort in the olive branch of sorts. And while he got cleaned up, I gathered everyone to talk.

68

Asher

"I haven't a clue, Love. The man was a lovable dope but always a bit scattered." William had arrived from wherever he'd been hiding out this week, while I showered and changed again. He struck me as the kind of guy who always had a place to hang his hat, no matter when or where.

I emerged from my basement quarters to find him holding forth at the kitchen island with Jocelyn, Laney, and Genevieve in attendance.

"I never thought of him as scattered." Jocelyn shook her head, then smiled at my approach. She offered me a glass of wine, but I declined.

"What on earth, pardon the pun, do you know about running a landscaping business?" Laney scoffed.

"What's this about?" I asked.

"Raphe has taken off and left his landscapers to William," Genevieve explained but reached across the counter to squeeze my arm in an entirely different statement.

I nodded in reply and put my arm around Jocelyn. "So, where'd he go?" I tried to look disinterested.

"Asher, old boy, I really couldn't tell you. He could be at the bottom of the ocean for all I know." William cackled at only he knew what. "And I don't imagine I'll ever hear from him again. But if I keep his business afloat, I don't expect anyone will ever miss him. I mean, other than me, of course." His face went stoic, but then he winked, and I'd swear he meant it as a message just for me.

Harry's face flitted across my mind and the hope she had taken care in her handling of the slippery William Atwater. Hell, I hoped she never told him her name. Surely, the overactive imagination of a suspense writer triggered the dastardly scheme that alleged Jocelyn's ex-husband confronted Raphe about remains that science says he couldn't have possibly found, but then did something unthinkable to tie up loose ends. Just in case. My brain skipped back to a recent movie night where the "good guy" let the bad one off for his misdeeds. I wondered how often life imitated art in that unfortunate way.

"You okay, Asher?" Jocelyn looked up at me, my arm still around her shoulders.

"What?" I pried my gaze away from William's scarily hypnotic leer.

"You look a little—green." She placed her hand on my stomach with an affectionate rub.

"Yeah, I'm never drinking Scotch again." I attempted a smile.

"Hey, me either," Jocelyn quipped.

"More for me," Laney cheered.

William voted first to keep the status quo. Hearing Mr. Bismarck, the person truly responsible for Darren Kolchek's death, was dead and that both the Kolchek parents were also deceased, no reason made sense to divulge the truth. Add to that, distant family believed the boy had happily gone off to play soccer in Mexico. It wouldn't help anyone to learn what really happened this many years later.

The decision ultimately came down to Genevieve, as she'd borne the weight of the tragedy all these years. Jocelyn, Laney, and I promised to do as Genevieve wished, and if at any time she changed her mind, we would support her choice. Knowing Jocelyn wasn't responsible for the boy's death was such profound relief. I'd swear Genevieve's whole posture changed, and she gained a youthfulness in her face no one could miss.

The observer in me watched as all three women breathed easier than they had the day before. Although I couldn't help but think of Raphe, coupled with worry for Harry Smith, burdening anyone with that unsubstantiated theory wouldn't do any good. I would have to live with that inkling all on my own.

"Will said his goodbyes. Sorry he missed you. Made me promise to remind you of his standing offer to take you out on a boat if ever you're interested." Jocelyn knitted her brows, then shook off the passing look of confusion.

Rest assured; I had no plans to go boating with William Atwater. Ever.

"And it looks like the rain has moved out, so the fireworks at the pier are a go. Have I mentioned I *love* fireworks?" She beamed.

I lifted Jocelyn onto the island and followed up with an eager kiss, taking my time. When I released her mouth, I nuzzled her ear. "You mentioned fireworks."

"Did I?"

I kissed her cheek. "You did."

"Yes. Laney and Gigi are changing. They're staying another

night, and I know you might not—"

"Joss, I think it's great they're staying. I think it's *great* William left. But your sisters' staying is great, too."

Her head back tilted with her laugh, and I took the opportunity to enjoy her neck, eliciting a pleasured gasp.

"And I think it's really great you make that sound when I kiss you here." I did it again.

"How many times are you going to say the word 'great'? Is the wordsmith losing his skills?" She sighed as I moved to her bare shoulder.

"I'll learn new skills."

"Your agent might take umbrage with that plan."

"Agent, *schmagent*." I returned to the spot just above Jocelyn's collarbone.

"Excuse me, Asher?" Laney had snuck down the stairs like only she could. "Jocelyn?"

Flushed, Jocelyn made a big show and little effort to wrest my lips from her skin.

"Oh, I see now. You two are in *cahoots*, huh?" My agent squinted at us.

"Yes, we are Laney Li. Yes, we are." I said with another kiss to Jocelyn's cheek.

"Yes, you are what? Ready for fireworks? Jojo *loves* fireworks." Genevieve came down the hall.

"Are *they* ready? Look at them. These two have already started, Gen." Laney rolled her eyes while Genevieve kissed her and dragged her by the arm without stopping on the way to the side door.

"Leave them alone now, Laney. See you two at the pier," Genevieve called. "Or not." And the duo closed the door behind them.

I grinned, enjoying that someone in this world kept Laney Li in line, but my heart catapulted to my throat when my eyes returned to Jocelyn and that lip between her teeth. Even as she undid a button on my shirt, my chest tightened. When her legs circled my hips and she pulled me close for a slow, soft kiss, I gave up on oxygen altogether. Jocelyn was my air now.

With her mouth still exploring mine, she slid off the counter in a way I'm sure must be illegal in some states. That's when my vision faded and I was sure this woman would be the death of me.

"Listen to that," she whispered against my lips, then pressed deeper—not that I could form words for a reply.

With yet another sense gone, I couldn't hear anything either. My palms skimmed her hips and my fingers bunched both sides of her sundress. At least my physical body held its own.

"That's the sound of *absolutely no one* interrupting us."

You know what else worked? My blasted inquisitive brow. Speech returned, too. "What about—fireworks?" I stammered. *Why, Asher? Why?*

But Jocelyn didn't disappoint, leading me upstairs to the most extraordinary July Fourth of my life. *Fireworks.*

THE END

Kelly Elizabeth Huston writes women-centric, genre-straddling fiction that always includes laughs and a love story. But sometimes there's heartbreak, a smidge of mystery, moments of suspense, and maybe a dead body... or two. Maybe. Above all, she hopes her protagonists are better for it in the end, and she entertains her readers along the way. She currently lives in Georgia with her husband and two nearly-grown sons, who are, hands down, the best cheer squad a writer could wish for. After spending a few years in the traditional publishing space, Kelly leaped to the indie side without looking back and is eager to dole out her book babies and get them read. She hopes you'll join her in the adventure. www.kellyelizabethhuston.com

Also by Kelly Elizabeth Huston
Tex Miller Is Dead

Coming soon: A GIRL, STUCK

1

He laughed as he folded his tall frame into that ridiculous vintage Tahiti blue MG. He'd made a joke, a funny one, I'm sure, but I missed it while my heart crumbled in the stifling July Fourth humidity on a sidewalk in Jamaica—Jamaica, Queens, that is. The morning mist had strengthened to spitting rain, and the whole scene turned absurdly appropriate. *Warning:* this next bit won't be pretty.

"Hey, Asher." Looking skyward, I cinched my droopy ponytail, kinking in the wet. I knew to avoid his face. Better to endure the increasing pelt of raindrops on mine.

"Yeah?" He'd closed the little car door but spoke out the opened window.

"*Uh,*" I sucked in hot, soggy air, wishing it wasn't. "Do me a favor."

"What's that, Harry? Name it." Sincere blue eyes met mine when, like a fool, I lowered my gaze.

"Lose my number." It sounded more like a question. I adjusted the messenger bag that weighed me down along with the summer heat and the leather jacket I wore, intent on some self-assured *Gloria Gaynor* moment. It didn't go that way.

"What?" Asher's shock came as a pleasant surprise, at least. "Do you mean that, Harriet? Really?"

Jesus, I hate it when people call me by my given name, except him. "Yes... Maybe... No." I tried for a chuckle, but it fell flat. I growled to loosen my tightening throat. "I mean, *yes*. Yes, I do. Don't call me again. Okay? Not sooner or later or—*ever*. Could you do that for me? Never call me again? Because I can't—"

"I hear you. I won't. But if you ever need anything—"

"I won't." I couldn't get those words out fast enough before I spun on the wet sidewalk to trudge through the St. John's University campus to my home three blocks south. The MG's engine rumbled to a start. "*Shit*. Shit, shit, shit, shit. I swear to God, Harry Smith, if you turn around, you will never get over the man. Just keep walking." Yes, I spoke the words aloud. To myself. I do that.

With a forceful head shake, I picked up my pace, proud of my restraint as I left the bestselling author Asher Cray, the man of my—*whatever*, in my wake. I took another damp breath and focused on getting home to email the last of that relationship out of my inbox so I could get on with the business of getting *over* the man who had unknowingly kept me under his spell for the better part of two years. *Ugh*. His *spell*? That sounded like a gooey romantic, and rest assured, I am anything but. Let's just say Asher is funny and smart and kind and an incredible, toe-curling lay, and now it's over. *Has* been over for more than a year... until he called yesterday. *Son-of-a-bitch*.

Pulled from my wallowing thoughts, I stopped short of bounding up the concrete stairs that led to my apartment when the muffled mews of one of the neighborhood's stray cats cried from under a boxwood hedge. The skittish animal didn't come out to greet me, having more sense than to step into the rain. I bent to say my hellos and pulled a folded napkin from my bag's front pocket.

"Hey, kitty. I brought you some bacon." I tore up my breakfast leftovers, placing the bits under the shrubbery for the homeless creature's easy access.

She hissed.

"To hell with you then," I jeered but continued to rip apart the salty strip of pork. When the mangey ingrate finished eating, it scurried deeper into the privet without so much as a head bump in thanks. I remained crouched in the rain until Mother Nature urged me indoors when she sent down a harder cloudburst.

My home had the outward look of a miniature asylum rather than a residence. I'd bought the lackluster two-story brick square for next to nothing four years ago. Originally a small industrial warehouse built early last century, I had the structure gutted and retrofitted into two two-story apartments—one for me, one for a stranger who had become like family. A wise investment of an unfortunate financial windfall.

I stomped water off my sneakers, meeting a frigid air-conditioned blast when I entered the building's vestibule, and spasmed at the chill. It wasn't a big deal in the grand scheme, but I decided I didn't care for any more surprises. Wet rubber soles squeaked on vintage penny tiles, announcing my arrival. I couldn't get my deadbolt unlocked and myself inside before the door across the hall flew open.

"Harry Smith." It was another hiss, but not of the feline variety.

With my forehead pressed to the still-closed door, I sighed, "Hello, Leo," prepared for the inevitable reprimand.

"Don't 'hello, Leo' me, missy. Did I see—"

"It's not what it looked like, Nosy Parker," I cut short my neighbor's scolding with an exasperated snap.

"Oh, thank sweet baby Jesus," Leo let slip his southern accent. "Cuz it *looked* like that famed writer who ghosted you over a year ago showed up here last night and didn't leave until this morning, and since it took you until like last *Tuesday* to actually get over the way-too-old-for-you-albeit-incredibly-hot man—that would have been a gut-wrenching wound to re-open, not to mention stupid as fu—"

"*Okay*, Leo. It was a *little* like it looked but not entirely, and he *didn't* ghost me, and *I'm* fine, and Asher's gone for good this time." With a slow turn, I faced unexpected silence. My neighbor Leo, that stranger-turned-family, leaned in his doorway with a hand on his hip, his head a few inches from the top of the frame. He wore a look of disdain and a flowing floral kimono identical to one I owned, thanks to a night of too much Manischewitz and some tipsy online shopping. And dammit, if he didn't look better in it than I did. I couldn't take the quiet. "Jesus, say something."

"Did you—"

"*NO*." I should have guessed he'd go there. "His visit was strictly for book research business."

"Really?"

"Well, I might have tried, but—" I confessed. I couldn't help myself. Leo possessed a priest-like quality, though rabbi would be more appropriate.

"*Really?*"

"Seems he's met someone," I explained.

"*Real*-ly?"

"And it's serious."

"Really?"

"As a heart attack. Asher's words, not mine."

"Well, the man is of a certain age," Leo snickered.

"Come on. He's not that old."

"Really?"

"Leopold Klein, so help me. Say '*really*' one more time. I dare you." My glare met his pursed lips.

He didn't. He said nothing for an agonizing moment. "You all right?" The soft-spoken question came laced with genuine concern.

"I'd be better if I had a summer session to teach, or my phone would ring with a PI case that didn't involve infidelity and the need for proof, but yeah, I'm alright." Sometimes the work schedule of an adjunct professor allowed for too much free time, and the private investigator side-hustle left me feeling dirty.

"What'll you do now?"

"I'll close out the last of the background research I did for Asher's next book—that he doesn't even think he's gonna write now— and send him his file with a *very* big invoice."

"Big, huh?"

"*Huge.* But it's the last one. Hand to—"

"I don't need to know where your hands have been, Harriet. Seriously." Leo waved his long fingers and *tsked* with a curled lip.

I laughed, relieved to find laughter still possible, and opened my apartment door.

"Hey, got plans tonight?"

"No. You?"

"Gantry Plaza. Fireworks. Independence Day?" He gave a pointed look before belting out a country song I'd like to think I'm too young to know.

"That's a hard pass." I forced a relaxed grin at my friend. "Thanks, though. Have fun."

Inside my home, I hung my messenger bag on a teak hat rack and peeled off my leather jacket before catching my reflection in a mirror. The older man's ability to say no wasn't so hard to believe when my sagging image stared back at me. The wide-receiver-on-game-day look my rain-smeared mascara provided forced an eye-roll. I wiped away the smudges, toed-off my sneakers in an ungraceful stumble, then trudged upstairs to my bathroom. The very bathroom Asher had showered in a few hours earlier. The rest of last night's Macallan 18 baited me from the coffee table in the middle of my bedroom. An unexpected night of drinking had landed the best-selling author in my bed, and me—on my sofa. Yeah, not my best work.

In a blink, I found myself downstairs again and across the hall, banging on Leo's door. When it opened, I thrust the one-third full bottle at my wide-eyed neighbor. "Take it."

"Oh, honey. I don't—"

"Take. It." I shoved it to his chest and held it there.

"You know I don't drink the dark liquor. It makes me—I mean I get—I go *wiiild*—"

"It's three hundred dollars a bottle."

"Well, if you insist..." Leo snatched the Scotch from my grasp, and I hurried back to my solitary sanctum, shutting the door with more force than I meant. Tripping over my shoes, I beelined to the shower before any sort of "Asher Cray shrine" status took hold, and I found myself bathing at the gym for the rest of my life. *Pathetic, Harry.*

Steam filled the tiled room, and I washed away what I hoped would be the last of the memory of a man who wasn't meant to be. Well, not for me, anyway.

2

I don't have many friends. Days lecturing university students on investigative tactics and criminal profiling with nights spent sneaking around in a surveillance van, or worse, seedy motels and bars, doesn't lend itself to a life full of age-appropriate pals who sing karaoke on Friday nights or brunch on Sundays.

Maybe I shouldn't blame my career choices for my lack of social life. I'm also a bit of a disaster and not very nice. Add to that, I'm *probably* too smart for my own good and *definitely* endowed with a firm ass and a perky rack that, when coupled with a clipboard, gain me access to just about anywhere I want to go. And as for humility, well—I might've skipped the day they gave that lesson.

People call me Harry, but my post-dated birth certificate reads Harriet no-middle-name Smith. I could tell you how I was *hashtag blessed* to be born to wonderful parents who, when they decided they *didn't* want me, dropped me at a police station instead of in a trash can. And how a young cop at that precinct fell in love with my hours-old red curls and blue eyes, so much so that, with some well-connected help, he was able to push through paperwork to foster and eventually adopt me. But none of that is very interesting. Suffice it to say, a cop raised me surrounded by more cops, and you'll never find a more loyal, protective, and supportive family. Ever. It also means I lack some social niceties, etiquette, a filter, and whether that is nature or nurture, I don't know, but Dad called it moxie. I *do* know that imparting hard-won wisdom about investigation practices and a lot of alone time in a junk food-laden windowless van suits me. So, despite any signs of *softness,* rest assured, I'm a tough-as-nails badass who handles her shit with serious skill, so you can kick your concerns about any apparent heartbreak to the curb. That's for damn sure.

My phone rang, my business line. It helped to keep the private investigator's life separate from my personal one in many ways. I answered without looking at the screen.

"Harry Smith Investigations. How may I direct your call?" Full disclosure, people looking for a PI tend to have some gender bias. Shocking, I know. So, until I suss out the details of a case, sometimes even after some initial sleuthing takes place, I don't disclose my identity. The number of first-time callers who assume I'm the "front-office girl" would... well, it shouldn't surprise you. Funnily enough, once I'd procured some much-needed information, often damning photographic or audio evidence, the client couldn't give a crap whether I sit or stand to pee. Investigative work is a results-driven gig, no matter who gets the goods, no matter who pays the bill.

"Hey, kiddo."

I pulled the phone from my ear and hit the speaker button, recognizing the number belonged to a local police precinct.

"Marty, why are you calling the work number? You good?"

"I'm *well*, and I debated which number to dial because this is a business call, *official* business." Martin O'Shea is one of the cops I mentioned earlier. A stickler for keeping official business *official* and his grammar correct, Marty was also my father's on-the-job partner. Harlan Smith, my dad, was shot and killed in the line almost five years ago. And I'm still not ready to talk about that yet.

"Official business, huh? Well then, *Detective* O'Shea, how may I officially be of service? And when are we doing this? Today works, right now even. I'm walking to the door as we speak." The relief at the mere prospect of something to fill my time, any length of time, washed over me, and breathing got easier.

"Slow down, Harry. Going off half-cocked won't fly with what I have in mind."

"Half-cocked is my middle name, Uncle Marty. It's part of my charm."

"I happen to know you don't have a middle name—or charm." The curmudgeon's smirk resonated through the speaker.

"Wow. With that kind of talk, you can forget the friends and family discount. Full bore for you, Smarty Marty." I flopped onto my bedroom's low sofa and kicked up my bare feet.

"I'm not looking for any special rate, kid."

"Aw, I'm just joshing. Besides, I've got a big payday on the way, and between you and me, I could use some distraction. What do you need? And when?"

"The *when* is tonight."

"Thank you, sweet baby Jesus," I mimicked Leo from across the hall. "Oops, sorry, Marty." I meant the apology.

Martin O'Shea is a devout Irish Catholic, a great man with a dry sense of humor, and he knows how to have a good time, but he prefers I keep my blasphemy to a minimum.

"What's the *what*?" I asked, eager to move on to the good stuff.

"Surveillance, but on foot, so I need you to blend in a crowd. No audio or visual evidence collection is necessary. Just follow, watch, and report back. No interaction. As a matter of fact, I'd rather you not make contact at all." The last part sounded more like an edict than a suggestion.

"*O-kay*. And who am I tailing? How will I happen upon the mark, and what am I looking for?" I took mental notes. Sometimes a paper trail gets complicated, legally-speaking.

"Let me be clear, Harriet. You're not *looking* for anything. Simply observing, watching, then reporting back to me." Marty's use of my proper name caught my attention, and I knew he wanted me to take notice.

"Okay."

"The target is a young punk. New on the scene. His name is Trey Popov. I'll send you a photo. Says he'll be at some July Fourth festivities. That's really my first question. Whether he shows or not. It could be a speedy job."

"Shows where?" I opted to focus on the business at hand and not the questionable longevity of the gig. At the moment, I'd take anything.

"Gantry Plaza. At the East River. Right across from—"

"The U. N.," I interjected.

"Yes."

"That significant?"

"No," he answered without skipping a beat. Maybe too fast.

"Marty?"

"No, Harry. He's just some young punk, and I'd like to get your take."

"How young are we talking?"

"Your age?"

"So, *very* young, then." I made the lame joke to gauge Marty's real mood.

"You wish," he teased. "He's no teenager, but it's hard to say. You're all young to me."

"Well, thirty is the new Forever Twenty-One," I quipped.

"Keep telling yourself that, Harry."

We both chuckled in a way that included more sigh than laughter. A tension Marty didn't want to concede bubbled underneath our banter, but our history said he'd tell me what I needed to know when I needed to know it, and apparently, that time was later.

"Are we clear on the particulars?" He returned to the need-to-know details.

"Got a time?"

"Let's say before dark. Easier to latch on when you can see, but it's a fireworks display, so that won't happen until well after sundown. Plus, there will be a crowd."

"Okay, blend in, just watch, note who he's with, how he acts, what he eats, drinks, smokes. Don't engage."

"Sounds about right," Marty confirmed.

"Do I follow him home?"

"No. Not this time. Just stick to Popov's social interactions."

I grinned to hear it might not be a one-time deal but kept a noncommittal tone. My eagerness was my concern. "How should I report back? Anyone else interested in my findings?" It was a bold question that may have tipped my hand, but Marty let it go.

"Let's keep this between you and Uncle Marty, okay, kid? We'll talk tomorrow. I'll call you."

"Yes, sir."

"And Harry?"

"Yep?"

"Be careful, but don't go armed. No firearm, I mean."

"Nothing but my Ivy League education, my wit, and bare hands. Promise."

"I think we both know your arsenal consists of far more than that, Harriet."

"What did you say about my *arse*?"

"Talk tomorrow, Harry," Marty O'Shea sighed and ended the call.

3

Eager to get to work, I plotted my travel. The majority-minority neighborhood I called home prided itself on being diverse, inclusive, and *not* gentrifying. And on that July Fourth, my apartment's bedroom view included wet walkways below but parting clouds with blue sky above. The fireworks would be a go. *God bless America.*

My trek to the park, several miles west of home, included two subway rides, an Uber, and some walking in between it all, but that's just smart tradecraft. I've mentioned my education, a master's degree in criminology, but I picked up lessons in surveillance by pounding the pavement and listening to my dad. Extreme tactics wouldn't be necessary, but my path to the surveillance spot would differ from the one I took home. Having followed, listened in, videoed, and photographed more people than I care to count, has instilled a healthy measure of paranoia. I take good care when I travel.

Destination: Gantry Plaza State Park. The reclaimed dockyard is a great patch of earth with Manhattan's skyline for a backdrop, right on the East River and popular with the Tai-chi-set, daily dog walkers, and seasonal concert goers. No doubt, thanks to the clearing skies, a mob would descend to celebrate the patriotic holiday, a crowd I needed to blend into, so my outfit mattered. I chose blue jeans, sneakers, and a white scoop-neck t-shirt with a red, white, and blue heart stretched across the bust. To be honest, my wardrobe lacked any flag-waving wear, and I'd bought the shirt out of necessity when I spilled coffee down my front at a café on the Champs-Élysées. In Paris. That's right, I flaunted French patriotism, not American, but a red, white, and blue heart is a red, white, and blue heart, right? I gave my reflection a reassuring nod.

After a rainy day, the hazy, sinking sun made the already steamy atmosphere downright oppressive as evening blanketed the city. A cold beer would go down fast, and I'd allow it—you know, to blend in with the crowd—more smart tradecraft. I smirked at my well-reasoned plan.

Time allowed me to take a circuitous path to my destination, and the closer I got, the denser the sidewalk traffic grew. With all I needed in my jeans pocket, including my phone, free hands could be advantageous. I had memorized the details of Mr. Popov's face, but if I had doubts, I could steal a glimpse with the swipe of a screen. Despite the sticky heat, it felt damn good to be working outside a van.

The trip, with all my zig-zagging, took nearly two hours. I didn't feel rushed, but I wondered if I had given myself enough daylight to set eyes on my target. The busier the streets became, the more finding Trey Popov felt like pinpointing a specific needle in a pile of needles. In moments like these, patience became my mightiest virtue. Patience is a teachable skill if one is willing to learn, and if not, I don't recommend a career in investigation. It's not for everyone.

I played that platitude on repeat as frustration's tune crept its way from a spot in my brain to a broader expanse in my chest. Fear of failing Marty joined in the lament, and I worried the night would end in a botched job. I breathed in more of that humid air, and my brows raised when the mugginess included the skunky aroma of some popular weed I'd noticed a lot recently. With flared nostrils, I headed straight to a line at a local craft brew truck. It was hot, and I was thirsty, and blending in was key.

Stepping to the end of the line, I pulled out a tenner and my phone in an attempt to look disengaged when I was anything but. A quick glance told me I had no missed calls or texts. Not surprising. The line inched ahead, and I looked forward to the cold beverage as the evening's next musical act conducted a sound-check on the nearby temporary stage erected for the event. The excruciating squawk of mic feedback jerked me to attention, and a loud groan from the crowd followed.

That's when I saw him.

I caught myself before I nearly stepped out of line with a quick reminder to the unusually jumpy investigator in me why I had come there and what I meant to do. *Focus, Harry.* Rooted in my spot in the queue, I was more intent than ever on that beer as my mouth had gone dry at finally laying eyes on the man. Now for the fun part.

From some distance, I would have said Trey Popov stood six foot nothing, maybe six-one. His build appeared slim, but I withheld judgment because of the oversized tracksuit draped on his frame. I never would understand that fashion choice unless it aimed to provide a silhouette that disguised all sorts of things. The wardrobe preference by a person of Popov's ilk made sense, and I took mental notes about the man and those gathered around him.

Keeping his circle in my periphery, I took a seat on a bright red Adirondack chair, the likes of which dotted that area of the park. Even if you've never been to New York City, I bet you'd recognize my surroundings. Ever seen a movie or television show where a character had some hard-thinking to do— in an urban setting—while jogging, let's say? The Manhattan skyline made for magnificent scenery and the park's well-lit East River boardwalk allowed for a spectacular long-shot. Sure, they may have edited out the namesake gantry with "Long Island" emblazoned on it and the gigantic neon Pepsi-Cola sign, but chances are you've seen the place.

I snapped a few pictures, faking selfies. Again, a girl's gotta blend in, right? Casually sipping my fast-warming beer, I kept a distant eye on Trey Popov, who quickly became a bore. It didn't appear he and his friends had plans to wander anytime soon. I may have sighed my disappointment out loud.

Marty's earlier admonishment echoed, "You're not *looking* for anything..."

Good thing, Marty, I thought. Cuz nothing to see here but a crowd of millennials with questionable taste in leisurewear.

Enough time had passed that I considered getting another drink, but a roar of laughter erupted from Mr. Popov's gang, catching more than just *my* attention. Indigo skies said the fireworks display would launch soon, and a few colorful starbursts had already shot off a barge anchored in the river. Pre-show test charges, I presumed. Curiously, Trey and his pals chose now to disperse. Why give up the prime locale with the night's main event about to begin? The group scattered a couple at a time, and I tossed my empty cup and followed the dark curls walking alone in the navy-blue tracksuit. With so many spectators seated and sprawled on blankets, tailing him proved easy, and I kept my distance.

Things looked to get interesting when he doubled back, but he only meandered his way to a line of Port-a-Johns. I may have cursed Martin O'Shea's name for the tedium oozing from the whole affair. A crowd gathered near the makeshift bathrooms. It wasn't a place I cared to linger, but I found an out of the way knee-wall and copped a squat with a clear view of Trey's stall. I'd wait for him to do his business and follow him a bit longer, but it seemed pretty clear the night was a bust. Whatever Marty thought about our boy Trey, it wasn't happening. At least, it wasn't happening that night. My target exited the restroom. I followed, disappointed when he veered away from the partying onlookers. Trey Popov had had enough fun and appeared to head out of the festivity zone.

I didn't enjoy having so little to report to Marty, so with the early hour and my adrenaline pumping, I continued surveilling my lanky mark. He traveled along the edge of the gathering, and I only checked-up a second when he strolled toward a darker tree-covered section of the park. My alert heightened as the population dwindled to near-nothing, but I maintained my laid-back pursuit.

Fireworks exploded more frequently, while piped-in music played on public announcement speakers hanging from light poles, replacing the earlier live bands. Behind me, the customary unison *oohs* and *ahhs* followed each colorful burst, and I worked to steady my mounting breath the further we wandered from the throng and the murkier our surroundings became.

Marty's growl calling me *Harriet* ricocheted in my ear, and I nearly tripped over my own feet when I heard my name called aloud, this time with more hiss than bark. I whipped around to see the unmistakable tall figure of my neighbor Leo and his fabulous crew. Another hurried turn and my unsuspecting date for the evening, Mr. Trey Popov, had vanished in the trees and inky nighttime light.

"Shit," I groused, then forced a smile when I faced Leo again. "There you are," I called.

"There *you* are, Miss Thing. Thought you weren't in the mood for all this frivolity."

"I wasn't, and then I was. But now, it turns out I'm not again. Think I'll head back home. Grab a Lyft." I wiggled my phone.

"No! Come out and play with Auntie Leo. We're headed to a bar. A bar where I promise *no one* will hit on you. Swear to Cher, honey. It'll be fun."

"Thanks, but no. It's getting late, and I have a meeting with Uncle Marty tomorrow." I'd known Leo long enough that he was familiar with my "family," making him well-aware of who and what Uncle Marty was to me. The fact my meeting with Marty would be a phone call didn't feel too much like a lie. I shrugged.

"I won't push, cuz you've had a day." Leo kissed my cheek, and I waved as his huge frame somehow scurried to join his friends, who'd continued to a park exit.

I watched for a second before making the slow stroll back toward the crowd. The tempo of explosions sped up, and the impressive display wowed the audience. Remaining on the periphery, I found a vacant park bench that allowed a view of the show with a little solitude in an acoustical hole where the booms jarred with less intensity. I tried to enjoy the colorful exhibit but couldn't help but dwell on the total failure the day had been... on so many levels.

Waking my phone, I read my recent call log and with it, Asher Cray's name. My thumb hovered over the contact icon as a bead of perspiration rolled down my breastbone. The ticklish sensation stirred memories of sexier, sweaty times when a red, white, and blue firework combination burst over the East River. "Independence Day," I muttered and hit *delete contact*.

Like some cosmic joke, another run-in with my pal Karma, the instant I confirmed the deletion, a man's voice floated out of the darkness. "You know that's a French flag you're wearing on your chest, don't you? I mean, it's America's birthday, and you're sporting some other country's flag. Not complaining, you wear it well, but..."

I expelled an unladylike huff through my nose, casually avoiding the confident man who joined me on the far end of my bench. I gave a short sigh. "That's quite the pickup line," I chortled, before I let my head turn to see what such a brazen man looked like.

The familiar stranger stopped my heart, and not just because of his devilish grin. The navy-blue tracksuit shouldered some responsibility, too.

"Trey Popov." He extended his hand in the introduction. "And if I didn't know better, I'd *swear* you were following me."

COMING EARLY 2024